TO THOSE WHO THINK, LIFE IS A
COMEDY, TO THOSE WHO FEEL, A
TRAGEDY
LORD MELBOURNE
1779-1848

For Jean Samuelson —

with every good wish.

— Henry Hurt.

August 25, 1989
Chatham, Virginia

Wruke
8-90

SHADRIN
THE SPY WHO NEVER CAME BACK

SHADRIN
THE SPY WHO NEVER CAME BACK

by Henry Hurt

READER'S DIGEST PRESS
McGRAW-HILL BOOK COMPANY

New York   St. Louis   San Francisco
Hamburg   London   Mexico
Sydney   Toronto

Copyright © 1981 by The Reader's Digest Association, Inc.

1 2 3 4 5 6 7 8 9 F G F G 8 7 6 5 4 3 2 1

LIBRARY OF CONGRESS CATALOGING IN PUBLICATION DATA

Hurt, Henry.
Shadrin, the spy who never came back.
1. Shadrin, Nicholas. 2. Spies—United States—
Biography. 3. Defectors—Soviet Union—Biography.
4. United States. Federal Bureau of Investigation.
I. Title.
HV7911.S46H87   327.1'2'0924 [B]   81-8339
ISBN 0-07-031478-0   AACR2

for Frances Hallam Hurt

Whenever it is made known to the President that any citizen of the United States has been unjustly deprived of his liberty by or under the authority of any foreign government, it shall be the duty of the President forthwith to demand of that government the reasons of such imprisonment; and if it appears to be wrongful and in violation of the rights of American citizenship, the President shall forthwith demand the release of such citizen, and if the release so demanded is unreasonably delayed or refused, the President shall use such means, not amounting to acts of war, as he may think necessary and proper to obtain or effectuate the release; and all the facts and proceedings relative thereto shall as soon as practicable be communicated by the President to Congress.

—United States Code

The Agency assumes an awesome responsibility when it takes under its wing any defector. . . . If bodily harm were to come to a defector inadequately protected by our Security Officers, there would be a devastating impact on all potential defectors.

—Robert W. Gambino
Director of Security
Central Intelligence Agency

Author's Acknowledgments

In early 1979, when I met Ewa Shadrin for the first time, there was no thought of writing a book about her travails. Even a long magazine piece seemed unlikely, given the stone wall of silence that surrounded the case. But the known elements of the story were haunting: a brilliant and handsome Soviet military officer; his love for a pretty girl in Poland; their daring escape from communism; their success as Americans; his life as a double agent; his sudden disappearance in Vienna. The gnawing problem was that no one seemed to know what happened to Nick Shadrin. Even the most reasonable theories were no more than that. But the story seemed increasingly worth telling—if for no other reason than setting down a record of a courageous woman's quest to find her husband. I was given an assignment to write a story on the Shadrin case for *Reader's Digest*, although not one of us knew quite what the story would be or how it would end. Almost inevitably the story, with all its complexities, grew in the process of research and writing until it was a book-length manuscript.

From the beginning I was determined to keep the focus on what could be learned of Shadrin's life—not on the myriad speculations about what happened to him. It is disappointing, of course, not to have found a solid solution to the enduring mystery of Shadrin's fate. But it is not really surprising, for the answer is one that no knowledgeable party to Shadrin's fate has an interest in seeing emerge.

The most challenging aspect of this undertaking was the scope of the project, the span of time over which the events occurred, and the hundreds of people involved in the story. It was impossible to locate all the witnesses to the events in the Shadrins' lives or even to conduct extensive interviews with all those who were located. However, I spoke with about 150 people who had some connection with the Shadrin case or knowledge of it. In numerous instances I conducted several interviews with the same source.

Memories, of course, had become foggy over the two decades that had passed from the time the Shadrins arrived in the United States. A major part of my task was to sift through these recollections, to evaluate the sources from various angles, and to decide what most likely was true and accurate. It was an extensive undertaking, an impossible one without the superb assistance of many people who have more to do with the merits of this book than I am comfortable admitting.

Quite simply, I cannot imagine a writer having more support than I have had in this project. Primarily I am indebted to the extraordinary global research facilities of *Reader's Digest*. From around the world—Paris, Melbourne, Toronto, Vienna, Capetown, Berlin, Montreal, Oslo, London—came prompt replies to queries seeking information on points pertaining to the saga of Nicholas Shadrin. It is of incalculable value to have such resources a cable away. This was especially true in view of the muddled details and predictable contradictions that were part and parcel of information tumbling in from so many diverse and honest sources.

It was in the United States that the largest measure of research checking was done. Few researchers can match the meticulous dedication shown by Nancy Tafoya, who possesses an indomitable reverence for accuracy. Nancy always seemed guided by the purest concept of research assistance—an understanding that her first obligation was to support what I wrote, testing every statement, never failing to challenge a soft spot. When she caught me in error, she was ready with a constructive suggestion for modification or correction.

In researching the book, Nancy was assisted by Mary Lyn Maiscott, one of the most skilled members of the *Reader's Digest* Research Department. Mary Lyn's perseverance in the pursuit of accuracy represents a major contribution to the integrity of the book. She and Nancy Tafoya are responsible for hundreds of modifications and corrections, and they are entitled to a considerable measure of credit for whatever merit is found in this work. In some of the more complex sections of the book involving counterintelligence matters and current investigations, I was not free to provide sources for them to check. I alone am responsible for that material.

Surely there are errors that have escaped us, for the opportunities range into the thousands. But it is not for a lack of our genuine effort to catch every one. On many occasions during this project I have thought of a comment I once heard from the late DeWitt Wallace, founder of *Reader's Digest* and the man who conceived this research checking process. "I hope we will never lose our mania for accuracy," he said to a gathering of his editors. No doubt he would be gratified to know that that mania lives on at the *Reader's Digest* Research Department.

Making sure these facts are set down in a readable fashion was the job of Steven Frimmer of Reader's Digest Press, editor of the book. His pencil is light and incisive, replacing cloudiness with clarity. I never challenged one of his editing changes but that he supported the change with sound reasoning. Usually I was convinced he sharply improved my work.

Any telling of the Shadrin story is fraught with legal questions. At every turn I had the patient and wise counsel of David O. Fuller, Jr., of the *Reader's Digest* Legal Department. His advice, as well as that of W. Barnabas McHenry, the magazine's general counsel, was valuable in keeping the book within the bounds of publishing laws. In the matter of our futile and frustrating legal attempts to force the government to release material on Shadrin, I appreciate the efforts of David Cohen of Warshavsky, Hoffman & Cohen, who pressed our court action under the Freedom of Information Act.

A significant aspect of the project was the work of Andrea B. Bennett, who typed the manuscript as well as hundreds of pages of interview notes. There are few typists who can equal her astoundingly low rate of typographical errors and her attentiveness to mistakes in the manuscript. Early in the project thousands of pages of interview notes were efficiently transcribed by Alice Anagnost of the *Reader's Digest* Typing Department. And at every step my efforts were facilitated by the exceptional secretarial assistance of Dorothy Kavanaugh, my faithful colleague of the *Reader's Digest* Pleasantville office.

Mail service took on an unusually significant importance in this project because I live in a little town in Southside Virginia and the rest of the team was in New York. Dozens of times my telephone rang at six in the morning—even on Sundays—with a message from one of the efficient and courteous men at the local post office that a special delivery envelope had arrived for me. Such exceptional service surely is rare.

Ewa Shadrin has shown remarkable patience during what must have seemed to her endless, tedious hours of interviews. (Notes of my interviews with her alone run to more than 500 typed pages.) Once I had completed my basic interviews with Ewa, the researchers spent as much time as I had in going over points on which she had pertinent knowledge. Sometimes hours were spent on a single fact. Ewa Shadrin's sole interest in the book is her desire to see a full account published of her personal tragedy. We tested and checked her version of events at every possible point, and she emerged from the process as an astonishingly credible witness. I cannot remember even once when she contradicted herself on an earlier statement. She was certain about what she knew, and she was just as certain about what she did not know. I deeply hope that this record of what happened in her life—as imperfect as the record may be—will provide Ewa Shadrin with a feeling of satisfaction that she has done all that she can do—and that she has done so with grace, vigor, and courage.

The most stalwart supporter of the project has been my editor at *Reader's Digest*, Fulton Oursler, Jr., managing editor. He was closely involved with every aspect of the book's development and provided guidance at each crucial point. The book is greatly improved by his ability to slice through fuzziness in my thinking and writing, going straight to the heart of some muddled point with questions and then suggestions for modifications or additions. Fulton's invincible support of my efforts is a contribution without which this book would not have been written.

No accounting of contributions is complete without my genuine thanks to Noel Oursler, my very special friend.

No one has shown greater faith in the project than Edward T. Thompson, *Reader's Digest* editor-in-chief. From the start he recognized the potential deficiencies of the Shadrin story—especially that it is a story without an ending. But he backed me without a flinch, over a far longer period of time than he had bargained for. Ed showed a rare confidence which I appreciate enormously.

Of course, there are many who deserve an expression of my appreciation but desire to remain anonymous. Some of these sources have acted out of a perceived patriotism; some out of friendship; some out of an interest in setting down an accurate historical record. Other sources have motivations that elude me, and their contributions were viewed with more caution than the others. In each case, our interests happened, for a time, to coincide. I am grateful for their help. Out of this melding of mutual interests, I hope there will emerge some contribution to the betterment of the American intelligence services.

My greatest gratitude must go to my wife, Margaret, and to our children—Robert, Charlie, and Elizabeth. Others involved in the book also should be grateful for Margaret's editorial contribution, for as the first reader and critic of what I wrote, her suggestions saved many extra hours of work for those to whom I submitted the material. But much more than that, my family's steady love and understanding through the long months of my neglect will always be an important part of this work.

Henry Hurt

Chatham, Virginia
April 1981

SHADRIN

THE SPY WHO NEVER CAME BACK

Chapter 1

IT WAS Christmas season in Vienna. The warm charms of the old city glowed softly from beneath a fluffy coat of fresh snow. Brightly colored lights and gleaming tinsel hung along the streets, which were echoing with the sounds of people and Christmas music coming from the shops. Vienna was one of Ewa Shadrin's favorite places. She was enchanted with her good fortune in being there at Christmastime. Brimming with happiness, Ewa told her husband what sights she hoped to see and what music she hoped to hear during the brief visit. Their taxi stopped at the door of the Hotel Bristol, across the street from the magnificent opera house. Moments later the Shadrins were engulfed by the warmth and elegance of the handsome old hotel.

The visit to Vienna was an unexpected and welcome diversion for Nicholas and Ewa Shadrin. They were on their way to Zürs, Austria, for a long-planned Christmas skiing vacation. A month prior to their departure Nick mentioned to Ewa that he would like to combine their vacation with a business appointment in Vienna. She was delighted. Ewa would have no trouble entertaining herself while Nick went about his business.

Small and energetic, with olive skin and intense dark eyes, Dr. Blanka Ewa Shadrin had established a successful private dental practice in a Virginia suburb of Washington. On evenings out she enjoyed the music and ballet that were bountiful in the U.S. capital. At home she took a special pride in being able to prepare the fish and game her sportsman husband brought back throughout the year. She also welcomed every opportunity to travel, to see new places.

Nicholas George Shadrin, her husband, was a widely acclaimed lecturer at the Naval War College as well as a former analyst and consultant for the Office of Naval Intelligence. His company and counsel were sought by some of the most important people in Washington's military and intelligence community. With a Ph.D. in international affairs and a master's degree in engineering, Shadrin was employed by the Defense Intelligence Agency, where he was considered among the best in his field. In addition to his intellectual prowess, Nick Shadrin excelled as a hunter and a fisherman. And at a height of more than six feet two inches, he possessed a commanding charm and presence that invariably won him acceptance in almost any company.

Seventeen years earlier, when fate first intertwined the lives of Nick and Ewa, they were strikingly different people. He was Captain Nikolai Fedorovich Artamonov, the youngest commanding officer of a destroyer in the history of the Soviet Navy. Soviet publications touted him as an example of the "New Soviet Man," a brilliant product of the Soviet system.

He was so highly regarded that the Soviets sent him to Gdynia, Poland, where he was charged with training Indonesian naval officers in techniques of destroyer operations. There, in 1958, at the age of thirty, he met a lovely girl named Ewa Gora, who was twenty-one and in her last year of medical school. They fell wildly in love.

In June 1959 they fled across the Baltic Sea in a small launch and sought asylum in Sweden. Their daring escape from communism was heralded around the world. A year later Nick and Ewa were married and living in the United States. Their rapid acclimatization to American life had been stunning.

The music and beauty of Vienna so admired by Nick and Ewa contrasted starkly with the city's renown as a cockpit of international espionage. When the Shadrins checked into the Hotel Bristol, about 3:00 P.M. on December 18, 1975, they were assigned a room on the third floor. They had been in transit for eighteen hours—from Washington to London, where they were delayed as a result of a violent snowstorm in Central Europe, and finally on to Vienna. After showering and changing clothes, they went downstairs for a drink and a light lunch at the bar.

2

Nick Shadrin explained to his wife that he would have to leave at 5:00 P.M. for a business appointment that would include dinner. He told her that his meeting was with the same person he had seen on earlier occasions when they traveled abroad. He mentioned, as he had prior to the other meetings, that the man was a Russian who had been working for the United States for twenty-five years. Shadrin told Ewa he was to meet his friend on the steps of the Votivkirche, the large church in direct line of sight from the United States consulate building.

That was all Nick Shadrin told his wife. But that was all she expected him to tell her. A gregarious, ebullient man, Shadrin was intensely private in other respects. It did not occur to Ewa to question him about his work. Although he had never told her, she assumed the meetings he had in foreign cities were somehow related to his work for the Defense Intelligence Agency. The fact that she usually got to go on the foreign trips was far more important to Ewa than badgering Nick for details about what he was doing.

As soon as Nick left the hotel to go to the Votivkirche, Ewa went out to stroll the snowy streets of Vienna, to enjoy the Christmas decorations, and to mingle with the throngs of shoppers who filled the sidewalks. Several of the prettiest streets had been closed and turned into pedestrian malls. "The city was magnificent that evening," says Ewa. "Everything was lovely in the snow." The chill in the air was invigorating after the long hours on the plane.

At about 6:20 P.M. Ewa returned to the hotel. Refreshed from her walk, she delighted in the creakiness of the old elevator, a quaint touch one rarely finds in the United States. Thirty minutes after she reached her room the telephone rang. The voice was vaguely familiar. It was Ann Martin, a woman Ewa had met in Washington ten days earlier.

Ewa recalled the strange visit to her home by Ann Martin and Jim Wooten, one of Nick's closest personal friends. Wooten had brought Ann Martin to the Shadrin home on December 8 specifically for her to be introduced to Ewa. Miss Martin had something to do with Nick's upcoming Vienna meeting, Ewa was told, and Miss Martin had wanted to meet Nick's wife. Ewa was fond of Jim Wooten, but she had found Miss Martin oddly remote, even cold.

That night in Vienna Ann Martin stated that she was at the Imperial Hotel five minutes away. She told Ewa she would like to

3

come to her hotel room immediately and to wait there for Nick's return. "Of course," said Ewa, thinking that perhaps Miss Martin would warm up a bit in a one-on-one setting. At 7:00 P.M. Miss Martin knocked on the door to the Shadrins' room.

Ann Martin was nearly six feet tall, very thin, with straight brown hair, and wore no makeup. She had little to say. Ewa soon saw that any hope she had of warming up Miss Martin was silly. However, during the three hours they were together it did emerge that Miss Martin had been in England for a few days before flying to Vienna and that she had studied in Germany. She said that she lived alone with a cat in the Georgetown section of Washington.

Ewa was relieved when finally, at ten-thirty, there was a brisk knock at the door. It was Nick, and he filled the room with warmth and graciousness. As always, Ewa felt flushed with pride at his obvious intelligence and grace, his ability to make things seem cheery even in the presence of the strange Miss Martin.

Shadrin was extremely enthusiastic about the success of his meeting. He mentioned no business details, but he did tell the women about the fish restaurant where he and the Russian had dinner. Although the establishment itself was rather dreary, he said, the food was exceptionally good. He related that he and the Russian each consumed three double vodkas and then feasted on carp. Shadrin said he had enjoyed the drive around Vienna so much that he was going to rent a car the next day so he and Ewa could go sight-seeing.

Then something strange happened. Miss Martin, who had stood by patiently as Nick told about the restaurant, got out a pen and pad and motioned toward the bathroom. Nick smiled at Ewa and went into the bathroom with Miss Martin and closed the door. Ewa settled down to read. She could hear muffled voices coming from the bathroom.

Less than ten minutes later Miss Martin and Shadrin emerged from the bathroom. She tucked her pad and pen into a purse. Nick resumed his enthusiastic description of the restaurant while Miss Martin put on her coat.

Before leaving, Miss Martin got out a street map of Vienna and explained to Shadrin how to reach the house where she was staying. Nick had a second meeting with the Russian on Saturday, and Miss Martin wanted to talk to him on Sunday before he and Ewa left the city to go to Zürs. Shadrin wrote down the specific

4

instructions so he could direct a cab to the address. He also wrote down Miss Martin's telephone number and assured her he would see her on Sunday afternoon.

Then Miss Martin bade the Shadrins good night and left. Nick stood at the door listening until he heard Miss Martin's footsteps fade away. When he turned to Ewa, there was a wide grin on his face. "I didn't tell Ann everything," he said. "I'll wait and tell the rest to Jim Wooten."

"Nick was jubilant," says Ewa. "I have never seen him happier. His meeting must have been tremendously successful."

Even though Ewa knew no details about her husband's work, she did know that these Vienna meetings were the most important he had ever had. Nick had told her a few weeks prior to their trip that if the meetings were successful, he could expect vitally important changes in the professional aspects of his life. For one thing, Nick indicated, at last he would be approved for a security clearance, something that had eluded him because of his background as a Soviet defector. He had been stunted in his development as an intelligence analyst because of this. Such a clearance would mark the realization of one of his most fervent aspirations.

It never occurred to Ewa to ask Nick what he was doing or why he was meeting a Russian in foreign cities. She sensed it was an area he did not want to discuss: "There were so many things we enjoyed talking about and wanted to talk about that it would have been silly to waste time on things either of us did not want to discuss." Besides, Shadrin did not like his work at the Defense Intelligence Agency, and Ewa had long since learned that the atmosphere was more pleasant if work was not discussed.

By the time Miss Martin left the exhaustion from their eighteen-hour trip finally caught up with the Shadrins. Even so, Ewa was glowing with good feelings about Nick's success and their good fortune to be on a holiday in Vienna. They went to bed and slept until ten the next morning.

At breakfast Nick told Ewa that the whole day was theirs. He had one more meeting with his Russian friend, but that would not take place until Saturday. On Sunday they would be off to Zürs to ski, after stopping at the house where Ann Martin was staying in Vienna.

When they had finished breakfast, Nick asked the concierge to arrange for two tickets for that evening's performance of a Johann

5

Strauss operetta and one ticket for *The Gypsy Baron* for Saturday evening. Ewa wanted to attend that while Nick went to his second meeting with the Russian.

The Shadrins spent the rest of Friday shopping. They bought tortes to send to Ewa's mother in Poland and to an old friend in Hawaii, Captain Thomas Dwyer. Nick bought a sweater for himself and a sweater and a dress for Ewa. They had an early dinner and went to the operetta. At some point toward the end of the evening Ewa began to notice that Nick seemed increasingly preoccupied, as though he were not paying attention to the operetta.

After the performance Nick and Ewa walked over to the bar at the Bristol. A man was playing the piano. Nick had a cognac, and Ewa ordered coffee. The hotel happened to have a favorite blend of hers that she rarely found elsewhere. While they were sitting at the bar, Nick slipped his hand into the inside breast pocket of his jacket and withdrew a bulky envelope. He patted it between his hands and smiled at Ewa.

"That's one thousand dollars," he said quietly, grinning. "I was supposed to give it to the Russian I met last night, but he told me to keep it."

"Good," said Ewa mischievously. "I know of plenty of things we can do with it." She reached playfully for the envelope.

"Oh, no," said Nick, laughing, pulling it away. "I have to try to give it to him again when I meet him tomorrow."

"I hope he still won't take it," said Ewa.

"Then I'll have to take it back to Washington and give it to Jim Wooten," said Nick. He smiled and ordered another cognac. The conversation then turned to a discussion of the operetta.

Before going to bed that night, Nick took a Valium. He told Ewa that his meeting the next day was so extremely important that he wanted to get as much rest as possible. He asked her not to awaken him on Saturday morning, to let him sleep as long as he could. Never before had Ewa known Nick to be this tense in anticipation of a business meeting.

They got a late start on Saturday morning. In keeping with a Russian custom that calls for buying something new for New Year's Day, Nick went out to buy a new shirt and tie. When the Shadrins returned to the Bristol, the concierge informed them that their car, a bright red Audi, was ready.

Around noon they set out in the car to try to find the marvelous fish restaurant. Their search was hindered because Nick could not recall the name of the place. They drove for miles and, after hours of searching, returned to the Bristol at about three-thirty. The hotel restaurant had just closed, so they went to the bar, where they had herring and vodka. They then went up to their room, where Shadrin took a shower and rested before his evening meeting.

Ewa continued to be aware of Nick's preoccupation and increasing tenseness as the hour for his meeting approached. He mentioned several times that he needed to be completely rested and relaxed. At 6:00 P.M. he got up and dressed.

After he had slipped on his jacket, he handed Ewa a card. "These are the numbers for you to call if anything happens," he told her. This was something he had done on previous occasions when he had a meeting in a foreign city. Once Ewa asked him what he meant when he said, "if something happens." He just looked at her and smiled, as if to say, "Who knows?"

Nick reminded Ewa that the numbers would put her in touch with Ann Martin, the person she should contact if she needed any assistance. The card he handed her had a notation in Nick's handwriting: "Ann Stays With Grimm." Above that were two telephone numbers—one to be used during the day and the other for night. There also were the precise address and driving instructions provided by Ann Martin.

"If the meeting is over early," Nick said, "I'll wait for you outside the opera house and we'll have a late dinner."

At six-thirty Nick kissed Ewa good-bye, looked into her eyes, and smiled. He mentioned that, as he had done on Thursday, he was to meet his Russian friend on the steps of the Votivkirche. Then Nick left the room briskly. Ewa could hear the creaky old elevator shudder to a halt on their floor.

Fifteen minutes later Ewa left the hotel to go across the street to the opera house for the seven o'clock performance of *The Gypsy Baron*. When she emerged at its conclusion, at about nine forty-five, she looked around for Nick. She was not surprised that he was not there. She thought it unlikely for his meeting to have been completed so quickly. She returned to her hotel room and settled down to read the libretto of *The Gypsy Baron*.

Ewa did not have dinner so that if Nick returned early enough, they could go out together. At 11:00 P.M. she concluded that he would not be back in time to go out. She undressed and got into bed and continued reading. By midnight she was vaguely concerned that she had not heard from Nick, but still, there was no reason for alarm. She established 12:30 A.M. as the time she would begin to worry.

The deadline was quickly upon her. The vague worry was turning into a nagging fear. Never before had Nick been this late without getting in touch. Ewa got up to check the card he had given her and looked at the night number. She did not like the idea of telephoning unless it was absolutely necessary. She told herself that she would wait until one-thirty—not a minute past. Then she would call the number.

It was then that she became aware of her attention being captivated by the old creaky elevator down the hallway. At that hour it was operating infrequently. Whenever she heard it, she would become tense—waiting, hoping that it would stop on the third floor. A few times it did stop there, and she could hear footsteps coming along the corridor. Each time the rhythm of the footsteps did not break as they passed her door.

Tears suddenly engulfed her. Thoughts of their past flooded her mind—their almost incredible escape across the Baltic Sea, the life they had established in America. She was frightened. Where could Nick be? What could have happened? For the first time her thoughts turned to a grim possibility. If Nick was meeting with a Russian who had "worked for the United States for twenty-five years," as he had told her, then was it not possible that the Soviets had captured this man—and taken Nick along with him?

Suddenly it was 1:30 A.M. Ewa reached for the telephone. At the other end of the line, she knew, would be Ann Martin. She felt a chill as she thought of the woman's cold aloofness. She wanted desperately to be composed when she called. She decided to wait until 1:35.

Her voice well under control, Ewa rang the desk and requested an outside line. She dialed the night emergency number on the card. She could hear the phone begin to ring. Ewa waited, poised. The phone rang perhaps a dozen times. There was no answer. Ewa hung up. A deep and frightening chill again swept through her, and she began to cry.

She might have dialed the number repeatedly, but each time

she would have to request an outside line from the hotel operator. She did not want to do that, so she waited exactly twenty minutes. At 1:55 A.M. she tried the number again. This time Ann Martin answered. Ewa identified herself.

"Have you tried to call before?" asked Ann Martin. They were her first words. Ewa said she had tried earlier. Miss Martin stated that she had been having dinner with friends and had just returned.

"Nick has not come back," said Ewa.

There was a moment's silence, and then Ann Martin said, "It is true that it's late, but there's no reason to worry. He came in quite late Thursday night." Ewa listened intently. It had not occurred to her that 10:30 P.M. was "quite late," especially since now it was 2:00 A.M. Then Miss Martin added, "Be sure to call me immediately when he comes in. It does not matter what time it is. Call me." Ann Martin told Ewa to make sure her room door was bolted and to open it for no one except Nick.

For the next three and one-half hours Ewa wept. What started as a joyful Christmas holiday had turned into an ever-deepening nightmare, one that became bleaker with each passing minute and no word from Nick. The only time Ewa stopped weeping was when she heard the elevator. Then she would hold her breath and listen, hoping it would stop at her floor and footsteps would come her way.

Finally, at 5:30 A.M., Ewa mustered her courage and telephoned Miss Martin. "Nick still hasn't come," she said. It sounded to Ewa as though Miss Martin had been awake when she called. Matter-of-factly Miss Martin said that still there was nothing to worry about, that once before in Vienna Nick had been gone overnight for a meeting. Ewa did not point out that on that occasion the overnight stay was planned in advance. No one had been surprised when he did not return until the next day.

In any case, Miss Martin said that she would "cable Washington" with the information that Shadrin had not returned to the Hotel Bristol. Ewa did not know what Miss Martin was talking about, and Miss Martin did not offer any explanation. She did tell Ewa to stay in her room and repeated that she should not open the door for anyone but Nick. Ewa hung up the phone and began weeping again.

As daylight broke, the elevator became active. There were increasingly frequent footsteps passing Ewa's door. Each one brought a rising hope that was dashed almost as soon as it began. Then, as Ewa held her breath and listened, some footsteps stopped at her door. There was a light knock.

"Yes?" Ewa said, holding her breath, listening intently at the door.

It was Ann Martin. Ewa let her into the room. Miss Martin's demeanor had not changed. Ewa tried to compose herself and not cry in front of the strange woman. All day Sunday the two women stayed in the hotel room. Miss Martin assured Ewa that Nick would probably return at any time. In the meantime, she said, people at the American Embassy were checking with all hospitals and the police in case there had been an accident.

Ewa explained her own theory to Miss Martin—that if Nick were meeting with a "Russian who had worked for the United States for twenty-five years," and if that Russian had been caught by the Soviets, it would seem logical that Nick could have been kidnapped along with him. The next step, Ewa felt, was to try to get in touch with the man Nick was meeting, to find out what had happened to him. Would he report that he had last seen Nick at dinner? Or would he himself be missing? Getting in touch with the Russian seemed logical.

Miss Martin stated that she had no way of knowing how to reach the man Nick was meeting. "But he was working for the United States," Ewa said. Miss Martin stared at Ewa and said nothing.

Throughout the day Miss Martin was making telephone calls. What Ewa could hear made no sense. Ann Martin kept referring to Washington, but that was all Ewa recognized. Whenever the phone rang, Ewa would answer. It always was the same man's voice, asking for Miss Martin.

At one point, in an apparent effort to make small talk, Miss Martin asked Ewa to tell her about the skiing plans she and Nick had made for the next day. Ewa felt something akin to revulsion sweep through her. No matter what, she knew they would not be going skiing. The question was cruelly insensitive, Ewa felt.

Around six in the evening Miss Martin ordered dinner sent to the room. She told Ewa that she herself was afraid to remain in the private home where she had been staying because Nick knew that address. If he had been kidnapped by the Soviets, he may have told them the address. Miss Martin explained to Ewa that she had left the place where she had been staying and moved to the home of the friends with whom she had dinner the night before. She gave Ewa that telephone number and told her to call if she heard from Nick.

Ewa was relieved when Miss Martin departed, but her hope that Nick would soon return was dying. She now listened only halfheartedly to the footsteps from the elevator. She lay across the bed and wept until she finally slept fitfully.

Ann Martin telephoned Ewa the next morning and stated that she would be spending all day Monday working at the American Embassy. She said the embassy staff would be in touch with officials in Washington to formulate a plan to try to find out what had happened to Nick. Ewa spent the whole day in her hotel room, as Miss Martin had advised. Her hope for Nick's early return had faded. She wept throughout the day.

That evening Miss Martin arrived at the hotel room to have dinner with Ewa. She reported that there was no news from the check of area hospitals and police. She told Ewa that efforts to find Nick were under way, though she did not offer a single concrete detail. She asked Ewa to be patient, that the United States government was working for a resolution.

Ewa made a great effort not to weep in front of Ann Martin, but she was suddenly overcome. It was all so wild, so crazy. No one would explain to her who he or she was or what Nick had been doing. Whatever Ann Martin knew, she clearly was not going to share it with Ewa. Ewa broke down in a great avalanche of sobbing.

Not once during the days they were together did Ann Martin make a single gesture of warmth. But at this moment, from across the room, Miss Martin offered a curious condolence. "Don't worry," she said. "You'll get used to it." Through tears Ewa looked up at the impassive face staring calmly at her. It was a moment Ewa would never forget.

Tuesday morning Ann Martin called Ewa from the embassy. There was no word about Nick, but it was the feeling of the United States government that his disappearance was not going to be resolved in Vienna. Miss Martin suggested that Ewa go to the Pan American World Airways office right away and book passage for the next flight to Washington, via Frankfurt.

After Ewa had returned to the hotel with her ticket, Ann Martin arrived. She had a list of questions from embassy officials:

Nick's date and place of birth; the description of his clothing when last seen; his address in Virginia; any birthmarks. Ewa answered the questions patiently. Almost as an afterthought, Miss Martin said that embassy officials felt that because Nick would not be returning to the United States right away, Ewa should turn over his passport to the embassy. Ewa handed it to Miss Martin. In addition to his passport, Nick had left behind his reading glasses and daily hypertension medication.

Then Miss Martin explained to Ewa that an engaging older gentleman from the midwestern United States had been dispatched from Washington to escort her home. Miss Martin said that the man, who she indicated worked for the U.S. government, was named Bruce. Miss Martin gave Ewa the impression she would find Bruce a comforting companion with whom to travel.

At 12:45 P.M. on Tuesday, December 23, Miss Martin called for Ewa at the Bristol Hotel. She was in a car driven by a red-haired man whom she identified as being the friend with whom she had been dining the night Shadrin disappeared. Ewa recognized his voice as that of the man who had called repeatedly for Miss Martin on Sunday. Miss Martin and Ewa got into the back seat and were driven to the Imperial Hotel a few blocks away.

There Ewa was introduced to Bruce, who joined them for the drive to the airport. Miss Martin explained to Ewa that she and Bruce should pretend that they did not know each other on the flight from Vienna to Frankfurt. They should keep up this charade until after they were through passport control in Frankfurt.

The cold aloofness of Ann Martin was quickly surpassed by the almost-sullen taciturnity of the bland, nondescript man called Bruce. On the flight to Frankfurt Bruce and Ewa did not sit together. At the Frankfurt airport Ewa observed Bruce as he wrote a name on a new luggage tag and switched it with the one already on his bag. After clearing passport control, they went to a hotel to spend the night before their early flight to Washington the next day. After a silent dinner with Bruce, during which Ewa softly wept, she went to her room. When she was alone again, Ewa's weeping turned to uncontrollable sobbing. No woman could have felt a greater security than that she had known with her husband. Nick Shadrin was powerful, poised, and intelligent. He always moved with confidence, and he usually seemed to do the right thing. As far as Ewa could now tell, she was in the hands of

12

graceless, fumbling functionaries from some murky department of the government.

Ewa Shadrin's roots ran deep into the heritage of Catholic Poland, where the most important personal observance each year was one's name day. Birthdays were hardly noted, but families traditionally celebrated a loved one's name day—that day of the year honoring the Christian saint for whom a person was named. When Ewa awoke that Wednesday morning, hoping for a fleeting moment that her nightmare was over, she looked around the depressing airport hotel room. It dawned on her that it was Christmas Eve, her name day. Those scattered people around the world who loved her were thinking of her that morning. Deep in her heart Ewa knew that somewhere Nick was among them.

Her thoughts were interrupted a few minutes before 7:00 A.M. by a knock on the door. It was Bruce, who said it was time for them to go. After a silent breakfast together they went to the Frankfurt airport.

When they changed planes in London, Ewa watched as Bruce scurried about putting a new name tag on his luggage. The most casual observer could have seen him writing the new name tag and then switching it. Then, in a rare personal utterance, Bruce told Ewa he needed to do some Christmas shopping for his wife and daughters. She watched as he selected various pieces of inexpensive jewelry from a souvenir counter.

Bruce and Ewa sat together on the long flight from Frankfurt to Washington. Not once did they have a substantive conversation. Bruce spent his time reading and staring ahead, while Ewa sat quietly, trying to suppress her tears. Her mind was focused tightly on Nick, never straying far. At first she had lived from minute to minute, hoping for some word. Then it had been from hour to hour. Now, at least, there was a span of seven hours that she was in flight and out of reach. Maybe there would be some good word when they reached Washington. This meager hope—in which she placed little faith—was her only consolation.

It was about 1:30 P.M. on Christmas Eve when Ewa and Bruce arrived at Washington's Dulles International Airport. They were met by Nick's friend Jim Wooten. It was clear to Ewa that Wooten was acquainted with the enigmatic Bruce. Wooten's was the first friendly face Ewa had seen since Nick had vanished. Even though she had met Wooten only twice, she had talked to him on the

13

telephone hundreds of times over the years he and Nick had been close friends.

Wooten's face reflected his grave concern. He walked Ewa to a car and driver that awaited them in front of the terminal. Bruce stayed behind; he always went through customs separately from Ewa. Wooten opened the back door of the car for Ewa and told her to wait while he went back into the airport terminal to locate Bruce.

The drive from the airport to the Shadrins' McLean home took about thirty minutes. Wooten and Ewa sat in the back talking quietly. Bruce sat in the front. It was then that Wooten wrote down two Russian names on a slip of paper and gave it to Ewa. The note stated:

> *Dec 18—Oleg Kozlov   Soviet*
> *Mikhail Ivanovich Kuryshev*
>
> *Dec 20 . . . left to meet again with above*

Ewa stared at the names. She had never seen them before. Wooten explained quietly that these were the men Nick was last known to have been with. He stated that Nick had known Kozlov in Washington and that he had previously met Kuryshev in Vienna in 1972. He also told her that Nick was performing a patriotic duty for the United States, although he did not explain just what that meant.

Wooten explained that the government's working theory on Nick's disappearance was that he had been kidnapped by the Soviets and was in their hands. He told Ewa that the strongest possible steps were being taken to bring about a prompt resolution. He reported that Secretary of State Henry Kissinger had agreed to see Anatoly Dobrynin, the Soviet ambassador to the United States, the next day.

Wooten told Ewa gently that he felt it was urgent to find some resolution because he believed it likely the Soviets would execute Nick within forty-eight hours of having him. Wooten reminded her of what she knew so well—that the Soviets had placed Nick under a death sentence following his defection sixteen years earlier.

They sat in silence. Bruce and the driver had hardly spoken. Ewa was comforted by Wooten's obviously warm concern over Nick. As the car neared the Shadrin home, Wooten became even

14

more serious. He told Ewa it was extremely important that she tell no one what had happened. The only hope of getting Nick back was to make sure nothing leaked to the press. Any published account could hopelessly tangle negotiations.

"But what can I tell our friends?" said Ewa, feeling again the great swell of futility.

"Tell them you were ill and had to come home early," said Jim Wooten. "Tell them that Nick stayed on to ski." It was a cockeyed explanation, Ewa thought, but at least it suggested that Wooten and the government seemed optimistic about an early resolution to the crisis.

As they turned into her driveway, Ewa saw the car of her friend Janka Urynowicz. She came each day to feed Trezor, the Shadrins' nine-month-old German shepherd, while they were on vacation. Suddenly Ewa felt frantic. "But what do I tell my friend right now? Who do I say you three men are?"

"Tell her we are your clients," said Wooten. The stupidity of it all rushed over Ewa. It was preposterous to suggest that she had arrived home a week early from a European vacation with three strange men in the car that she announce to her best friend the men were her dental patients, if that is what was meant by "clients." Ewa said nothing. She figured it would serve no purpose.

The three men sat in the car while Ewa went into the house. Janka's twelve-year-old daughter also was there. Alarm and confusion radiated from Janka's face. She had seen Ewa and the men drive in, and she knew something was terribly wrong. Even before she spoke, Janka burst into tears as she and Ewa embraced.

"What has happened?" cried Janka.

"I cannot talk," Ewa said. "Go home! I will call you later." Janka and the girl rushed from the house and drove away, trying not to look at the strange men who sat watching from their car.

It suddenly dawned on Ewa that she was without a car. A few weeks before going on their trip, Nick's jeep had been stolen. He had ordered a new one that he was to take possession of upon his return from Europe. But that was not scheduled until January 3. As for their automobile, Nick always disconnected the battery cables when they went away. Ewa had no idea how to reconnect the cables.

She asked the men if they could do that for her. They agreed, and she opened the garage door. Bruce and the driver worked at

15

getting the cables hooked up while Wooten went into the house with Ewa.

"Since you'll find out who we are soon enough," said Wooten, "I might as well tell you now." He explained that the strange man named Bruce was actually an officer with the Central Intelligence Agency. Wooten identified himself as an agent with the Federal Bureau of Investigation.

"But what was going on in Vienna?" cried Ewa.

Wooten would say only that Nick was working honorably for his country, that his work was in the highest tradition of patriotism. He had strong hopes that Nick would soon be returned.

Out in the garage, Bruce was proving as deft at working on the battery cable as he and Ann Martin had been in taking care of Ewa in Vienna. "They just didn't seem to know how to hook up a battery cable," says Ewa. Finally, Wooten went out and helped Bruce and the driver. Once Ewa's car was started, the three men drove away.

Ewa came back into her house. Trezor nuzzled into her. She was alone. In the myriad confusion there was one clear focus to her thoughts: Nick. Somewhere, she believed, he too was thinking of her on her name day.

In all this Jim Wooten was a bright spot. Clearly the strange people Ewa had seen in Vienna—the enigmatic Bruce, the chilling Ann Martin, the indifferent red-haired driver—did not care about her. She could guess only that they cared nothing about what happened to Nick either. But Jim Wooten was a friend of at least ten years' standing. Nick had held him in the highest esteem. Before leaving the Shadrin home on Christmas Eve, Wooten gave Ewa telephone numbers for her to use to reach him day or night. He promised to be in touch with her at least once a day.

That night Ewa went to Janka's house for a traditional Polish Christmas Eve dinner. On Christmas Day she took Trezor and moved into Janka's home. This way she could avoid the routine telephone calls from friends inviting them out or asking to speak to Nick.

The next seven days were as terrible as any Ewa Shadrin would ever know. She was alone with the numbing belief that her husband had been kidnapped by the Soviets. She didn't dare tell even Janka that Nick apparently had been working for the CIA and the FBI when he vanished. Janka was aware that Nick had defected from the Soviet Union, and she now believed he had been snatched back by the Soviets. Ewa could share this much of her secret.

Good to his promise, Jim Wooten telephoned each day, often twice. There were no startling developments in the first few days, but it was certain that the resolution of the matter did not lie in Vienna. Then, about 2:00 P.M. on New Year's Day, Ewa stopped by her house, where she found a telegram from the Department of State. She ripped it open and read: "Please contact Mrs. Leslie Fort . . . concerning a cable from the American Embassy, Vienna, Austria." Ewa frantically dialed the number given in the telegram, only to find it was not operable except during normal office hours. The torment of the past ten days, capped by this, swept her into an agonizing mental frenzy, her imagination racing to every possibility.

In Ewa's mind the cable from Vienna could mean only one thing: Nick's body had been found. She seized a calendar and stabbed her fingers along the dates. Because of the long holiday weekend, she believed that she faced three full days and four long nights until the first business day of 1976. Ninety-one hours of anguished mental torture would pass before she would finally have word of Nick.

Her sturdy resolve, which had provided a certain numbness, burst with a convulsion of tears.

Chapter 2

"Ewa, the State Department would never inform anyone of the death of a loved one with a telegram. *Never!*" Mary Louise Howe was trying to soothe her young friend. "If they had found Nick's body, they would send someone to your house to tell you."

In utter despair, Ewa Shadrin had telephoned William and Mary Louise Howe for consolation and help. It was not easy for the Howes to convince her that the United States government had such a humanitarian standard. Ewa thought that if the State Department did send a representative, the person would be someone like Ann Martin. As the two women talked, William Howe telephoned the home of a highly placed friend at State. The friend immediately contacted the department's cable room and had the cable read to him.

It turned out the cable that had wrought such desolation upon Ewa was purely benign. In the highest bureaucratic tradition, the Department of State wished to inform Ewa Shadrin that the U.S. Embassy in Vienna had possession of Nick's passport—something Mrs. Shadrin had known inasmuch as she had turned it over to them a few days earlier.

That the Howes were the first people Ewa turned to in her despair is a true measure of her regard for their friendship. From the Shadrins' earliest days in the United States, Bill and Mary Louise Howe had opened their handsome Washington home to them. As a senior electronics analyst for the Office of Naval

Intelligence, Bill Howe was one of the first to debrief Shadrin in 1959. After one of his early sessions with Shadrin, Howe told his colleagues: "If he is a typical Soviet Navy captain, the United States is in deep trouble." Fortunately, Howe would later say, Shadrin was not typical; he was perhaps the best destroyer captain in the Soviet Navy.

Out of this grew a friendship that spanned sixteen years. There were frequent visits to each other's homes, and the two couples even took trips together. Nick taught the Howes' son to hunt and fish. Ewa was the Howes' dentist. When Nick encountered a snarl in becoming a citizen, Mary Louise Howe moved quickly to have a friend and neighbor who also was a U.S. senator sponsor a bill to alleviate the difficulty.

Ewa's tremulous, frightened voice on the telephone on New Year's Day instantly alerted the Howes that something was terribly wrong. It was puzzling enough that she was back early from the Shadrins' much-anticipated Austrian skiing vacation. More telling, however, was the way coherence eluded Ewa as she tried to speak. The Howes rushed from their house and sped across the Potomac River to the Shadrins' suburban Virginia home. The story, as Ewa knew it, cascaded through her tears. The Howes sat in stunned astonishment.

Ewa's appeal to the Howes, though largely instinctive on her part, could not have been more effective. Both were well connected with high government officials. They had friends in the Republican administration. Few people command a greater respect in the field of technical and electronic warfare than does William Howe. And Mary Louise possesses a genteel brashness that is undaunted by Washington's smoothest bureaucrats—or their secretaries.

The socially active, independently wealthy Howes have entertained hundreds of prominent people at frequent dinner parties in their elegant home. Mary Louise's activities have brought her into regular contact with many other wealthy, charitable Washingtonians. Ewa did not doubt the goodwill of FBI Agent James Wooten, but it was only after she had impulsively brought the Howes into her confidence that she began to see things a little more clearly. Their presence and concern strengthened her emotional well-being and permitted her a more balanced perspective.

There was a frenzy of activity in the early days of 1976 to find out what had happened to Nick Shadrin and to get him back.

19

Secretary of State Henry Kissinger was in touch with Soviet Ambassador Anatoly Dobrynin. Kissinger also talked to Soviet Foreign Minister Andrei Gromyko. Brent Scowcroft, President Ford's national security adviser, was briefed. President Ford himself was informed and later would make a direct appeal to Soviet leader Leonid Brezhnev. One hopeful plan was to try to involve former President Richard Nixon, and a direct contact was made with one of his personal advisers.

Despite these overtures—and dozens of other efforts by less prominent officials—the Soviets' response was essentially the same: They had not seen Shadrin in Vienna on December 20 and knew nothing about what had happened to him.

Ewa's intense frustration was deepened by the fact that she still did not know what Nick had been doing for the U.S. government. And she realized that if there was not an early resolution, she would be in the increasingly uncomfortable position of having to deal with Nick's friends and associates who would be asking about him. It was simply impossible to continue saying that he had remained in Europe to ski.

Bill Howe, who had spent twenty-five years in various areas of the intelligence business, was able to make more sense out of the clues than Ewa could. But even Howe did not know for sure what was going on. His counsel to Ewa was to bring into the fold of confidence Robert and Helen Kupperman, mutual friends of the Shadrins and the Howes who had excellent connections at the Department of State.

At the time of Shadrin's disappearance Robert Kupperman was chief scientist for the Arms Control and Disarmament Agency, located at the State Department. Helen Kupperman was an attorney for the National Aeronautics and Space Administration. They had first met the Shadrins about eight years earlier.

Kupperman and Shadrin had enjoyed a variety of activities together, but primarily their friendship was based on the long conversations they enjoyed, often at lunch. Although they saw each other during 1967 and 1968, when Kupperman was working for the White House, it was not until the early 1970's that their friendship blossomed. Today Kupperman is executive director at Georgetown University's Center for Strategic and International Studies.

"Nick Shadrin was a brilliant, warm, and compassionate

person," says Kupperman. "He was a man of extraordinary professional and intellectual gifts." Kupperman recalls seeing Nick and Ewa at the time they were about to cast their first votes as Americans: "Their discussions about who they were going to vote for was a poignant demonstration of their love for being in this country."

Kupperman was repeatedly impressed with Shadrin's distinguished connections. He recalls, for instance, that Shadrin introduced him to Admiral Stansfield Turner, who later became Director of Central Intelligence. Kupperman was also aware of Shadrin's close association with Admiral Rufus Taylor, who in the late sixties held the second highest positions at the CIA and the Defense Intelligence Agency. Taylor also served as the director of the Office of Naval Intelligence.

Upon hearing the startling news of Shadrin's disappearance, Kupperman felt a particular shock. He and Shadrin had planned to have lunch just before Nick left for Vienna. Shadrin called Kupperman a few days prior to their date and canceled, saying he had pressing business to take care of before his departure. Shadrin told his friend there had been recent developments that assured him of a better life in Washington. Kupperman assumed that this meant Shadrin's getting a more significant job with the government. Shadrin said he would be able to tell Kupperman more about it when he returned from his Vienna trip.*

Kupperman's first step was to begin calling personal friends in sensitive positions at the State Department. But even those friends would not tell Kupperman anything specific about the case. One did express horror over "the government placing an American citizen in such extreme jeopardy." Another told him the situation was none of his business, adding that "it is a sad and hopeless case."

Jim Wooten not only telephoned Ewa at least twice each day but frequently stopped by to see her. He seemed to keep her informed of every development, and she was sure his warm concern was genuine. Wooten clearly felt a deep personal distress at the strange disappearance of his friend.

---

*In all, Shadrin told at least a half dozen friends separately that his professional situation would greatly improve following his trip to Vienna. Shadrin was not a casual optimist, and all of his friends believe he must have been certain about something in order to make such a statement. In each case, he told the friend he would tell him more when he returned from Vienna.

But even Jim Wooten declined to explain specifically what had been going on in Vienna. It remained unclear how Shadrin had been serving the United States. Still, Wooten had revealed to Ewa that Ann Martin, the red-haired driver and Bruce all were with the CIA. Indeed, it seemed certain there was more to what had happened than a simple kidnapping.

Ewa Shadrin's distress deepened. Her counselors, the Howes and the Kuppermans, insisted that her quandary was intolerable. On January 6, at their urging, Ewa telephoned Jim Wooten and told him that he must give her a better idea of what Nick had been doing. It was essential if Wooten expected her to continue putting off people who already were asking repeatedly about when Nick would be back. She begged him to sit down with her, the Kuppermans, and the Howes.

That evening, promptly at nine o'clock, Jim Wooten arrived at the Kuppermans' home. Bill and Mary Louise Howe were there along with Ewa and the Kuppermans. It was a solemn, hopeful gathering. They sat around the Kuppermans' dining-room table, and Helen Kupperman served coffee and cake.

A trim, sturdily built man, James P. Wooten stands no taller than five feet nine inches. His rather large black eyes peer intently from beneath the high dome of his balding head. All this, combined with a roundish face, is in striking contrast with the stereotyped image of the tall, lean and lantern-jawed agent of J. Edgar Hoover's FBI.

For several years Wooten's wife had been ill with a debilitating disease. Several of their children were of college age, and Wooten had indicated to Ewa the financial difficulties presented by the combination of his wife's illness and the children's educations. Still, on this cold winter night, he seemed readily willing to drive a long distance from his Virginia home to the Kuppermans' house in northwest Washington. This willingness was seen as a measure of his goodwill.

After shaking hands with the Howes and the Kuppermans, Wooten explained that he considered the meeting off the record. He said he was doing it purely with the hope that it would assist Ewa to face her ordeal. He said that he was not going to make any report of the meeting to his superiors at the FBI.

There was not the slightest doubt in anyone's mind about Wooten's sincerity. "He was clearly as deeply concerned as we were," says Mary Louise Howe. "He was terribly agitated over the slowness of the government in resolving the matter. And we could all tell that Jim was absolutely devoted to Nick as a friend." Ewa, of course, had told them of the great admiration Nick felt for Jim Wooten.

What Wooten revealed that evening was an extraordinary story spanning nearly ten years. Nick Shadrin, reporting each day for his job at the Defense Intelligence Agency, had also been operating as a double agent for the FBI and the CIA. While under the direct supervision of the FBI, Shadrin had worked with the CIA in preparing "soft" information on the U.S. Navy to be passed to the Soviets.

Wooten told the gathering that during the summer of 1966 Shadrin was approached by a Soviet intelligence agent in downtown Washington. The agent proposed that Shadrin go to work as a spy for the Soviet Union. Instead of rejecting the overture at once, Shadrin stalled the agent and then reported the approach to the FBI, which had its Washington field office in the building where Shadrin's DIA office was located.

The Soviet Counterintelligence Section of the FBI took a great interest in what Shadrin told it. Immediately an opportunity to exploit the situation was seen. The FBI proposed that Shadrin play along with the Soviets—that he pretend to redefect to their ranks while continuing to work for DIA. Wooten said the FBI proposed to have Shadrin feed the Soviets CIA-doctored information about the U.S. Navy.

At this point, Wooten stated, Shadrin refused. According to the five people at the meeting that night, Wooten stated that for "close to a year" Shadrin refused the FBI's request that he play a double role with the Soviet agent. Finally, Wooten told the gathering, Shadrin's friend and mentor Admiral Rufus Taylor "twisted his arm" and persuaded him to cooperate with the FBI.

Wooten, who at every turn mentioned his admiration for Shadrin, emphasized that Shadrin finally agreed to play the game when it was clear that it was an opportunity to perform an extraordinary service for his country. Wooten said that the officials masterminding the operation did not perceive it to be particularly dangerous, especially since there were no plans for Shadrin to leave the United States.

Nick's role in the operation was to pass CIA-doctored informa-

23

tion on the U.S. Navy to the Soviets. What the United States was supposed to get in return—beyond the advantages of ultimately misleading the Soviets about U.S. naval capabilities—is far from clear. However, Wooten suggested that there would be great value in knowing the sorts of questions the Soviets would ask Shadrin. The questions alone could reveal areas of Soviet interest.

The five stunned listeners sat in awed silence. It was all so overwhelming that there were hardly any questions. Over and over, though, the same question arose: How could someone as intelligent as Nick Shadrin ever have consented to become involved in a dangerous counterintelligence operation? The answer was always the same: patriotism and Rufus Taylor.

Wooten said he became Shadrin's FBI case officer about six months after the operation had started. One of Shadrin's earliest Soviet case officers, Wooten related, was Oleg Kozlov, who was a diplomat at the Soviet Embassy in Washington from May 20, 1968, until December 15, 1972. Kozlov also was one of the two men Shadrin was last thought to have been with in Vienna. Wooten explained that on evenings when Shadrin would leave home for brief periods, he was taking material to a dead drop near his house, where it could be picked up by the Soviets.

Their heads already spinning with these revelations, the five were nearly incredulous as Wooten described how Shadrin had actually been sent out of the country in the early seventies on missions to meet with the Soviets. To experienced minds like those of Kupperman and Howe, the extreme danger of the basic operation was magnified hundreds of times by allowing Shadrin to meet with Soviet agents outside the country. The slightest indication that Shadrin was playing the Soviets for fools could be his downfall.

Shadrin's first meeting with Soviet agents outside the country took place on a trip to Montreal in 1971, Wooten said. Indeed, Ewa recalled a "business meeting" Nick had during their vacation in Canada. Wooten said that Shadrin again met with Soviets in Vienna in 1972. On that trip Shadrin was away from their hotel overnight so that the Soviets had time to train him in the use of sophisticated espionage equipment. Again, Ewa remembered a "business meeting."

In each case, Wooten emphasized that the foreign meetings were only supportive adjuncts to the major operation, which was being handled in the United States.

Bewildered by grief and despair, Ewa Shadrin could say only that her husband would never have done anything so stupid as to become involved in the madness described by Wooten. If he had, she said, he must have been grossly deceived or subjected to enormous pressures. Indeed, Jim Wooten agreed that the pressures from Rufus Taylor had been not only extraordinary but crucial to persuading Shadrin to go along with the scheme.

It was past midnight when the meeting was over and Jim Wooten departed for his long drive home. Although dazed by the revelations, Ewa and her friends shared a great feeling of gratitude for Jim Wooten. "He was just wonderful," says Ewa.

During those early days in January Ewa told Wooten that Nick had said he did not tell Ann Martin everything he learned from the Russian during his first meeting—that he was saving the most important information to tell Jim. Wooten listened carefully to this. Although he never offered any substantive comment, he did ask a few questions. In the course of doing so he made reference to "Cynthia."

"Who?" Ewa asked quickly, demandingly.

Jim Wooten looked at her, shrugged, and explained that the woman's name was not Ann Martin at all. Her name was Cynthia Hausmann. In comparison to everything else, the deceit seemed minor, but it angered Ewa to learn that the woman who had caused her so much discomfort had done so while cloaked in a false name.

Ewa also asked Wooten about the $1,000 in cash. He theorized that it was money the Soviet agent had given Shadrin at the first meeting to cover his travel expenses. Normally Shadrin would have turned it over to Wooten later. Wooten told Ewa that if she found the money, she could keep it.

It was then that Ewa thought about the courtly gentleman named John Funkhouser who called so often on the telephone. In her mind, Ewa always connected Funkhouser with Wooten. She had seen Funkhouser only three times, but she had talked to him hundreds of times over the years. Funkhouser would exchange pleasantries when he called and then say, "Is Nick around?" It happened that Wooten always used those exact words. Like Wooten, Funkhouser was a pleasant voice on the phone.

Ewa also knew that Nick was fond of Funkhouser and considered him a brilliant authority on naval affairs. They had had lunch together several times each month. Ewa finally asked Wooten if Funkhouser had something to do with the operation.

"He's with the CIA," replied Wooten, adding that Funkhouser was the agency's expert on the U.S. Navy. He indicated that Funkhouser worked with Shadrin to create the "soft" information that was being passed to the Soviets. "But," added Wooten, "it is very important that you never mention Funkhouser's name to anyone."

Ewa Shadrin meekly agreed, but her puzzlement deepened.

One evening around seven, a few days after the meeting at the Kuppermans' house, Jim Wooten dropped by to see Ewa. This was not unusual except that he brought another FBI agent along with him. Wooten told Ewa that following Nick's meeting with the Soviets in Vienna in 1972, he had been given some espionage equipment. It had been sent by diplomatic pouch to the Soviet Embassy in Washington and then turned over to Nick by his KGB contact. Wooten said the FBI thought it best to remove the equipment from the house now that Nick was gone.

Ewa readily agreed, although she could not imagine what could be in the house that she did not know about. Wooten strode directly to Nick's study and reached unerringly for a single book on a shelf packed with other books. He flipped it open with satisfaction. From the doorway, Ewa saw that the inside of the book was hollowed out, creating a cavity where something could be stashed.

Then Wooten told her they needed to find a piece of white paper that would appear blank. He said it contained important information written in an invisible ink—apparently a code. They searched unsuccessfully for the piece of paper.

Wooten told Ewa that somewhere in the attic there was a large radio transmitter. Listening to his description, Ewa felt certain she would have seen something that size, but she had not. She took the men to the attic, but they could find nothing. Then Ewa happened to pick up a box of things one of her friends had stored there. Beneath it was a cardboard box which Wooten instantly recognized as containing the transmitter. It seemed heavy. Wooten and his assistant carried it down from the attic.

Standing at her living-room window with Trezor, Ewa could see the shadowy figures of the two men as they loaded the radio transmitter into the trunk of their car. It was not difficult for Ewa to accept that Nick would conceal from her his participation in a frightening operation such as this. He had always been scrupulous about shielding her from his worries, from any difficulty that would impinge upon her happiness.

What she could not accept was that Nick could have been persuaded to become involved in something as mad and seemingly senseless as this. Although Wooten had stated repeatedly that the operation was tremendously important to the United States, that did not seem plausible to Ewa, on the basis of what she had been told. She was convinced that something more was going on than met the eye.

But her faith in Jim Wooten was resolute. His sure presence provided both comfort and hope. At one point when Ewa was at the depths of her despair, she had sobbed to him: "I just don't understand how Nick could have gotten into this. Did he ever think about what would happen to me? There were just the two of us. No relatives, no family. We just had each other."

Wooten replied that Shadrin had addressed himself to this very point. He had once asked Wooten how much help Ewa could expect from the FBI if something happened to him. Wooten assured him that the bureau would absolutely take care of Ewa's every concern.

It seemed to Ewa that Jim Wooten was living up to that compact. Not only had he been one of Nick's closest friends, but he seemed to be in a position to ferret out the truth, to pursue lines of inquiry that would lead to results. And he was absolutely committed to helping her. "No one could have worked harder," says Ewa. Wooten assured her he would not leave Washington until he found the answers.

At the core of Ewa's shock and confusion there glowed a steady faith that Nick was alive. As events swirled madly about her—the situation becoming more bizarre by the day—she clung to her belief that even the Soviets would find Nick more valuable alive than dead. Her touchstone with the murky past and the hopeful future was Jim Wooten. He was the bedrock upon which Ewa Shadrin built her faith. With Wooten's wisdom and guidance, Ewa believed the day would come when she would be reunited with her husband.

Chapter 3

THE silence of the chauffeur seemed heavier than usual to the young man and woman who sat in the back seat of the black Warsaw limousine. Holding hands, heads together, they spoke in hushed voices. It was early evening on May 19, 1959, in the Polish port of Gdańsk. The heavy car pushed through the crowded streets. In charge of the limousine was Soviet Naval Captain Nikolai Artamonov, and with him was Ewa Gora, a dark-haired, bright-eyed woman of twenty-one who was in her last year of medical school. Passing the outskirts of town, the dark car sped northwest along the sparkling Gulf of Danzig toward the town of Sopot. Their destination was the elegant Grand Hotel, where Captain Artamonov had planned a sumptuous dinner for just the two of them. The occasion was his thirty-first birthday. His purpose was to present an extraordinary proposal, one so fraught with trauma and danger that level-headed, intelligent Ewa Gora found it almost impossible to contemplate.

That Ewa Gora was merely in the company of Captain Artamonov was intensely traumatic for her family, especially her father. The historic resentment of the Poles for the Russians had reached a pitch so feverish in recent years that there had been rioting at Poznań protesting Soviet domination. Hatred for the Russians among the Polish population was so great that Captain Artamonov—the commander stationed at Gdynia to train the Indonesian Navy in destroyer techniques—felt it was too dangerous to walk the streets in his Soviet Navy uniform. Except for official functions, he wore civilian clothes when he went ashore.

For Ewa's father, an officer in the Polish merchant marine, the association of his daughter with the dashing Soviet commander was a disgrace. In fact, had Captain Zygmont Gora not been on a merchant voyage to China when Ewa first began seeing Captain Artamonov, it is likely that the relationship never would have developed. Captain Gora could imagine little worse than for his only daughter to marry a Russian and spend the rest of her days living in the hated Soviet Union, her spirit stifled by the Soviet system, her hopes of ever again seeing her family virtually nil. When her father did learn about the courtship—and when he had seen the couple together and suspected the seriousness of their relationship—he told close friends that if Captain Artamonov were not a high Soviet military officer, he would make plans to murder him.

Much of Ewa Gora's life in Poland had been comfortable, if not affluent. Nevertheless, she could remember Warsaw in 1944. She was seven years old, and the city was in flames. Her family and others were packed into trucks by the Germans and hauled to the train station. Ewa's head was shaved.

But the family had survived the ravages of World War II and acquired the financial security to provide the girl with almost any material thing she wanted. Life became so comfortable for Ewa that she came to largely discount the horrors she had seen as a child in war-torn Poland. Her doting mother—pampering her pretty dark-eyed daughter at every turn—would even grind carrots daily so little Ewa could have an abundance of fresh carrot juice. As a child Ewa never knew a Polish family that was not devoutly Catholic.

When Ewa grew older, she became an excellent tennis player. Jadwiga Gora would dispatch her son, Roman, two years younger than his sister, to the courts to deliver fresh strawberries and sour cream to Ewa so she would not have to interrupt her tennis and return home to eat. And Jadwiga Gora—an overbearing sort by most accounts—was so determined that her daughter become a dentist that she actually trained the girl to look forward to routine visits to the dentist's office.

Although Ewa's father was away much of the time, he, too, doted upon his daughter, bringing her expensive treasures from his voyages to the far reaches of the world. Her fancy was his command, and the little girl would give him long lists of the things she wanted him to bring her. Captain Gora took pride in filling her orders, down to the last whimsical detail. One of Ewa's most prized possessions was a coat made of extremely expensive fur from China. Ewa returned thanks for all this by being a satisfying child—excelling in sports and studies, reaching her last year in medical school with top grades.

One of Ewa's closest friends was married to Polish Navy Commander Janusz Kunde, who was in charge of liaison with the Soviet Navy. At the time there was a substantial contingent of Soviet naval men in Gdynia working with the Polish Navy to train Indonesians. On hand for training purposes were a Soviet submarine and destroyer, the latter commanded by Captain Artamonov.

Commander Kunde introduced Ewa to the Soviet commander at a party in October 1958. Ewa found Nikolai Artamonov an exceptionally striking-looking man. He stood about six feet two inches tall. Above his prominent black eyes were eyebrows that arched, as Ewa thought, "like a man always surprised." In a flash his eyes could race from good-humoredness to somberness. But he had an even temper and a quick wit that won him privileges denied other men of his rank. And by all accounts, he could be devastatingly charming.

On this first occasion, Ewa paid little attention to Captain Artamonov. He was, after all, a Russian.

Commander Kunde and his wife, however, thought their dear friend should give Artamonov another chance. They told Ewa that in addition to being handsome and charming, Artamonov had reached the rank of captain in the Soviet Navy at the age of twenty-six—the youngest in Soviet history. Some of the Kundes' praise was borne out later when Ewa heard from other friends who were tremendously impressed by the sharp wit and gentle grace of a speech Artamonov made to hundreds of women on International Women's Day.

The Kundes also pointed out that Captain Artamonov enjoyed privileges that were rare by any standards. He had a seemingly free hand in how he spent his off-duty time, a private limousine and chauffeur (compliments of the Polish Navy), and his own launch and engineman to take him to and from his destroyer. If he pleased, he could use the launch to take friends fishing or on sight-seeing excursions. He also was able to secure tickets to any cultural event, and he seemed to have unlimited funds for elegant dining and entertainment.

The privileges Captain Artamonov enjoyed were exceptional, even for a destroyer commander. Normally Soviet officers are not allowed such freedom in foreign ports, but Artamonov seems always to have been able to win concessions. This, no doubt, was due largely to his friendship with Admiral Mikhail Pavlovich Gladkov, who for years had been Artamonov's mentor. Admiral Gladkov seemed always willing to intercede on Artamonov's behalf, and it was rare indeed that Artamonov did not succeed in doing exactly as he pleased. There were occasions when he was reported for violating Soviet Navy rules—such as his fraternization with Ewa—but no punishment ever seems to have been levied.

All this had a strong appeal to Ewa Gora, a girl accustomed to getting what she wanted and doing as she pleased. She next met Artamonov at a small birthday party given by Commander Kunde in December. Ewa knew that Captain Artamonov had declined to come—preferring to go boar hunting—until Kunde told him that she would be there. That night they got along well, and Artamonov offered to take Ewa home. She agreed. Instead of taking the limousine, they walked the mile to Ewa's house. The rapport was instantaneous, and they talked the whole time. A few days later, a Soviet musical group arrived in Gdynia; Artamonov easily obtained tickets, and he and Ewa attended.

On these occasions, however, Jadwiga Gora refused to meet the Soviet commander when he came to call on her daughter. It was simply a scandal for the daughter of a respectable Polish family to associate with the Soviets—especially with a man who was playing such a prominent role in the Soviet presence in Poland. Ewa's brother, Roman, was given the job of receiving the new suitor when he came to the house.

Not long after she began seeing Artamonov, Ewa became bedridden with influenza for a few days. Pampered as she was, she had never imagined anything like what was to occur. No sooner had word reached the Soviet commander that she was ill than the cascade of gifts began. A virtual parade of Soviet naval officers came to the front door of the Gora house, bringing fresh flowers, grapefruits, and oranges. Something new arrived every hour throughout the day. Mrs. Gora rushed about trying to find places for all the flowers, which were soon spilling out of Ewa's bedroom.

Soon Jadwiga Gora began to have softer feelings toward Captain Artamonov. However, she was exceedingly glad that her husband was away in China.

Following this, Mrs. Gora consented to meet Captain Artamonov. Later she told Ewa that he was not really a Russian at all—that he was really a Georgian and just did not know it. She soon became nearly as fond of the Russian as her daughter was.

The fruits and flowers were but the beginning of a quietly extravagant courtship. It was against Soviet naval regulations for Artamonov to fraternize with a Polish woman, so it was prudent for him to be circumspect in his relationship. He always wore civilian clothes when they were together, but that did not interfere with their wide attendance at parties and cultural events. Not content with the many hours he spent talking to Ewa in person, Artamonov installed a secret private telephone in his quarters aboard the destroyer. He could call Ewa directly without going through the ship's telephone system. They spent many hours talking late into the night when they were not together. Ewa had taken eight years of Russian in school, and that was the language they used.

Nikolai Fedorovich Artamonov, whose Russian nickname was Kolia, was born on May 19, 1928, in Leningrad, which he would always regard as one of the world's most beautiful cities. His parents were well educated—his mother, the former Aleksandra Grigoryeva, a teacher and his father, Fedor, a mechanical engineer. Prior to the Revolution, the family had known an affluence which could be seen in the few remaining pieces of antique furniture and fine rugs in their home. As he grew up, Nikolai was the only child. Later there was a foster daughter who lived with the family after the siege of Leningrad.

Baptized in the Russian Orthodox Church, the boy enjoyed a warm family life. For many years he retained fond memories of his grandmother's religious teachings. Quite early his voice was thought worthy of cultivation, and he was encouraged to sing. Later he learned to accompany himself on the guitar, giving him and his friends pleasure for years to come.

For generations the family had been voracious readers. Nikolai's grandfather had owned an extensive library, which was passed along to family members, and the boy became an avid reader. Thoroughly knowledgeable in the Russian classics, he also developed a keen appreciation of classical Western literature. Among his favorite Western writers were Charles Dickens, O. Henry, and James Fenimore Cooper. Of all stories, his favorite was "The Ransom of Red Chief" by O. Henry.

Among the family tales in Artamonov's repertoire was one that involved his grandmother during Stalin's purges. Soldiers appeared at her home one day and demanded that she turn over a certain individual known to be in her keeping. Certain that the soldiers were going to take the man out and shoot him, she explained that the individual was ill, far too ill to be taken out and shot. She promised to nurse him back to health so he could be more properly executed. When the soldiers returned, the man was nowhere to be found, having recovered so thoroughly that he had escaped, the old woman claimed.

Apocryphal or not, the lightness of this recollection could not mask the horrors of living through those purges. Nikolai would always have a vivid memory of an uncle who was an economist. In 1937, after having expressed economic views that were counter to Soviet policy, he was seized in his home and sent to an insane asylum in Siberia. The family never again saw him.

Nikolai attended elementary school and became a member of the Pioneers, a Communist organization for children. He was an exceptional student, and in 1941 he was enrolled at a special secondary naval school on Vasil'evskii Island. He began to dream of becoming a naval officer and never gave serious consideration to anything else. It was considered an honor to attend the premilitary school, and during this period Nikolai first learned something about real war.

When the Germans were attacking Leningrad, Nikolai and his fellow students stood on the rooftops of the school buildings and fired small weapons at the attacking German planes. Not only were the weapons ineffective, but for the rest of his life Nikolai's legs would bear small scars from the shrapnel he and his classmates caught as their weapons misfired and ricocheted off the buildings.

From the time Nikolai was about ten years old, he had a pet German shepherd named Alfik. He taught the dog a host of tricks and later recalled that he would make Alfik perform his tricks so endlessly that the poor dog collapsed from plain exhaustion. Nikolai loved the dog dearly, especially since he had no brothers and sisters.

Then came the invading Germans, and Soviet military officials went through Leningrad conscripting all large dogs for military service. Alfik was taken away to a "training camp," where Nikolai was allowed to visit him on certain days. At the camp the dog's proclivity for learning tricks was put to good use. He was taught first that he could always locate food beneath an armored tank. Later he was taught that the only place he could eat his food was under the tank. Finally, Alfik and the others were trained to seek food beneath the tank as it was moving and to run along under the tank to retrieve the food.

When the German tanks finally thundered through the streets of Leningrad, Alfik and his comrades raced beneath the moving tanks in search of food. Upon the dogs' backs were strapped canisters of gasoline that exploded under the tanks, often immobilizing them. Alfik presumably died in this manner.

Many years later Artamonov would recall his last visit to Alfik at the training camp. "He was so sad," Artamonov would say. "He actually was crying when we said good-bye."

The siege of Leningrad bore down hard on the Artamonovs, as it did on nearly every family. Nikolai's father had to trade his prized stamp collection to feed his family; even so, he watched his own mother die. Starvation was so severe that young Nikolai lost some of his teeth. Many of his classmates died.

Years later Artamonov would recall an occasion when he was assigned to go out and scrounge up food for his classmates at the military school. He walked for a long time, looking for something he could take back for a meal. His search took him into a darkened cellar, beneath a heap of rubble, where he heard the sound of a cat. The meowing became louder, and then Artamonov felt the cat rub against his leg. He picked it up.

Here's dinner, thought Nikolai. The cat began to purr. He put the cat down and shooed it away. When he returned, he informed his classmates that he had not been able to find any food. But he told them about the cat and asked if he had done the right thing. They told him that he had.

Following his secondary education, Artamonov was again honored by being selected to attend Frunze Naval Academy, an institution roughly comparable to the U.S. Naval Academy at Annapolis. He started his classes in 1945 with major emphasis on radioelectronics, weaponry, and naval science. Other subjects included physics, higher mathematics, astronomy, and hydrology.

Artamonov was graduated fifty-seventh out of a class of 550 and was named to the rank of lieutenant, junior grade. He also won the "right to select fleet and privileges in assignment."

Artamonov was graduated from Frunze in 1949, the same year he became a member of the Communist Party. That fall he was assigned as the commander of a destroyer's combat unit. By 1952 he had been promoted to deputy commander of a destroyer. In 1954 he was assigned to take special courses in nuclear physics and nuclear weaponry, which he passed with honors. He was twenty-six when he was appointed commander.

In September 1955, at the age of twenty-seven, Artamonov was given the command of a Soviet Red Banner Baltic Fleet destroyer. He thus became the youngest man ever to hold such a high position in the Soviet Navy. He received many commendations, and his accomplishments were heralded in the Soviet press. *Red Star*, the Soviet Ministry of Defense newspaper, lauded the rising young officer. So did *Soviet Navy*, another publication.

Such commendation was unusual. These articles cited Artamonov for his outstanding performance and leadership as well as for his high competence in antisubmarine warfare. Significantly, the newspapers also praised him for his proficiency in propagandizing Communist Party decisions among his officers and men.

Years later Artamonov, tongue in cheek, would use various Soviet clichés to describe his image: "I was a one hundred percent Soviet citizen of the new generation, unmarred by . . . capitalist money."

Beneath this well-polished veneer of allegiance to the Soviet state drummed a deep and steady love for Mother Russia and her rich heritage. In the most difficult of times Artamonov would hark to an enduring touchstone: his abiding love for Russia—her people, her culture, her land. This love, perhaps more than anything else, nurtured his quietly growing resentment of the Soviet government.

Despite this deepening resentment, the brilliance of Artamonov's performance on the Soviet stage was never diminished. He and his destroyer were selected as one of two ships to represent the Soviet Union on official visits to Copenhagen and Malta. Twice Artamonov sailed his destroyer to England, again representing the best of the Soviet Union. The Soviet Navy seemed almost as proud of Artamonov as it was of the destroyer he commanded.

Three years after having been named commander, Artamonov

was assigned to Gdynia to work with the Polish Navy in training Indonesian sailors. At this time the Soviet government was wooing the Sukarno regime with more than a billion dollars' worth of arms and military training. Artamonov's assignment was to train the Indonesians in basic destroyer operations. A month after reaching Gdynia, Artamonov met Ewa Gora.

The courtship between Artamonov and Ewa went along blissfully once Mrs. Gora had been won over by the avalanche of fruits and flowers. Nevertheless, the couple did not flaunt their love. Then, in the springtime, Ewa's father returned home for Easter—a major religious observance in Poland. Captain Gora had been away many months and had not been told his daughter was seeing a Soviet naval captain. He was unhappy with the news, but Ewa protested that she and the Russian were only friends. Captain Gora said he would wait to see for himself.

While Captain Gora was in Gdynia, he hosted an Easter party aboard his merchant ship. A special feature was the food prepared by the Chinese cooks who worked on board. To reach the ship from Gdynia, Captain Gora's guests had to drive about six miles around the coastline. But Captain Artamonov generously offered his motor launch to ferry the guests directly out to the merchant vessel for the party. It was on this occasion that Captain Gora was first exposed to the gracious charm of the tall, handsome Soviet commander.

After the party Ewa found it futile to try to tell her father she was simply a good friend of Artamonov's. For two hours Captain Gora lectured Ewa about the dangers of falling in love with Artamonov. "Do not tell me you are just friends!" raged her father. "I am a man, and I can tell the way he feels about you. He will never go back to the Soviet Union without you!"

Captain Gora's anger and humiliation were so great that he told friends it was impossible for him to sleep. Then, abruptly, he set sail for China.

Although Ewa had not told her father, Captain Artamonov had indeed proposed marriage to her in March, suggesting that they could live in the Soviet Union. He had explained to Ewa that he had a wife in Russia from whom he was estranged and that he had no children of his own; he said a divorce could be arranged.

Ewa told him she could never live in the Soviet Union—not even for five minutes. She pointed out that Soviet citizens were not allowed to marry foreigners. Artamonov stated that he had some

36

connections to a relative of Premier Khrushchev's and could easily arrange special permission for the marriage. But because Ewa declared adamantly that she would never live in the Soviet Union under any circumstances, the discussion went no further.

As the Warsaw limousine sped toward Sopot and the elegant Grand Hotel, Ewa had no illusions about the future of her relationship with Artamonov. There would be no marriage. This, she thought, was heartbreaking. She loved Artamonov for his charm, his good looks and his considerate nature. Most of all, she loved him because he was the most sensitive and intelligent man she had ever known. But, short of marriage, she could still make the most of the companionship they had come to enjoy so much. And tonight there would be candlelight and champagne and fun—a celebration of his thirty-first birthday.

All these feelings were surging through Ewa when Artamonov lowered his voice and asked her if she would be willing to go away with him, to desert Poland and Soviet control and escape to the West.

"I was as shocked as if the Pope had asked me to marry him," says Ewa. She was certain she had misunderstood him. Artamonov repeated the proposition, adding that he had been thinking about it since March, when she told him she would never go with him to the Soviet Union. Whispering, he told her that he did not expect an immediate decision, that all he asked was for her to think about it and tell no one of his proposal.

He also said that he did not want to discuss any aspect of his plan. He stated that he would need to know her decision twenty-four hours prior to the time of departure. After that Artamonov changed the subject, leaving Ewa's mind spinning in confusion.

The momentousness of the proposal did not escape Ewa Gora. It stirred in her emotions ranging from elation to pure terror—if caught, they could be executed. Even living under Soviet domination there was a comfortable certainty to her life. And from a selfish standpoint she had everything a twenty-one-year-old girl could want—doting, almost affluent parents who catered to her, an education that would secure her future economic and social independence, and an ability to get along, even prosper, in spite of Soviet control. This was a lot to give up for the uncertainty of life in the West.

But such considerations paled in comparison with the sacrifice of Captain Artamonov. She could not comprehend how he was willing to give up his brilliant future in the Soviet Navy—a future that Soviet Navy journals had intimated could well take him to the helm of one of the world's greatest navies. The perquisites that went with such a military position in the Soviet Union were extraordinary. And, Ewa Gora knew, Artamonov loved the Navy and the sea perhaps more than anything. If he defected to the West, he would never again belong to any navy. She was awed that he was willing to give up these things to run off with her.

In making such a proposal, Captain Artamonov was placing extraordinary trust in a woman he had known for only seven months. However, he kept many thoughts to himself. Surely, during some of the time he spent alone with Ewa his thoughts must have ranged over deep-felt emotions and experiences. Yet he never voiced any secret thoughts about the system that could not tolerate the true thoughts of a man like Nikolai Artamonov.

Hard as it is to imagine, Artamonov never once shared with Ewa his deep hatred of the Soviet government. Those expressions would not appear until they were beyond Soviet control, and then they would come out gradually, tiptoeing from his mind in a cautious fashion that left Ewa uncertain exactly when she first heard them. They spent many hours talking about theater, listening to music, going to plays. She taught him how to play bridge. But there was such a deep-rooted terror of the Soviets that even a girl in love with a man who happened to be a Soviet military officer would not dare broach the subject. It was as though his being a Soviet were a stain that she tried to overlook. The only motivation for defection that Artamonov ever mentioned to Ewa was his love for her.*

The weather was warm and sunny on Friday afternoon, June 5, 1959. Captain Artamonov and Ewa Gora were strolling through a park along the bay, admiring the spring weather. It had been more than two weeks since his proposal, and now he brought it up again.

---

*An Indonesian naval officer was an unsuccessful suitor of Ewa's during those days. She had been introduced to him by Commander Kunde, who also introduced her to Artamonov. Later there would be speculation that the officer was an agent of the Central Intelligence Agency and that he had some contact with Artamonov prior to his defection. Indeed, the CIA did have various agents within the Indonesian Navy during those years, and it would not be surprising if Artamonov on some occasion had been introduced to a CIA agent. However, there is no substantial evidence that he was recruited.

He told Ewa that he was ready, that his plans were set and could be put into motion at any moment. He was scheduled to return to the Soviet Union in a few weeks, to spend a year at school preparing him for promotion to a higher rank. Conditions were at their best for his escape.

"I begged him not to do it then, to think about it," says Ewa. "I told him that he should return to the Soviet Union and that if he still felt this way, we could go away the next time he was in Poland." Artamonov responded that he absolutely could not return to the Soviet Union, that now was the time. He would not make the escape unless she joined him. He begged her to flee with him to the West.

But Ewa was terrified by the prospect. In a final plea, she reminded Artamonov that he would be abandoning forever his career as a navy man, that no other navy would accept a defector from the Soviet Navy. Captain Artamonov, his deep brown eyes looking down at her, nodded. He was aware of what he was giving up. He told her that he loved her and that he would not go without her.

Ewa's thoughts were essentially selfish, focusing on how much she had to lose. But Artamonov explained that a factor in his deliberations was her graduation from dental school, which had taken place just a week earlier. He had decided not to make his escape until she had her diploma in hand. Ewa knew that with her training as a dentist she could succeed in the West. Still, she needed time to think.

All of Artamonov's talents as a skilled seaman were brought to bear on his plans for escape. The vessel would be the twenty-two-foot motor launch assigned to ferry him from ship to shore at Gdynia—the same boat he had used to convey guests to Captain Gora's Easter party. The route would be across the Baltic Sea at night, toward Sweden, through water crisscrossed by Soviet and Polish ships and constantly scanned by Soviet radar. Artamonov spent hours studying the traffic and weather patterns of the Baltic and sharpened his consummate knowledge of the areas covered by Soviet radar. Even more hours were spent studying the currents of the Baltic. The voyage would take twenty-four hours, half that time in the daylight, when the boat could be quickly spotted by search planes.

Relying upon only the stars and a simple compass, Artamonov

planned for a landfall at Öland, an island off the southeastern coast of Sweden. He felt sure that until they were past the Hel Peninsula, not far from Gdynia, they would be safe—if questioned, he could argue that they were simply on a fishing excursion. After that there would be no excuses for his presence in those waters, though he would claim he had taken Ewa against her will. Therefore, it was essential that she take nothing with her to suggest her complicity.

But Ewa Gora still could not make up her mind. A level-headed, intelligent person, she found herself torn to the core by indecision. She had a great love for her home and family, and her life had seemed gratifying—until now. To leave made no sense from a practical standpoint. Artamonov repeated that he needed twenty-four hours to complete the preparations. The final word had to come from Ewa Gora, the pretty Polish girl who had everything she could dream of, everything to lose.

The next day was Saturday, and Ewa spent hours pondering her decision. By then she knew she wanted to go, but she was terrified that at the last minute she would not be able to go through with it. Never again would she see her loving mother, her doting father, her brother, her home, her friends, or her considerable possessions. She would be adrift in the world with only Artamonov as her anchor.

Finally, she decided, that alone was enough. She was sure she would never know a man she loved more than Artamonov.

That night, at an officers' club party attended by many of Artamonov's colleagues, including his mentor, Admiral Gladkov, Ewa whispered to him that she was ready, that she would go. Artamonov told her to act as if everything were normal. He would tell her the plans in the morning. After he took her home at 2:00 A.M., Artamonov returned to the party, where he continued drinking and talking with his friends, just as he normally would have done.

If he felt any guilt over his impending action, it was when he considered the wrath that would be heaped upon Admiral Gladkov for having befriended him and granted him special concessions. But in the end he knew this allegiance could not govern his life. The only thing that might have stopped him was his genuine love for his parents, but his father had died the previous year and his mother two years before that.

At midmorning the next day Artamonov appeared at Ewa's home. He was there only long enough to tell her that their plans were set, that he would return for her at 7:00 P.M. Ewa spent a nervous day, but she believes she never gave her family the slightest hint of what was planned.

She was at home alone when Artamonov arrived that evening. As usual, he was cheerful. He told Ewa to write a note for her mother, stating that they had gone to the International Fair at Poznań, a town about 260 kilometers south of Gdynia.

To cover his tracks further, Artamonov had informed other ship's officials that he would be gone all night with the motor launch—another night fishing expedition, he said. It was his hope that when he did not return the next morning, the Soviets would first check Ewa's home. There, he hoped, they would be thrown off the trail by the note. Artamonov knew that once the Soviets realized he had set out across the Baltic for Sweden, they could easily intercept him with airplanes and speedboats. It was essential to delay the discovery of their escape for as long as possible.

After she wrote the note, Ewa ran to a closet and got her new fur coat, possibly the most extravagant possession she had. She begged Artamonov to be allowed to take just that, nothing else. He smiled and said that he was sorry. She could take nothing except her diploma, which could be easily destroyed if they were seized. It was essential, he said, for her to take nothing that would cast suspicion on his assertion, if they were caught, that he had taken her against her will.

As they were about to leave the house, Artamonov called Ewa to him and looked at her for a long moment. He asked her to sit down beside him and to be very quiet, just to sit for a moment and think. They sat there for several minutes, saying nothing, as they contemplated what they were about to do. "It was a wonderfully composing time," says Ewa. "I suddenly felt relaxed and knew I was doing the right thing." After several minutes Artamonov looked at Ewa, smiled, and said, "Let's go."

From that point on the couple hardly spoke.

Leaving the house, they took a cab to the spot where the launch was anchored, about five miles from Artamonov's destroyer. Awaiting them was Ilya Aleksandrovich Popov, a twenty-five-year-old sailor assigned to operate the motor launch for Captain

Artamonov. Although Popov and Artamonov had known each other for several years, protocol in the Soviet Navy dictated that Popov never initiate a conversation with his superior. On this occasion he had been told that the commanding officer wanted to go fishing, and he was standing by to operate the boat. It did not seem unusual that food prepared by the ship's cook had been brought aboard, as well as extra gasoline. Popov started the engine, turned the launch away from the dock, and headed out of the harbor. At that moment Ewa Gora knew she would never again see her home or family or set foot in Poland.

The night was magnificent, with stars gleaming down through a clear sky. Artamonov had taken the helm, and the launch churned steadily through the Gulf of Danzig. For the first several hours he set a northeasterly course, heading toward Leningrad, in order to navigate around the peninsula of Hel. Artamonov's eyes scanned the horizon. His only weapon was a finely crafted pistol that he had treasured for years.

Artamonov told Popov to go below. He asked Ewa to keep an eye on him, to try to observe whether the young sailor knew what was going on. Although Popov never uttered a word, Ewa thought he seemed very nervous.

By 11:00 P.M. they had reached the tip of Hel, at which point they would enter the open waters of the Baltic Sea and take a northwesterly course for Sweden. It was the point of no return. If they were stopped, there would be no excuse ingenious enough to explain what they were doing.

Just as they passed the tip of Hel, a tremendous storm erupted. Lightning emblazoned the now black and roiling skies, and thunder crashed down upon the tiny vessel. Powerful gusts swept the little boat between pounding waves. Suddenly the bright night had become dense with heavy clouds. No longer were there any stars to guide them. A deluge of rain soaked Artamonov.

Below, Ewa quietly kept her eyes on the young Russian sailor. "Poor Popov," she says. "He was so young and confused." The storm raged on as they beat through the black Baltic waters.

Through the early part of the voyage Artamonov was constantly calculating where he might expect to encounter a Soviet or Polish ship. He also was aware of the radar coverage of the area. As they pressed into the black night, now well past the peninsula of Hel, Artamonov indicated to Ewa that so far all was well. He set the course, using only his compass and his instincts, and put Popov at the controls. In the open Baltic the risk of being detected by radar was minimal. Still, the tension was so great that neither Artamonov nor Ewa ate or drank during the entire voyage.

By dawn the weather had cleared, leaving the blue waters shimmering in the sunshine. Popov, though silent, obviously was upset. Artamonov told him that the violent storm of the night before had fouled the compass, that they had taken a wrong course. They pressed on steadily to the northwest.

Meanwhile, back in Gdynia at midmorning, Ewa Gora's mother heard a banging on her front door. She opened it to find several Soviet naval officers and other men she believed to be agents of the KGB, the Soviet secret police. They asked if she knew the whereabouts of her daughter and Captain Artamonov. She said she knew nothing more than what was contained in a note left her by Ewa. She showed it to the officers. The one in charge read it hastily. He turned abruptly and left, taking the note with him.

At 11:00 A.M., more than halfway across the Baltic, Popov indicated that he had spotted a vessel in the distance. Artamonov leaped to his feet and grabbed the binoculars. He studied the ship for a long time. It was quite a distance away, too far for Ewa to see it clearly. She could feel the tension rising. Then Artamonov relaxed, saying that he believed it was a West German ship which seemed not to have spotted them. Still, he knew that by this time the Soviets could have dispatched planes and speedboats to search for them.

At 7:00 P.M., twenty-four hours after leaving Gdynia, the vessel reached the Swedish island of Öland, only one-half mile from Artamonov's intended point of landfall. At first they could find no people, so they made their way in the boat along the western side of the island. Finally, they came to a tiny fishing village where they found a few families. Artamonov had expected that by this time word of their escape would have spread and that people would be on the lookout for his party. But the fishermen saw them only as friendly visitors.

Unable to find a common language, Artamonov communicated with the villagers through gestures and facial expressions. He gave them food from the boat and even broke out a bottle of cognac he had on board. The fishermen were delighted and could not fathom what he was talking about when he indicated he wanted them to summon the police. The party continued for nearly an hour. Ewa could feel her tension increasing as she realized how completely her life, her destiny, lay in the hands of Nikolai Artamonov. And during all this, Popov's confusion deepened.

Finally, Artamonov was able to get the villagers to send for a taxi. The driver took the couple to a tiny police station, where Artamonov was able to explain that he and Ewa were seeking asylum and that Popov hoped to return to the Soviet Union. For their safety, they all were placed in cells overnight. The next morning there arrived a Russian-speaking Swede, to whom Artamonov explained the whole situation. Among other things, Artamonov requested that an officer of the Swedish Navy be summoned. He would feel more comfortable dealing with a fellow navy man, regardless of nationality.

A few hours later an officer of the Royal Swedish Navy, Commander Sven G. T. Rydström, arrived. An excruciatingly thin man who stood nearly six feet tall, Rydström had served from 1952 to 1955 as a naval attaché at the Swedish Embassy in Moscow. In addition to his native Swedish, he spoke excellent Russian and English. In his mid-forties, he was much older than Artamonov and Ewa. The young couple instantly felt secure in his hands.

Clearly in charge of the case, Rydström immediately had them moved to a larger, more comfortable jail at Kalmar. He explained in detail why it was so important that they be lodged in a jail—that the Soviets were frighteningly skillful at grabbing recent defectors off the streets. Rydström quickly dealt with Popov, who had become deeply depressed as he grasped what was going on. Exercising full precautions and protocol, Rydström arranged for Popov to be returned to the Soviets. Meanwhile, after two days at Kalmar, Artamonov and Ewa were moved to much better facilities at Stockholm.

There were obvious practical reasons for Artamonov to have insisted that Ewa take nothing with her on their escape from Poland. But his own reasons for taking nothing were purely ideological. Artamonov later explained to Ewa that he detested the common practice of Soviet KGB and military men defecting to the West with satchels of information that they used to barter their way into favorable positions in their new countries.

In addition, Artamonov despised the KGB officers with whom he had been in contact in the Soviet Navy. He wanted to be certain his flight to the West bore no resemblance to the almost-commercial leave-takings of Soviet intelligence officers. Not only had Artamonov left behind all his possessions, but he declined to wear his Soviet Navy uniform. He left it hanging neatly on a rack aboard the motor launch, and wore a plain blue business suit. And just so it could never be claimed that he had taken *anything* belonging to the Soviets, he left his own pistol—a weapon he had bought personally and treasured—aboard the launch.

When the Soviet representatives in Stockholm requested permission to interview Artamonov, he refused to see them. He sent a messsge to the Soviets telling them where they could find their launch, adding that they would find his uniform and pistol on board. He never again wanted to speak to a Soviet official.

Back in Gdynia, Jadwiga Gora was gctting used to unexpected banging on her door. On six separate occasions she was taken from her home for interrogation. Early each morning she was driven to Gdańsk, where the KGB interrogated her for hours about Ewa's relationship with Captain Artamonov. On one occasion she was told that all eight of her questioners were specially sent from Moscow. The KGB took every photograph Mrs. Gora had of her daughter. KGB agents began interviewing Ewa's relatives all over Poland. Several days into the interrogation, the KGB agents told Mrs. Gora that her daughter and Artamonov had been captured by the Soviets. "Wonderful," Mrs. Gora replied. "Now I will get my daughter back!"

It was during her second interrogation that Mrs. Gora was led into a room where she saw a man wearing a Soviet naval officer's uniform slumped in a chair, his face buried in his hands as if he were sobbing. She was told the man was Artamonov's mentor, Admiral Gladkov. He was led away as Mrs. Gora was being seated for her interrogation session.*

On another occasion, when Mrs. Gora was questioned for an entire day, the Soviets made her give them all her keys. Later, when she returned to her apartment, Mrs. Gora discovered minute particles of plaster dust on the floor, which led her to conclude that

---

*The fate of Admiral Gladkov is unclear. However, it appears certain from the absence of any subsequent mention of him in available Soviet naval records that he was transferred into official oblivion, at the very least.

the Soviets had secretly installed listening devices in the walls of her home.

News of the defection flashed around the world. In China, Captain Zygmont Gora heard a mere snatch of a broadcast, saying only that a very high Soviet naval officer had escaped with his Polish fiancée. Captain Gora had no doubt that it was his daughter, whom he would never see again.

Deep inside Russia, two attachés from the American Embassy were aboard a train with two Soviet naval officers—one of them a KGB agent. They were traveling through far eastern Siberia en route to Nakhodka. One of the Americans, Marine officer Leo J. Dulacki, pulled from his pocket an account of the Artamonov defection, which he had clipped from the Paris edition of the *International Herald Tribune*. Smugly he showed the article to the KGB man, who perused it.

"I have known about this," said the KGB man, shaking his head sadly. "There is but one tragedy here, and that is that Artamonov has deserted his wife."

Ironic glances flashed between the Americans. When the KGB man asked if he could keep the newspaper article, Dulacki declined.*

All over Russia there were "closed party meetings" at which Communist Party members were briefed on the defection. Fifteen years later a former colleague of Artamonov's at Frunze Naval Academy would recall being instructed at one of these meetings that Artamonov had "fallen into evil temptations," that he had been lured to the West by a prostitute. But aside from party meetings, there apparently were no reports in the Soviet Union of the Artamonov escape.

In Stockholm the treatment given the couple was exceptionally good. A woman who spoke fluent Polish was assigned to take Ewa out sight-seeing or to lunch whenever she wanted to go. The interrogations went on every day, but otherwise Artamonov and Ewa were allowed as much time together as they wanted. Their guards and guides would take them sight-seeing on weekends.

But their home was the jail, and this was deeply depressing to

---

*Both Dulacki and Paul Adams, the second attaché, years later would become friends of Artamonov's.

Ewa. She began to question the wisdom of what she had done. She longed for her home in Gdynia and her mother. Her only comfort was Artamonov, and he spent many hours being questioned by Swedish naval and intelligence officials.

Her spirits improved considerably a couple of weeks later when Rydström invited them to come to his summer home at Göteborg and stay there until they could decide on their next move. He even arranged for them to have a separate house in the country, near his own. The transfer from the jail to the country was made with the greatest security precautions, including stopping to switch license plates on the way. Ewa was beginning to feel that the Soviets must be everywhere, and indeed, Rydström told her, they were. It was becoming clear that Sweden probably was not the best place for the couple to try to get established.

Until now there had been so much activity that Artamonov and Ewa had not discussed their specific final destination. Their entire focus had been on the first step—escaping from Poland. That accomplished, they could now consider the options available to them. Sven Rydström informed them that his government would do its best to accommodate them in Sweden. However, he explained, because of its proximity to Soviet-controlled countries, Sweden is a difficult place to relocate defectors. He told them that England would be receptive to them and that the Swedes could expedite their transfer if the couple wished.

It was Ewa who proposed that they go to the United States. Artamonov expressed indifference, as long as they found a safe haven, a place where Ewa could practice dentistry. He felt he could get along anywhere.

But Rydström had grave reservations about their going to the United States. "The Americans are the kind of people who will use you and abandon you," he warned, according to Ewa. This was a curious cloud, something neither Ewa nor, probably, Artamonov had ever thought about Americans. Ewa had a good impression of Americans, but Artamonov said he had too little firsthand knowledge to form an opinion. He listened carefully to Rydström's warnings, seeming to file them away in his mind.

After three weeks near Rydström's country home Artamonov and Ewa returned to Stockholm. The interrogation by the Swedes had neared completion, and consideration was being given to the move for permanent relocation. By this time they had become quite friendly with Rydström, who invited them to stay at his apartment in Stockholm.

Because Rydström had expressed negative feelings about their going to the United States, the couple did not inform him of their plans. One morning Ewa slipped out alone and went to the American Embassy. There she asked to see someone who spoke Russian. The receptionist asked her what she wanted. Ewa, so young, away from home for the first time, struggling in a foreign language, stood her ground and stated that she would see only someone in charge.

A giant of a man, Russian by birth, emerged from the inner offices and invited her to sit down. Ewa explained to him in Russian what had transpired so far. She stated that she and her fiancé would like to go to the United States. He listened politely, almost warmly. He told her to come back the next day, and to bring Captain Artamonov.

Ewa returned to the apartment with this news. That evening, when Rydström returned home, Artamonov informed him that they had taken steps to go to the United States. Rydström urged them to reconsider, according to Ewa, begging them to realize that the Americans could be nearly as callous as the Soviets when it came to using people for their own goals. He implored them to think more about going to England or even to consider staying in Sweden instead of going to the United States.

By that time Artamonov and Ewa shared a great liking and respect for Rydström. Nevertheless, they declined his advice. But his counsel would echo in Ewa's mind for the rest of her life.*

The Americans were exceedingly cordial to the couple when their Swedish guards delivered them to the embassy the next day. Ewa was astonished at the size of the Americans, for they all were strikingly taller than Artamonov. They said that officials in Washington had been contacted and that permission for the couple's acceptance by the United States was expected at any moment. They were told to go back with the Swedes to Rydström's apartment to await word.

---

*At the time of this writing, two decades later, Rydström insists that Ewa Shadrin has misinterpreted his position. He has stated to the author: "Nikolai said he wanted to start a new life in USA as a pure civilian far from his former existence, and to this I made the short remark that he could not possibly come to the USA without being thoroughly interrogated and probably more or less involved with U.S. Naval Intelligence." Ewa Shadrin, however, stands by her interpretation.

When Rydström returned home from work that evening, he was gloomy but matter-of-fact. He was bearing official word from the Americans to the Swedes that Artamonov and Ewa Gora had been granted their request for political asylum in the United States. Rydström told them to get their things together, that they would leave at once.

As soon as it was dark, and under heavy Swedish guard, Artamonov and Ewa were driven to an isolated section of what appeared to be a military airport outside Stockholm. They were met by several Russian-speaking Americans who explained that they were being put on a secret flight to Frankfurt. Artamonov and Ewa were led onto the airfield and taken to a small cargo plane. Ewa had been told to wear slacks so that from a distance she would appear to be a man. They and their escorts climbed into a compartment of the plane that was concealed from the crew. The cargo of the plane was lumber and some plain logs, and they sat on boxes amid the wood.

There were no seat belts, so the passengers were knocked about during the takeoffs and landings. The flight was very unpleasant, and in the darkness Ewa could think only of the days long ago in Warsaw when, as a little girl, her head was shaved by the Germans and her family was herded into the back of a dark truck.

When the flight reached Frankfurt, Artamonov and Ewa waited silently until the crew had disembarked. Then they were led off the plane and into a building where they were given an exceptionally warm welcome by the Americans who would be their hosts. The date was August 1, 1959.

In the dead of night they were driven to the handsome house that would be their home for the next three weeks. It was a lovely place on the outskirts of Frankfurt, with a beautifully kept garden. Their host was a former Russian, and the three guards assigned to them were courteous and helpful. Artamonov and Ewa were the only guests. A congenial Polish woman was assigned to Ewa, and she was a constant companion.

Their days were tightly filled with interviews and interrogations. As many as a dozen people would come to the house on a given day. The young couple never left the grounds of the house, but the lawn and gardens were ample for taking walks and relaxing. Ewa's outlook improved considerably.

To be sure, there were disagreeable aspects to their three-week stay in Frankfurt, which presumably was directed by the CIA's

Defector Reception Center. Artamonov and Ewa were given polygraph tests, but they were never told the results. Both were given extensive psychological tests, and there were long, seemingly pointless interviews with psychiatrists. Artamonov's debriefings lasted many hard, exhausting hours, but Ewa found it delightfully easy to entertain herself around the spacious house.

Within three weeks, a remarkably short time, Artamonov and Ewa were informed that they had been cleared for transfer to the United States.

The secret flight from Frankfurt to Washington was luxurious compared to the earlier one from Stockholm. Though the plane was small, it was not loaded with logs. And there were seats, although the compartment where the couple and their escorts sat was concealed from the flight crew. When the plane stopped for refueling in the Azores, the passengers were taken off the plane in a manner that prevented the crew from seeing them.

Toward the end of the eighteen-hour flight, as the plane neared Washington, the escorts began pointing out sights that Artamonov and Ewa had seen only in books. Although it was past midnight, brilliant floodlights illuminated the Washington Monument and the Capitol. Whatever happiness the couple felt at seeing America paled beside the larger relief that at last they were reaching a final destination.

The plane landed at Andrews Air Force Base at 2:00 A.M. on August 22, 1959. When the doors opened, the heat that rushed in was so torrid that Ewa actually wondered if they had reached Africa instead of America. No one had told her about Washington summers. She was still wearing a wool skirt and sweater that had been comfortable in Germany.

A marvelously warm and friendly man named Walter Onoshko greeted Artamonov and Ewa. Speaking fluently in Russian, he stated that he would be their host and interpreter. On behalf of the United States, he welcomed them. Onoshko led the couple to an enormous black limousine—so large it reminded Artamonov of a tank—that would take them to their first home. Inside the car it was cool and comfortable. Silently they were swept through the hot Washington night toward the Virginia countryside.

It was three o'clock in the morning when the limousine turned into the long driveway leading to the safe house. The large, rambling white frame house was located a few miles outside

Washington in the gently rolling hills of Virginia. The car's headlights illuminated the spacious grounds as they drove in. The lights of the house itself looked inviting to Ewa.

Inside, the dining table was covered with good food. There were wine and vodka in abundance. Walter Onoshko introduced them to a couple who were the cook and housekeeper. Three men who would constantly guard the couple were introduced, and Ewa found them warm and courteous. They sat down and had their first meal in America. Ewa felt good about being in the United States—the first time she had felt really good since leaving Poland.

At last there was a sense of security, of satisfaction, even though exhilaration was numbed by their physical and mental exhaustion. What stretched ahead was a long and uncertain road that led to the rest of their lives. But in spite of the uncertainties, the future seemed much more secure than it had the night they set out from Gdynia—a night that seemed a long, long time ago.

Chapter 4

At the Office of Naval Intelligence, on the fifth floor of the Pentagon in Washington, Lieutenant Commander Thomas L. Dwyer studied with growing astonishment a highly classified cable from Stockholm. In it the Central Intelligence Agency advised that Captain Nikolai Artamonov, commanding officer of a Soviet destroyer, had escaped from Poland to Sweden. He was in protective custody and undergoing interrogation by the Swedes. The CIA indicated that British intelligence officers were making a strong pitch to have Artamonov and his Polish girl friend, with whom he had fled across the Baltic Sea, come to England for resettlement. But, the cable advised, if the Office of Naval Intelligence (ONI) was interested in Artamonov, the CIA would use its influence to try to get him to come to the United States.

Dwyer, the Eurasian Area desk officer in ONI's Intelligence Collection Section, felt a tremor of excitement. This was not his first tour behind a desk in Washington, but the pace was slower than that of the earlier days of his gallant career. For instance, he served aboard the destroyer USS *Hugh W. Hadley*, which, during the Okinawa campaign during World War II, was attacked by more than 100 Japanese aircraft. Though bombed and hit by three suicide planes, the *Hadley* shot down twenty-three Japanese aircraft in a single ninety-minute engagement before being knocked out of action. Dwyer had subsequently held intelligence posts around the world. His adrenaline quickened as he sensed a major intelligence bonanza.

Dwyer went to the office of Jack Leggat, a former commander and deck officer who had seen battle as a member of both the Royal Navy and the U.S. Navy. Leggat was now a senior civilian analyst in ONI's Foreign Navies Branch who specialized in Soviet naval developments. "Jack," said Dwyer, "how would you like to have a *Skoryi*-class destroyer commander dumped on your desk?"

Well known for his wry, sometimes boisterous sense of humor, Leggat was always wary of being caught on the short end of a caper. He looked up at Dwyer and smiled. The *Skoryi*-class destroyer, considered the workhorse of the burgeoning Soviet fleet, was a prime intelligence target of the United States. More than that, the commanding officer of such a ship would possess a staggering amount of knowledge about the whole Soviet Navy. No one could seriously hope for such a superlative intelligence achievement. Leggat calmly waited for the punch line to Dwyer's question.

But Dwyer shook him off, insisting that he was not kidding. He explained that just such an officer had defected from the Soviet Navy and was within the grasp of U.S. Naval Intelligence. "You cannot imagine the jubilation," says Leggat. "It was like a dream coming true. And what's more, we knew all about Artamonov. We knew from Soviet publications that he was considered one of the brightest young officers in their whole navy."

Almost immediately a positive recommendation began its way back up the chain of command. Captain Rufus L. Taylor, then assistant director for foreign intelligence, concurred with his subordinates, and the recommendation went on to Rear Admiral Laurence H. "Jack" Frost, then the Director of Naval Intelligence. There was unanimous agreement that Artamonov be brought to the United States and turned over to Naval Intelligence as quickly as possible. Within days Artamonov's westward journey had begun.

After making their enthusiastic recommendations, Dwyer and Leggat—along with a few other analysts at ONI—settled back to savor just what Artamonov's defection could mean to Naval Intelligence. To their knowledge he was the highest-ranking Soviet naval officer ever to defect to the United States. Not only would his knowledge be vast, but it would be fresh. He would bring with him hundreds of details about the technical aspects of his own *Skoryi*-class destroyer as well as the latest developments in tactics, weaponry, and communications systems. Off the top of his head Artamonov would be able to answer questions and fill gaps that analysts had puzzled over for years. His basic knowledge could possibly save the United States millions of dollars through more efficient spending of research and development funds.

Even more important from an intelligence standpoint, Artamonov, as a senior officer, would possess information about Soviet naval strategy and theory that no degree of abstract analysis could ever determine. It was known to ONI that Artamonov had been a protégé of the Baltic Fleet commander and had been privy to some of the highest military thinking in the Soviet Union. He had attended a number of seminars for select Soviet naval officers at which Admiral Sergei Gorshkov, commander in chief of the Soviet Navy, had expounded upon secret Soviet policies and intentions. Indeed, if the debriefing were handled properly, Artamonov could become one of the most important military defectors in United States history.

But this aside, Dwyer and Leggat, as two former seagoing deck officers, shook their heads in wonderment and admiration that Artamonov was reported to have crossed the Baltic and made land only one-half mile from his intended destination. States Dwyer: "It was pretty courageous, escaping in a small open boat with a magnetic compass and maybe a sextant to navigate by, crossing some hundred fifty miles of open ocean with the ever-present threat of being discovered by a Soviet naval patrol craft. Nick was distressed he missed the landfall by so much. For me it would be a miracle."

A staggering amount of detailed planning must have gone into the feat. Artamonov would have had to make precise calculations of the Baltic currents, estimations of wind velocity and direction, the plotting of Soviet patrols. Dwyer and Leggat were anxious to meet the extraordinary Captain Artamonov.

The defection of Nikolai Artamonov coincided with a crucial period in the development of the Soviet Navy—a period when naval intelligence analysts were more interested than ever in learning Soviet techniques and intentions. Although the United States maintained a strong naval superiority, there was no question that the Soviets were gaining broadly and rapidly.

Writing in *The New York Times* eighteen months prior to

Artamonov's defection, military affairs analyst Hanson Baldwin summed it up this way:

> The United States has a tremendous numerical and qualitative naval superiority over the Soviet Union, and far more global naval experience. But, since World War II, Russia has out-built the United States in new submarine tonnage by six to one, in destroyer tonnage by nine to one, in cruiser tonnage by 14 to one.

By September 1964 the same military writer stated in an article in the *Atlantic Monthly* that "the Soviet Navy . . . has been transformed from what was essentially a coastal defensive force into a blue-water offensive fleet."

During those intervening years of tremendous Soviet naval expansion, the United States had at its fingertips a brilliant man with a stunningly good memory who could provide a firsthand glimpse into the Soviet naval mind. Indeed, Nikolai Artamonov's value to the United States was inestimable. "He was the most knowledgeable defector in ONI's history," says Dwyer. And of course, Artamonov's greatest contribution could be realized in the future, as an analyst for U.S. Naval Intelligence, assessing Soviet moves and anticipating future ones.

From the start the CIA seems to have had little active interest in Artamonov. Spies have an insatiable hunger for documents, and Artamonov had not brought a shred of paper with him when he defected. What he did bring, of course, was a vast and vibrant store of knowledge about the Soviet Navy. But that alone seems not to have been sufficient for the CIA to want to develop Artamonov into one of its own resources—as it did with a number of important defectors from Soviet intelligence services.

And Artamonov seems to have had little interest in dealing with the CIA. More than simply having no background in Soviet intelligence operations, Artamonov appears to have scorned the KGB officers he knew. He took great pride in his advanced education, his technical training, and his high position in the Soviet Navy. Indeed, he clearly thought the skills of his intelligence counterparts—whether American or Soviet—were crude compared to those of highly trained military men. There are also indications from his earliest days in the United States that Artamonov harbored a distaste for, if not an outright suspicion of, many of the CIA people he met.

Still, it was up to the CIA to pass judgment initially on the subject of Artamonov's bona fides. The Soviets had become increasingly skilled at sending out phony defectors who, if accepted, could do considerable damage by conveying disinformation as well as by transmitting fresh information back to the Soviets. This apparently was a major point of concern in Frankfurt at the Defector Reception Center.

The three grueling weeks of interrogations, psychological evaluations, and polygraph tests at the Defector Reception Center certified Artamonov's bona fides in the minds of the senior CIA officials in charge of the case. Three weeks is a relatively short time for this process, but one former CIA counterintelligence officer has stated there is nothing unusual about this swift handling in view of Artamonov's prominent position in the Soviet Navy. His case would have been expedited to get him into a useful position as quickly as possible.

But on at least one occasion in Frankfurt Artamonov flunked his polygraph test, a fact that was resolved at the time but would pop up nearly two decades later as evidence to suggest doubts about his bona fides.* Nonetheless, the senior officers handling the case obviously considered the polygraph problem resolved because Artamonov was sent on to the United States and turned over to Naval Intelligence. Within weeks of his arrival in America he was being questioned by senior intelligence analysts who prepared their own questions. If there were doubts about his bona fides, the CIA never would have allowed senior analysts to be exposed to him.

From the time they set foot in America, Artamonov and Ewa underwent a gradual cultural metamorphosis. They, and their handlers, knew that English would have to become their language, that their customs would have to be Americanized. In order to get along, they would have to learn as much about their new country as possible. It was a goal with which everyone involved was in agreement.

---

*Simple failure of a polygraph test certainly carried no great significance in the minds of the top CIA management under Admiral Stansfield Turner. When one of his appointees for chief of a major division was unable to pass a polygraph in 1979, Turner waived the results and put him in the post anyway—after ordering new questions and a new polygraph operator. The case is not dissimilar to what appears to have happened in Shadrin's case in Frankfurt as well as in other cases of initial polygraph failure.

Almost immediately the name Nick rolled from the lips of the people who dealt with Artamonov. In Russia he had been called Nikolai or Kolia, a Russian nickname for Nikolai. But to an American looking at the name Nikolai, Nick seemed natural. Thus, from the start he was called Nick, a name that stuck and evolved into Nicholas when he finally put together the full name that would be his in the United States.

It was months later that he and Ewa selected the name Shadrin—and even then it was done as a fluke, with the thought that it would be only temporary, something they could change later. Ironically, the name Shadrin comes from the archvillain in Russian novelist Aleksander Pushkin's *The Captain's Daughter*. But the name stuck—evolving into Nicholas George Shadrin—and became the only name Artamonov would ever use in the United States.

The first days in the United States were comfortable for Nick and Ewa. Their biggest complaint was about the cook at their safe house, a grumble few Americans were in a position to make. But the American handlers were friendly and helpful and seemed willing to assist them in anything they wanted to do. Walter Onoshko, who was known as Benson to Nick and Ewa, had been joined by an equally amiable man named Walter Sedov. Onoshko and Sedov were their chief handlers and interpreters, and through them Ewa and Nick made all their plans and appointments. Indeed, Onoshko and Sedov were a window on America for the newcomers.

The first days Nick and Ewa spent much of their time walking the grounds of the safe house, always with at least one of the guards. Altogether there were nine armed guards working in three rotations. Even then Nick found the presence of the guards annoying, a small point that later would grow into a major issue. Ewa could hardly tolerate the constant cigar smoke she associated with the guards.

As soon as Nick had rested for a couple of days, he began the long and strenuous business of debriefing. It lasted at least eight hours each day and often more and was an exhausting experience for him. Ewa, meanwhile, was beginning to have an enjoyable time. The CIA assigned a Polish-speaking woman, who went by the name of Mrs. Forrester, to be her companion.

"Everybody, even the guards, made fun of Mrs. Forrester,"

says Ewa, who describes her as an amusing, officious woman who always wore loud Bavarian hats with feathers. Mrs. Forrester claimed to be from Colorado. "She was from Colorado like I'm from Peking," says Ewa.

But Mrs. Forrester did her job well. She was strikingly successful in teaching Ewa to speak English. She also took her shopping or to the movies or out for lunch. She even taught Ewa how to cook. Mrs. Forrester attracted much teasing from the CIA guards, who sometimes made vicious fun of her pretentiousness.

One person who did not find Mrs. Forrester amusing was Nick, whom she was also supposed to tutor in English. He would become so agitated over her silly antics that Ewa feared he would be rude to her. It soon became clear that Nick would have to polish his English elsewhere.

While everything suited Ewa superbly, Nick Shadrin was beginning to have reservations about his new status. A person's motivation for defecting is rarely positive in any pure sense, and Shadrin was no exception. In his case, the primary goal had been a negative one—to get away from something, to flee a system he could no longer tolerate. A positive aspect of his defection may have been his love for Ewa, but that is probably the only one.

Although Shadrin's actual escape was planned meticulously, there is no evidence that he had given much thought to what would happen to him in the West. He had never discussed his feelings about the Soviets with Ewa, but Shadrin's debriefers immediately recognized that in his heart there was an intense, intelligently thought-out hatred of the Soviet system—a hatred that had propelled him westward into a highly uncertain future.

During his first weeks in the United States Shadrin finally began to consider his future. Although Onoshko and Sedov were pleasant enough hosts, Nick's pleasure with what he was seeing in America stopped there. The guards assigned to the house were, in Nick's eyes, not much different from Soviet security personnel. They seemed sloppy and spent much of their time watching television and smoking cigars.

Worse that that, the CIA interrogators were making a poor impression. One of the earliest English words Shadrin learned was "plumber," and that was the name he applied to some of the people who came to interrogate him. To Nick, the term suggested a person who was primarily a technician, a man who exhibited no depth of understanding of larger issues, a man sent to perform the technical job of asking a list of questions and making note of the answers. This was quite different from the highly skilled process of elicitation practiced by some of the analysts from ONI.

Shadrin became deeply frustrated over the fact that the Americans had issued them no papers. He had nothing to show his identity. His security was utterly in the hands of the technicians handling him. No one was able to discuss with him what he finally would do in the United States. No one seemed to know whether Ewa would be able to practice dentistry in the United States or even what had to be done to get her enrolled in the proper school.

Worst of all, the CIA people Nick was dealing with—primarily the guards and the "plumbers"—began to remind him of the KGB officers he had despised in the Soviet Union. He thought of them as officious and not very smart, yet readily willing to pontificate on any point. And the pretentious Mrs. Forrester was a constant irritant to Nick, who could hardly refrain from throwing her bodily out of the house.

In all, it was a time of great confusion and trauma for Nick and Ewa.

Much more thought was being given to Shadrin's situation than he could know. By mutual agreement, a defector with Shadrin's particular expertise would fall into the province of Naval Intelligence; nevertheless, the CIA retained authority over Shadrin's resettlement and adjustment to life in the United States.

The job of coordinating the overall debriefing of Shadrin went to the firmly affable Tom Dwyer. He decided who would question Shadrin on which days and tried to avoid a wholesale duplication of interrogation on the same subject. Dwyer was also in charge of seeing that Shadrin was happy and that his debriefing would be of maximum value.

At the Central Intelligence Agency, Leonard McCoy, an officer in the Reports Section of the Soviet Bloc Division, was assigned as a liaison officer to work with ONI on Shadrin's debriefing. McCoy was an expert on the Soviet Navy. In this case his job was to take the reports generated from ONI debriefings, edit them, and disseminate them to the proper parties.

From the beginning McCoy told the ONI officers that he did not want to meet Shadrin or have any personal contact with him. He preferred to stay in the background, reading the debriefing reports. McCoy said that he could remain more objective if he did not become personally associated with the Soviet naval captain. His position was not unusual; this was a standard posture taken by CIA counterintelligence personnel.

In addition to debriefing Shadrin, Tom Dwyer decided to make a determination of the former Soviet citizen's fitness to go to work for ONI as an analyst. Never before had a defector been employed as an analyst for ONI, but initial indications were that Shadrin possessed such a wealth of knowledge and analytical instincts that he could be of primary usefulness for many years to come.

Dwyer was aware that Shadrin had flunked one of his polygraph tests in Frankfurt. In fact, the polygraph operator, who happened to be a navy captain, had since returned to Washington and told Dwyer about the incident. Although Shadrin had been cleared, the polygraph operator seemed to harbor some lingering suspicions. He recalled that once when he left the room and observed the Russian through the two-way mirror, Nick was smiling broadly, causing him to wonder if he was perhaps taking some pleasure from duping his interrogators.

By the time Shadrin was turned over to ONI no serious question remained about his bona fides. There had been at least two other polygraph tests given Shadrin in the United States, and the presumption is that he passed them. It was generally understood that he would not be turned over to senior analytical personnel at ONI if there remained any substantive questions about his bona fides.

The initial CIA interrogations, which had so irritated Shadrin, were aimed at eliciting all perishable information. The questioners picked his brain for every shred of cryptographic information. He was asked about codes as well as about everything he knew on the subject of current operating plans for the Soviet Navy and his particular division in the Baltic Fleet. Much of that sort of information would have been changed by the Soviets upon learning of Shadrin's defection, but still, it had value as an analytical device for measuring the Soviet reaction to Shadrin's defection.

About ten days after Shadrin's arrival Tom Dwyer was notified that he could begin his long-term debriefing. Leonard McCoy told Dwyer where he could meet the driver from the CIA's Security Office who would take him to the safe house, using an ingeniously circuitous route so that even Dwyer never knew the location of the house.

Shadrin, who had become depressed over his dealings with the CIA officers, was elated when told that he would be meeting a navy man. Tom Dwyer arrived one morning with Walter Onoshko and Walter Sedov, who served as interpreters. "Nick was the picture of confidence," says Dwyer. From the first moments the two navy men got along splendidly. They spent the morning in the living room of the house talking informally. At lunch that day Ewa joined them.

"It was as if there was no language barrier with Tom Dwyer," says Ewa. "Tom was so gracious, so friendly, such a gentleman. We immediately understood each other. Tom could talk with his hands and his eyes and his face. It almost didn't matter that we did not have a common language."

From that day forward both Nick and Ewa felt much better about their future in the United States.

With his introduction to Tom Dwyer, Shadrin began nine long months of steady debriefing by ONI. Because Shadrin had been a high Soviet naval officer, there were myriad areas where he had extensive knowledge and expertise. To dissect the *Skoryi*-class destroyer alone took weeks of discussion. Proper debriefing required a virtual parade of naval officers and civilian analysts, each with his own intelligence specialty, each assigned to explore a different compartment of Shadrin's vast store of knowledge.

One of the first intelligence analysts to debrief Shadrin was Jack Leggat, who was as awed as his colleagues by the wealth of information the Russian seemed to possess. At first Leggat was surprised by the scowl on Nick's face, especially since he had heard Tom Dwyer talk about what an amiable chap Nick was. "He looked angry when I first met him," sayd Leggat. "But it turned out he was under the impression I was another 'plumber' from the CIA. He cheered right up when he found out I was a navy man."

Leggat points out that a distinct difference between Shadrin and many of the defectors from Soviet intelligence services was that he held back nothing. Perhaps it would have been to his advantage to adopt the technique of some of the skilled KGB defectors who managed to spend years bartering what they knew. But the knowledge cascaded from Shadrin in torrents that swelled the information coffers of Naval Intelligence.

"There was never any question of his keeping back anything," says Leggat. "And he was meticulously honest. When there was something he wasn't sure about, he wouldn't hesitate to tell you.

But when he told you he was sure about something, you could count on it."

Once Shadrin was firmly in the hands of Tom Dwyer and the navy men, friendships began to grow that offset much of the unpleasantness in his life. From the earliest interrogation sessions, the grueling day would be capped by generous libations of vodka and good conversation, ranging from world history to modern geopolitics. Many of these early friendships would continue to sustain Shadrin throughout his time in the United States.

Commander Robert Herrick was serving in Hawaii as the chief of intelligence collection for the commander in chief of the Pacific Fleet when Shadrin first reached Washington. Herrick, who was well aware of Shadrin from Soviet publications he had read, was recalled to Washington for a six-week stint to participate in Shadrin's debriefing.

"Nick was a fountain of valuable information," says Herrick. "And he and I hit it off immediately. He liked anything having to do with the navy, and he enjoyed talking about the Soviet Navy. We ended almost every session by opening a bottle of vodka."

A point of contention between Nick and Ewa that seems to have reached back to their first days together was Nick's smoking, which he went at with the same enthusiasm he showed for everything else. Not only did it bother Ewa, but it gave her considerable cause for worry about his health. Tom Dwyer was also a heavy smoker and was convinced it was doing him no good. Dwyer and Shadrin entered into a pact to stop smoking on October 1, 1959, only a couple of months after Nick's arrival. Dwyer bought a box of Bantron tablets, which are supposed to help one give up smoking.

"I took the box of pills out to the safe house and took one of them in front of Nick on the day we were going to quit," recalls Dwyer. Then he gave the box to Nick. Dwyer managed to quit on that occasion, but the pressures on Nick were too great. "Fifteen years later Nick still had that box of tablets in his pocket, and he was still smoking," says Dwyer. When Dwyer looked in the box all those years later, there still was one tablet missing—the one he had taken.

From the time they first met, Dwyer and Shadrin were friendly. What started with Tom's trying to be helpful to the two strangers in his charge quickly grew into something warmer. Nick and Ewa observed their first Thanksgiving celebration at the

Dwyers' home that November, a festive occasion that set the style for many future gatherings.

Shadrin's knowledge was so vast that experts from many fields were brought in to question him. Among them was William E. W. Howe, one of America's most brilliant scientists in the field of electronic and technical intelligence. A small, energetic, eccentric man, Howe began his career with the Office of Naval Intelligence in 1949. In 1974 he switched from Naval Intelligence to become the top man in the technical division of Army intelligence. On more occasions than one, Howe's middle initials have been said to stand for "electronic warfare." Indeed, that was his specialty.

Trained as a physicist and an electronics engineer, Howe has been responsible for some of the most successful technical efforts of U.S. intelligence. Many of his accomplishments remain highly classified, but one top former naval intelligence man flatly describes Howe as the "electronic warfare wizard" of the U.S. Navy.

When Shadrin arrived in the United States, Bill Howe was the senior electronics analyst for the Office of Naval Intelligence. While old sea hands like Jack Leggat and Tom Dwyer obviously had much in common with Shadrin, one would not expect tiny, intellectual Bill Howe to find any great rapport with the large, gregarious Russian. But the two hit it off splendidly. Howe was deeply impressed with Shadrin's knowledge of electronics and the technical aspects of the Soviet military establishment. Even more than that, Howe was astonished at Shadrin's superior intellect.

The friendship between Bill Howe and Shadrin seemed instantaneous. Mary Louise Howe, Bill's outgoing wife, took an immediate liking to Nick and Ewa. Some of the young couple's earliest social visits in America were at the Howes' elegant home in the Kent section of Northwest Washington. There are many superlative aspects to the hospitality offered by Bill and Mary Louise Howe, including an extensive collection of wines from around the world and more particularly an after-dinner cordial list of 100 different selections. Nick spent many happy evenings savoring the wines and cordials at the Howes' home.

Over the years William Howe had been involved in the interrogation of other defectors, and he found Shadrin to be exceptional. Howe says that the information brought by Shadrin was "extremely valuable" and that all of it has held up over the years.

Howe emphasizes the point that the information produced by

Shadrin was so damaging to Soviet interests—and has continued to be so even to this day—that it is inconceivable that he could have been a disinformation agent. In fact, some of the information Shadrin gave to the United States is so sensitive that it remains highly classified. Howe also says that not only was Shadrin's information unique, but it was universally accepted.

Usually an amiable fellow, Shadrin rarely suffered fools lightly. William Howe was aware of that. "Nick had an intellectual snobbery about him that could irritate his colleagues," he says. "And he was extremely intolerant of stupidity." More than one associate over the years found this out, starting with the "plumbers" who so infuriated Nick.

Howe also was impressed with Shadrin's meticulousness in describing what he did *not* know about a subject in which he was well versed. "That was one of his greatest strengths," says Howe. "He was always sure about what he did know and what he didn't know."

Bill Howe is positive that Shadrin's bona fides had been accepted by the CIA at the time they turned him over to ONI. "There is no way they would expose senior analytical personnel like me to him if they had any questions," he says. He points out that a trained agent could pick up sensitive information just from the questions a man like Howe might ask. Howe recalls that during his years in the intelligence community there were defectors who were under suspicion, and analytical personnel were not allowed to question them directly.

One of the important areas of information Shadrin could discuss concerned surface-to-surface guided missiles. At that time the U.S. Navy had been experimenting with the concept of a supersonic pilotless airplane, but the developments were not significant. Moreover, the United States did not regard it as a top-priority item for development. But Shadrin reported that the Soviets had perfected this type of missile—one that could fly at a low altitude at great speed for long distances. He was able to describe the technical aspects of the development in precise detail.

Not only did everything that Shadrin reported about missiles turn out to be true, but the analysts at ONI were wise enough to accept his information at that time. Accordingly, U.S. plans were modified, and new emphasis was placed on the research and development of this type of missile. As a result, the United States was able to produce a missile that effectively countered the Soviet effort quite a bit earlier than it would have without Shadrin's help.

Tom Dwyer states that this is a prime example of the sort of vital information—hard intelligence crucial to the security of the United States—that Shadrin provided. Dwyer, as well as other intelligence analysts, claims there are additional examples to support this point, but they remain highly classified.

The scope of Shadrin's information was stunning, ranging from technical aspects of missiles and communications systems to the strategic and tactical thinking of Soviet military leaders. One of the Soviets' most closely held military secrets was their zones-of-defense concept, which is described in a book* by Robert W. Herrick, one of Shadrin's early friends.

At a time when the Soviet Union was officially denigrating the importance of developing a navy capable of traversing the globe, in reality it was carefully constructing its whole military establishment around just that theory. In 1959 Premier Khrushchev placed his imprimatur on this massive ploy by making this official statement: "Military ships are good only to make trips for state visits. From a military point of view they have gone out of fashion. They have become obsolete! Now they are only a good target for missiles!"

Fortunately for the United States, Nicholas Shadrin was able to provide important details about the Soviets' real plans for overall strategy, which was based on the recognition of the necessity for the very ships Khrushchev had ridiculed.

In his book Herrick observes that the reason for the Soviets' secrecy about their zones-of-defense strategy was that:

> to acknowledge the existence of such zones is to admit that all the Soviet claims that the military-technical revolution has outmoded the surface component of naval power are purely propaganda—and so too, obviously, does their existence admit the falsity of the Soviet claims that submarines and aircraft alone provide all the necessary ingredients for supremacy at sea.

A significant aspect of Soviet weakness was revealed by Shadrin's assessment of the Soviets' first zone, which included an area 150 miles off the coastline. This zone, according to Herrick's

---

*Soviet Naval Strategy, (Annapolis, Md.: Naval Institute Press, 1968).

account, "is considered to be the only maritime area in which the USSR can expect, even under favorable circumstances, to exercise command of the sea against the superior power of the NATO naval forces. . . ." Knowledge of this secret was vital information for U.S. naval analysts and strategists.

An important point Shadrin was able to clarify concerned the Soviet position in those years not to build aircraft carriers. U.S. Intelligence knew they were not being built but remained puzzled as to why. Shadrin had heard the official explanations in highly privileged meetings. The Soviet view was that carriers simply were too costly and vulnerable in comparison with other warships, and the same money could be spent more wisely on destroyers and submarines. The orders were directly from Khrushchev, who, Shadrin once told Robert Herrick, "knew no more of naval matters than did a pig about orchids."

In addition to the major areas in which Shadrin could help, there were myriad small ways that, less obviously, were tremendously useful. U.S. intelligence operatives in the Soviet Union had tried to find the location of the offices of the submarine headquarters of the Soviet Navy in Leningrad but had been unsuccessful. It took Shadrin perhaps thirty seconds to explain just where it was. It turned out he was right.

In the bureaucratic maze of the Defense Department, there have always been squabbles over the size of Soviet military components relative to those of the United States. An important reason for these debates is that they bear upon the size of military budget being requested. From a bureaucratic standpoint it is important to describe and estimate what the Soviets have as a basis for requesting adequate funding to establish proper countermeasures.

Such a squabble had festered for years over the question of whether the Soviet Union had a Marine Corps. Some argued feverishly that it did, while a more objective handful said that it did not. A quick question to Shadrin settled the issue. There was no Soviet Marine Corps at that time.

The area of Shadrin's greatest immediate contribution concerned Soviet antisubmarine warfare tactics. In keeping with Khrushchev's espoused notions about large surface ships being nothing more than sitting ducks for missiles, there had been a tremendous expansion of the Soviet submarine force. And there had been a considerable buildup of submarines by the United States.

Shadrin was in a unique position to know as much about Soviet antisubmarine warfare tactics as any person inside or outside the Soviet Union. He had been considered one of the most skilled destroyer commanders in the Soviet Navy. He was so good that he was selected to train the Indonesian Navy in destroyer operations. Without question, there was no better expert on the subject in the United States.

Great intelligence resources had been expended in trying to anticipate what a Soviet destroyer commander was trained to do in a confrontation with a U.S. submarine. In Shadrin, the United States now had the answers. "He brought us great insight into likely reactions under certain contingencies," says Tom Dwyer. "He could tell us how Soviet destroyers were going to react to our best submarines. The information was invaluable."

Dwyer also points out that more specifically, naval intelligence analysts wanted to know what a Soviet destroyer captain's instructions were if he discovered an American submarine in the Baltic Sea. Shadrin was able to report that the orders were to radio Moscow for approval and then drop depth charges.

Never before had the U.S. Navy had such a source for information. And what Shadrin provided was so fundamental, so pervasive, that no simple switch in strategy on the part of the Soviets could counter the information. The damage to the Soviets was devastating and irreparable. "The Soviets must have been in a hell of a bind," observes Jack Leggat.

At the time of Shadrin's debriefing there was one naval intelligence officer who had gotten a rare firsthand look at the *Skoryi*-class destroyer, the same class Shadrin had commanded. It had happened several years earlier, when the Soviets took the vessel to a foreign port to show it off as part of their "New Navy." The host country solemnly promised that there would be no monkey business, that intelligence security would be maintained. Word was passed along that no efforts were to be made among U.S. intelligence people to glean information about the destroyer. Thus, with some confidence of security, the Soviets invited a select group of tourists on board to marvel at Soviet technical brilliance.

Among those on the tour was a man from Naval Intelligence, who was well aware that he was violating all the rules by being there. He dawdled along at the end of the tour until he saw a chance to split off and dash below for a look around. He found the electronics department and was busily studying the depth charges when a Soviet security officer discovered him. The Soviets detained him, raged for a bit, and then threw him off the vessel.

The intelligence officer had an opportunity to look at some vitally important features of the *Skoryi*-class destroyer, although he could not understand much of what he was seeing under the circumstances. An important part of the Shadrin debriefing occurred when this intelligence officer was brought to Shadrin and reconstructed his visual examination of the destroyer. Shadrin was able to give him detailed information about everything he had seen, providing a stunning, collaborative bird's-eye view of one of the Soviets' best destroyers.

Another of Shadrin's significant contributions was his detailed account of the secret Soviet decision, in February 1955, to adopt a doctrine of surprise nuclear attack against the United States. He reported that the doctrine had been published in a document seen only by Soviet military officers of flag rank and above.

Shadrin was able to tell his interrogators that contrary to Soviet propaganda claims, he had never known a single Soviet officer who really believed that the United States would make a first strike against the Soviet Union. Therefore, whatever attack plans the Soviets had were purely offensive.

He also confirmed what U.S. intelligence specialists had long believed: that the Soviet fishing trawlers that hovered off the coastal areas of the United States were really espionage units sent to spy on naval operations. He reported that the vessels were loaded with fish before they left the Soviet Union and that actually the trawlers were a special part of Soviet Naval Intelligence. One of the trawlers' specific goals was to follow various aircraft operating in the U.S. early warning system. They also monitored the frequencies used by radio and radar stations in the United States and gathered information about combat preparations of American naval forces, fleet composition and structure, and the types of weapons carried by the various ships. The trawlers made regular reports on the locations and activities of U.S. naval patrols as well.

At the very time that Shadrin was providing fresh details about the Russian fishing trawlers, the floating spy units were spotted in the vicinity of U.S. submarine maneuvers off the East Coast.

Analysts state that Shadrin's information was of timely significance.

There were, of course, cases in which Shadrin delivered information that was already known to Naval Intelligence. This was true to some extent of his information on the trawlers. But this duplication was valuable in that it provided a confirmation of intelligence already in hand as well as served as a basis for judging Shadrin's reliability.

Officials at ONI did not restrict Shadrin's usefulness to the long hours of interrogation and debriefing at the safe houses. They found other ways in which he could perform vital training functions to help prepare the United States Navy for possible combat with the Soviet Union. In the spring of 1960 Shadrin went to Newport, Rhode Island, for antisubmarine maneuvers.

There was a dual purpose to the mission, according to Captain Raymond D. Smith, then a lieutenant commander involved in Shadrin's debriefing, who accompanied him to Newport. Smith, a former destroyer commander, has explained that the exercise was to be the ultimate test of Shadrin's bona fides, that it was considered virtually impossible for the KGB to train one of its dispatched agents to command a destroyer. The second purpose was to allow the officers aboard the destroyer to benefit from watching a skilled Soviet commander handle himself. The Americans could see precisely how the Soviets were trained to respond to certain situations. They, as well as their fellow Americans on board the submarine below, could get an idea of what to expect if they went into combat against a Soviet destroyer.

The plan called for Shadrin, Walter Sedov, and Captain Smith to fly from Anacostia Naval Air Station, outside Washington, to Newport. Captain Smith recalls that there were some sailors at Anacostia hoping to catch a free ride to Newport on the plane, since there were extra seats. "But the CIA considered this a very secure mission," recalls Captain Smith. "Sedov wouldn't let them go. It really irritated Nick that we couldn't take the sailors along."

The operation of a destroyer is a tremendously complicated business. Anyone can stand behind the controls for a few minutes, but it takes an exceedingly skilled officer to execute the maneuvers properly. It requires a basic instinct known as seaman's eye—an innate ability most naval officers agree someone is either born with or not.

Destroyer combat operation is also a matter of being able to assimilate all the information that is cascading in—details about engine speed, precise positioning of the "enemy," raw data needed to project his next position. The conning officer must evaluate information regarding the range and bearing of the submarine, the range rate, and various other factors to get and keep his destroyer in the correct firing position for the antisubmarine weapons. All this must be done with rapid and effective coordination so that the destroyer keeps in range with the submarine, which is moving as fast and erratically as possible.

In addition to all these complications, the destroyer commander and conning officer are standing on a ship 300 or 400 feet in length, perhaps sixty feet wide, and displacing 5,000 tons. Once it is moving, its momentum is crushing. An important ingredient for success is the "dash" of the commander. He must be so confident of what he is doing that he can move quickly and decisively, spending barely perceptible time making his precise calculations. Under optimum circumstances, the conning officer has a supreme challenge.

Facing Shadrin that day was not only a vessel he had never seen before but a crew with whom he could communicate only through an interpreter, in this case Captain Smith. A further complication was the fact that ahead-speeds for U.S. destroyers are measured in quarters, while Soviet destroyer speeds are measured in thirds. But Shadrin exuded confidence.

With the easy grace of a man coming home, Nick Shadrin—Captain Nikolai Artamonov again for a few hours—took the conn of the destroyer. Not long into the exercise, he had the submarine in the position he wanted it. Quietly, calmly, he stated his orders to Captain Smith, who passed them along in English to the crew.

Two hundred feet below, the submarine rolled erratically as she spun and sped from the destroyer. With almost instant precision, Shadrin's destroyer pushed through the waters, keeping its position on the submarine. When the exercise was over, the American navy men were deeply impressed by what they had seen. With greater familiarity with the vessel, Shadrin, they agreed, could be as good as anyone in the U.S. Navy.

Captain Sidney Merrill recalls that Admiral Laurence Frost, then the Director of Naval Intelligence, had specifically asked Merrill to put Shadrin through the paces, to determine that he was indeed a destroyer commander. Captain Merrill, the commander of the destroyer, recalls the incident. "Admiral Frost gave me a lot of latitude in finding out if Shadrin was who he said he was. Basically I was trying to see if he reacted as a skipper would. We gave him surprises, and he reacted properly. It turned out he was everything he said he was. He really knew his antisubmarine stuff and signals and acoustics. I had no doubt he had years of command."

Captain Smith says that on the trip back to Washington Nick told him that one reason he had done so well was that the Soviet Navy had many of the top secret destroyer manuals from the U.S. Navy and that he had studied them intently while rising through the ranks of the Soviet Navy.

Although it had been an excellent training experience for the U.S. Navy men, Shadrin confided to his friend Tom Dwyer that he really had not been overly impressed by what he had seen of the Americans. It was his feeling that there was a serious lack of discipline, which translated into a certain shoddiness in operations. On the other hand, various observers of the exercises at Newport had been impressed by Shadrin's ability to get along with the personnel. Indeed, he seemed to be able to get along quite well with anyone he wanted to.

During the long months of interrogation, it is significant that Shadrin was largely in the hands of the Office of Naval Intelligence. Although the CIA maintained official jurisdiction over him, the true extent of the agency's interest in Shadrin is not known. Leonard McCoy of the CIA's Soviet Division continued to receive the debriefing reports with apparent interest and made no secret of his admiration for the quality of Shadrin's information.

But there is no indication that the CIA's interest in Shadrin went beyond receiving the reports. This could be because Shadrin provided no information of direct counterintelligence value. Nevertheless, the agency remained completely in charge of Shadrin's personal security and his plans for resettlement as an American. This continued association with the CIA was a gnawing, growing source of irritation to Shadrin, and his frustrations often found vent in his contact with the guards from the CIA's Security office. More than once his contempt for them flashed openly.

While most of the official attention was on Nick, Ewa was quickly becoming acquainted with America. Every other day the loud and funny Mrs. Forrester would arrive, parading about in her outrageous hats, taunting the guards, irritating Nick if he was within earshot. But Ewa's command of English was developing quickly, and she was beginning to like what she saw of the United States.

At the end of September they were moved from their first safe house into another house near Leesburg, Virginia. It was an old farmhouse that had not been lived in for a while, and there were mice scurrying about in it.

Both Nick and Ewa were fond of animals, particularly dogs. They made friends with a handsome boxer while strolling through the woods on the grounds of their second house. Nick was especially happy to see the dog, which began visiting on a regular basis. The dog apparently belonged to someone who lived in the area, for he was well fed and cared for. Nick, still struggling with English, noticed that the boxer had a tag attached to his neck which apparently bore his name, spelled M-a-l-e. Trying several pronunciations, Nick found one that sounded right and from that point on called the dog Male.

Several days later Ewa, whose English was coming along more rapidly than Nick's, informed him that "Male" was a reference to the dog's sex, not his name at all. One of the guards explained that the small metal plate actually was a vaccination tag.

"How stupid!" cried Nick. "Anyone can tell the sex of a dog. Why does he have to have a sign?"

Although they continued to enjoy Male—and call him by that name—Nick began to feel that the United States was no more immune to bureaucratic foolishness than was his homeland.

Of all the colorful characters in the U.S. Navy, Jack Leggat was one of the most liked and respected. After having compiled a stunning combat record in both the British and the American navies, Leggat went on to become a highly regarded intelligence analyst. A California native, Leggat joined the Royal Navy in 1940, before the United States entered the war, then resigned and joined his own country's navy.

A lifelong bachelor, Leggat was living in what has been described as the thinnest house in Washington. It was so narrow, it is said, that whenever he hosted a party, all the guests had to stand up. There was never much furniture, and what was there was dominated by a large piano. No one could understand how it had got into the house. There was also a refrigerator that normally held little more than a bottle of gin and a jar of olives.

But something traumatic happened to the footloose Leggat in 1959. He met an engaging woman with light brown hair, named Peggy, who was about to end his status as one of the navy's most eligible bachelors. During the late summer and fall, while Leggat was busy debriefing Shadrin, Peggy was visiting her sister in Baltimore—and seeing quite a lot of Leggat. It had not occurred to her to ask what Jack was doing for the U.S. Navy, and he had volunteered nothing.

According to Peggy, she and Jack were at his house one Saturday morning when Tom Dwyer telephoned. She had met Tom and knew he was one of Jack's close friends. Tom said that Nick Shadrin wanted to have a luncheon gathering that noon and would like to have Jack come. He thought it would be all right for Jack to bring Peggy.

"The drive to the house was wild," says Peggy. "A car picked us up and we drove and drove out into Virginia, and then the car stopped and we all jumped out and jumped into another car. Still, Jack hadn't told me anything about the Shadrins. I had no idea what was going on."

Peggy recalls that the Shadrins' home was a huge country house with servants. It had a long, graceful driveway. On the large screened porch was a Ping-Pong table. At one point that day Peggy found herself struggling in high heels to play Ping-Pong with a man who turned out to be a CIA guard.

"I'll never forget the first time I saw Nick," Peggy says. "He was the sort of person you just don't forget—so handsome and intelligent and boyish-looking. And he seemed so clearheaded and open, and I loved his eyes. He looked straight at you." Peggy never had the slightest doubt about Nick. Instinctively she knew he was someone she could be fond of. She also noticed how much Nick seemed to like Jack.

Peggy knew there was supposed to be a young woman with Nick, but she had not appeared. When Peggy asked Tom Dwyer about it, he indicated that Ewa had become a little tired of having so many people around. He said that she was upstairs keeping busy with a new sewing machine he had just acquired for her. "I don't know why she isn't happy with that new sewing machine," Peggy remembers Dwyer saying.

"The poor girl," says Peggy. "Here she was, away from home for the first time in her life, surrounded by strangers talking in a foreign language, thinking she never again would see her family.

And all I could see she had to talk to were these men—all these men who were just paying attention to Nick."

Peggy insisted that Tom send for Ewa right away. "She was just darling," recalls Peggy. "She was so shy, but she had very pretty eyes and dark hair and olive skin. There was something energetic and bright about her prettiness. But above all, she seemed so *young*."

Ewa told Peggy that she had been learning to sew and was working on fashions made popular by a current celebrity. Peggy was impressed with how much English Ewa had learned in a short time, and the two of them got along splendidly. Peggy was one of the first non-CIA women Ewa had talked to since arriving in the United States. She found her a welcome change from the imperious Mrs. Forrester.

The luncheon was a great success, with the ebullient Nick Shadrin playing the role of host *and* guest of honor. In the center of the table was a large bottle of vodka with a spigot on it, and many toasts were offered as the afternoon wore on. Peggy spent most of her time talking to Ewa, and by the time she departed it was her feeling that Ewa was happy and thoroughly optimistic about her future in America.

In general, there were remarkably few frustrations for Ewa, but Nick often found himself stewing in anger. He told Ewa he was furious that they still had not been given papers to show who they were. He was holding back nothing from his interrogators—the ultimate expression of good faith. In return, he had no reliable assurance about his and Ewa's future. He began to fear that the CIA was deceiving him. Harbored deep in his mind was the awful thought that once the United States had got from him everything he had, they might be abandoned, cast off without a penny. More than once Nick and Ewa recalled the warnings of their Swedish friend Rydström.

Shadrin's toleration of incompetence was exceedingly slim, a factor that would contribute to his frustration for years to come. During his interrogation his irritation focused on the presence of the CIA security guards. They were so omnipresent—and, in Nick's eyes, incompetent—that he wondered aloud to Ewa whether the guards were there to protect them or, as seemed more likely, to protect the United States from Nick and Ewa. His dislike of the guards simmered constantly as they wandered about the house smoking, drinking beer, and watching television soap operas. He felt they were utterly incapable of protecting anyone.

On one occasion Nick was traveling by car through the one-and-a-half-mile-long Baltimore Harbor Tunnel with one of the CIA men driving. Midway through, moving in heavy traffic at a high rate of speed, the driver slumped over the wheel. Cars were streaming toward them. Nick was able to grab the wheel and control the car until they were safely through the tunnel. It turned out that the driver was not ill; he had just gone to sleep.

Finally, one night Nick had enough. He woke up in the middle of the night and tiptoed down the steps. The guards, who had spent a routine evening drinking beer and watching television, were sound asleep at their posts. Carefully Nick removed the ammunition from each weapon and returned it to its proper place. He slipped the ammunition into his pajama pocket and went back upstairs. The next morning, after eliciting a few comments from the guards about their vigilant night, Nick returned the ammunition to them.

Whatever satisfaction he got from this did little to ease his growing bitterness. Perhaps, he told himself, he should have planned things better, perhaps he should have been a hard bargainer with the Americans.

On the other hand, the living conditions had been good from the start. Then, in December 1959 Nick and Ewa were moved into a magnificent safe house much closer to Washington, in McLean, Virginia. It was a large stone Tudor house, one of the most elegant places Ewa had ever seen.

Tom Dwyer knew that Nick was having his ups and downs, although his attitude was remarkably balanced compared with that of most defectors. Then one day, as Dwyer was being driven to the safe house, he saw Nick sitting off in the woods by himself. He apparently had shooed the guards away, as he often did.

"Nick was sitting on a stump all by himself with his head in his hands," says Dwyer. "He was extremely depressed, and I felt terribly sorry for him. I knew how much he disliked some of the CIA people he dealt with, but there was just so much we could do about it. They were primarily in charge of the case."

Dwyer sat down on a log nearby and had a long talk with Nick about his situation. He tried to cheer him up. For starters, a trip to Florida was discussed, a vacation from the long daily debriefings.

Dwyer suggested that they buy some lumber and tools and that Nick undertake to build a boat. Although Nick had never built anything in his life, he brightened at the prospect. He would get a book and learn how to build a boat.

After a trip to Daytona Beach, Florida, Nick settled down to spend all his spare time building a boat—not just a small boat, but a twenty-seven-foot cabin cruiser. "The boat was a godsend," says Ewa. "From then on Nick's whole outlook improved. He loved building it, and everybody was amazed at how well he could do it."

Dwyer, Leggat, and the guards marveled at how a man they regarded as an "intellectual" could so successfully put his hand to something as complicated as building a boat. Certain skeptics saw Nick's manual dexterity as evidence that this man was not exactly who he claimed to be. But Bill Howe, the navy's electronics genius, belittles this suggestion. "Highly intelligent people often are good at everything," he says, adding that it is a myth that intellectuals are stumblebums with their hands.

In an effort to make Shadrin feel more comfortable, one of his guards took him to a golf driving range, something Nick had only heard of. His natural balance and hand-and-eye coordination made him potentially an excellent golfer. Indeed, he greatly impressed the guard with his natural abilities. But after that single experience he told the guard, "When I'm an old man, I'll come back and play with you again." He told Ewa that it was one of the most boring pastimes he could imagine, that "it's so stupid to spend an afternoon beating a ball across a field with a stick." Tom Dwyer, an avid golfer, says Nick could have been an excellent player, given his extraordinary coordination. However, Dwyer finds it completely predictable that Nick detested the game. He never even tried to get him to play.

Chess was a game that Shadrin loved and played very well. Tom Dwyer also enjoyed chess, but he never found it much fun to play with Nick. Says Dwyer: "I even remember once when we played that I had made just two moves. Then Nick made a move. I was concentrating on my next move when I realized he was sitting there, grinning at me. I looked back at the board. I was checkmated."

Despite all of Shadrin's complaints about the CIA, there is little question that a great effort was being made to keep him and Ewa happy. Not long after arriving in this country, they were introduced to Ashford Farm, a magnificent country estate in coastal

Maryland that served the CIA for many years as a safe house.* At Ashford Farm, Nick found hunting and fishing opportunities that he would enjoy for the rest of his years in the United States.

Operated during most of its service by the CIA's Pete Sivess and his wife, Ellie, Ashford Farm was a first haven for dozens of Soviet bloc defectors through the years. Stories of drama and treachery haunt the twenty-six-room mansion overlooking the Choptank River in Talbot County, only a few miles away from a home owned by author James Michener and next to an estate once owned by Gene Tunney. In 1962 the sixty-eight-acre estate was used for the debriefing of Francis Gary Powers when he was returned from Russia. Some neighbors also tell of alcoholic defectors rowing many miles upriver in search of a liquor store or roaming the sedate neighborhood, speaking a strange language and searching for some sexual outlet.

Ellie Sivess recalls the first time she saw Ewa at Ashford Farm: "She was standing at the top of the long stairs in the house. She looked so young, so pretty, with her great dark eyes that were wide-open with excitement and expectation."

Ashford Farm was not used as a facility to debrief Nick, and he and Ewa never lived there. They could arrange to go there only when it was not being used to house defectors. Still, there was ample time for Nick to enjoy the marvelous duck and deer hunting during the fall and winter. In the spring and summer he would spend many hours there fishing with his friend Pete Sivess.

The nine months of debriefing were an exhausting time for Shadrin as well as for the ONI officials. From an intelligence standpoint, Tom Dwyer was highly satisfied. And the CIA was satisfied with the language skills Nick and Ewa had developed. At last the couple was ready to be settled into American life.

Tom Dwyer knew how fortunate ONI was to have a man with Nick's extraordinary intellectual strength and independence. He was distinctly different from so many other defectors, people who were sometimes paranoid or even mentally unbalanced. Some of the CIA's most highly regarded defectors were, at best, neurotic, paranoid, often alcoholic.

Shadrin was none of these things. Moreover, he was refresh-

---

*The CIA's official position is that Ashford Farm was only a "conference facility and training site."

ingly forthright in delineating just what he did know and what he did not know. "He was simply an exceptional human being," says Dwyer. "He was brilliant; he was funny; he was always in control. And if he liked you and respected you, he was delightful to work with." Without question, Dwyer believes, Shadrin was one of the most valuable military defectors in U.S. history.

In addition to technical information, Shadrin possessed a stunning knowledge of Soviet naval thinking and strategy. Even though he had brought no documents, in his head were answers to questions that had puzzled U.S. analysts for years. And his assessment of new situations and conditions, which developed after he had come to the West, were probably more cogent than those of any analyst at ONI or anywhere else in the U.S. intelligence community.

Measuring the value of a man like Shadrin is always difficult, but a clear example of his value was shown in October 1962, during the Cuban missile crisis, say several naval intelligence analysts. Advice based on ONI's assessment of Soviet naval strength was critical to President Kennedy in judging Soviet reactions. Shadrin was able to state with great confidence that the Soviet Navy did not have a range that would effectively include Cuban waters. An inaccurate estimate of Soviet naval strength at this juncture could have contributed to a much grimmer outcome in the tense standoff between the two powers.

That Shadrin would provide such critical information—in other instances as well—is a significant point in favor of his legitimacy as a defector. However, few in the intelligence community would ever be willing to swear absolutely to a Soviet defector's loyalties. "That's just something you can never do," says Tom Dwyer.

The consensus among ONI officials was that Shadrin's contribution had been extraordinary. There never had been a single source like him for high-grade intelligence on the Soviet Navy. Many of the senior analysts felt it was important to bring Shadrin into ONI in an official capacity, one that would allow the United States to continue to benefit from his knowledge and to draw upon his enormous capacities as a consultant and analyst. One senior naval officer who later was acting director of ONI put it this way: "We had been looking at the Soviet Navy from the outside in. With Shadrin, we could see it from the inside looking out. He was a gold mine—absolutely invaluable."

But ONI had never hired a Soviet defector. There was an initial reluctance to taking a former Soviet Navy captain into one of the most sensitive branches of the U.S. Navy. Tom Dwyer and Bill Howe were among the chief proponents for hiring Shadrin, and apparently there was no widespread dissent from their position.

However, William Abbott, then the senior civilian adviser on counterintelligence for ONI, felt it would be a grave mistake to allow Shadrin to go to work for Naval Intelligence. Abbott prepared a report containing a strong recommendation against hiring him.* Tom Dwyer submitted an equally strong report urging that he be hired. Dwyer's recommendation was quickly accepted by his immediate superior.

The next step in the bureaucratic chain was the approval of Captain Rufus L. Taylor, then assistant director for foreign intelligence. Taylor, who became Director of Naval Intelligence and then second-in-command at the Defense Intelligence Agency (DIA) and who later held the same position at the CIA, had a distinguished military career that Shadrin greatly admired. All signs are that this respect was mutual.

"Rufus Taylor and Nick would get together for lengthy discussions about Soviet and world affairs," recalls Tom Dwyer. Others vouch for the fact that even in those early days Shadrin and Taylor were fast becoming close professional associates. Captain Taylor quickly gave his approval to hiring Shadrin as a consultant and analyst for ONI.

There was no ready niche at ONI for a man like Nick Shadrin. He was not eligible for the security clearances required by a consultant or analyst in the standard sense. To create a suitable slot, Tom Dwyer turned to the Translation Unit of the Scientific and Technical Intelligence Center (STIC) of ONI. Its offices were located at the old Naval Observatory in Northwest Washington.

Shadrin was assigned to the Translation Unit, but his job was unique. He was to be an analyst, available for consultation and also on hand to assess Soviet material that was made available to him. His supervisors understood that he was on call by the various

---

*Abbott, now retired, refused to discuss or even acknowledge his role in the hiring of Shadrin. Other analysts close to the case state that it was completely predictable that a counterintelligence officer would oppose hiring Shadrin. "Those guys don't get paid to take chances," said one. Another, speaking specifically of Abbott, stated, "Bill Abbott would have said no simply because of Shadrin's background, no matter what value he could have been."

intelligence agencies of the government that might find him useful for any given project.

There is nothing unusual about the fact that even some of Shadrin's closest friends and associates did not favor granting him significant security clearances. Says Tom Dwyer: "It is just something that is not prudent if there is even one chance out of a hundred that the man is not who he claims to be. And with Nick's background, you could never be more than ninety-nine percent sure." Dwyer adds that his feeling was that Nick's value in the early days would not be seriously stunted by his not having clearances, and he hoped that as time went on, Nick's exceptional analytical powers would retain their vitality.

For months Shadrin had been steaming to leave the safe house and be allowed to live without any protection from the CIA security guards. On one beautiful spring morning in May, Nick and Ewa were out strolling along a lane near the safe house when two of the guards drove up behind them and told them they would have to return to the grounds of the safe house. Nick turned on them angrily and told them to go away, to leave Ewa and him alone. He told Ewa that day that he had had enough, that he could no longer stand living with the guards.

With a lump-sum payment from the CIA for his months of consulting services, Shadrin made a down payment on their first home, a small house in Arlington, Virginia. The CIA had assigned an intelligent, amiable young man to help them find a suitable place. It took only a few days.

Adding to Nick's joy of starting his new life was the fact that he and Ewa were married in a civil ceremony by a justice of the peace. For them to be legally married, it was necessary to bring about a technical dissolution of Nick's marriage in Russia. This was arranged with a Mexican divorce. Later Nick and Ewa were married in a church ceremony with a few friends present.

Finally, the CIA granted Nick a degree of satisfaction by providing him with a Social Security number. His rate of pay was adjusted to coincide with that which an American naval officer of similar rank would receive for his services. By all accounts, the Shadrins were exuberant over their prospects for a new life in America. Nick was pleased with the job he was getting at ONI, and Ewa was making plans to return to school and earn the necessary credits so that she could practice dentistry in the United States.

Of all the people who admired Nick Shadrin, no one felt more strongly about him than Tom Dwyer. There was a respect, an affection between the two men that was extraordinary. Dwyer saw in Shadrin a man of courage, a man of honor and decency, of good humor. He recognized him as having exceptionally great intellectual powers. And he remained highly impressed that Shadrin—Nikolai Artamonov—had been prescient enough to overcome the intellectual shackles of Soviet communism and see the difference between communism and freedom.

One thing worried Dwyer a great deal, although he hesitated to discuss it with Shadrin. For most of his career Dwyer had worked in Naval Intelligence, principally in areas of collection and analysis. But he was aware of some of the CIA's counterintelligence operations. And he knew some of the people involved in CIA counterintelligence. He knew something about their instincts, their values, the kinds of situations they might be tempted to exploit.

Dwyer felt instinctively that Nick Shadrin was ideally suited for use in a counterintelligence operation. Given Nick's extraordinary qualities, Dwyer thought it conceivable that the CIA could concoct some exceptional role for him in working against the Soviet Union. Dwyer knew the agency would be skillful at playing on Shadrin's fierce anti-Soviet attitudes, as well as on his patriotism toward the United States, in convincing him to work against the Soviets.

Dwyer had listened patiently to all of Shadrin's loud complaints about the CIA but had never said anything in agreement or disagreement in these points. He had taken the position that he represented the U.S. Navy and simply had no influence on how the CIA conducted its business.

Shadrin seemed a little surprised when, for the first time, Tom Dwyer broached the subject of the CIA's possible interest in him. Dwyer explained somberly that in his opinion the CIA was wont to become involved in various counterintelligence schemes that, as far as most people could see, served purposes of obscure validity. He warned that Nick Shadrin looked like a perfect man to be used in some such operation, and Dwyer urged him to resist any such overture should it ever be made.

Dwyer explained to Shadrin that no matter how noble the ultimate goal might appear, there was no way he could ever benefit from cooperating with any counterintelligence operation. He warned that Nick would be running a great risk for his own safety, that the Soviet counterintelligence people against whom he would be working were very skillful. Even more serious, Dwyer warned, was his feeling that the CIA counterintelligence officers would not necessarily have Shadrin's welfare foremost in their minds. After all, Dwyer counseled, Shadrin was not one of the CIA's favored defectors. As a military defector he had not made any special friends at the CIA. Indeed, his relationship with the CIA had been poor from the beginning.

Leonard McCoy, the Soviet Navy specialist at the CIA's Soviet Division, was soundly impressed with everything gleaned from Shadrin. But he still had not met Shadrin and insisted that he did not want to. McCoy told Dwyer his feeling that meeting the Russian might affect his objectivity in evaluating the debriefing reports. "But McCoy probably knew more than anyone about Nick," says Dwyer. Many years were to pass before McCoy and Shadrin would meet. And for now, McCoy's admiration was not enough to assure that Shadrin would have someone looking out for his interests at the CIA.

In short, Dwyer's message to Shadrin was that given an opportunity, the CIA might use him in some risky manner, that he should never become involved with them. Shadrin looked somber. He accepted Dwyer's warning gravely, pensively. Surely, he was thinking that all this sounded familiar. It was almost precisely what his friend Rydström had told him when he left Sweden nearly one year earlier.

Chapter 5

THERE was something comical, almost surrealistic, to Ewa about her husband sitting patiently as cosmetologists from the Central Intelligence Agency worked on his face. Wearing makeup seemed utterly incongruous to a man as large and masculine as Nick Shadrin. But for two days the cosmetic specialists labored over their subject, attempting to alter his appearance so radically that no one who saw him would know what he actually looked like.

The occasion was Shadrin's appearance in September 1960 before a subcommittee of the House Un-American Activities Committee (HUAC). It was the CIA's plan to present Shadrin five days before Soviet Premier Nikita S. Khrushchev's arrival in the United States. And the Shadrin presentation was welcomed by the fierce anticommunists of HUAC, who were eager to promulgate a view of the Soviet system strikingly different from the propaganda line expected to be espoused by Khrushchev.

The cosmetic specialists quickly realized that Nick's eyebrows, the ones that Ewa said "made him always look surprised," were in the greatest need of attention. Fake eyeglasses would help obscure them, but eyebrow liner and false brows also were needed. One of the cosmetologists spilled some chemicals onto a table that still bears the marks of the accident. It gave Ewa chills to think the stuff was being used on Nick's face.

Although now officially named Shadrin, he would for a few

days return to his role as Captain Nikolai Fedorovich Artamonov, Soviet naval commander. For this congressional appearance, the CIA deemed it best to move the Shadrins from their new home to the Holiday Inn on Glebe Road in Arlington. The CIA explained that by doing this, there was less chance that the Soviets could follow them to their new home and learn their identity. To confuse observers further, it was announced at the congressional hearing that the Shadrins were living in the New York area.

Not content with the work done on Shadrin at home, the cosmetic specialists arrived at the motel, where more hours were spent working on Nick's face. Even if his photograph were taken, it would not be an accurate representation of his true appearance. In fact, a photograph of Nick that appeared in the Washington *Post* and another in *The New York Times* in conjunction with his congressional appearance did show a man who appeared slightly built and thin-faced, studious behind spectacles and a carefully coiffed mustache. His striking eyebrows had been muted by being made far thicker, the accent on the sharp peaks in the center having been lessened. The alteration was substantial, although Ewa believes anyone who knew him could still recognize him.

But none of this really would have made any difference to the Soviets. Shadrin appeared publicly using his birth name, Nikolai Fedorovich Artamonov, and nothing was obscured about his background. Of course, the Soviet KGB had a full dossier on Artamonov, including photographs. If there were any surprises for the Soviets—and that seems doubtful—it is that Artamonov had finally surfaced in the United States. The last official information the Soviets had was that he had fled to Sweden. Where he had gone after that was supposed to be a secret. "We never did understand who the CIA was trying to hide Nick from," says Ewa.

As hard as it is to imagine, Shadrin had never shared with Ewa, prior to their escape, his deep feelings of hatred for the Soviet government. That was a subject no intelligent Polish girl would ever discuss with a Soviet, even if she loved him enough to run away with him forever.

But since reaching the United States, Nick had gradually told Ewa of his real feelings. And he had discussed them at length with people like Tom Dwyer, Bill Howe, and Jack Leggat as well as with his CIA handlers. All this was an important part of understanding how such a high-ranking Soviet naval officer could relinquish his enormous class privileges for an uncertain future in the United States.

Still, the occasion of the congressional appearance would be the first time Ewa heard Nick fully articulate his reasons for coming to the West. The amusement over the cosmetics specialists spending hours on Nick's face subsided as the time neared for him to be driven to Capitol Hill for the session. His appearance before Congress was a rare and solemn occasion for the Shadrins as well as for the United States government. Although she wanted to attend the hearing, Ewa was told to stay behind and watch her husband on television. There was no reason to expose her to the Soviets, the CIA security officers told her.

There was nothing subtle about the intended counterpoint of presenting Shadrin less than a week prior to the Khrushchev visit. In the stately caucus room of the Old House Office Building, Congressman Francis Walter of Pennsylvania, chairman of the committee, opened the session with this statement:

> Mr. Khrushchev will quote the scriptures of democracy with the hypocrisy of the Devil. He has sowed the fiction of class struggle, so that he may reap the personal privilege of class power. He will continue to paint a falsely glowing picture of his Communist paradise, but he will not let in the light of the western free world to reveal its shabbiness, its shame, and the miserable view of tortured souls who are made to kneel in worship to the Baal of materialism.

After a glowing introduction of Shadrin in which he described his astonishing rise through the Soviet system, Chairman Walter —who had heard Shadrin in an earlier executive session—added this:

> Listening to this young man's statements about the Soviet military and political intentions, strategy, capabilities, Soviet espionage, and the present lot of the Soviet citizen, we are reminded again of the aggressive and deceitful threat to world peace the Soviet Union represents.

After having been sworn in, Shadrin, speaking through an interpreter, gave the committee a synopsis of his life up to the time of his defection. Seated in the audience facing Shadrin was a secretary from the Soviet Embassy who was busily taking notes. Shadrin stated that he had no connection with any foreign intelligence agency and that he had not fled the Soviet Union under any duress. He stated:

> On the contrary, I was given favored treatment by the Soviet authorities and had a bright future ahead of me—having been publicly described as one of the brilliant young career officers of the Soviet Navy. My defection was also not prompted by the prospect of greater material gain or security or an easy life, for I gave up what promised to be a successful career in the Soviet Navy to come here.

Shadrin then gave the committee a description of his indoctrination since childhood by the Soviet government:

> As a child I was taught to be ever vigilant, that enemies were all about; if necessary, I should denounce even my own father. I witnessed arrests and noted that people whom I had known disappeared into the torture chambers of the NKVD, but in my immaturity I was pleased that our motherland was being made more powerful through this crushing of the "enemies of the people."
>
> Early in World War II, I felt the strong national pride of all Soviets, at times mixed with bitterness for our suffering. In spite of the hard times caused by the blockade of Leningrad and our evacuation from the city, I never once doubted the policies of Stalin and our government. My friends and I were prepared to do anything for our motherland and our leader. Like any other Soviet citizen, I welcomed our victory with joy and hope for the future.
>
> But in the Higher Naval School [Frunze] . . . I began to have my first doubts—as I began my courses in Marxism-Leninism and political economics. I saw that the Soviet system was constructed without valid foundations and that there was a great breach between the theory of Soviet communism and its practice as we saw it every day. Still, as a loyal Soviet I sought to justify things by lame analyses of the country's current needs.
>
> Many other questions were born as a result of my cruises abroad, but Soviet propaganda and political education managed to quiet them, to the point that I often acted as a defender of party policies in arguments with my father and friends.
>
> As the years passed and my views matured, more questions arose, and with them the gradual feeling that my government's policies were wrong. But when I raised the questions as to why, the usual propaganda answer was: "for the people" or "for a brighter future."
>
> Events in 1956—especially the revolution in Hungary and

the unrest in Poland—finally gave rise to the conviction that the government's foreign policy statements were untrue. They showed the aggressive character of that policy. All this was somewhat covered up by conditions inside the country, when it appeared that Khrushchev was making an effort at bringing the country to a normal state, normalizing and improving the relationship between the government and the people and trying to introduce domestic measures and, to a certain degree, bring to life the existing constitution.

Then, his voice rising, Shadrin spoke with ringing eloquence of the basic human fraud of Soviet communism:

> The Russian people have no use for [the Soviet system]. The Russian people are gifted and industrious, mighty and strong. They are not interested in wasting their energies and talents by solemnizing the dictators of the Kremlin or enslaving other nationalities for the sake of the very same dictators. They are not interested in surrounding themselves with bereavement and tribulation for a concept that is profoundly antidemocratic and which is bringing misery to them and to others; the concept in which no one, especially the leaders of the party themselves, believes. . . .

Shadrin then delivered a stirring soliloquy about his position as a bright star in the Soviet system:

> The question arose—where is my place, what am I to do? Should I pursue the "brilliant" career promised me as a naval officer?
> Should I keep on saying things which I myself do not believe to be true, things which I know are absolute lies?
> Should I keep spreading ideologies which I do not share, which I detest?
> Should I keep on helping the Kremlin to accumulate more and more power, to deceive my people, to dominate my people; and help the Kremlin to perpetrate crimes on an international scale?
> But I was an officer; wouldn't I be betraying my own people by running away from them?
> No. I shall never betray my people and I shall never forsake them. I was, I am and I shall always remain, a Russian—but not a Soviet Russian, not a toy in the hands of Khrushchev and the company in the Kremlin.

Shadrin then went head to head with Premier Khrushchev, stating that he understood—as did all Americans who were reading newspapers—that the Soviet leader was coming to the United

States to speak in favor of disarmament. Shadrin told the congressmen that such a position by Khrushchev was simply a "propaganda trick" and that he was "trying by all means to weaken or to dull the vigilance . . . of western countries."

Shadrin told the congressmen about the doctrine of surprise attack promulgated by the Communist Party leadership in 1955—a secret doctrine known only to Soviet military officers of flag rank. Under this doctrine the Soviet Union was prepared to knock out the United States in a surprise attack if it was deemed feasible.

Shadrin stated:

> The Soviet dictatorship would undertake a surprise attack if she felt that she could win in one stroke. Make no mistake, they are power seekers, not political idealists. Khrushchev does not wish to wait indefinitely for the United States to become a socialist state by evolution; moreover, he does not believe this will happen. He would like to see it take place in his lifetime.

In addition to these matters, Shadrin detailed for the congressmen the true activities of the Soviet "fishing trawlers" that so often hovered off the shores of the United States. For the first time the American public was informed in detail of these espionage activities—news that made front pages all over the country. But it was not news to the intelligence community, for everything Shadrin presented to the committee he had presented to his debriefing officers over the past year.

Still, as Committee Chairman Walter pointed out, much of Shadrin's information was far too sensitive to be made public. Even today some of the information brought by Shadrin remains highly classified.

The following week Khrushchev arrived.* Among other things, he spoke warmly to the United Nations about his hopes for total disarmament, reassuring Americans of the fervent desire for world peace he and other Soviet leaders felt. He also assured Americans that their greatest enemy was mindless expansion of a defense establishment.

---

*Arkady N. Shevchenko, the United Nations Under Secretary-General for Political and Security Council Affairs, defected to the United States from the Soviet Union in April 1978. He is the highest-ranking Soviet diplomat ever to defect. Shevchenko was a disarmament expert who accompanied Khrushchev on his 1960 trip to the United States. Shevchenko has stated to the author that he has no recollection of Khrushchev's being informed of Shadrin's statements, although he does have some vague memories of the incident.

News and propaganda organs all over the world carried the story of Shadrin's direct verbal assault on the Kremlin. In the United States the story of Shadrin's appearance was bannered in more than 500 newspapers, including page one coverage in *The New York Times*. It was beamed into Communist bloc countries by Radio Free Europe. If the KGB had wondered what had become of Captain Nikolai Artamonov, it now knew.

Carefully staged upon the most respectable podium in America, Shadrin's words surely pierced deeply into the wrathful Soviet psyche. This orchestration of Shadrin, with choreography by the Central Intelligence Agency, obviously served a high purpose for the United States. But it could bode nothing good for Shadrin.

Shortly after his appearance a Soviet court sentenced Captain Nikolai Artamonov to death.

Nick and Ewa Shadrin burst headlong into American life with an almost insatiable appetite for freedom. Their first year had been spent in a sort of captivity, and from that experience Shadrin would remember the guards and safe houses with a loathing he would never get over. Few defectors had ever been so eager to escape the protection of the CIA and to get on with building a new and independent life.

About a year after assuming his job at the Office of Naval Intelligence, Nick wanted to see America. No one could have been more willing than Ewa. They bought a Studebaker Lark and set off alone on a twenty-eight-day driving tour of the United States. Their itinerary was practically nonexistent, and their journey became more joyful each day.

"We could hardly keep moving," says Ewa, although by the time the trip was over they had driven 10,000 miles. "We loved everything we saw. It was wonderful. Colorado was one of my favorites, and Nick loved Oregon and Washington. He even stopped to go fishing in the Pacific."

One destination was California, where they visited Jack Leggat, one of their first friends from ONI. Leggat had retired from ONI and returned to California, where he and Peggy were married. While there are common threads among all of Nick's friendships, each one has its individualistic traits. Clearly, Jack and Peggy Leggat were the friends Nick had the most exuberant, slaphappy times with.

On the occasion of this visit they all stayed at a little cottage on Balboa Beach in Southern California. There was much laughing and singing and drinking. Nick was clearly delighted to be back in the company of Jack, the man who had given up the thinnest house in Washington to settle down with Peggy.

One evening during a visit later in the 1960's some young people who were friends of Peggy's son came by the cottage. This was during the time of the violent demonstrations at Berkeley and the overt flirtation with Communist Party doctrines. The Students for a Democratic Society (SDS) was formed and active at Berkeley and other campuses. Peggy and other parents she knew of felt frustration in trying to make their children understand the virtues of America.

Peggy had told Nick of her concern, and he responded with his characteristic intensity. "Nick's eyes were always alive," says Peggy. "But that night they were blazing. The kids were all sitting on the couch of the upstairs of the little house. Nick was striding back and forth in front of them, smoking a cigarette and waving it around. He explained to them that he had been born into communism, that communism was his heritage, a heritage that he rejected. He told them that he had defected from his country because he wanted to find truth and that one would never find any truth in communism." Peggy says she was deeply stirred as she sat listening to Nick.

"The kids were absolutely transfixed," says Peggy. "Here was this magnificent, handsome, intelligent man obviously speaking the truth. He was an excellent speaker, even in his new language, and knew just how to drive home points. The kids had such admiration for him.

"And they hung on every word he said. He told them if they were disillusioned with the free enterprise system or with the political system of the United States, they should keep in mind just one thing—that it is the best system in the world, despite its faults.

"He talked to these kids about America like no one else could. You had to have an enormous respect for anyone who would give up what Nick gave up as a matter of principle, and the kids could understand that. They knew it took an extraordinary sense of values to do what Nick had done."

Of course, the most important factor to Peggy was that Nick was saying all the things she had been trying to say for so long. She was grateful that the young people had readily accepted what Shadrin had to say.

Another subject that came up that night was the use of marijuana. The old arguments surfaced that using pot was really no different from smoking cigarettes and drinking alcohol on the part of adults. But Shadrin ventured forth with a persuasive argument—that the key difference was that one was against the law and the other was not. He explained to them that under any system of laws, citizens had an obligation to obey them, if they were people of principle.

Again, the children listened to an argument they had often heard from their parents. This time, Peggy believes, it seemed to make a difference.

During the Shadrins' first visit Jack and Peggy caught a rare glimpse of the residual terror that must fester in the heart of every person who has escaped from the Soviet Union. The Leggats and the Shadrins were walking along the beach about midnight, enjoying the cool surf and invigorating air. Nick and Jack had cans of beer in their hands. Suddenly, moving rapidly in their direction, there was a beach patrol jeep and a couple of policemen.

"We could all feel Nick go tense," says Peggy. Out of the calm, beautiful night had suddenly come a symbol from Shadrin's past: the police arriving to interfere, to question—or perhaps something worse. "We told Nick it was routine, that the police came by every night to keep the kids on the beach in line." He docilely acquiesced when Peggy concealed his beer for him, covering it partly with sand. She told him there was an ordinance against drinking on the beach. The police jeep passed without stopping.

Shadrin had a hard time reconciling the incident with his notion of what freedom was supposed to be all about. "He just couldn't understand how we could accept the police patrol as a normal occurrence," says Peggy. "It really shook him up."

The incident was minor compared to the indignation Shadrin expressed a few weeks later when he learned it was against the law for him to mail a bottle of vodka to the Leggats to thank them for their hospitality. It called to mind the dog tag that specified the sex of the animal. Shadrin was never comfortable with laws that made no sense to him.

During these first months of real freedom Shadrin's personal life seems to have been a special pleasure for him. Although he and

Ewa had been married in a legal ceremony earlier, they decided to have a quiet church ceremony at a Polish Catholic church in Baltimore. In addition to Tom Dwyer and his wife, Nick invited Tatiana Sciugam, a former Russian lady who worked at the ONI office where Nick was posted. After the brief ceremony Tom Dwyer and his wife had to depart right away. Nick, Ewa, and Miss Sciugam went to a Georgetown restaurant for a quiet dinner.

Miss Sciugam, much older than Nick and an aristocratic refugee from the Soviet regime, has been described by her colleagues as representing the old order in Russia—in contrast with Shadrin, whom the Soviets had viewed as the "new Soviet man." But Nick and Miss Sciugam had much in common, and they enjoyed speaking in Russian and discussing Russian literature and history. They compared their upbringings and how things had changed.

In the course of their friendship Shadrin left Miss Sciugam with a clear impression of why he had fled the Soviets. "He could not breathe; he could not think for himself," she states. "His intellectual potential was being dampened, and that prompted him to leave."

Friendships were easy for Nick Shadrin. This was not so much because of his quick assimilation of American habits as it was because of his old Russian ways. He possessed an old-world graciousness that seems to have enchanted both men and women as well as little children. "Anything you admired of Nick's," says Tom Dwyer, "he would want to give it to you—right there on the spot. He was forever trying to give me his fine Swiss navigator's watch just because I admired it and said how hard it would be to find one like it." Many times Dwyer saw Nick's eyebrows arch sharply and heard him say, "You like? I give!"

"And our kids loved him," says Dwyer. On one occasion Dwyer and his children were visiting the Shadrins at their home and were enchanted with the pair of parakeets Nick had. He had bought them on an impulse with the mistaken impression that he was going to teach them to speak English as he himself learned to speak—an effort soon abandoned as he became better informed about the little birds. Nick was insistent upon giving the birds to Dwyer's children, but Tom was able to resist.

As the years passed, Nick developed his skills as a hunter and fisherman. He enjoyed getting better acquainted with the CIA safe house, Ashford Farm, and became close friends with Pete Sivess, the CIA man who ran the farm. When the secret facility was not being used for debriefing and orientation, Nick and Pete would spend many happy hours there hunting for deer.

One of Shadrin's favorite hunting companions was Nicholas Kozlov, who later owned some land in Virginia that the two enjoyed hunting on. Kozlov, himself a former officer in the Soviet military, had come over many years before Shadrin and had served U.S. Intelligence in Germany after World War II.

Shadrin became so proficient as a sportsman that as late as 1980 there were freezers in the Washington area that held fish and venison he had presented to friends. Other homes have racks and trophies from the large bucks he brought down. Shadrin finally became such an avid hunter that it was not uncommon for him to hold hunting licenses in Maryland, Virginia, and Pennsylvania and go to all three states for the opening of deer season.

Tom Dwyer was constantly amazed at the new skills he would find in Shadrin. On one of Shadrin's trips to Hawaii, Dwyer drove him home after meeting him at the airport. "We picked up my kids and went to Barbers Point to take a swim," Dwyer recalls. "Nick hit the water and was gone. He was swimming south and just kept on going, slashing through the water like a boat. He must have gone a mile before turning around and coming back with just as much grace and ease." Shadrin seemed to master anything that required coordination—whether it was mental or physical.

In everything, Nick Shadrin showed a striking, often playful sense of humor. But it is clear that he was facile in showing whatever side of his rich personality would most appeal to the person he was dealing with. Tom Dwyer, for example, has a hard time imagining some of Nick's antics with droll, fun-loving Jack Leggat.

One such antic occurred on an occasion when Shadrin went to California to visit Jack and Peggy Leggat. Shadrin was in California to make a speech while Ewa stayed home to attend to her dental office. Jack Leggat had seen virtually nothing of his boyhood chums since that day in 1940 when, impatient over America's reluctance to enter the war, he dashed off and joined the Royal Navy. It happened that Nick was in California on the occasion of the twenty-fifth reunion of Jack's class at South Pasadena High School.

At the reunion party Jack gave his badge to Nick to wear as he strolled among these people Jack had not seen in twenty-five years.

Nick took the greatest pleasure in having people who had never seen him before walk up, look at his badge, and say, "Gee, Jack. You haven't changed a bit. How have you been?" Nick, who looked absolutely nothing like Leggat, would answer in his heavy accent that he had been fine, that it was good to be back with the old crowd at South Pasadena High. The person would agree heartily.

Later, at the high school reunion dance, Jack retrieved his name tag from Nick. But Nick had had so much fun pretending to be Jack Leggat that he attended the dance and told all comers that his name was O'Higgins—a friend of Jack Leggat's. When people would ask where he was from, "O'Higgins" would answer that he was from New York.

"But you don't sound like an O'Higgins from New York," stated one girl, obviously taken with this handsome man.

"Oh," replied Nick, smiling down at her. "We talk many different ways in New York." Then he danced with the woman.

Throughout the evening Jack Leggat would encounter his old friend "O'Higgins," and the two would pound each other on the back as if they had not set eyes on each other in twenty-five years. Inevitably other classmates—undaunted by the large "Irishman's" Russian accent—would step forward and proclaim vivid recollection of them both.

Later, on the way home, Nick became somber as they talked about how much fun they had had at the class reunion. "Nick told us that more than ninety percent of the boys who had been in his high school class died during the siege of Leningrad," says Peggy.

The Leggats were particularly fond of Shadrin, and, says Peggy: "He had such a sense of fun about him. And he was so intelligent, so good-hearted, so loyal. He had such a love of life. And his sense of humor was wonderful."

It was a great tribute to Shadrin that he had been given a five-year consulting contract to work for ONI. Not only was it a salute to his knowledge and potential analytical skills, but it spoke volumes for his ability to work well with others—in striking contrast with most defectors. Moreover, his command of English was exceptional for someone who had been exposed to it for only a year.

"Nick was an extraordinary person as well as being extraordinarily well informed about Soviet naval strength," says William Howe, who also was working for ONI at the Naval Observatory during those years. "There was no ready place for a man like Nick, so we made a special slot for him at ONI."

From the start, the tiny, sharp-eyed electronics genius got along superbly with the big, amiable, brilliant Russian. And Howe's gracious wife, Mary Louise, was instantly taken with the Shadrins. Soon the four formed a friendship that went far beyond the professional relationship that was developing between the two men.

Although Shadrin was the first—and perhaps still the only —defector to be given such a high position of trust at ONI, this did not include a security clearance. Even his strongest supporters seemed to accept this as a routine safeguard. As long as there was the slightest chance that Shadrin could be a dispatched agent, prudence could not allow such a clearance.

Thomas Koines, a linguist who spent thirty years with ONI, was directly in charge of the Translation Unit to which Shadrin was assigned. The mission of the Scientific and Technical Intelligence Center (STIC) was to learn as much as possible about the scientific and technical aspects of the Soviet Union as they related to U.S. naval capabilities. Although Shadrin was assigned to the Translation Unit, says Koines, his primary purpose was to be available for consultation with officials from any of the myriad departments of the navy as well as officials from the intelligence community. He was a highly regarded expert on Soviet naval matters, which was an area of principal concern throughout ONI. In addition, Koines points out, Shadrin's exposure to the best Russian-English linguists in the country was designed to help him with the English language. Shadrin improved his English with a speed that awed his colleagues.

Koines found that Shadrin was "a natural learner, a man with a tremendous intellect and a great intelligence." He and others were astounded at the amount of information Shadrin could absorb —and the strikingly high percentage of it he could retain. Koines adds that Shadrin's unique value was that everything in his experience and training "was a reflection of Soviet strategic thought."

The work Shadrin was assigned to was a far cry from his former duties as the commanding officer of a destroyer, and he never pretended that he did not miss those duties. He cherished being a navy man, and he clearly possessed a residual pride in the Soviet

Navy. It came naturally to him to fall into debates with his ONI colleagues about the comparative virtues of the Soviet and U.S. navies. He believed there were areas where the Soviets were sharply ahead, and he was quick to say so.

"But this could be very good," states Jerry Edwards, a former ONI official who worked with Shadrin. "Any residual pride he had in the Soviet Navy that encouraged him to point out weaknesses in our navy was to our benefit. That's what we had him there for." Edwards, who spent four years across the hall from Nick at ONI, knew and worked with numerous defectors during his twenty years in the navy. To his mind, Nick was in a class by himself. "What was unique about Nick was his commander's point of view," says Edwards. "He understood how the Soviet Navy worked from the executive level."

Edwards was intent on keeping up his own language skills in Russian, and he and Nick often went to lunch together. Nick would speak in English, and Edwards in Russian, the idea being that they both could sharpen their skills this way. But Edwards was constantly amazed at Shadrin's staggering knowledge of everything going on around him. For example, Shadrin was usually fully informed about what was going on in county government —including proposed changes in tax schedules and ordinances— and he had a consuming interest in these things.

More than one of Shadrin's friends has commented on his incisive interest in all civic affairs. They seem humbled that a newcomer could have mastered the often boring intricacies of county government. It was not unusual for Nick to know minute details about something going on in the local government outside his own bailiwick, such as a proposed change in the tax structure of a neighboring county. He was always informed about the most obscure local elections.

It is clear that initially Shadrin was satisfied with his job at ONI. He no doubt expected it to be a starting point from which he would launch his career in service to the United States. And he was generally fond of Americans, he told Ewa, finding them to be very much like Russians in their instincts and feelings. This was surprising to Nick, but he believed it had something to do with the large geographical size of the two countries.

Nick, who made friends easily and quickly, loved to communicate—to talk, to argue, to pontificate, to pound the table, and to discuss world issues. He fell easily into the Washington lunch circuit, and his company was sought by a great variety of people, many of them prominent in the military and intelligence community. Whether it was simply getting a pizza around the corner from the Naval Observatory or going to a restaurant for several hours of drinking and talking, Nick was always anxious to go.

His new friends saw him as an unusually warm and open man, who, above all, hated the lies and deceit that characterized the Soviet regime. He told more than one friend that the greatest thing about being in America was that he never again would have to lie.

Ewa entered dental school in September 1960. She received credit for some of the courses she had taken in Poland, but still faced four years of dental school in the United States. At Georgetown University, where she was enrolled, she found herself the only woman in her class and one of two women in the whole dental school. This was a shock to her, having become accustomed to being in dental school with other women—fifty of the fifty-seven graduates in her Polish dental class had been women. "I was just miserable at Georgetown," says Ewa.

One elderly professor made things particularly difficult for her. "One time he even told me I should be home ironing my husband's shirts," she says. On two other occasions, when Ewa was a little late to class, he told the others in the class that he presumed the "woman" had dropped out. The class erupted into laughter when Ewa came in, and the professor feigned great surprise. "I would be shaking every morning when I would leave for school," she says. It was terribly humiliating.

This problem worried Nick greatly, but it was particularly difficult for them to deal with. Finally, according to Ewa, their dear friend Tom Dwyer tried to elicit some understanding from the dean, some promise that he would try to rectify the situation. But it became clear to Dwyer that nothing was going to be done. After one semester at Georgetown Ewa transferred to Howard University, where there was another woman in her class and many other women in the dental school. "Everything was fine after that," Ewa says.

Ewa was graduated in 1964 and soon passed her certification board examinations in Maryland and the District of Columbia. Soon after her graduation she went to work in a dental clinic and began earning a salary. In 1967, when she decided to set up a private practice in Virginia, she passed the board examination in that state.

Nick returned to school in 1961, studying engineering at George Washington University during the evenings. Although his proficiency in English was developing, he did not feel comfortable writing his master's thesis in his new tongue. Therefore, he wrote it in Russian, and some of his friends at ONI helped him translate it into English.

Nevertheless, it was considered quite an accomplishment to be awarded a master's degree in engineering from an American university only five years after having arrived in the country with hardly a word of English. Nick and Ewa received their degrees only two days apart. The degrees represented for them highly important tools of access to acceptance in American society.

A deep chill swept through Nicholas Shadrin, stirring his adrenaline, setting in rapid motion the reels of his memory. There before him, in downtown Washington, was Lieutenant Commander Lev Aleksandrovich Vtorigin. Shadrin knew him well. They had been friends at Frunze Naval Academy, and they had roomed together on their first naval assignments. Their paths had split when Vtorigin married the daughter of a high-ranking KGB official. He had left the Soviet Navy to attend the Military Diplomatic Academy for training in diplomacy and espionage. In 1959 Vtorigin had been posted to Buenos Aires as an assistant naval attaché at the Soviet Embassy.

Precisely two months after Shadrin's congressional appearance —and only a few weeks after the Soviet death sentence had been issued—Commander Vtorigin was assigned as an assistant naval attaché to the Soviet Embassy in Washington. In addition to any diplomatic skills he might have had, Vtorigin was a highly trained Soviet agent. In fact, he had the reputation for being the best pistol marksman in the Soviet Baltic Fleet.

Tom Dwyer remembers the Vtorigin incident vividly: "We believed the man had been sent to kill Nick."

Shadrin was not certain that Vtorigin saw him that day in downtown Washington, but he immediately reported his sighting to the FBI agent in charge of keeping track of Soviet attachés operating in Washington. Some consideration was given to whether Shadrin could induce Vtorigin to defect to the United States, but Shadrin thought it would be difficult.

Apparently Vtorigin's presence was very much on Shadrin's mind, but he never discussed it with Ewa. It was characteristic of Nick that he would not burden his wife with the awful fear that a trained assassin might be in Washington on a mission to murder him. It was a burden he would carry alone.

Even so, he presented Ewa with a small snub-nosed .38 caliber Smith & Wesson and told her to carry it whenever she took their dog, Julik, walking. He said the pistol was for her protection, but he also wanted her to be able to protect Julik in case he was attacked by a larger dog, a rather remote possibility, given Julik's disposition. Eventually the pistol rubbed a hole through the lining of the leather jacket she usually wore when she walked the dog.

Shadrin himself often carried one of the nine guns he kept in his house. When he was going out to walk Julik, Ewa occasionally saw him strap on a holster that housed his heavy nine-millimeter Walther automatic. For all Ewa knew, he always did this. Nick once explained to her that he, too, worried about Julik being attacked, and he wanted to be ready to defend him.

It is highly unlikely that these measures simply reflected Shadrin's concern over Julik, a powerful German shepherd always eager to protect his domain. It is much more likely that the weapons were related to the five long years that Lev Vtorigin's presence in this country cast a shadow on Shadrin's equanimity. No disguise could hide Shadrin from the eyes of a man he had lived with. Nor was there any way for him to forget his former friend's skill as a pistol marksman. However, there is no evidence that Shadrin and Vtorigin ever actually met in this country.

On August 2, 1965, Commander Vtorigin left the United States, according to the State Department. No public diplomatic records show that he has returned.

Shadrin's apprehension over Vtorigin was unusual. Few men have exuded more confident courage than did Nick Shadrin. From the start he appeared to ignore the threat of the KGB, despite the order of execution he faced. He leaped so openly into the mainstream of American life that for the next twenty years other Soviet defectors would express suspicions about him on the basis of that alone.

"You have to wonder about a guy who had no fear of retaliation from the KGB," says a former KGB colonel who made his flight to the West more than two decades ago. He was speaking in 1979, as he sat in an apartment building near Washington which he described as the most secure residential building in the area. A few days earlier he had been terrified by a man he met in the building corridor—a man who looked at him in a peculiar way. The defector believed the man might have been sent by the KGB to kill him. He, too, lives under a Soviet death sentence.

Shadrin's life was the antithesis of this. "He was the most fearless man I ever met," says Tom Dwyer. "And I met a few during World War Two." Ewa Shadrin believes that Nick was afraid of nothing. But as his closest friends knew, Shadrin was far too intelligent to believe that he was immune to the danger that comes from living under a Soviet execution order or immune to the sharp eyes of a Soviet assassin.

Tom Koines first saw it at the office on the day following a dinner party at Howard University on the occasion of Ewa's graduation. Grimacing in pain, Shadrin asked Koines to drive him to the office of a doctor whose name he had been given by his CIA contact. "Nick really felt terrible," recalls Koines. "And he was afraid. He thought the KGB had poisoned his food." Shadrin explained that the KGB was capable of reaching almost anywhere for someone they wanted. It turned out that Shadrin had come down with a standard case of intestinal flu, but Koines would never forget the apprehension that he saw in his friend's eyes.

Other close friends can remember instances, especially in dark places, when Shadrin would almost jokingly mention that someone might easily be kidnapped if he were not careful. While Shadrin never allowed his life to be guided by such considerations, he was certainly aware almost constantly of the danger he was in. But this was an awareness he never shared with Ewa.

In December 1961 a Soviet defector named Anatoli M. Golitsin arrived in the United States. At the time of his defection he was a major in the First Chief Directorate of the KGB, the department that specializes in Soviet clandestine activities abroad. Golitsin defected to the West from his assignment in Helsinki, Finland, and his revelations about Soviet penetration were to have thundering reverberations throughout Western intelligence services.*

Golitsin's revelations about Soviet penetration of the French

---

*Golitsin is perhaps best known as Boris Kuznetov, the "fictional" defector who is the central character in *Topaz*, a best-selling novel by Leon Uris.

government, including the Cabinet, were so convincing to President John F. Kennedy that he dispatched by personal courier a private letter to President Charles de Gaulle. The letter, of which there was only one copy, contained allegations so serious that some of De Gaulle's top advisers fell under dark suspicion. P. L. Thyraud de Vosjoli, then a high-ranking French intelligence officer posted in Washington, says in his autobiography, *Lamia,* that Golitsin exhibited "an all but encyclopedic knowledge of the secret workings of the French intelligence services." He offered precise details to support his claims.

Senior French intelligence officers, all highly trusted by De Gaulle and his staff, were rushed to Washington secretly to interrogate Golitsin about his dreadfully serious allegations. From his knowledge of specific documents, the officers were satisfied that what he was telling them was indeed true. The implications were awesome. Evidence emerged of a well-placed and efficient Soviet spy ring operating at the top of SDECE, the French intelligence service. Given the code name Sapphire, the spy network was to occupy the attention of Western counterintelligence analysts for years to come.

Golitsin's leads touched other countries. Kim Philby, the infamous Soviet spy in British Intelligence, was exposed with his help. Golitsin's information contributed to the downfall of Stig Eric Wennerström, the Soviet spy whose treachery scandalized Sweden. Some of his leads in other cases continued to prove useful as late as 1979.

American intelligence officials appear to have largely accepted Golitsin's bona fides and were disturbed that in spite of strong evidence implicating certain French officials, nothing was happening in Paris. Six months after President Kennedy dispatched his alarming letter to De Gaulle, General Paul Jacquier, director of SDECE, arrived in Washington to meet with U.S. intelligence officials. At an elegant dinner in his honor at the 1925 F Street Club, General Jacquier was told bluntly by a top American intelligence official that his service was infiltrated by the Soviets and that the Americans expected appropriate action to be taken. If not, Jacquier could expect cooperation between the French and American intelligence services to cease.

Golitsin was questioned repeatedly about every allegation he made. Undoubtedly the pressure on him grew as time passed and the French did nothing. Did they know something the Americans did not? Or was the Soviet penetration so thorough that any investigation could be stopped in its tracks?

Golitsin also provided leads to a high-level penetration of U.S. Intelligence.* He was so convinced of this that he insisted upon speaking only to President John F. Kennedy, but had to settle for an audience with Attorney General Robert F. Kennedy. The leads were not sufficient to bring about the exposure of any American intelligence personnel. Golitsin's tension must have been heightened by his wondering if in fact he was dealing with secret Soviet agents operating in the CIA.

On the other hand, Golitsin's living conditions were almost extravagant. He and his wife had been given a fine house in McLean, Virginia. The CIA also furnished a car and a chauffeur to drive them and their seven-year-old daughter around Washington. Mrs. Golitsin had a maid. Golitisin had two fierce German shepherd dogs that were often at his side. The dogs had no names.

While the CIA had catered to Golitsin's material desires, it could not give him a friend. On the surface, Golitsin was not an attractive fellow—short, squat, powerfully built, intensely paranoid, and reportedly foul-tempered. His background in the KGB was enough to make him anathema to a distinguished and intelligent military defector like Nicholas Shadrin. But as it happened, Nick Shadrin was then feeling a strong need for companionship with a native Russian. He wanted someone with whom he could have wide-ranging discussions in Russian. His best American friends—Tom Dwyer and Jack Leggat—were no longer in Washington. And some of the bloom of his ONI job was fading. He had been complaining to Ewa, saying he wished he had someone he could talk to.

Although he knew Golitsin was likely to possess qualities he detested, Shadrin felt that there must be something good about him if he had decided to defect from the Soviet Union. Moreover, Golitsin's managing to defect with his wife and daughter indicated to Shadrin that he was a man of extraordinary cunning. Shadrin agreed to meet with Golitsin.

---

*The first details of this were described in *Legend: The Secret World of Lee Harvey Oswald*, by Edward Jay Epstein, published in 1978 by Reader's Digest Press. Subsequent details appeared in *Wilderness of Mirrors*, David C. Martin, published in 1980 by Harper & Row.

The time was early October, possibly the same week that General Jacquier was in Washington being warned by the Americans to heed Golitsin's revelations. The pressures and fears churning within Golitsin that week must have been unimaginable. The scene of the initial meeting, hardly the fare of spy thrillers, was a sprawling asphalt parking lot in northern Virginia.

The introduction was orchestrated by the CIA to accommodate Golitsin's extensive security precautions. In the company of a CIA man known to Golitsin, Shadrin was driven to the Seven Corners Shopping Center in Falls Church, Virginia. There, in the parking lot, Shadrin and his escort encountered Golitsin and his chauffeured car. The introductions were made.

From the start the two men got along splendidly, much to Shadrin's surprise. They shared a love for long conversations involving an intricate knowledge of politics and history. They discovered a mutual appreciation for good food and drink. Golitsin's ebullience and graciousness made him thoroughly companionable with his friends. And both men had a great interest, for different reasons, in German shepherd dogs. If Shadrin was provoked by the CIA's manner of dealing with him, he soon realized his complaints were trivial. Legitimately or not Golitsin was developing a towering resentment of the CIA.* He was angry with its people, its methods, what he perceived to be its procedural inefficiency. His faith was so shaken that in spite of the exceedingly elaborate security measures, he believed that at any moment he could be plucked off the streets by the KGB. But what bothered him most was the CIA's "stupidity," the most common descriptive word Ewa would hear from him.

The intensity of the friendship between Shadrin and Golitsin was almost like that of long-lost friends, although there is no evidence that they had ever known each other in the Soviet Union. But Ewa did not get along well with Golitsin, who seemed to harbor an innate disliking for Poles. When she was present, he seemed to take special pleasure in talking about Polish generals, whom he considered to be particularly inept as military men. This

---

*Although his treatment by the CIA was extravagant, Golitsin remained critical of the amenities surrounding his reception. Once, after a French interrogator had presented him with a huge container of caviar in order to win his good grace, Golitsin sniffed: "The CIA would never do this for me." He went on to explain to the Frenchman that the CIA did not seem to recognize that he was used to an extravagance of caviar.

was always enough to send Ewa on her way. Says Ewa: "I didn't like him, and he didn't like me." But she got along superbly with Golitsin's wife, Svetlana.

A large and gregarious woman, Svetlana Golitsin was exceptionally friendly and gracious. She enjoyed cooking and was enthusiastic about shopping and buying clothes. She and Ewa spent hours in the elegant stores around Washington. On one occasion Ewa and Svetlana and her daughter attended a performance of the Bolshoi Ballet. Anatoli stayed home, however, on the grounds that the event would be swarming with Soviets.

Tolka, as the Shadrins called Anatoli, and Nick spent many hours together. Men of exceptionally broad knowledge in many areas, they would speak in their native tongue late into the night. Because Ewa did not get along with Tolka, she rarely stayed up to listen to them. She does know, however, that a favorite subject was their mutual hatred of the Soviet regime.

Nick was also fond of Svetlana, and he enjoyed singing while she played the piano. She had brought with her a new popular song from Russia called "Moscow's Windows," which Nick quickly learned. If anything, Svetlana was even more outspoken than her husband about the horrors of living under the Soviet regime.

But there was always a great fear that marred any occasion with the Golitsins. Few people knew better than Golitsin the terrifying efficiency of the ubiquitous KGB. The Shadrins and the Golitsins rarely went to restaurants; once when they did, Ewa can recall that Tolka appeared frightened the whole time. He kept wheeling about to look behind him. He did this even as they walked along the street from the car to the restaurant. He seemed constantly afraid that the CIA's Office of Security was too incompetent to take care of his safety. Shadrin's tales about his own experiences with the Security Office did not help ease Golitsin's fears.

The loneliness of the Golitsins was almost pitiful, Ewa felt. They did not have a single couple in the United States with whom they were friendly except for the Shadrins.*

Contrary to his expectations, Shadrin found nothing evil about

---

*P. L. T. de Vosjoli recalls vividly that during that period there was great concern over the misery of the Golitsins. Both the French and the Americans were interested in easing their discomfort. However, De Vosjoli does not recall Golitsin's introduction to Shadrin, though he hastens to explain that there was no reason for him to know about it. In his recollection, no friends were ever found to help the Golitsins ease their loneliness.

Golitsin. In fact, he came to believe that Golitsin possessed a certain integrity that had led to his daring defection. They seem to have found a bond in their mutual abhorrence of the Soviet regime and the KGB. And of course, Shadrin had enormous respect for Golitsin's knowledge and intellect. But Shadrin did not overlook the irony of his friendship with a man with whom he would have been at such odds back in the Soviet Union.

It is not unreasonable to suppose that Golitsin counseled his friend Shadrin about the best ways to deal with the CIA. Considering what is known of Golitsin's feelings about the agency, he probably would have told Shadrin he needed to be very cautious, that he needed to strike a better bargain than the one he had.

Golitsin had worked out possibly the best settlement of any defector in history.* But Golitsin had a great batch of documents and many bargaining chips—assets Shadrin neither had nor would apparently have understood how to use to his advantage. Still, it seems likely that Golitsin, in those long private conversations, advised him to be more canny in dealing with the CIA.

While it is known that Golitsin was then immersed in his allegations that were of such intense concern to several governments, it is not known how much of this, if any, he shared with Shadrin. It is clear, though, that Shadrin was one of the few people Golitsin ever relaxed with during this period of his life in the United States.

The Shadrins watched Golitsin's fear and frustration grow into a consuming passion to set a distance between himself and what he perceived to be the towering incompetence of the CIA. What worried him as much as his personal protection was the agency's apparent failure to get other intelligence agencies to follow the leads he had provided. And despite his warning, the agency had made no progress in rooting out its own penetration by the Soviets.

Finally, Golitsin told Shadrin he could take no more. "He was beside himself with how stupid the CIA people were," Ewa recalls. Golitsin told the Shadrins he believed he would be safer and happier in England. Plans were made to leave in February, and

---

*Initially Golitsin demanded $1 million for his information, according to De Vosjoli, but the CIA balked at this. In 1975 Jack Anderson reported that the CIA paid Golitsin $200,000 in compensation for his information and spent at least $500,000 more in protecting him and creating a "superbly contrived false identity." Other sources reliably report that Golitsin continues on the government payroll as a consultant to this day.

after their house was sold, Svetlana and her daughter stayed with the Shadrins while arrangements for their departure were finished.

Golitsin knew how much the Shadrins admired his lovely home, and he tried to sell it to them for a price far below the market value. It was a figure the Shadrins could have afforded. But Nick felt this would be an improper gift, and he stoutly declined the generous offer. Later, after Shadrin had also refused to accept an expensive color television set Golitsin had decided not to take to England, Ewa found it sitting on their doorstep one morning. Golitsin had sent it over by his chauffeur.

The most lasting gift from Golitsin was one of the nameless German shepherds that had served as a guard. Shadrin was delighted to have the dog and immediately named him Dzhulbars. (When Nick was small, there had been a series of movies in Russia about Dzhulbars, a character roughly comparable to Lassie in the United States.) Quickly the dog came to be known as Julik, a Russian word meaning "little cheat." Nick's joy over Julik grew every day. He became as attached to him as he had been to Alfik so many years earlier, before the siege of Leningrad. Julik would remain one of Shadrin's closest companions for the next thirteen years.

Two decades later Golitsin told the author that in one of his last talks with Shadrin he warned him that he should stop Ewa from making telephone calls to her parents in Poland. Golitsin apparently felt this could provide the KGB with clues to the Shadrins' whereabouts. However, Ewa says that Nick never passed along these warnings to her.

The friendship between Shadrin and Golitsin lasted for only about four months, but for years it would stand out in Nick's mind as one of the closest he enjoyed in the United States. Later Tom Dwyer would recall hearing Shadrin speak of his fondness for Golitsin. "But," Dwyer adds, "Nick did think he was a strange man, a very brooding type of person."

Professionally as well as socially, often mixing the two conveniently, Nick Shadrin cultivated friendships among the powerful and distinguished. For example, Captain Thomas L. Dwyer, was on his way to becoming the executive assistant to the commander in chief of the Pacific Fleet (CinCPac), one of the highest defense posts in the United States. During the last fifteen years of Dwyer's distinguished career he counted Nick Shadrin as his best friend.

Dwyer was but one of the extraordinary number of highly placed people Shadrin got to know. There was his exceptionally close relationship with William "Electronic Warfare" Howe and his gregarious wife. A prolific entertainer, Mary Louise Howe was always eager to include the Shadrins at her frequent dinner parties, which would routinely seat at least twenty guests. It was not uncommon for the Shadrins to meet U.S. senators, congressmen, and top military and intelligence officials at the Howes' handsome house. The gatherings frequently included officers from the military service as well as officials from the State Department and the intelligence community. By all accounts, Shadrin thrived on meeting these people and was warmly accepted by many of them.

One friend of the Howes who enjoyed Nick and Ewa's company was Marine Lieutenant General Leo J. Dulacki, who had been posted to the U.S. Embassy in Moscow when Shadrin defected. It was he who had shown the clipping about the event to the KGB man on board the train to Siberia.

Dulacki first met Shadrin in the summer of 1960 while on leave from his Moscow post for thirty days in Washington. He spoke Russian and was introduced to Nick, as were many of the attachés from the American Embassy in Moscow. Among other things, they talked about the beauty of Leningrad, and Nick asked Dulacki to bring him some prints of the city; the general did so on his next trip to Washington.

In 1961 General Dulacki was detached from his Moscow post for a Pentagon assignment. A lifelong bachelor, General Dulacki had Polish immigrant parents, and he thoroughly enjoyed sharing the observance of Polish holidays and customs with Ewa Shadrin. He was a guest at the Shadrins' home on Christmas Eve, when there were just the three of them, plus an empty chair at the table, a custom observed at the Polish Christmas Eve dinner.

On other occasions Dulacki celebrated Easter at the Shadrins', once with a succulently roasted goose that Nick had shot. For the Easter observances Ewa would color dozens of eggs for the dining room. "They always treated me with great warmth and friendship," says General Dulacki. He also notes that Shadrin was a large man in every sense—physically, in his gregariousness, his openness, his willingness to be friendly. "He was the sort of guy you would want on your side in a pinch," Dulacki says.

On many occasions Shadrin and Dulacki stayed up late into the night, conversing in Russian and drinking Metaxa Greek brandy. "Nick had a brilliantly analytical mind," says Dulacki, adding that he had lost none of his analytical balance by rejecting the USSR for the United States. He still could weigh the pros and cons of the systems very carefully. He knew that from a military standpoint the Soviet system had sharp advantages over the American —especially in terms of discipline and the rugged Spartan life expected of the soldier in the field. "Nick decried the pampering of the American serviceman, with the exception of the marines, whose discipline and toughness he highly respected," recalls Dulacki. "He admired American military leaders with combat experience or those who had served in troop-leading commands, but he scorned those whom he considered managers."

Dulacki lived alone, and it was not easy for him to reciprocate the Shadrins' hospitality. So he often took them out to dinner or would invite them to his apartment and send out for Chinese food. On one occasion when the Shadrins visited Dulacki at his Crystal City apartment near Washington, Ewa Shadrin got quite a jolt. There in the elevator with them was the Polish woman who had been assigned to Ewa during the period of Nick's debriefing in Frankfurt. Ewa says the Polish woman recognized her and then turned away. Ewa did not speak.

Predictably Nick Shadrin was graciously expansive when it came to entertaining. General Dulacki recalls an elegant dinner party Nick hosted for him and another couple. They were at the Shoreham Hotel, and Dulacki cringed when he thought of the final bill as they stayed and talked, fresh rounds of after-dinner drinks coming constantly. The bill apparently was staggering, but Nick was chipper about paying it, refusing all attempts from his guests to share part of it.

Another well-placed acquaintance was Admiral Sumner Shapiro, today the Director of Naval Intelligence. Admiral Shapiro recalls being impressed with Shadrin as a "very outgoing, personable man" whose observations were of "considerable value . . . at a time when relatively little was known about the Soviet Navy." He also recalls that Shadrin "was very proud of his Russian heritage, but at the same time conscious and most appreciative of the freedom he enjoyed living in this, his adopted country."

Another distinguished military man with whom Shadrin became friendly was General Sam V. Wilson, later director of the Defense Intelligence Agency. General Wilson had had a magnificent military career, including service with Merrill's Marauders in Burma. Later he was a defense attaché to the U.S. Embassy in Moscow. He first met Shadrin in the early sixties, when one of his friends told him he thought he would enjoy the company of this remarkable former Soviet naval officer. They got together for a weekend of shooting at Ashford Farm.

General Wilson, who at that time was deputy assistant for special operations to the secretary of defense, recalls the weekend and has a picture of a couple of the geese shot that day. "I got to know Nick as a human being," he says. "I just wanted to get a general feeling for him. I felt he was probably genuine. He appealed to me as many Slavs do. He was straightforward, once he sized you up and felt comfortable. He was gregarious, jovial, pleasant, friendly. He gave you straight answers and looked you straight in the face. My general impression was a positive one."

The occasion and the geese shot that day prompted a long-standing joke between General Wilson and Nick Shadrin. By his own account, Wilson did not get up as early as Nick, who had bagged a couple of Canada geese and had them in the yard by the time the general was up and about. Then Nick, laughing and teasing Wilson, accusing him of being a sleepyhead, insisted on having the general photographed holding the geese Nick had bagged. "Nick just rode the hell out of me over that the next time I saw him," says Wilson. To this day there is a picture in General Wilson's study of him standing with a couple of geese he supposedly shot. In Shadrin's home there is a picture of Nick holding the same two geese. "When people admire the geese, I have to admit I posed with them as a gag," says Wilson.

Wilson says that although he saw Shadrin on five occasions, he was not really close with him. He never worked directly with him, although in 1966 Shadrin did become a part of an analytical branch of the Defense Intelligence Agency that had been created by General Wilson.

Wilson and Shadrin had a mutual friend in Nicholas Kozlov, with whom Nick frequently enjoyed hunting. Kozlov had originally worked under General Wilson in Berlin while operating as an agent for the United States against his native Soviet Union. Wilson, who regards himself as a close friend of Kozlov and considers him "extremely intelligent," has stated that he was responsible for getting him to come to the United States. Over the years Kozlov became closer with Shadrin, and even today he continues to be a dental patient of Ewa Shadrin's.

A great professional pleasure for Nick Shadrin was his association with Rufus L. Taylor, a career man who was graduated from the U.S. Naval Academy, remained in the navy for thirty-two years, and advanced to the rank of vice admiral. He served on various battleships and destroyers and had a thoroughly distinguished career.

It is not clear exactly when Taylor and Shadrin first met, but it is an association that many ONI colleagues believe went back to Nick's earliest days. Admiral Taylor did, of course, have to give his approval for Shadrin to go to work for ONI.

"I could not tell you just when their friendship started," says one naval officer with security clearances who worked near Nick's office at the Naval Observatory. "But I do know that during those early years Taylor, who was then in charge of the Intelligence Division, would be in there for an hour at a time talking to Nick. Even when they had the door shut, especially at the lunch hour, you could hear them."

The naval officer, who greatly admired both Shadrin and Taylor, reports that there were "dozens of times" when he heard Nick's loud voice booming as the two men discussed matters. According to this officer, Shadrin and Rufus Taylor were often heard conversing about subjects that should never have been discussed. "It was quite routine for them to be talking about classified naval intelligence," he states.

Normally, in the office where Shadrin had his desk, there were eight or nine other people, but when Rufus Taylor came in, it was an unspoken point of protocol that the others would leave the room. The naval officer who observed this reports that these frequent visits stopped after Rufus Taylor became Director of Naval Intelligence.

"It was perfectly obvious they had a very high regard for each other and would talk about things you should not talk about without having the proper clearance," he says. "There was clearly a bond, a professional and personal bond, between them—as well there should have been. They were two good men."

Many of Shadrin's good friends heard him speak fondly of his association with Admiral Rufus Taylor. Shadrin admired him above all as a professional navy man. However, there is no evidence that their friendship ever extended to social connections or to hunting and fishing.

Rufus Taylor died in 1978, so it is impossible to know how he might have assessed his friendship with Shadrin.* However, in early 1966 Taylor did recommend to David Abshire, then executive director of the Georgetown University Center for Strategic and International Studies, that Shadrin be considered for a position there.†

Admiral Arleigh Burke, another prominent acquaintance of Shadrin's, also made a similar recommendation to Abshire. Years later Admiral Burke described Shadrin as "a very bright, sincere, honest person. He was a very good naval officer, and I thought he was sincere when he defected."

During the early sixties Shadrin's value to the United States ranged far beyond his consulting duties at ONI. He addressed members of the Joint Chiefs of Staff about Soviet naval strategy and capabilities. He briefed the commanders at Atlantic Fleet headquarters and on several occasions flew to Hawaii, where he gave briefings at the Pacific Fleet headquarters. He spoke with the commander in chief of the Pacific forces.

Shadrin took pride in briefing the highest officers in the United States military establishment, and he made his presentations with considerable skill and flair, according to those who witnessed his lectures. But perhaps, of more importance to him were his frequent invitations to lecture at the Naval War College. The staff there seems to have readily understood that there could be no more effective authority on the subject of the Soviet Navy than Nicholas Shadrin.

Shadrin's association with the Naval War College was to become one of his most significant contributions to the United States. As of the close of 1980 he was the only Soviet defector who had ever lectured there. These occasions provided the basis for his

*Captain Wyman Packard, who knew Shadrin vaguely from an investment club, the Capital Investment Association (CIA) at ONI, sat down the hall from Taylor's office at the Pentagon after Taylor became Director of Naval Intelligence. Captain Packard never once saw Shadrin visit Taylor there. But it is not illogical that as Taylor's administrative duties increased, he had less time to spend with analysts in Shadrin's position.
†Abshire indicated that a "full-time post-doctoral fellowship" might be available. At the time Shadrin was just beginning his doctoral program at George Washington University.

professional relationship with Admiral Stansfield Turner, president of the Naval War College from 1972 until 1974, who later became Director of Central Intelligence.

Captain Paul A. Adams is the man who first arranged to have Shadrin lecture at the college. He had followed Shadrin's career from that day in 1959 when he was on board the train from Moscow to Siberia and his associate Leo Dulacki showed the newspaper clipping on Shadrin's defection to the KGB man. Subsequently Adams became a personal friend and supporter of the Shadrins.

Shadrin delivered his first lecture at the Naval War College on October 27, 1961. To this day the lecture is classified secret, but it stimulated such a positive response among the students that other classes were canceled so that the afternoon could be spent questioning Shadrin. "We had never seen such enthusiasm," says Captain Adams. It was the first of many appearances, each of which won Shadrin numerous glowing letters of thanks from the staff.

But even during these good years there were those who had reservations about Shadrin. One of them was Captain William Hatch, a senior officer at ONI, who, in spite of his reservations, did not stand in Shadrin's way when it came to utilizing his analytical abilities. In fact, Hatch had warm personal feelings for Shadrin, although he could never bring himself completely to accept the Russian's bona fides.

"Nick knew I had these feelings," Hatch says. "And when I would see him socially, I always had the feeling he was seeking approbation from me. But I think he knew I just couldn't quite accept him for what he claimed to be." Hatch, who speaks Russian and had assignments that took him to Murmansk during World War II, doesn't have any specific reasons for his reservations—only an awareness of Soviet tactics combined with his knowledge of Shadrin's background.

His devoted colleague and friend Tom Koines, Shadrin's immediate supervisor at ONI, acknowledges that Shadrin's acceptance was not universal: "There was quite a split of those who had a really high regard for Nick and liked him very much and those who just didn't trust him at all. And there were those who respected him for his information and were able to check the reliability of his information—but still didn't trust him. These feelings existed almost entirely because of Nick's origins—nothing else."

Generally, though, Shadrin was widely accepted and respected in the military and intelligence community. He even became a regular at the annual Red Tie Luncheon, a strictly unofficial observance of Soviet Navy Day by U.S. Naval Intelligence personnel. One of the founders of the Red Tie Luncheon was Herman Dworkin, one of Shadrin's acquaintances and coanalysts at ONI. The festivities took place each year on the Monday following Soviet Navy Day. Usually there were about 200 guests, mainly from the intelligence community, all wearing red ties on their necks and smirks on their faces. Traditionally the final toast was: "Sink the Soviet Navy!"

During the first half of the sixties Shadrin's life was enriched by new experiences and associations, endearing friendships, and much hunting and fishing. He was able to travel all over the United States. His pride in Ewa's success was unabashed. But Shadrin's friends began to sense his growing frustration over the professional limitations he faced without a security clearance. With the passage of time—and his increased distance from his service in the Soviet Navy—Shadrin's potential as an analyst and consultant was increasingly stunted. His store of knowledge, from which he had spent so lavishly, was not being replenished with fresh classified information being gathered on Soviet naval technology.

On one occasion William E. W. Howe raised the issue with then Director of Naval Intelligence Rufus Taylor, who was sympathetic and agreed to see if he could assist in getting a clearance for Shadrin. Taylor apparently took the matter to the proper authorities, but the response was negative. However, no one considered this a poor reflection on Shadrin. No prudent security agency could afford to risk the minuscule chance that he was a phony defector, really a Soviet agent.

"In something like that," says Howe, "it is always better to make a negative ruling than to go out on a limb."

Many of Shadrin's friends quickly recognized that he should consider work outside the government. A think tank would have been the perfect spot, but that would have required a security clearance similar to the one he could not get at ONI. Several urged Shadrin to consider working at a college or university because he was a gifted speaker and was fond of young people. He told some friends he was interested in the merchant marine, and he mentioned to others that he would like to own and operate a fishing marina.

In spite of his frustrations, Shadrin indicated outwardly that he continued to enjoy his work at ONI, even without a security clearance. He was in professional contact with some of the highest officials in U.S. defense and intelligence, men like Rufus Taylor and Sam Wilson. Among his closest personal friends were men like General Leo Dulacki and William E. W. Howe. His lectures at the Naval War College were widely admired.

One of Shadrin's greatest sources of pride was the accomplishments of his wife. It meant a great deal to him that she had quickly mastered her dental program, that her language skills exceeded even his own, and that she was readily compatible with her American patients and friends. In return, Ewa was extremely proud of Nick's broad intelligence, his prowess as a hunter and fisherman.

But Shadrin did speak to some of his friends about Ewa's success compared to his own. She was earning more money than he and had established herself in a career that would continue for the rest of her life. It deeply concerned Nick that his own professional life was strikingly less successful. It seemed to offend him as a man that he really was not taking care of his wife.

Ewa Shadrin was aware of her husband's growing despondency, but there was little she could do about it. More than once she heard him say how much he missed the happy hours he had spent talking to Anatoli Golitsin. "I only had Golitsin," Nick told her many times. But Julik—the German shepherd given him by Golitsin—remained a source of pleasure for Shadrin, and he spent many enjoyable hours out walking the dog. Increasingly Shadrin spent his spare time hunting and fishing.

Shadrin was working at ONI under a five-year contract that was due to expire in June 1965. He was the only defector ever to work as a consultant and analyst for ONI, and he had been consistently praised for his exceptional contributions. In fact, in March of that year Shadrin's friend and colleague Admiral Rufus Taylor, then Director of Naval Intelligence, arranged for him to address the Naval War College. On that occasion there was a luncheon in Shadrin's honor. Admiral C. L. Melson, then president of the college, was stimulated to write to Admiral Taylor:

Once again, the students and staff officers of the college found Mr. Shadrin's lecture and answers to questions of the highest possible interest and of great relevance to their course of work here. His lecture was received with enthusiasm, and a barrage of questions continued through the luncheon in his honor and the afternoon post-lecture conference, right up to his evening departure.

The letter also contained a statement that shed considerable light on Taylor's own opinion of Shadrin's continued usefulness to ONI. Melson stated:

> Obviously, as you remarked in your kind letter of 9 March, Mr. Shadrin's presentation is unique and, I believe, not likely to suffer in its intrinsic value with the passage of time. It certainly affords incomparable insights into the many persisting attitudes and problems of Soviet naval personnel, and of the Army and Party leaders who dominate the military picture.

But when one of his supervisors tried to convince ONI officials that Shadrin's value was so great that he should be given a new contract, he got nowhere. The intimation was that Shadrin's usefulness had diminished because he had been out of the Soviet Navy for more than five years. "This just wasn't true," says the supervisor. "There was no one in the office who could surpass Nick when it came to analysis of Soviet strategy, and things like that do not change overnight." But the appeal was to no avail.

A top ONI official, one of Shadrin's strongest supporters, believes that no particular significance should be attached to the fact that Shadrin's contract was not renewed. He points out that by this time the Defense Intelligence Agency (DIA) had been established and that many former functions of ONI were being taken over by the new intelligence agency.

"ONI was left only with things that were terribly sensitive, which Nick could not have dealt with without a clearance. The broad, general Soviet naval intelligence concern was in the hands of DIA. The function at ONI had become more specialized, and there just wasn't a place for Nick."

Although Tom Dwyer was not in Washington when Shadrin's contract ended, he could readily see that his value as an analyst would have been reduced by the passage of time. "But," Dwyer adds, "there is no question in my mind that Nick could have qualified as the top Soviet naval analyst, limited only by the amount and quality of information he was permitted to deal with."

Already becoming despondent over his situation, Shadrin was profoundly depressed at the prospect of losing his ONI job. There was nowhere else acceptable that he could go. A job had been offered to him at DIA, but it was in a department basically concerned with translation—a department filled with defectors of all stripes. Shadrin was insulted at the prospect. Neither he nor his friends considered him in the same league with other defectors.

A few days before Shadrin was to leave his office at the Naval Observatory, there was a farewell party. Shadrin did not know where he would find a suitable job, so it was not a particularly joyful occasion. Then, a day or so after the party, while Shadrin was still at the office, word came that he had been given an extension of six months on his contract. This, of course, was good news, but he and his friends knew there would be no extension beyond that.

It was a gloomy fall for the Shadrins. "They were so stupid, the way they never utilized Nick," says Ewa. "There was so much he could have done." Nick's many friends echoed her feelings, but there was no hope of his staying on at ONI. He spent hours walking with Julik, brooding over his situation, no doubt thinking of what he had given up for this. Again, he must have thought about the warning from his Swedish friend Rydström, with whom he corresponded occasionally.

The job at the Defense Intelligence Agency was still available, but Shadrin could not imagine taking it. His opinion of other defectors was not high. Like many intelligence officers, Shadrin viewed them as too often neurotic and paranoid. His dilemma brought to mind his great fondness for Golitsin, and he no doubt compared his own miserable situation to the cushy deal Golitsin had managed.

Various friends made diligent efforts to help, some even sending out letters and résumés to large corporations with analytical departments. Always, it seemed, a promising job prospect had the basic requirement of a security clearance. Shadrin was hampered in considering jobs outside the Washington area because Ewa's dental licenses would allow her to practice in Virginia, Washington, and Maryland. His frustration was heightened by the fact that he had worked so hard at George Washington University to earn

116

his master's degree in engineering. Still, he could not find a job.

A perfunctory letter arrived from Rufus Taylor, as director of ONI, in which he thanked Nick for his work. Curiously, it was addressed "Dear Mr. Shadrin":

> You have demonstrated most outstanding capabilities as a special consultant and lecturer on the theory and practical application of the many aspects of modern naval science, tactics and engineering.
>
> I therefore wish to take this opportunity to express our complete satisfaction with the job you have done for our Navy through the application of your unique experience, knowledge and concepts. Your intelligence and outstanding ability are certain to ensure your future success, as they have during your past association with my staff.

This did little to cheer up Shadrin. To Ewa, it simply made no sense. "It was just crazy," she says. "They had nothing but praise for his work, and then they fired him and wanted him to take a demeaning job translating newspaper and magazine articles at DIA." Ewa longed to be able to help her husband, but there was nothing she could do except work hard at her own job to bring in enough money for both of them. This, she knew, was not Nick's idea of how he should take care of his wife.

Shadrin, burying his frustrations, became increasingly popular as a public speaker all over the United States. His normal patterns of speech were those of an orator, and he possessed a true speaker's sense of timing. He would pound the rostrum as he thundered eloquently about the evils of communism or the strengths and weaknesses of the American system.*

According to those who heard Shadrin speak, he was intelligently balanced in his presentation. His chief concern was what he perceived to be the lethargy of the American people toward the awesome threat of Soviet domination. And, according to Tom Dwyer, Shadrin could support his points with "a remarkable knowledge of the philosophies of the founders of the Republic."

In 1965, while he was in California visiting Jack and Peggy

---

*Shadrin apparently was on a list of FBI-approved speakers. Evidence of this is seen in a three-page FBI report discussing the details of a request for a Soviet defector as a guest speaker for the Junior Chamber of Commerce in St. Cloud, Minnesota.

Leggat, Shadrin addressed the Los Angeles Women's Division of the Freedoms Foundation at Valley Forge. He told his audience that much of the laxity and passivity he had seen in the United States had their origins in the home. According to an account in the Los Angeles *Herald-Examiner*, Shadrin stated:

> Children must be taught the goals and responsibilities of freedom and Americanism, and the seat of learning is in the home. The school cannot be a substitute for a family, but all too few people bother to teach patriotism to their children.
>
> United States citizens take freedom so for granted that they dare put aside great problems of our day in favor of trivia. I am shocked that so few people vote. And that so many give passive acceptance to the dangers of communism.
>
> There is a bland acceptance here of co-existence, whereas it really has the important goal of giving Communists time and strength to bury the capitalist system. Passive support can create opportunity for communist action.

Shadrin called the student rioting of the sixties a reaction "to a poor education on the bases of Americanism and communism." But he did not suggest an ostrich approach to communism: "We must not forbid education of communism. The Communist Manifesto should be read and then analyzed intelligently."

Two months after giving this speech, Shadrin officially became an American citizen. Ewa had become a citizen in October 1964, but Nick was delayed by a technical problem—he had been a member of the Communist Party. The law stipulated that he had to wait ten years before becoming naturalized. Several of his friends recall Shadrin's indignation and outrage when it was suggested to him by someone in the Immigration and Naturalization Service that he could simplify matters by stating that he had not been a member of the Communist Party.

"I came to this country so I would not have to *lie!*" stormed Shadrin. So Mary Louise Howe prevailed upon her friend and neighbor Senator James O. Eastland of Mississippi to introduce a special bill into Congress that exempted Shadrin from that particular provision of the Immigration and Nationality Act. On November 24, 1965, Nicholas Shadrin became a naturalized American citizen.

A telephone call on October 15, 1965, provided one other pleasant break in Shadrin's gloom. The telephone rang at about

7:00 P.M., and Ewa, who answered, told Nick that his dear friend Anatoli Golitsin was on the line. Golitsin said that he was calling from Canada.* Ewa Shadrin heard Nick's enthusiastic greeting to Tolka, and then she went about her own business. The only part of the conversation she could understand concerned Julik. Shadrin and Golitsin talked for about an hour. Presumably, Shadrin told his dear friend about the professional problems he faced. What advice Golitsin gave him is unknown.†

Beneath the Christmas festivities that year gloom permeated the Shadrin home—a despair on Nick's part that things had not worked out well in his new country. It was a mystery to him why the Office of Naval Intelligence refused to renew his contract. An even greater mystery was why he was under pressure to take a job at DIA that was a catchall for maladjusted defectors, virtually a sinecure to keep them pacified.

In early February Shadrin received an unsigned to-whom-it-may-concern letter from Brand W. Drew, assistant officer in charge of the Naval Scientific and Technical Intelligence Center. Of Shadrin's performance, Drew states:

> Mr. Shadrin performed excellent to outstanding services for the technical and scientific personnel of this activity, especially in areas associated with marine engineering, ordnance, and translation services of technical articles printed in the Russian language. Mr. Shadrin has a remarkable background in technical, engineering and scientific areas pertaining to the USSR and provided much valuable information, analysis and interpretation to all units of this activity during the period of his contract.
>
> Mr. Shadrin is a reliable and sincere person, and gets along with all with whom he comes in contact. His services for STIC left nothing to be desired.

---

*Golitsin had returned from England by then, but he was not yet ready to settle in the United States. According to P. L. T. de Vosjoli, the French government remained so angered over what it considered humiliating exposures of Soviet penetration within its own intelligence service that it wanted a firsthand crack at Golitsin. Paying him a large amount of money, the French had him move to their country, where he spent eighteen months to two years undergoing interrogation. De Vosjoli states that the French hoped to utilize Golitsin to root out the Soviet penetration in U.S. Intelligence and thus return the humiliation it had felt in 1962 as the Americans lectured the French about *their* penetration.

†In the spring of 1980, the author located Golitsin and requested an interview to discuss, among other things, his relationship with Shadrin. Golitsin declined, though he did state that the telephone call was only to say farewell to Shadrin.

It was not exactly a gold watch, and it did nothing to lift Shadrin's despair. Nor was it of much help as he tried desperately to find a dignified job. In the meantime, his paychecks stopped. However, a number of Shadrin's friends learned of his termination at ONI and did what they could to help him.*

Norman Precoda, a General Electric engineer who worked on government research projects, had come to know Shadrin four years earlier, when Nick read a report Precoda had prepared for General Electric on the threat posed by the Soviet armed forces. Precoda, who has written widely on subjects pertaining to national defense, was gratified that a man of Shadrin's stature read his work so carefully. They sought each other out and became friends.

When Shadrin was facing the bleak prospect of the DIA job, Precoda was one of the friends who rallied to his aid. Nick told him that he would like to find a job in private industry, something more rewarding than working for the government. Precoda, doubtful that Shadrin would be comfortable sending out résumés and applying for jobs, did this for him. He made copies of Shadrin's résumé and began responding to promising ads in the *Wall Street Journal* and other publications.

"But the mid-sixties apparently were not a good time for job hunting in Nick's areas of expertise," says Precoda. There were no favorable responses to his efforts.

"I've often thought that things would have been so different for Nick, much better, if he had not always thought of me first," says Ewa with tears brimming in her eyes. She was well settled in her job at the dental clinic and had made close friends in the Virginia suburbs. Nick often told friends how important it was to him that Ewa realize her dream of a successful career in the United States. He would do nothing to hinder that, such as taking a job in a jurisdiction where she was not licensed to practice dentistry.

After brooding for three months, Shadrin decided to take the job with the Defense Intelligence Agency. As depressing as he felt the job would be, it was less of a humiliation than failing to draw a salary. Ewa recalls that during that period Nick spoke often of Rufus Taylor. No doubt Shadrin was gratified that Admiral Taylor himself had agreed to accept a job at DIA. In March Shadrin

---

*Other friends—even the Howes—never knew Shadrin was without a job. It was so humiliating to him that he seems to have told as few friends as possible.

reported for work at the DIA offices in the Old Post Office Building in downtown Washington.

A few months later Admiral Taylor stepped down as Director of Naval Intelligence and became deputy director of DIA. Taylor would be there only a few months before leaving to accept the second highest position in the Central Intelligence Agency. Taylor's departure from DIA must have been a great disappointment to Shadrin.

Chapter 6

Early one Saturday morning in the spring of 1966 the telephone rang in the Northwest Washington home of Richard M. Helms. It was about eight o'clock, early enough for the caller to be reasonably certain Helms would not have left his house. Julia Bretzman Helms, a sculptress of some note and at the time the wife of Richard Helms, picked up the telephone. The caller, a man who came to be known as Igor, asked to speak to Helms.

Igor described himself as an officer of the Soviet KGB. He stated that he was going to be in Washington for only a few more months and that he wanted Helms, who had just been appointed Director of Central Intelligence, to be aware of his desire to work as an agent for the United States. Helms expressed interest and relayed Igor's proposition to the appropriate intelligence officers for immediate handling.

Within the hour, top counterintelligence and security officers had been notified. James Angleton, the chief of CIA Counterintelligence, for whom Helms had a long-standing respect, and Bruce Solie of the CIA Security Office were informed. Solie was intensely involved with Angleton in pursuing leads given by Anatoli Golitsin about a Soviet penetration of the CIA. The sudden emergence of a new source from the Soviet side was fortuitous and tremendously important—especially if he came bearing clues that would ferret out the Soviet agent believed to be spinning a poisonous web of treachery deep within the CIA.

Five hours later there was a meeting between Igor and U.S.

intelligence officers at a safe house in the Washington area. There to listen to Igor were Bruce Solie and Elbert T. Turner of the Soviet Counterintelligence Section of the Federal Bureau of Investigation. Bert Turner would serve as Igor's case officer because the FBI normally handled such cases in the United States. Solie would be Igor's chief CIA contact, an unusual position for a security officer.

Over the next several weeks Igor revealed an exciting potpourri of intelligence that opened one of the most confounding unfinished chapters in modern espionage. He generated powerful allegiance and trust in some quarters, while experts in other areas remained doubtful. But even those whose initial doubts began hardening into suspicions could not ignore Igor's tantalizing array of information —a variety so choice that it seemed he had brought something for everyone. Decades may pass before a detailed description of Igor's total package reaches the public domain, but it is known that there were three prime areas in which his messages were immediately pertinent.

Festering in the inner sanctums of the intelligence community was the debate over the legitimacy of Yuri Nosenko, a Soviet who had defected to the United States in early 1964 and claimed to have been a KGB officer. The case would remain hidden from public view for another decade, but at the time of Igor's appearance it was creating a wrenching division between those who believed Nosenko to be legitimate and those who did not. Igor possessed information that would help settle the debate.

His second major contribution directly concerned the intense investigation that was under way to uncover a Soviet penetration agent believed to be working at a high level of American Intelligence. Few things were more welcome to Angleton and Solie than fresh leads for this investigation.

But it was the third aspect of Igor's 1966 appearance that was at once tantalizing and bizarre. Igor's purported willingness to work secretly for the United States was sharply enhanced by the fact that he was relatively young and could anticipate fruitful decades of rising through the ranks of the KGB—an advance that would be to the direct advantage of the Americans. But to accomplish this, Igor said, he had to succeed in what is surely one of the most curious and complex missions in the annals of espionage—the recruitment of Nicholas Shadrin. Not only was Shadrin now a well-adjusted American citizen, but his contributions continued to strengthen the

United States in its position vis-à-vis Soviet naval capability. Igor's mission would have profound repercussions.

An atmosphere of great expectancy characterized the early days of Igor's 1966 debriefing. The depth and diversity of his information seemed extraordinary, supporting his claim that he held a high position with the KGB. His credibility was enhanced by precise reports on current, sensitive activity involving U.S. intelligence officers in Europe, information that would not reach CIA head-quarters through normal channels for weeks. And there was much more. It must have been difficult to remain professionally circum-spect in the face of such timely, convincing evidence of credibility.

Embedded in the blizzard of information was a clear message concerning Yuri Nosenko, whose most timely information had encouraged the conclusion that the KGB had nothing to do with Lee Harvey Oswald during the period of Oswald's defection to the Soviet Union from 1959 through 1962. By the same measure, the Soviets had nothing to do with the assassination of President Kennedy. This was a message FBI Director J. Edgar Hoover was anxious to embrace as fact, for it would relieve the FBI of responsibility for Oswald. No one expected the FBI to keep track of "a lone nut," if that was what Oswald really was.

But from the time Nosenko reached American soil, he had fallen under serious suspicion in the eyes of most of the CIA officers involved with his case. Senior officers in the Soviet Division, along with most of James Angleton's counterintelligence staff, suspected that Nosenko was a prime example of Soviet provocation. The feeling was so strong and widely held that Nosenko was placed in detention for years while suspicious CIA officers worked unsuc-cessfully to get him to confess his duplicity.*

Thus, it must have been with special urgency that Solie and Turner reported to their superiors that Igor's information certified that Nosenko was not a provocateur but, in fact, was just who he claimed to be. It was a sorely needed foundation block for the FBI's acceptance of Nosenko. Still, in view of the almost unanimous distrust of Nosenko by the CIA at that time, Igor's certification of Nosenko's bona fides should have set clanging the bells of suspi-

---

*For a full account of the Nosenko case, see Epstein's *Legend: The Secret World of Lee Harvey Oswald*, op. cit.

cion. Perhaps it did, but Igor's total package—if not entirely convincing—was apparently so intriguing that few were willing to discredit him just because of his message about Nosenko. Moreover, it appears that Igor won some powerful support to Nosenko's side, for only a few months later a major directive went out from CIA Director Richard Helms to resolve the Nosenko question.*

In spite of this erratic signal in the quality of Igor's information, there was no reason for James Angleton or anyone at the CIA to let Igor know of any suspicions. It was far better not to spook him, but to let him run, to listen to all he had to say. Even if he was a provocateur, his satchel of information had to contain a tempting variety of good-grade intelligence designed to enhance his credibility, to aid him in selling himself to the Americans.

It was in just this context that Igor brought forth his second bombshell, which he dropped squarely into the laps of James Angleton and Bruce Solie, who were embroiled in their search for a Soviet penetration agent. Igor's astounding piece of information pertained to what has come to be known as the Sasha case, which has its origins in post-World War II espionage activities in Germany.

According to Golitsin, who had defected in late 1961 and remained the CIA's premier defector, an American intelligence agent working for the Soviets and known to them by the code name Sasha had betrayed numerous pro-Western undercover agents to the KGB. Some men had died as a result of this. Others were in prison. But the Americans' purpose in tracking down Sasha was a bit more complicated than just catching a lone traitor from the past.

It apparently was Golitsin's contention that the positive identification of Sasha would be a major step toward the exposure of Sasha's boss within American Intelligence as a highly placed Soviet penetration agent. The theory was that many years earlier this man—one of several who handled Sasha—had been compromised by his principal agent and then recruited to work for the Soviets.

Thus, there was urgent emphasis on exposing Sasha primarily because it would give investigators a quantum leap toward the

---

*Helms has told the author that his desire to resolve the Nosenko question was not prompted by any external influence—that Nosenko's detention was a glaringly unsatisfactory situation that called for an immediate resolution.

more significant penetration. So, in this context, Igor's promise to provide new information on Sasha was not only timely but stunningly important. "It was truly an instance of deus ex machina," says one former CIA officer.

On the basis of Golitsin's leads, the CIA and FBI were virtually certain that Sasha was one Igor Orlov. Bruce Solie's diligence in combing the old espionage files on CIA activities in Germany had turned up confirming details that quite distinctly pinpointed Orlov as Sasha. A former American intelligence agent, Soviet-born, Orlov had retired from his espionage activities in Germany and settled into a quiet private life in Alexandria, Virginia. Ironically, he had actually been known by the name Sasha during his early days in Germany. A small, sturdily built man with silvery hair and great gray eyes, Igor Orlov operated a small picture framing gallery with his wife in the Old Town section of Alexandria.

Despite weeks of intense investigation by the FBI, including polygraph tests, Orlov technically remained nothing more than a suspect. At one point, in the spring of 1965, the investigation became so grueling and ostentatious that according to the Orlovs, the FBI had two agents sitting in their tiny framing gallery studying each customer. "They wouldn't even take off their hats!" Mrs. Orlov recalls with indignation. Meanwhile, the shop was under constant surveillance.

On two occasions during this period the FBI sent one of its prized double agents, John Huminik, into the shop to browse and to observe the Orlovs. "The FBI wanted me to see if I could spot any of the Soviet spies I had been meeting with in Washington," says Huminik. "But I never saw anyone I recognized."

In the final analysis there was no conclusive evidence to prove Orlov's alleged treason. "There was a significant amount of high-grade circumstantial evidence, but nothing more," says one of the counterintelligence officers involved in the investigation.

It was not illogical that after long months of ardent and fruitless investigation the FBI's interest began to wane. After all, not only was Orlov out of the spy business, but his alleged potential danger must have been neutralized by the pervasive investigation swirling about him. It was difficult to imagine how, guilty or not, Orlov and his law-abiding wife and small children posed any threat to the United States. Moreover, there was little chance that his current activities would yield clues to the higher penetration—even if

Orlov *were* Soviet agent Sasha. The FBI was expending enormous resources in pursuit of a goal that seemed ever-elusive. Some FBI officials were beginning to draw back from the investigation, to question whether it was worth all the effort.

Over at the CIA James Angleton and his counterintelligence staff did not see it that way. Perhaps Angleton had his own reasons for considering Orlov a continuing threat or believing that he would yet yield evidence leading to the higher penetration. He also had another reason for pressuring the FBI to keep up the investigation. If an absolute determination could be made that Orlov was Sasha, it would be another star in the crown of that prince of defectors Anatoli Golitsin. Fresh information from Igor conclusively proving the guilt of Orlov was perceived as supremely important to the CIA Counterintelligence staff. Thus, counterintelligence officers were undoubtedly pleased when Igor announced he was prepared to provide damning collaborative evidence that Orlov was the long-sought Sasha.

According to the account of numerous sources, including published ones, Igor stated that Orlov had paid a personal visit to the Soviet Embassy in Washington. Among those who heard this, at a joint FBI-CIA debriefing of Igor in 1966, was the FBI's Bert Turner, one of the prime agents involved in the 1965 investigation of Igor Orlov. Turner, among others, reportedly told Igor that this was not possible, that the FBI photographed every person who entered or left the Soviet Embassy and Orlov had not been among them. Igor urged the Americans to return to the surveillance photographs and study them with a fresh eye; he insisted they would find a picture of their suspect.

With expressed skepticism—and perhaps with some masterful playacting for the CIA—the FBI agreed to review the surveillance photographs of the Soviet Embassy. Sure enough, the bureau soon reported, there was a picture of Orlov at the Soviet Embassy.

At this point the sequence of events is befogged by grinding inconsistencies that are best presented forthrightly. Certainly to those who believed that Igor's 1966 appearance represented his first contact with American Intelligence, this news of Orlov's visit to the Soviet Embassy was a revelation. But to others—namely, the FBI men handling Igor—the news of Orlov's visit to the Soviet Embassy was more than a year old.

The date of Orlov's visit to the Soviet Embassy—and the FBI's

127

frenzied investigation of that visit—was actually the spring of 1965, a year before the KGB's Igor made his gambit with a telephone call to Richard Helms. This date is supported by Orlov's extensive business and personal records and corroborated independently by FBI double agent John Huminik, today a respected business consultant. If there was a second investigation in 1966, Orlov and his family claim convincingly that they were not aware of it. Independent evidence indicates that by the spring of 1966 the FBI investigation of Orlov had ceased and his life had taken on a certain normality.

In any event, the standard account is that the FBI in 1966 —after reviewing the surveillance photographs again—reported that the KGB's Igor was indeed correct. A photograph had been found showing Orlov at the Soviet Embassy. If the FBI did tell the CIA that the visit had occurred a year earlier and that a full-scale investigation had been made then, there is no evidence that this year-old information dampened the enthusiasm of the CIA men pursuing the penetration case. The "news" was viewed as highly encouraging by the officers who were handling Igor. Not only did they feel it added weight to the evidence against Orlov, but it greatly enhanced the credentials and credibility of Igor, the KGB man.

Igor Orlov's peripatetic life began in the Ukraine in 1925 as the child of a prominent military family. By the time he was eighteen Orlov had been trained as a Russian military intelligence officer. This, in Orlov's mind, is strikingly different from working for the KGB. Orlov was one of the youngest Russian agents parachuted into Germany on intelligence missions during World War II. He speaks of his record with quiet satisfaction, even pride.*

On a drop in 1944, Orlov was fired upon by antiaircraft weapons as he drifted toward German soil. He was hit repeatedly, one piece of shrapnel even passing through his neck. He bears the scars of his wounds, which took months of hospitalization to repair. By the time he was well he had been convinced to go to work for German Intelligence. He did this until the end of the war, when he

---

*In a series of exclusive interviews with the author, Igor and Eleanore Orlov provided details about their tumultuous lives in Europe and the United States. Wherever possible, the account has been corroborated by independent sources.

became involved in the activities of the SBONR—Union for the Struggle for the Liberation of the People of Russia, an émigré organization. Among various other duties with the émigrés, Orlov worked as a writer for a Russian-language newspaper. It was during this period that he and Ellie met and married.

Five years after the war Orlov was recruited as a contract agent by the CIA and put to work against the Soviets, recruiting and running agents in Berlin. Those who knew his work say he was a brilliantly versatile agent. Known commonly by his nickname Sasha, Orlov based his operations in Berlin until November 1956, when he was transferred to Frankfurt. During these years he had a variety of bosses from the American intelligence services, several of whom were later subjected to intense, ultimately fruitless investigations in the CIA's frantic search for a penetration agent following the revelations by Golitsin.

Proud of her German heritage, Ellie Orlov felt a simmering resentment at the frequency with which she and her husband were required to assume new names and identities. Her resentment was transferred to the Americans when she realized they were responsible for so much of the turmoil in their lives. Her one unalterable demand was that each new name begin with the letter *K*—a simple enough request for a woman who, as the young bride of Lieutenant Alexander Kopazky, had been given linens embroidered with the letter *K*. (The name Orlov was not used until much later, and Kopazky was not his original family name.)

The greatest indignity for Ellie Orlov was that with her new identities, she was considered stateless. Although she was German, she had to register each year with the police as a stateless person. She recalls that the CIA was dependable about acquiring new documents, such as marriage certificates, bearing the new names. But they would not give her a forged American passport, which would have solved her problems.

After the birth of the Orlovs' first son, Ellie lost her temper; in fact, she created such a commotion that some American intelligence officers, long retired, still recall it. "How would my poor baby ever know what his name was?" she asks incredulously. Ellie announced she was going to leave her husband and take her baby back to her mother in Munich and live there. Finally, the one American she admired and found congenial mollified her—Orlov's chief superior, General Sam V. Wilson.

"General Wilson was an excellent intelligence officer and a real gentleman," states Orlov, who placed great value on his association with the distinguished American military figure. Ellie Orlov agrees, recalling fondly that it was General Wilson who later encouraged them to move permanently to the United States and paved the way for their doing so.

During these years Orlov carried out many sensitive missions for the United States in addition to his primary duty of running agents. Following one mission of several weeks' duration with the International Youth Festival in Vienna in 1959, Orlov returned to Frankfurt to discover that his private compartments in an office safe had been opened while he was away. Orlov, who shared the large safe with another former Soviet military officer recruited by the CIA, Nicholas Kozlov, had placed tiny chips of mica along the drawers of his locked private compartments so that he could determine if anyone had entered them during his absence. Inside the compartments were the code names of agents as well as descriptions of operations currently under way. The possibility that his agents and operations could have been compromised by this breach, following his final departure from Germany, still haunts Orlov.

He reported the incident to his immediate superior, the only person other than Nicholas Kozlov who had access to Orlov's private compartments in the safe. The superior, from the CIA's Soviet Division, was a man for whom Orlov had respect. The CIA officer told Orlov he had not entered the compartment. The only other possibility was Kozlov, but the CIA officer dismissed that possibility—citing the esteem in which Kozlov was held. He recommended that Orlov not write a report of the incident.*

The relationship between Orlov and Kozlov, never very good, soured after this incident. However, the two former Russians continued to have much in common—particularly their close relationships with General Wilson, which, in each case, culminated in moving to the United States and becoming an American citizen. And two decades after that, the names Kozlov and Orlov would again be curiously linked—this time by the KGB—with the disappearance of Nicholas Shadrin (see Chapter Eleven).

---

*Kozlov, who today holds a sensitive position in the U.S. government, has declined to discuss the safe incident with the author.

The Orlovs' permanent move to the United States was sudden. Through the thoughtfulness of General Wilson, they had visited the United States in 1957 for the birth of their second child. It was a luxurious experience for them, and it included a relaxing stay at the CIA's Ashford Farm, where they were visited by General Wilson. Three years later Orlov became embroiled in the prickly business of insisting that a report he had prepared describing misuse of funds by a superior, a CIA officer, be sent to Washington. Even though it turned out that Orlov was correct—the superior was later disciplined—it effectively spelled an end to Orlov's career. Several months after his report on the misuse of funds, Orlov was told to pack up, that he and his family were being sent to the United States.

His first impression was that he was being transferred to the United States, where he would continue his work for the intelligence services. He and his family were put aboard the SS America, traveling with first-class accommodations. "We had five steamer trunks and two children and our old Ford car—everything we possessed," recalls Ellie. They landed in New York on January 17, 1961, packed their belongings into their car, and drove to Washington. Every hotel for miles around was booked because of President Kennedy's inauguration. Finally, the Orlovs found a motel miles away from Washington.

When Orlov tried to report to people he knew at the CIA, he discovered that there was no job for him. It was soon clear that he was finished working for U.S. Intelligence. A young man from the CIA was assigned to help the Orlovs find a place to live. The agency paid for him to take a crash course in English at the Berlitz Language School and offered him $2,000 as a lump-sum settlement for his years of service. Insulted, Orlov turned it down.

Speaking hardly a word of English, Orlov took the first job he could find to support his family. It was long, hard hours of moving furniture. Later he got a job with the Washington *Post* as a truck driver for the circulation department. In his spare time he learned the picture framing trade and, in 1963, opened a small framing gallery. He and his wife operated it as he continued driving the newspaper delivery truck—a schedule that kept him working eighteen hours a day. It was a grueling life for the Orlovs. But their goal was clear and simple: to own their own property and to send their two sons to college.

Around eight o'clock one morning in early March 1965 there was a knock at the door of the Orlovs' apartment in the Old Town section of Alexandria, Virginia. The two callers identified themselves as agents of the FBI. They explained that they could easily get a search warrant but asked Orlov's permission to search his home and shop without one. Orlov quickly agreed. The agents made a telephone call, and within a few minutes four or five more agents arrived. Ellie Orlov was terrified and took the children away. Orlov was confused. The team of FBI agents spent about six hours searching the apartment and shop.

Thus began a harrowing six weeks during which Igor reported each morning, after finishing his job at the Washington *Post*, to the FBI Field Office at the Old Post Office Building in downtown Washington for five or six hours of interrogation. He was questioned on every aspect of his past. The framing gallery was staked out, and two agents were posted in the back room to look at each customer who came in.

The FBI carefully checked even Mrs. Orlov's personal correspondence, including an elaborate investigation of a small hand-drawn map agents found in her purse. The map led them to the home of a German-speaking couple who were members of Ellie's Lutheran church. The agents seemed especially interested in a letter Ellie had received from a former maid in Germany who had since moved to Australia. Bert Turner, who became the case officer of the KGB's Igor, interrogated Mrs. Orlov for hours on end.

The investigation nearly wrecked the Orlovs' lives. Each day the fear and frustration grew worse. The questions the agents asked Orlov seemed to be the same ones over and over; it was clear to him that they did not believe his answers. His confusion deepened.

Finally, in desperation, Orlov concluded that the FBI had him mixed up with someone else. He decided that if he could get in touch with relatives in Russia, they might know something that would help him to understand what was going on. That, he claims, is what took him to the Soviet Embassy some time in April 1965. Orlov insists that the decision to go there was impulsive and desperate—a measure of last resort to find out what was going on. That morning, while he was at the loading dock behind the Washington *Post* building, he noticed men emptying garbage cans at the rear of the Soviet Embassy, about fifty yards away. A thickset man wearing a fedora was holding the door open, watching the men emptying the trash cans.

Orlov approached the man in the doorway. Speaking in Russian, Orlov stated that he was a former Soviet citizen and that he needed help. He asked to speak to someone in the embassy. The man in the fedora motioned for him to come in. He led Orlov to a small room with a table, two chairs, a desk, and a large mirror on the wall. Still wearing his fedora, the embassy employee listened to Orlov's story about wanting to find his relatives in Russia. Orlov claims he did not tell the official his Russian name—only his American name. The man asked Orlov if he was an American citizen, and Orlov stated that he was. He also told the Soviet that he was the subject of an intense FBI investigation of his past activities and that was what had driven him to seek help at the embassy.

The official told Orlov to wait, that he had to confer with others, and left the office. While he was gone, Orlov heard a series of distinct clicks from behind the mirror, leading him to believe the Soviets had photographed him. When the official returned, he explained that the embassy was not in the business of helping former Russians find relatives. But he gave Orlov an address in Moscow he could write to for assistance. Then the official led Orlov to the front door and bade him farewell. Igor Orlov walked straight out onto Sixteenth Street, a site rivaled by the Grand Canyon for the frequency of photographs taken there each hour.

The following day, when Orlov reported for his interrogation session at the FBI, he noticed a new reserve in the attitudes of the two agents who handled his questioning. "I could tell they had something on their minds," says Orlov. "Then one of them said, 'Where did you go yesterday?'"

"I told them I went to the Soviet Embassy," claims Orlov. The agents informed him that they were aware of his visit and wanted to know why he had gone there. He gave them his explanation. Orlov says a great deal of time was spent going over each detail of his story. The agents expressed astonishment over his ready statement that he had told the Soviets about the FBI's investigation of him. The agents questioned him closely about why he had done this and precisely what he had said. Orlov claims he was cooperative and explained to the agents that he knew of no reason not to tell

133

the Soviets. He had never been told that there was anything secret about the investigation. Finally, in Orlov's opinion, the agents seemed satisfied with his explanation.

The day after this incident, following a polygraph test, one of the FBI agents invited Orlov to have lunch with him. According to Orlov, the agent stated that he personally believed the FBI had been on the wrong track in its investigation. He said that Orlov would no longer have to report for interrogation, that the investigation was over. The FBI man told Orlov to be sure to report any further contact he had with the Soviets, that he was obligated to do so. Greatly relieved, Orlov went back to his normal routine —working long nights delivering the Washington *Post* and diligently making picture frames during the day. Whatever the reason, Orlov's visit to the Soviet Embassy seemed to have brought the FBI's investigation of him to a close.

What happened next in this curious saga remains open to interpretation. The FBI refuses any comment, and obviously, the Orlovs are not impartial observers. However, they have placed in the possession of the author their detailed business records from the mid-sixties as well as their personal calendars showing dates when customers brought in work to be framed and the dates the work was picked up. The ledger books, filled with thousands of obviously contemporaneous entries, were kept to satisfy the regulations of the Internal Revenue Service. These regulations were so frighteningly complex to the Orlovs when they opened their business that the records they kept are meticulous.

On April 24, 1965, according to these records, a Mr. Johns came into the gallery with an ocean watercolor he wanted framed. He requested a particular mat and frame. In case there were questions, Ellie Orlov always noted her customers' telephone numbers. Mr. Johns provided the number for his home, located in North Arlington. However, the number he provided is listed in the telephone directory not for Johns but for the home of Courtland J. Jones, an FBI agent assigned to the Washington field office. Later Jones was made supervisor of a national security team and assigned to create and maintain an index of all persons who entered or left the Soviet Embassy.

Although the Orlovs did not know at the time that "Mr. Johns" was with the FBI, over the years he became a regular customer, even a friend to them. It was never clear whether he had clouded his identity on purpose, inasmuch as he later told them he was with the FBI. The significance is that Courtland Jones was the first of nearly a dozen FBI agents—most of them from the original unit that had investigated Igor Orlov—who became regular, friendly customers of the Orlovs.

This no doubt represented a shift in the FBI's strategy to secure evidence against Orlov. By becoming customers the agents might pick up new leads. In fact, routine reports were filed by the individual agents after each visit to the gallery. One might have expected a certain discretion on the part of these new customers, but there was rarely any doubt the customers were from the FBI.

On May 3, 1965, Joseph D. Purvis, special agent in charge of the FBI's Washington field office, walked into the Orlovs' gallery with his gray poodle, presented his business card, and left four pictures to be framed. According to the ledgers, Purvis gave the Orlovs his home telephone number and directions to his home, in case they ever needed to reach him. He also gave them an emergency FBI number they could call if anyone from the government ever again showed up and asked to search their home and gallery. These were hardly the normal amenities one would expect the FBI to offer a suspected Soviet agent.

"Mr. Purvis was a wonderful man," says Igor Orlov. "He told us he wouldn't be doing business with us if he didn't think we were all right. He said he wanted us to telephone him personally if we ever again had trouble with people coming and asking us questions. He gave us three numbers so we could reach him anytime." Purvis remained a faithful and friendly customer until he retired and moved away years later.

Strange as all this seems, one thing is clear: Joe Purvis wanted to know instantly if anyone began questioning the Orlovs.

Purvis and Jones were but two of an astonishing array of FBI agents who became regular customers. Indeed, the names—Fred Tansey, William Lander, Bill Branigan are a few—read like a roster of the FBI's Soviet Counterintelligence Section. But Joe Purvis, who became head of the Washington field office in December 1964 and later was promoted to assistant director of the bureau, was the most faithful customer, bringing in a great deal of official business. In July 1965, for example, Orlov framed eight different photographs of J. Edgar Hoover posing with agents. In August

1966 Orlov framed six photographs of scenes in the Washington field office, and Ellie delivered them to Purvis on a rush basis at the Old Post Office Building in downtown Washington. Purvis even gave Ellie his parking slot number for her convenience. He told the Orlovs he needed the pictures in time for a party marking the occasion of the redecoration of his office—that of the special agent in charge—at the FBI field office. (Nearly fifteen years later an official FBI spokesman was able to confirm that such a party was held in August 1966.)

A number of other high officials, including Hyman Rickover, Elliot Richardson, and former Senator Mike Mansfield, have become regular customers. On the wall of the shop hangs a thank-you note from Richardson for the high quality of Orlov's work. In addition, there are a number of customers who were high officials in the Nixon and Ford administrations. The Carter White House sent notes of appreciation for work well done.

Orlov has no explanation for this avalanche of distinguished customers; he is simply grateful to have the business. He has invested hardly anything in advertising his framing gallery, and he is in an area with many other such shops. He believes that somehow his distinguished customers signify that he has been exonerated of the suspicion that caused him and his family such misery.

Orlov is incredulous that his 1965 visit to the Soviet Embassy could be seen as evidence of espionage activity. He believes it is absurd to imagine a suspected deep-cover Soviet agent operating undisguised out of the Soviet Embassy—a building any Washington schoolboy knows is under constant photographic surveillance by the FBI. Orlov made no effort to conceal his broad daylight visit there, and he claims he never denied it to anyone. He explains that he had reached a period of desperation and was willing to try anything.

Since that terrible spring of 1965 Orlov has not been aware of any continuing investigation of him. His business has improved each year, and he and Ellie have seen the fulfillment of their greatest dream: the successful education of their children and the promise of their good lives ahead.

The excruciatingly intense investigation of Orlov's past connections—aimed ultimately at the exposure of a high Soviet penetration agent in American Intelligence—has yielded no lasting suspect. To this day, however, there seems to be a unanimous belief that Orlov is Sasha.

But if, indeed, Igor Orlov is *not* Sasha, then at least two people have gained a significant sense of security from suspicion being placed so squarely on him. The real Sasha has escaped suspicion, and, worse, the higher penetration agent, tied to Sasha's exposure, has also escaped the attention he richly deserves. He either remains active or has passed honorably into retirement.

By the early summer of 1966 Igor's handlers from the CIA and FBI were enthusiastic about his information. James Angleton and his counterintelligence staff were never directly involved in the debriefing of Igor, but they kept abreast of developments through the debriefing reports. Igor's leads on Sasha and their promising implications had enhanced his position. His certification of Nosenko coincided with a commitment by top CIA officials to resolve the situation. With his credibility at its zenith, Igor dropped his most intriguing news. He informed his handlers that he was in line to rise through the KGB's ranks, perhaps even to become head of KGB counterintelligence in the United States, the most important Soviet espionage post in this country. It would be an unparalleled coup for the CIA and the FBI to have in their pockets the KGB's top spy working in this country. Short of that, he might reach a high position in the KGB's American Department. Without question, Igor could become the most significant Soviet defector in American history.

As the euphoria over this prospect engulfed his handlers, Igor mentioned a specific mission he had to accomplish to ensure his rise through the ranks of the KGB. Igor told his handlers that there was a Soviet defector living in the United States whom the Soviet Union regarded as extremely important. In fact, the KGB had given Igor the assignment of recruiting the man and had made his future promotions contingent upon his success in this assignment. The defector's name, said Igor, was Nikolai Artamonov, now known as Nicholas Shadrin.

Igor described Shadrin's life in the United States during the six years since his defection. He was familiar with his distinguished service at the Office of Naval Intelligence, and he knew Shadrin had just recently gone to work at the Defense Intelligence Agency. He was aware that some of Shadrin's friends were at the highest levels of the military and intelligence communities. Significantly he added that Shadrin was absolutely miserable with his new job and the people he was working with. While his wife was enjoying great success, Shadrin's enchantment with the United States had faded. The glowing promise he felt during his first years in America had been dulled by the steady decline of his usefulness as a vital source on the Soviet Navy.

For these reasons, Igor's superiors in Moscow believed that Shadrin should be ripe for recruitment, highly susceptible for redefection to the Soviet Union. And, Igor indicated, the KGB was willing to allow Shadrin to return home, provided he serve his motherland for a while as a defector in place, passing information from his job at the Defense Intelligence Agency and from the many other friendly sources he had developed during his years in the United States.

Igor stated that Shadrin's defection in 1959 had been a great embarrassment to the Soviets. Indeed, there was no military defector more skilled or distinguished. It was highly important to the Soviets to get Shadrin back. If Igor could carry out this mission successfully, he would be rewarded with the choicest of KGB promotions.

But, Igor explained, there was one hitch. This Nicholas Shadrin was an unusual sort. Despite what Igor's superiors might believe, he himself was not at all sure he could recruit Shadrin, no matter how miserable Shadrin had become in the United States. In fact, Igor said, he could hardly imagine recruiting him on his own. Shadrin's hatred of the Soviets was just too great. But, Igor suggested, the recruitment might be feasible with a little help from the FBI and the CIA. After all, they would be the ultimate beneficiaries of Igor's successful mission. Could the Americans render such assistance? Could they arrange to have Shadrin redefect, even as a ploy? If Shadrin would just *pretend* to redefect, that would be all Igor needed to satisfy his superiors.

Mysteries hang like cobwebs over what happened next. However, it is certain that in the very beginning only a select few U.S. intelligence officials were familiar with Igor's request that the Americans assist him in the recruitment of Shadrin. At the CIA there were Helms, Angleton, Solie, and two of Angleton's counter-intelligence associates, Ray Rocca and Newton S. Miler. At the FBI, which would actually run any case that developed, there were at least six men involved: J. Edgar Hoover, Clyde Tolson, William Sullivan, William Branigan, William Lander, and Elbert T. Turner.

The presence of Bruce Solie of the CIA Office of Security was something of an anomaly. Solie, of course, was heavily involved in Angleton's search for the penetration agent; apparently Angleton liked Solie's work, finding him skilled at handling the details of the investigation. But, primarily because Angleton firmly believed that the lair of the Soviet penetration agent was the Soviet Division of the CIA, every detail of the investigation was kept from that division.

By the same token, Igor was kept secret from the Soviet Division. Angleton obviously did not want the penetration agent to know of Igor's contributions to the investigation. From the FBI's standpoint as well, it was desirable to exclude the Soviet Division simply because the division was chiefly responsible for the trouble Nosenko was having. The continuing investigation by the Soviet Division stood squarely in the path of Nosenko's acceptance as a legitimate defector to the American side. If they knew of Igor's certification of Nosenko, surely they would tend to discredit Igor.

Under normal circumstances, officers from the Soviet Division would have been intimately involved in the CIA's handling of the Igor case, which was given the cryptonym Kitty Hawk. But there was nothing normal about Kitty Hawk, and Bruce Solie found himself in the role that usually would have been filled by an officer from the Soviet Division.

There were multiple, if diverse, incentives for going along with Igor's seemingly preposterous request, and from the start it was inevitable that the reasons for proceeding would prevail. The FBI had the greatest interest in accommodating Igor because his primary value would most benefit the bureau in its Soviet counterintelligence efforts inside the United States. It seems clear that almost from the start the bureau completely accepted Igor as a legitimate defector to the American side. There was, of course, tremendous pressure from J. Edgar Hoover to shore up the wavering Nosenko, and Igor had done just that.

Like Santa Claus at Christmas, Igor also produced a marvelously tempting morsel for the CIA's counterintelligence staff. His information supporting Golitsin's fingering of Orlov as Sasha was just what CIA counterintelligence needed to fan the lagging investigation of Orlov. Even if the KGB's Igor was acting under Moscow's control, the CIA reasoning went, it was reasonable to expect that Moscow had decided to throw away Sasha, to sacrifice him to the Americans in order to promote their new agent provocateur, Igor. If so, Angleton and company would anxiously await Igor's return with additional clues on the Sasha case.

Indeed, there is evidence that even at this early juncture James Angleton had concluded that Igor probably was a provocateur. However, this was no reason to stop dealing with him. In any event, Angleton reasoned, Shadrin's life would not be endangered as long as he never left the United States. The FBI also seems to have reasoned that Shadrin would not be in danger. Because it firmly believed in Igor's bona fides, the FBI concluded that he would not betray Shadrin's true role to the Soviets.

Out of this murkiness emerges a single certainty: A decision was reached by the United States to assist Igor in the recruitment of Shadrin. Moreover, Shadrin would not be trusted to know that Igor supposedly was acting in the ultimate interests of the United States. But of course, Igor would be trusted to know that Shadrin was acting in concert with the wishes of American intelligence officials.

Deciding to play Igor's game could not possibly have been as prickly as figuring out how to get Shadrin to cooperate with the ploy. It is difficult to imagine a more extremely sensitive situation. Shadrin, of course, had never been shy about expressing his scorn for all counterintelligence officers, hardly making a distinction between the Soviets and the Americans. Anticipating the intelligence bonanza of the century, the Americans could have scarcely been faced with a tougher problem than Nick Shadrin. It would require superlative cunning to get him to go along with the scheme.

The cobwebs again thicken on the point of just how he was persuaded. But there is one line of reasoning worth contemplation. If the officers considering how best to approach Shadrin had consulted CIA files, they would have quickly discovered one officer who had been privy to every debriefing report filed on Shadrin. He was Leonard McCoy, who then worked in the Reports Section of the Soviet Division—the very division Angleton would not allow to participate in the Igor operation.

Several former counterintelligence specialists agree that it is not unfeasible that at this juncture a decision was made to draw upon Leonard McCoy's deep knowledge of Shadrin. McCoy had a great admiration for Shadrin's value as an expert on the Soviet Navy, according to comments he made to at least one senior man at the Office of Naval Intelligence. Surely, though, the officers masterminding the Igor operation must have been disappointed when they discovered that McCoy had never actually met Shadrin. Indeed, as recently as 1979 Leonard McCoy maintained that he never met Nick Shadrin. Captain Thomas L. Dwyer, a mutual friend of both men, believes McCoy is telling the truth.

But there is another side to the story.

On August 5, 1977, twenty months after Shadrin had vanished in Vienna, Ewa Shadrin and her attorney, Richard Copaken, went for an appointment at CIA headquarters at Langley, Virginia. This was during a period when the CIA ostensibly was giving full support to Mrs. Shadrin in her search for Nick. On this occasion she was introduced to a man who had been designated by CIA Director Stansfield Turner to assist her. It was Leonard McCoy. To Mrs. Shadrin's knowledge, she had never seen or heard of McCoy.

But when they were introduced that afternoon, McCoy bowed politely and volunteered to Mrs. Shadrin that it had been a long time since he had seen her. Mrs. Shadrin smiled receptively and indicated that it had indeed been a long time. McCoy proceeded to recall convincingly the occasion of their earlier meeting. It had been at the Shadrin home, he said, where he spent two hours with Nick in his basement study, "looking at Nick's books." McCoy also recalled a German shepherd lying under a table with a television set on it. He even remembered that Nick said the dog always lay under the television set.

"I never remembered meeting him," says Ewa Shadrin, who had met dozens of Nick's friends over the years. "But McCoy was right that Nick kept his books in the basement and that Julik, the German shepherd, stayed under the television set."

More telling is the fact that these two conditions existed only in the Shadrins' first house, which they moved out of in 1967. McCoy's two-hour visit would have had to occur prior to that time. The effort to recruit Shadrin took place in 1966.

While McCoy's role in Shadrin's recruitment is conjecture, that is not the case with Admiral Rufus L. Taylor. It would not have taken the intelligence officers much casting about to learn of the great mutual respect that existed between Shadrin and Admiral Taylor. And Shadrin was working at the Defense Intelligence Agency, where Admiral Taylor was serving as deputy director. The admiral was held in high regard by most members of the intelligence community, including the men who were trying to determine the best way to trick Shadrin into playing the primary role in the Igor operation. Richard Helms may even then have been considering Taylor for the post of deputy director of the CIA, for Helms named him to that position a few months later. Admiral Taylor agreed to approach Shadrin and try to convince him to serve his country by pretending to be recruited by a Soviet agent.

Despite Shadrin's enormous respect and affection for Admiral Taylor, he balked. There can be little doubt that Shadrin had vivid memories of the warnings he had heard from his close friend Tom Dwyer. What Admiral Taylor proposed sounded just like the sort of dangerous counterintelligence operation Dwyer had urged him to avoid. Sometime during this period Shadrin had a chat with Tom Dwyer in the course of which he recalled Dwyer's warnings about getting involved with the CIA. "But what about the FBI?" Shadrin asked. "Would it be okay to work with them?" Dwyer told Shadrin that in his opinion, there was a significant difference between the FBI and the CIA, that the men he knew at the FBI were highly professional, efficient and honorable. From his own observations and experience, Dwyer could tell Shadrin nothing sinister about the FBI.

Dwyer did not ask Shadrin why he was wondering about the FBI. "He never mentioned what kind of work was involved, and I didn't ask," says Dwyer. "I figured he couldn't tell me, and I didn't want to embarrass him by asking." Moreover, Shadrin was not the kind of man who evoked paternalism. He seemed well able to take care of himself.

Technically, the operation Rufus Taylor described to Shadrin would be run by the FBI's Soviet Counterintelligence Section. There was no reason for the CIA to be involved directly with Shadrin, except in the event he left the United States. Apparently no one believed he would ever travel outside the country, considering the enormous risk involved.

(Many years later one of the highest people involved in the

running of the Shadrin case insisted adamantly that Admiral Taylor was "innocent" of any complicity in the recruitment of Shadrin. What this suggests is that perhaps the admiral, although used to recruit Shadrin, never knew the full implications of what he was getting his friend into. Although there are five witnesses to a statement by FBI Agent James Wooten that Taylor was used in the recruitment effort, there is no specific evidence to controvert the proposition that the admiral may have been duped into aiding in Shadrin's recruitment.)

A supremely tricky part of the deception and recruitment of Shadrin was how to make sure he would not reject the first Soviet overture so harshly that there would be no later chance to make a reconnection. It appears that an ingenious scheme was devised to prevent him from making an outright rejection, while at the same time making certain that he did not know that the whole ploy was being masterminded by the CIA and the FBI. Apparently he was told there had been a sharp increase in the Soviets' surveillance of the Old Post Office Building which housed the DIA office where Shadrin worked. He was told that although there were a number of defectors working there, he was the only one with sufficient stature to interest the Soviets. There was the suggestion that the Soviets might make an approach to him. If so, he should avoid an outright rejection and report the approach to the FBI, which has its Washington field office in the same building.

The deception played on Shadrin's well-known soft spot—his resentment at having to work with less distinguished former Soviets. Indeed, he believed he was the only defector of any stature working in that building.

Shadrin must have felt that someone was particularly prescient when, a few days later, in the late summer of 1966, he was approached by Igor in a public place in the Washington area. Shadrin immediately reported the contact to the FBI. Agents met him and suggested that he play along with the Soviets. He finally agreed, thus launching himself on a decade-long operation as a double agent.

Igor's first questions to Shadrin concerned Yuri Nosenko and Anatoli Golitsin. Igor wanted to know anything Shadrin could report about them. He specifically inquired about their current locations, their new identities and employment. Nosenko, of course, was then in detention. Shadrin apparently knew little of

Golitsin's situation, although he could report that he had last heard from him when he telephoned from Canada.

The meetings between Igor and Shadrin continued for several months. Then, in the late fall, there was a change for Shadrin. Not only did Igor turn him over to another KGB handler, but the FBI assigned him to his permanent case officer, James Wooten, whom he would come to value as one of his closest friends. Shadrin's regular meetings with the KGB continued as before, with him passing "soft" information on U.S. naval matters to his KGB contact.

Meanwhile, Igor and his American handlers could consider the recruitment of Shadrin a success, the mission accomplished. Igor's tour of duty in the United States was at an end, but he would return at some point in the future to run the KGB's counterintelligence operations in the United States. One can only imagine the glowing satisfaction felt by the FBI and CIA masterminds who had managed to recruit Shadrin into the ostensible service of Igor.

It is not difficult to understand Igor's announced reason for wanting to recruit Shadrin: Such a coup would allow him to move upward in the hierarchy of the KGB. But why did the Soviets want Igor to recruit Shadrin? What did they envision as their advantage in Shadrin's defection?

In any unhurried defection it is fairly standard to request that the prospective defector remain "in place" for a period of time, usually as long as possible. During this period the defector can gather information for the country of his new allegiance and fulfill requests for specific information. Even though Shadrin did not hold a high security clearance, he could still provide significant military and intelligence information to the KGB. Even if the Soviets knew his information was carefully prepared for their consumption, it would provide them with a classic study of American techniques of disinformation. Either way Shadrin's value would be significant.

But of perhaps greater value would be his vast store of personal knowledge of top men in the United States military and intelligence community. His relationships with these men were continuing, in some cases growing. The Soviets could spend years plumbing Shadrin's knowledge of military and intelligence personnel. In addition, the Soviets would find valuable any information he had on other Soviet defectors living in the United States.

Then there was the impossible dream. The Soviets would consider it a stunning intelligence coup to induce Shadrin to return to the Soviet Union, renounce his allegiance to America, and denounce the whole capitalist system. Following that, he would spend the rest of his life in service to the KGB, advising it on matters regarding the United States. That would be the script written at KGB headquarters on Dzerzhinsky Square. It would be a chance to promulgate the Soviet view that the United States is a terrible place—especially for Soviet defectors with distinguished careers. But there was no chance of getting Shadrin to do that willingly.

There was yet another way he could be used to serve the purpose of the KGB. He could represent the ultimate proof that the KGB always gets its man, that it can reach into American society and snatch a defector back to the Soviet Union and put him on trial, secretly or publicly, as a traitor. Such an example would stand as a vivid lesson to every potential defector that the tentacles of the Soviet KGB can reach deep into the bosom of America—into the inner sanctums of the U.S. intelligence community—and pluck back *any* defector. It could signify that the days of the KGB's murdering defectors by staging suicides in hotel rooms were over, that now the KGB could return the offender to the Soviet Union for justice. It would be a starkly effective lesson for any Soviet considering defection.

Best of all for the Soviets, of course, would be to have it both ways: Allow Shadrin to function as a defector in place for years, relaying information to his Soviet handlers in Washington. Convince him that he was safe and secure, proving it by enticing him out of the country for meetings. With this relationship established, the Soviets could play Shadrin for as long as they liked before blowing the whistle to bring him home. And there could be no daintier fillip than to achieve this through the courtesy of top U.S. intelligence officials.

But what were the Americans to get out of their deception of Shadrin, their sending him out to play a deadly game with one arm tied behind his back? Just what was worth this sort of callous duplicity toward an American citizen?

It would be a brilliant intelligence accomplishment if, by providing Shadrin to the Soviets, the United States managed to help catapult its man Igor upward through the ranks of the KGB. If Igor became the top KGB counterintelligence officer in the United States, it would be the fulfillment of a dream few spies would dare to dream. It would rival the KGB's coup in having Kim Philby as a head of counterintelligence at Great Britain's MI-6.

But this was an extremely long-term proposition. It would require the continuing production of sensitive material to be fed to the Soviets in order to maintain Shadrin's credibility. This in itself would represent an ongoing, cumulative loss to the Americans.

What else could the Americans hope to realize from the operation?

There was, of course, some value to the Americans in debriefing Shadrin after each of his Soviet contacts. It enabled the FBI counterintelligence specialists to identify Soviet agents operating in this country, to pinpoint dead drops, to study the KGB's domestic intelligence operations. And there was value in knowing the questions the Soviets were asking Shadrin, the kinds of information they were requesting of him.

But all this was secondary to the extraordinary prospect of future contact with Igor, especially if he returned to the United States in charge of KGB counterintelligence. Enduring patience was the key to success, perhaps the only key. It also required a very steady hand on the part of Nicholas Shadrin, who knew nothing about the ultimate goal of the operation. It was essential, of course, that his true role as a man working for American interests never be revealed to the Soviets, for that could jeopardize Igor in his relations with the KGB. And the jeopardy to Shadrin would be just as great.

In the end, against all his known instincts, Shadrin agreed to become a double agent. Doing so violated his own judgment and the advice he had heard over the years from his friends. But he could not resist the request of someone as distinguished as Admiral Rufus Taylor, whose overtures to Shadrin's patriotism were on behalf of the highest officials in American Intelligence. It was an extraordinarily courageous act of patriotism on the part of Nick Shadrin.

Once the operation was under way, it would not have been difficult to convince Shadrin that what he was doing was of urgent value to the United States. He had every reason to believe that the information he retrieved for his American handlers was hard, useful intelligence. The Americans certainly told him that it was, and the constant attention from his handlers would have reinforced any doubts he may have had. Shadrin would never know the real reason for the operation: the eventual reconnection with Igor, the long-term placement of an American penetration agent deep within the Soviet KGB.

Formal meetings were extremely rare within the CIA Counterintelligence staff during the many years it was run by James Angleton. Indeed, it appears that Angleton perceived a certain strength in this informality. Whatever confusion this spawned was offset by the fact that it prevented thorny little fiefdoms from sprouting up, cliques that might threaten the total control he managed to wield over the 200 or so members of the staff.

So it was highly unusual when, on a summer day in 1966, Angleton called a meeting of fewer than a dozen of his highest counterintelligence officers.* Unusual security precautions were taken, including requiring each officer present to sign a special secrecy oath that nothing discussed in the meeting would ever be revealed. Angleton explained Operation Kitty Hawk to those assembled, including his reasons for keeping the whole operation away from the Soviet Division. He said that the most important goal of the hour was to find out everything possible about Igor. Little was known about the mysterious Soviet at that juncture, and the officers present were asked to begin work assembling facts about him.

While Angleton and his men may have been in the dark about Igor, that does not appear to be the case with the FBI. There are some indications that the Soviet diplomat who came to be known as Igor actually offered his services to the United States much earlier than the spring of 1966, that he brought with him a certification of Nosenko as well as clues to Sasha, clues which the FBI pursued immediately and which were the basis for the intense investigation of Igor Orlov in the Spring of 1965.

However, it is not difficult to understand such concealment when one considers the nearly open hostility and mistrust that existed between the two intelligence services during those years.

---

*Angleton has declined to confirm or deny any aspects of this meeting or whether the meeting even took place.

147

In fact, there are precedents for such concealments, as in the case of Fedora. Edward Jay Epstein, in *Legend: The Secret World of Lee Harvey Oswald*, describes the atmosphere that prevailed when J. Edgar Hoover was informed that the best thinking at the CIA held that Nosenko was a Soviet disinformation officer:

> [Hoover] realized that unless this verdict was immediately reversed, it could have very serious ramifications for his bureau. For one thing, it would completely destroy the credibility of the FBI's agent in place in the KGB, code-named Fedora. For more than six years Fedora, officially a Soviet diplomat with the UN in New York, had been supplying the FBI with information about Soviet espionage activities. Indeed, a large part of the bureau's counterespionage effort had been built on Fedora's tips. The information Fedora provided was so prized by Hoover that on many occasions he forwarded it directly to the White House.
>
> Fedora . . . had gone out of his way to back up Nosenko's story when he defected in 1964. If Nosenko was now ruled a fraud, then Fedora would seem to be part of the same Soviet deception. And if Fedora were really under Soviet control, it could bring down the entire FBI counterespionage structure like a house of cards.

In view of this, the FBI would surely be reluctant to let the CIA know about yet another Soviet source who was certifying Nosenko. It was far wiser to keep him out of the CIA's hands—much as Hoover had managed to keep exclusive jurisdiction over Fedora in order to have his own private stock of intelligence tidbits to feed to the White House. The difference this time was that he would not allow the CIA even to know about Igor.

Why, then, did the FBI finally decide to bring Igor into contact with the CIA? When Igor informed the FBI of his mission to recruit Nicholas Shadrin, there may have been an examination of the feasibility of such recruitment and a decision that it was impossible without CIA assistance. It is even possible that earlier, unsuccessful efforts were made to crank up the Shadrin operation and that the FBI turned to the CIA only as a last recourse. Such an effort would explain FBI Agent Jim Wooten's subsequent statement that Shadrin resisted going to work as a double "for close to a year." It also would explain the various reports that Shadrin strenuously resisted giving up his prestigious position at ONI for the boring DIA job. A variety of intelligence and counterintelligence experts agree that it would be unheard of to run a double agent out of ONI, just as it would never be acceptable to run such an operation from the CIA headquarters building. If all this were so, it would be essential to force Shadrin from ONI to DIA before the operation could begin.

The FBI had to be extremely cautious about how it brought the CIA into the case. Nosenko remained in detention, and it was highly undesirable to have those who were intensely suspicious of him suddenly learn that the FBI had a second Soviet source, in addition to Fedora, who certified him. There was also the question of how to keep the ever-suspicious Angleton from discrediting the whole Shadrin recruitment because of his suspicions of Igor over the Nosenko certification.

But there were two opportune factors at work for the FBI as it considered its approach to the CIA. The more important was Igor's collaborative details shoring up the common belief that Orlov was Sasha. Angleton, intensely involved in the search for the penetration agent, would be anxious to follow Igor's clues on that case.

It would appear that the whole charade would be exposed if Igor's information on Sasha were presented as more than a year old. So the FBI apparently pretended that the information was fresh. To this day various CIA officials insist that the investigation of Orlov—and his visit to the Soviet Embassy—took place in 1966, presumably because their knowledge of the investigation came to them from the FBI. According to a high former counterintelligence source, Angleton's staff never debriefed Igor, relying, instead, solely on the reports given to them by the FBI and Bruce Solie of the CIA Office of Security. (Under statute, the CIA would have been on ambiguous legal ground if it had participated in the physical investigation of Igor Orlov within the United States.) This scenario would explain the convincing evidence from Igor Orlov and John Huminik that the actual investigation took place in 1965, a year earlier than is generally believed.

The second factor working for the FBI was Angleton's belief that the Soviet penetration agent was harbored in the Soviet Division—the very division that had placed Nosenko in solitary confinement. It is possible that the FBI would have drawn back from its plans if it had meant exposing Igor to the Soviet Division, the very men who would begin to build their case against him the moment they learned that he had certified Nosenko. But the bait used to attract Angleton also served to guarantee that Nosenko's prime detractors would be denied any information about Igor. Because Angleton was determined to exclude the Soviet Division from any source bearing information on Sasha and the penetration, he certainly would not allow the division to find out about Igor.

It therefore is possible that when Igor telephoned the home of Richard Helms in 1966, he was acting with the knowledge of the FBI. If so, it was a ruse that worked marvelously well for the FBI. If there was a greater beneficiary, it was Igor.

A key question is whether U.S. intelligence officials believed that Igor's overture was legitimate—that he was not another in the series of suspected Soviet provocations. A burning belief in Igor's bona fides would somewhat mitigate the accountability of those men who took custody of Nicholas Shadrin's future. At the least, an argument could be presented that the potential payoff was such a tremendously crucial intelligence accomplishment that there was justification for manipulating Shadrin's life.

But James Angleton has told Ewa Shadrin's attorney that he had concluded that Igor was a provocateur. Richard Helms sets a distance between him and the question by explaining that he turned the case over to subordinates and is not sure what happened after that. William Colby, a former Director of Central Intelligence, says flatly, "I don't recall the name Igor at all." William Branigan, a top FBI counterintelligence official who was in on the operation from the start, looks convincingly quizzical when he says, "Who's Igor?" Bert Turner and Bruce Solie refuse any comment at all. At least Shadrin's FBI case officer, James Wooten, seems to have believed fervently that Igor was working for American interests.

Only the passage of time will show whether Igor was acting under control of Moscow or on his own and in the interest of the United States. In either case, there is one certainty. Nicholas Shadrin, the sturdy fulcrum upon which this operation rested, had not even a hint of the truth. He believed he was serving his country patriotically, working in a rather standard double agent operation against the Soviets he so despised. He probably could not imagine the truth: that Igor—and perhaps the KGB—knew that Shadrin was only *pretending* to be working for them, that he had been duped and put to work by the highest intelligence officials in the United States.

Chapter 7

Without question Nicholas Shadrin was capable of leading several successful lives simultaneously. Indeed, he had shown this brilliantly as Captain Nikolai Artamonov, moving easily toward the top of the Soviet Navy while planning his defection to the West, secretly harboring hatred of the system to which he proclaimed fervent allegiance. In America, his richly varied personality enabled him to maintain relationships with a variety of friends from astonishingly diverse backgrounds—friends who, if thrown together, would have had little in common beyond their mutual admiration and affection for Nicholas Shadrin.

His hunting and fishing companions rarely crossed paths with those friends with whom Shadrin discussed philosophy and literature or debated world issues late into the night. Others recall him as a master craftsman—an exceptionally gifted carpenter who constructed his wife's dental office in the basement of their house. Even those admirers were amazed to learn that he had built a seaworthy boat or that he could dismantle an automobile engine, improve on it in ingenious ways, and then reconstruct it. And his closest friends were astonished that Shadrin could write a lengthy, widely admired doctoral dissertation in English. His skills as an orator—he would boom away eloquently in his new tongue —suggested an earlier time, when speeches were delivered with style and spontaneity.

As if to complete a picture of shining excellence, Shadrin loved dogs and little children. There are countless examples of youngsters taking to him instantly because of his cheery and sincere interest in them—an interest many friends believe was heightened by the fact that he and Ewa had no children of their own.

Then, in the summer of 1966, at the age of thirty-eight, Nicholas Shadrin embarked upon yet another life, so covert that apparently not a single friend had even a hint of it. Conceived and promulgated at the highest levels of U.S. Intelligence, this secret life required that Shadrin never divulge any aspect of his role, even to his wife, though he knew she had such faith in him that she would accept any answer if his peculiar activities mandated some explanation.

But Shadrin's life seems to have gone along with remarkable equilibrium—even at times when the stress must have been great, the temptation to confide in a friend tremendous. In July, for instance, Shadrin drove to Vermont with William E. W. Howe to visit one of Howe's children at summer school—a boy Nick was fond of and had taught to hunt and fish. The story is recalled by Howe as an example of the remarkable perception Shadrin seemed to have about everything, but it also illustrates his continued normal behavior under what must have been the wrenching pressures of the hour.

Bill Howe was at the wheel of the car as he and Shadrin wound through back roads. They became hopelessly lost. Seeing a local farmer standing along the road, Howe pulled his car to a stop and leaned across to ask him how to reach their destination.

What ensued sounds like a caricature of the hackneyed jokes about New England farmers. The old man's directions went something like this: "You go up this road about two miles, and you'll pass a road going off to the left just beside a big red barn. Well, you don't take that road. Keep going straight. Now go for another three miles, and you'll come to a big stack of milk cans sitting beside a road that goes off to the right. Do you follow me?" The old farmer peered across Nick at Howe.

"Yes, sir," said Howe, slight impatience rising in his voice. "And I turn there?"

"Nope," said the farmer, his cadence hardly changing. "You don't turn there. You keep on going straight."

Shadrin entered the conversation for the first time. "Excuse me, sir," he said with smiling forthrightness. "Are you by chance an Armenian?"

153

"Why, yes, I am," said the startled farmer. "How on earth did you know that?"

"I could tell by the way you give directions," said Nick.

The story was to delight Bill and Mary Louise Howe for years.

An example of the diversity of Shadrin's friendships can be seen in the contrast between the tiny, intellectual Bill Howe and Pete Sivess, a huge, loquacious former professional baseball pitcher. Assigned to the CIA's Domestic Contact Division, Sivess—who speaks fluent Russian—and his wife, Ellie, held the hands of dozens of terrified Soviet bloc defectors as they took their first steps into American society.

Surely, a great part of Sivess's appeal for Shadrin was his complete access to the marvelous hunting and fishing opportunities offered by Ashford Farm. Despite Shadrin's dislike of most CIA people, Sivess remained his friend, a sometimes counselor, but more often a hunting and fishing companion. Over the years they spent countless hours stomping through fields and swamps hunting duck and deer or fishing the waters of the Choptank River.

After Shadrin had become inextricably bound to his role as a double agent, Pete Sivess received a telephone call from one of his superiors at CIA headquarters. First confirming that Sivess and Shadrin remained on good terms, the caller asked Sivess to take Shadrin to a certain location and introduce him to a senior CIA officer. Sivess readily agreed and was given details of how the meeting was to take place.

On a weekday Sivess drove Shadrin to the Hains Point area of the Potomac River, near the Jefferson Memorial in Washington. Hains Point, a spacious, parklike area dotted with benches, was the site of an early CIA installation. There, at a parking area near the river, Sivess spotted the car he had been told to expect. He got out and went over to establish that the lone occupant was the officer Shadrin was to meet.

Then Shadrin walked over to meet the frail, emaciated man waiting in the car. It was John T. Funkhouser, a top maritime specialist who had spent most of his career with the Central Intelligence Agency. In fact, Funkhouser had worked at the Hains Point installation. Sivess left Funkhouser and Shadrin alone in Funkhouser's car to complete their business. About an hour later Sivess and Shadrin departed.

Thus began the long and close association between Nick

Shadrin and John Funkhouser, a man Shadrin would come to value as one of his closest professional friends. Formerly with the Maritime Commission and an expert on Soviet naval affairs for the CIA, Funkhouser seems to have found much of interest to discuss with Shadrin.*

Regarding her husband's work, Ewa Shadrin had only a vague notion of what was going on. However, she does recall that in the late sixties she became aware of receiving frequent telephone calls from Funkhouser, for she especially remembers his telephone manner. "He had such a beautiful voice, and he was always so polite," she says. She noticed that Funkhouser, after exchanging pleasantries with her, always used precisely the same words when asking to speak to her husband. "Is Nick around?" he would say. Something else also struck Ewa; Funkhouser always telephoned in the evening and for only the briefest of chats. He called so often in the evenings that Ewa assumed he probably never called Nick at work.

There was one other oddity that Ewa noticed about Nick's friendship with Funkhouser. They seemed to have lunch together several times a month, usually on Wednesdays. What was unusual was that Funkhouser preferred to have lunch in his car. He would pick up Nick at his DIA office at the Old Post Office Building, and they would buy sandwiches and drive around and talk as they ate them. Or they would go to a place such as Hains Point and sit in the parking area. This was peculiar behavior for a man like Shadrin who treasured the midday hours when he could drink and enjoy talking with friends.

It seems that Shadrin was always highly indulgent of Funkhouser, a man many years his senior. Ewa came to believe that Nick's admiration for Funkhouser led him to put up with such peculiarities. In addition, Funkhouser seems by all accounts to have been in very frail health, and Nick often mentioned to Ewa his concern over this. He took the position that he always wanted to do whatever suited the older man.

But there were rare occasions when Shadrin convinced Funkhouser to go with him to Danker's, the boisterous steak house downtown where Nick and his friends often spent their noons. They once met Shadrin's friend Robert Herrick there for lunch,

---

*Funkhouser has refused to discuss with the author his association with Nicholas Shadrin.

and Herrick's chief impression of Funkhouser was that he was "quite elderly" and appeared to be "very tired and tuckered out." But Herrick recalls that Shadrin and Funkhouser seemed to have a sharp mutual respect for each other.

John Funkhouser has told Ewa Shadrin and others that his association with Shadrin was purely friendly, that they had no professional association whatsoever. But no doubt their association was useful to Funkhouser in writing an article that appeared in the December 1973 *U.S. Naval Institute Proceedings* entitled "Soviet Carrier Strategy." The focus of the article was on Soviet doctrine and strategy, which indeed were two of Shadrin's chief areas of expertise.

On the other hand, it was common in other counterintelligence operations against the Soviets during this period for the double agent—in this instance, Shadrin—to have assigned to him a person with a particular expertise with whom he could prepare material that could be handed over to the Soviets. It is ticklish under any circumstances to formulate information that will appear to be significant, that will be totally convincing to the Soviets, and that at the same time will not vitally compromise United States interests.

Several former CIA officers have confirmed that John Funkhouser was never an official part of the clandestine side of the agency. However, the same officers agree that given the description of the meetings—and given Shadrin's role as a double agent—it seems likely that Funkhouser had been assigned to him as the conduit for the agency-approved soft information to be passed on to the Soviets.

It was several years after Funkhouser began telephoning the Shadrins' house that Ewa finally met him. She and Nick had gone to the Alamo Steak House in the Virginia suburbs for dinner. By chance they encountered Funkhouser and his wife. Ewa found Funkhouser as charming in person as he had been on the telephone, although she thought he appeared terribly old and frail. She could readily understand Nick's concern for his health and why Nick seemed so solicitous of the elderly man's wishes.

During the years when Shadrin's friendship with Funkhouser was blooming, he was also becoming very close with James P. Wooten, the FBI agent from the Soviet Counterintelligence Section who had been assigned as his case officer. Ewa Shadrin knew nothing of Wooten's profession, but she did know that Nick was extremely fond of him. He considered Wooten superb company, bright and congenial. But Wooten's wife was ill during those years, and the Wootens and Shadrins never became social friends.

In fact, for eight years Jim Wooten was just a voice over the telephone to Ewa Shadrin. Like Funkhouser, he only telephoned Shadrin at his home in the evenings, and then only for brief chats, apparently to arrange meetings. Ewa occasionally found herself wondering about Wooten and Funkhouser, whom she naturally linked in her mind because of their common telephone habits. They shared none of the interests Nick had with his other friends, such as hunting and fishing. And for reasons Ewa could not understand, they never got in touch with Nick at work and they never came to see him at home.

All this reflects the great tolerance for each other that prevailed between Nick and Ewa. He had an enormous respect for her endeavors, and she seems always to have been supportive of whatever he wanted to do. Although she did not fully understand Nick's friendship with Wooten and Funkhouser, it was no more unusual than many of his relationships. She had grown accustomed to his being utterly at ease with such diverse personalities as Bill Howe and Pete Sivess; that ability was the essence of Nick Shadrin.

Filled with resentment and humiliation, Shadrin reported for work at the Defense Intelligence Agency in the spring of 1966, just a few months before being locked into his life as a double agent. For nearly one year he had resisted accepting the DIA job, which consisted primarily of translating Russian articles into English. These duties were demeaning for an intelligent, highly trained naval officer who, just a few months earlier, had been keenly appreciated as an analyst and consultant.*

---

*It is possibly significant that James Wooten later told Ewa Shadrin in the presence of the Howes and the Kuppermans (see Chapter Two) that Shadrin resisted going to work as a double agent "for close to a year." There is no evidence that he resisted accepting the role as a double for that long, once his friend Rufus Taylor appealed to him on the grounds of patriotism. But Shadrin did resist accepting the DIA job for precisely "close to a year"—from April 1965 to March 1966. The possibility that it was necessary for Shadrin to be moved out of his truly sensitive job at the Office of Naval Intelligence and into the more mundane job at DIA, which was located downtown and, conveniently for covert contacts, in the same building with the FBI field office, cannot be overlooked. All this suggests the possibility that a decision to use Shadrin in some capacity was made considerably earlier than the dates indicated by most sources in describing Igor's request for Shadrin. Moreover,

Surely there was some satisfaction for Shadrin in the fact that his friend and mentor Admiral Rufus Taylor was the second-in-command at DIA. If Admiral Taylor did no more at DIA than to persuade Shadrin to play the starring role in the Igor operation, he would win the gratitude of the top intelligence officials in the United States. But Shadrin could not know how his acquiescence to Rufus Taylor's wishes would enrich the admiral's stature in the intelligence community.

Shadrin was no doubt disappointed when, in October of 1966, Admiral Taylor resigned from DIA to take the more prestigious post as deputy director of the Central Intelligence Agency, which he held until February 1969. This left Shadrin afloat in his special section at DIA, which he considered a catch-all for Soviet bloc defectors who he believed were incapable of doing anything else. A few American analysts were in supervisory positions. The exact cover name of Shadrin's unit was the Handbook Analysis Division of the Soviet Directorate of DIA.

Despite Shadrin's deep resentment over being assigned to the External Research Project, as the group was called, the work done in the group was respected and considered valuable. In fact, General Sam V. Wilson, Shadrin's old goose-hunting companion, is credited with having conceived and organized the group when it originally was started some years earlier, long before General Wilson became the director of DIA.

According to General Wilson, the office was originally called the Soviet Consultant Group. The concept called for exposing the ex-Soviets to a great variety of documents—none highly sensitive —that had been acquired from the Soviet Union. The belief was

---

it supports the possibility that Igor was in the United States and in touch with intelligence officials earlier than is suggested by his spring 1966 telephone call to Richard Helms.

This looser time frame also could explain the hour-long telephone call Shadrin received from Anatoli Golitsin in October 1965. It was the only telephone call Shadrin ever received from Golitsin after the latter left for England in 1963. If intelligence officers were considering how to persuade Shadrin to take the DIA job—and thus the role as a double agent—they could find few more powerful advocates for their position than Shadrin's friend Golitsin, that prince of defectors in whom counterintelligence officers had placed exceptional trust.

One of the great questions surrounding Shadrin's career developments is why he was removed from a job to which he was so perfectly suited and transferred to DIA. While there are plausible explanations, they are not wholly satisfactory. But moving him for operational purposes would tend to explain the anomaly.

that the defectors would be deft at interpreting and analyzing trends, developments, and schools of thought.

From a theoretical standpoint, General Wilson explains the External Research Project and how a man like Shadrin would fit into it: "You pick a well-educated military man and feed him intellectually with contemporary documents in a field he has previously worked. He can tell you more about what they mean and what is going on in most instances than can one of our analysts who has never actually been in that field. When you pair a man like that with a topflight professional analyst, you frequently can come up with understandings and insights into things with greater acuity than if you don't have that kind of advice coming from that highly singular point of view."

It may have worked that way in theory, but Shadrin was far too proud an individual to be lumped into an assembly-line process such as this. As he expected, he found the group filled with neurotic and paranoid defectors—a number of them in varying stages of alcoholism—as well as an abundance of the bureaucratic "plumbers" he had detested among CIA personnel. In addition, there were career bureaucrats, who, on some occasions, drove him into seething rages with their seemingly absurd procedural habits. Shadrin hated the time he spent at the External Research Project. But true to his nature, he made some friends there anyway.

It is a remarkable measure of Shadrin's character and ability that his loathing for the work did not seem to interfere with the quality of his performance. "He was probably the brightest and most capable person we had in the office," says Colonel Bernard Weltman, a career intelligence officer with service at CIA, DIA, and the Air Force. Weltman was in charge of the project for several years while Shadrin was there. "Nick also was an intellectually stimulating man to have around," Weltman adds. "He was the most brilliant man I've ever been associated with."

One of Shadrin's greatest contributions at the External Research Project was to the production of a special weekly summary that went to the White House. Drawn from nonsecret sources, the information was intended to reflect the Soviet press's interpretation of whatever was going on in the Soviet Union.

Lieutenant General Daniel Graham, director of DIA for the last fifteen months of Shadrin's employment, states: "I would always call on him with any questions on the Soviet Navy. Nick could tell us what things meant in cases where our own analysts could not. In the area of Soviet naval operations and doctrine, Shadrin was the best we had." Although General Graham was shocked, after Shadrin's disappearance, to learn that he had been used as a double agent, he says that the FBI told him it had been given permission years earlier by one of his predecessors, Lieutenant General Joseph Carroll, to run Shadrin as a double while he was working at DIA.*

General Graham has pointed out that although Shadrin never had a high security clearance, he still was given classified material whenever it was necessary for him to do his job properly. There was a precedent for this, of course, in that Admiral Rufus Taylor had taken Shadrin into similar confidence when he visited him at the Office of Naval Intelligence. And others who worked at ONI with Shadrin confirm that he was provided classified material on a need-to-know basis.

But Shadrin's consultations with men of General Graham's stature did not typify his work at DIA. More often he was dealing with people like Reginald Kicklighter, a respected career bureaucrat and supervisor with whom Shadrin seemed destined to lock horns. One person also assigned to the External Research Project who knew both Shadrin and Kicklighter—and observed their relationship over several years—described Kicklighter this way: "He's the sort of guy who wears suspenders, a belt, overshoes and always carries an umbrella. If anything is going to happen, he is sure it is going to happen to him."† That description is the antithesis of Shadrin's personality.

However, Shadrin seemed to have felt strongly that if he had to accept the indignity of working for DIA, he was going to reap the greatest possible benefits from it. Part of Kicklighter's responsibility was to get a civil service status for all the defector employees so they would be eligible for retirement benefits and other perquisites available to government employees.

To do this for defectors, it was necessary to create histories for them, showing an appropriate length of government service that would qualify them for proper benefits. Kicklighter was the liaison

---

*Contacted by the author, General Carroll declined to comment on these matters.
†Contacted by the author, Kicklighter refused to acknowledge that he had ever been associated with Shadrin.

160

with the CIA, which was supposed to create the bogus histories on each man. In Shadrin's case, the delays seemed interminable. Each month Kicklighter traveled to the CIA headquarters to check on these matters. He would return and tell Shadrin to be patient.

This irritated Shadrin mightily, and one day he and Kicklighter got into a furious argument. Shadrin took the position that the delays were inexcusable, that perhaps no one would ever take care of his case, that he could be left with nothing after his tour of duty at DIA. At the height of the argument, Shadrin bellowed that he was going to throw Kicklighter out the window.

In response to this, Kicklighter is said to have shouted back that if Nick were not careful about his behavior, he might find himself dropped into another country without any identification. This was a suggestion—surely an idle one—that would ring in Nick's ears for years to come.

On another occasion Shadrin lost his temper with another defector and began bellowing at him in imperious tones. According to one witness, "Nick was suddenly the imperial Russian again." The reason for the argument has been forgotten, but it raged on to the point where Nick picked up a metal bar from one of the open safe drawers nearby and threatened the other man. Several spectators stepped in, took away the bar, and told Shadrin to calm down. At that time Kicklighter muttered within the hearing of some, including Shadrin: "If these defectors get out of hand, all the agency usually does is put them somewhere without a passport."

While there is no reason to believe these words were uttered seriously, they were recalled vividly by men who were already paranoid. In any case, Kicklighter was not in a position to be taken seriously. There is not the slightest evidence that he was, by government standards, anything other than a loyal and efficient bureaucrat. Nevertheless, he was the man immediately in charge of Shadrin, perhaps an impossible position for anyone who failed to command Shadrin's respect.

Such incidents illustrate the deep frustrations Shadrin felt as he reported for work each day at the Old Post Office Building. Arguing with petty bureaucrats was a far cry from commanding a destroyer on the high seas or conferring with the top men in the U.S. military and intelligence establishment.

In spite of his intense professional frustrations, Shadrin did make some lasting friendships among his DIA colleagues. One was with William R. Whittington, a young army intelligence officer assigned to Nick's unit at DIA. A native Mississippian, Whittington was delighted to find that like himself, Nick was an avid hunter and fisherman. They spent hours together hunting and camping on the Eastern Shore.

At work, Whittington found Shadrin energetic and capable of far more than simply translating material. He realized that Shadrin was deft at interpreting the material, illuminating the innuendos in a way that was more valuable than mere translation. He also was impressed with Shadrin as an American citizen who retained a deep respect for his Russian heritage.

In 1974 Whittington was transferred to a unit in the Middle East, but Shadrin remained his source for securing hunting and fishing gear in the United States. He recalls once sending Nick a check for a certain fishing knife. Shadrin went to the sporting goods store to buy it, but, as he wrote to Whittington, the only knife left in the store was the one in the case, and the owner would not sell that one. Nick said that he would go back each day and try to badger the storekeeper into selling it but that Whittington would have to be patient. A few weeks later Whittington received the knife with a note that said, "Good fishing, Nick." The note was written on Whittington's check, which was wrapped around the knife.

Whittington still speaks longingly of his association with Shadrin: "He and I shot geese on the Eastern Shore and tromped through the mud and caught a few bluefish. I guess we did some very American things together."

Shadrin spent a lot of time during these years seeing his old friends from the Office of Naval Intelligence—most often at lunch at Danker's on E Street. To most of them, Shadrin's brilliance was undiminished by his gloomy job at DIA. One frequent lunch friend, Colonel Bernard Weltman, still marvels at Shadrin's perception: "The amazing thing about Nick was that he could read the newspapers today, analyze what had been said by key people, and then predict what those people would be saying the next day. It was astounding how often he would be right. We used to joke that he was writing Henry Kissinger's lines for him."

There were some professional bright spots for Shadrin. His expertise as a consultant and analyst had not been forgotten by such people as Rufus Taylor, who continued to telephone Shadrin long after he himself had moved on to the CIA. "I don't know how much they were seeing of each other during those days, but they certainly used to talk a lot on the telephone," says Colonel Weltman, the man in charge of Shadrin's DIA unit for several years.

Also at this time, Nick and Ewa were present at numerous social gatherings, including a party at the elegant Alexandria home of David Abshire, chairman of Georgetown University's Center for Strategic and International Studies. In addition, Shadrin must have felt considerable professional satisfaction over his growing relationship with Admiral Stansfield Turner. While it is not precisely clear how Shadrin felt about Turner personally, it is certain that the admiral held Shadrin in the highest regard.

Throughout the sixties and early seventies Shadrin addressed the Naval War College numerous times. His value to the students and faculty obviously had not diminished by the passage of time. In fact, in the spring of 1975 Admiral Julien LeBourgeois, president of the college, noted in a letter to Shadrin that he had "become somewhat of a permanent speaker at the Naval War College for which we are very appreciative."

Shadrin's value was recognized even earlier by Admiral Stansfield Turner, who served as president of the Naval War College from June 1972 to August 1974. Turner invited Shadrin to lecture on several occasions and at least once held a luncheon in his honor. Shadrin stayed at the Flag Cabin at the college, a facility reserved for distinguished guests and flag officers. When Admiral Turner was resigning from his post as president of the college to become commander of the Second Fleet, he wrote a friendly "Dear Nick" letter to Shadrin, thanking him for his lectures at the college. The admiral signed his letter "Stan." In expressing his regrets over leaving the War College, Turner's enthusiasm for academia reached a fevered pitch when he added:

"The relentless search for intellectual truth and the foment of ideas which surround one on a college campus provide an atmosphere of excitement and challenge which I personally find exhilarating."

The friendship between Admiral Turner and Shadrin was also noted by Robert H. Kupperman, today the executive director of Georgetown University's Center for Strategic and International Studies. It was Shadrin who first introduced Kupperman to

Stansfield Turner. Kupperman recalls that Shadrin and Turner obviously had warm feelings for each other, and he assumed they were friends. Another witness to the association between Shadrin and Admiral Turner is Colonel Weltman, who recalls perhaps a dozen occasions when a telephone call came to the DIA office from Admiral Turner for Shadrin.

Again and again, Shadrin's immense energy and capabilities burst through the drudgery of his job. In 1973 he contributed a paper to the Joint Economic Committee of the U.S. Congress that became part of a congressional report called "Soviet Economic Prospects for the Seventies." Few of Nick's friends knew about this paper, which Senator William Proxmire, vice-chairman of the committee, called "a valuable contribution."

Another example of the continued respect Shadrin enjoyed in high defense circles is his inclusion in a panel of experts on Soviet military strategy at Georgetown University's Center for Strategic and International Studies. On June 8, 1966, precisely when Igor was asking for U.S. assistance in recruiting him, Shadrin attended the first meeting of the panel. Others present included David Abshire, Cornelius D. Sullivan, and Brigadier General Robert Richardson. Also present were Raymond L. Garthoff, later President Carter's ambassador to Bulgaria, and Thomas W. Wolfe, who became a high Treasury Department official.

Shadrin also kept up his friendship with General Sam V. Wilson, who had lunch with Nick in 1973, upon his return from duty as an army attaché at the U.S. Embassy in Moscow. "Nick talked about some of the things he was writing, some of his theses, that sort of thing," says General Wilson. "I sensed Nick was looking for something more substantive to do, but I didn't have anything to offer him at the time." Indeed, Shadrin was growing increasingly desperate over his mundane duties at DIA. "The poor guy was bored to tears with his job," says Commander Robert Herrick.

During these years Nicholas Kozlov—the man General Wilson had been instrumental in bringing to the United States—was also working in the Old Post Office Building. But Kozlov had a far more interesting job than Shadrin, one that required a security clearance. It is not clear how much Shadrin knew about Kozlov's work, but it is certain that on occasion he mentioned Kozlov as an example of a former Soviet military officer who had been given a greater degree of trust than he had. Shadrin could not understand why Kozlov could be given such trust when it was denied him.

Shadrin's greatest goal through these years was to attain a security clearance that would allow him to rise to his natural level as an analyst and consultant. Although many people tried to help him reach this goal, the clearance remained elusive. It is important, however, to note that the absence of such clearance did not signify any particular suspicion of Shadrin; it was only the standard prudence that usually denies giving such trust to a man with Shadrin's Soviet background. Alas, if he were going to make a significant contribution to the United States, it seemed it would have to be as the principal actor in the ever-murky operation spawned by the elusive Igor.

Through all these years of high-level friendships and associations, Shadrin met regularly with Soviet intelligence officers who presumably believed him to be their agent. A careful examination of the contents of Shadrin's desk in 1980 revealed tiny scraps of paper with minutely detailed diagrams—written in a casual mix of Russian and English—indicating drop and signal sites in the Virginia suburbs of Washington. The papers were tightly folded and placed at the bottom of a card file box. Some of the sites were near bus stops; others were in shopping centers; still others were at utility poles in purely residential areas.

One of Shadrin's long-term KGB handlers was Oleg Alekseyevich Kozlov, who in the spring of 1968 was assigned to the Soviet Embassy as an attaché. Soon Kozlov was promoted to vice-consul, and by late summer of 1970 he had been promoted to third secretary as well as vice-consul. Kozlov first lived in Arlington, not far from the Shadrin home.*

---

*Oleg Kozlov is known to have gone to extraordinary lengths to entice former Soviets to return home. One American citizen, a former Soviet, describes a nearly incredible story of an incident that took place while he was raking leaves in his backyard one November afternoon in 1972. An impeccably dressed man, attired in formal business dress, strode out of a wooded area and across the lawn. He introduced himself as the third secretary of the Soviet Embassy, presented his credentials, and proceeded to give a most engaging account of how badly one of the American's old acquaintances in Russia longed for some contact with him. Kozlov even brought mail from the former acquaintance. The shocked former Soviet, long settled usefully into American life, gave Kozlov a drink of water and sent him away. He even refused to open the mail, turning it over to the proper authorities. Kozlov had stated that it mattered little to him whether the former Soviet reported him since he was due to leave the United States very soon anyway.

An extremely open, engaging man, Oleg Kozlov has been described by those who knew him then as in his early thirties, blond, of medium build, and about five feet nine inches tall. He has also been described as exceptionally well informed, someone with whom Nick Shadrin probably enjoyed dealing. Not much is known of their association, but one of Kozlov's last official acts before leaving the United States in the late fall of 1972 was to deliver sophisticated espionage equipment to his agent Shadrin, equipment that the KGB had trained Shadrin to use during his meeting with them in Vienna some months earlier.

Dr. Blanka Ewa Shadrin's professional success brought her new friends and associates, professional satisfaction, and considerable happiness. Indeed, only one negative cloud loomed in Ewa's life: the immense dissatisfaction her husband felt with his career. In 1967, the year after Nick went to work at DIA and began his role as a double agent, the Shadrins bought a new house in the Washington suburb of McLean, Virginia. Ewa was anxious to open a private dental practice, and Nick promised her that by the start of 1968 he would build her an office in their basement. Once again exhibiting surprising skills, Shadrin constructed the convenient dentist's office that still fills the basement. And keeping his promise, he completed it virtually on New Year's Eve. With his customary flourish, Nick presented the office to Ewa on the first day of 1968.

Many of the people Nick knew professionally came to Dr. Shadrin for their dental work and soon began to send their whole families. Tom Koines, the Herricks, Nick Kozlov, and the Howes are but a few examples of early patients who remain to this day. Word spread about Dr. Shadrin's competent, efficient practice, and soon Ewa had a strong and faithful clientele. To this day the facilities Nick constructed are holding up superbly under Dr. Shadrin's burgeoning practice.

Having the dentist office in the basement of the house proved especially useful on one occasion. Ewa was serving a roast goose that Nick had shot, and William and Mary Louise Howe were the guests. William bit down on a piece of meat only to hit a piece of lead shot and break off one of his teeth. Ewa escorted him to the basement, where she remedied the condition so that dinner could continue.

Although Ewa did not enjoy hunting and fishing, it is clear that she took pride in Nick's prowess as a sportsman. She enjoyed preparing the venison and ducks and fish that he regularly brought home. She was especially pleased when he was able to present game and fish to their friends. And it is abundantly clear that Nick was extremely proud of Ewa's quick mind, her successful career, her constant hunger for learning, and her skills at cooking.

A number of their friends have remarked with a touch of sadness that it is too bad the Shadrins had no children because Nick was so fond of them and enjoyed dealing with them. But Ewa has stated that she has little interest in children, and on several occasions she has told others that she did not want to have children.

Through the years the fancy dinner parties at the Howes' home continued, as did other social functions around Washington. Nick and Ewa enjoyed cultural events at the Kennedy Center. Special treats were the occasions when they were able to travel to Hawaii and California to see old friends like the Dwyers and the Leggats.

One of the most important features of being an American citizen—especially for Nick—was the right to vote. He was meticulous about never missing an opportunity to vote for any-thing—whether it was for President or for local coroner. Robert Kupperman, who saw much of the Shadrins during this period, recalls the intensity of their excitement over voting. He also was impressed with Shadrin's extraordinary range of abilities, and it made him gloomy to realize his friend could never have a security clearance. "He could have done so much for his country. It was clear to anyone who knew him that he was being underused," says Kupperman. Like so many others, Kupperman did what he could to help Nick find some other work.

The more successful Ewa's practice became, the more reluctant Nick was to consider moving from the Washington area. Many of his friends tried to convince him that his professional life would improve sharply if he could just get away from Washington, away from government-related work. At one point it appeared that he might be offered a full-time position at the Naval War College in Rhode Island, where his lectures clearly were received with resounding enthusiasm. But Shadrin discouraged the offer. It would mean moving from Washington and disrupting Ewa's practice.

One recurring pipe dream that surfaced whenever the Shadrins visited Tom Dwyer was for Nick to operate a fishing vessel off the Hawaiian shores. Dwyer would navigate and his wife would sell tickets. Ewa would render dental assistance to distressed fishermen. But in the end they all knew Nick would not leave Washington—for this or a more serious pursuit—now that Ewa's practice was established and thriving. It would just be too difficult and disruptive.

Increasingly Nick turned to the pleasures of hunting and fishing. Nearly every weekend he spent at least one day—often staying overnight—in these pursuits, while Ewa spent time with her own friends. But spending time apart did not seem to strain what appears to have been a strong marriage. While there were spats over minor things such as Nick's smoking, no friends of the Shadrins can recall any broad disagreements over important matters. No friend reports ever hearing Nick express a negative opinion about Ewa. He was devoted to her.

The fierceness of Shadrin's independence was legendary, and it comes as a surprise to hear from so many friends how Ewa governed his spending habits. Often at lunch, Nick would peer into his wallet, his eyebrows arched with anticipation, to see how much money he had. He claimed he never knew until he looked. Many times his friends heard him say, "If Ewa needs, she takes. When she doesn't need, she puts." But as a backup, Nick always had a $50 bill tucked in a compartment of the wallet in case Ewa had not put in enough.

Shadrin's spirits brightened considerably in 1972, when he bought a boat. With this he had complete freedom on weekends to roam the Chesapeake Bay, fishing when and where he pleased. He kept the boat at a marina in Deal, Maryland, but the fees charged by the marina were a constant source of irritation to him. On Sunday afternoons he would return from an overnight fishing trip with an ice chest filled with fish for his and Ewa's friends. Increasingly irked by how much it cost him to dock his boat, Shadrin began to look around for property where he could keep the boat without having to pay the charges. In 1973 he and Ewa purchased a cottage at Solomons Island, Maryland, where Nick could put the boat in the water directly across the street.

From the start, he rarely spent the night at the cottage, preferring to stay on the boat and to rent out the cottage for income. The rental was handled almost entirely by an agency, so the Shadrins normally were not acquainted with the people who lived in the cottage. More frequently now, Nick was gone overnight. He almost always found a friend or two to go with him, but sometimes he went alone.

After the CIA closed Ashford Farm as a safe house, Shadrin and Pete Sivess found they could still hunt its perimeters. Nick had a good friend living on the edge of the property who would let him stay there whenever he wanted. It was a superb location for hunting deer.

One constant source of pleasure for Nick was Julik, the German shepherd dog given to him years earlier by Anatoli Golitsin. Julik remained as faithful and dependable as any person Nick knew. Shadrin's affection for Julik was extraordinary, and he spent many hours walking him, the nine-millimeter Walther nestled against his body. It distressed Shadrin to see Julik grow older, to become slower and less alert. He often reminded Ewa to carry the little pistol he had given her so that she could defend Julik if he were attacked by a more powerful animal.

Julik's presence also was a constant reminder to Shadrin of his friendship with Anatoli Golitsin, whom he had not seen since 1963. Shadrin often spoke fondly of Golitsin and asked various people if they knew where he was. But no one was able to help him find his old friend or even confirm his general whereabouts. He had gone into deep hiding.

Shadrin took great pride in being awarded his Ph.D. in international affairs from George Washington University. His doctoral dissertation was a massive work on the "History of Soviet Naval Power," which he dictated in English. Tom Koines, who helped him get the thesis into final typed form, states that he had to do very little more than insert missing articles, a common bugaboo in making the shift from Russian to English. Professor Vladimir Petrov, his doctoral adviser at George Washington University, considered Shadrin an exceptionally good scholar—a man who learned quickly where to go for information and how to discard useless information rapidly. Petrov believes Shadrin's thesis was an important contribution to understanding the Soviet Navy.

Despite his hatred of his work and his discomfort among the other defectors, Shadrin's performance at DIA was considered superior by those directly above him as well as by men like DIA Director Daniel Graham. Still, there was no security clearance. On

169

some occasions, according to General Graham, Shadrin was provided with classified material necessary to assist in his analyses. But this was not enough. Without the clearance, Shadrin proved himself to be a stunningly good analyst. With a clearance, his professional associates agree, he would have been among the top analysts in the United States government.

During their first ten years in the United States the Shadrins restricted their travel primarily to within their new country. These were the years of Ewa's grueling studies, and there was not much money for travel. Also, there was the safety factor. In certain parts of the world the Soviets could kidnap them with little difficulty. And they had provocation in Shadrin's pointed denunciation of Khrushchev before Congress and even more in the likelihood that he had revealed the most crucial secrets of the Soviet Navy to the Americans. Moreover, the death sentence from the Soviet Union forever hung over Nick's head.

On three occasions, however, the Shadrins did leave the United States, but only for brief vacations in benign holiday spots. They went to Jamaica for a week, spent a week in Barbados, and took a short cruise to Caribbean islands with their friends Pete and Ellie Sivess. Ewa states that she was with Nick at every juncture during these trips and that there were no opportunities for Nick to engage in any secret meetings. These were the only times they ventured out of the United States during their first ten years.

In 1969, three years after Shadrin began his role in the Igor operation, he seemed to feel free to undertake some European travel. Perhaps he was so confident that he had duped the Soviets into believing that he had redefected that he had no fear of reprisals. Whatever Shadrin's reasoning, Ewa was jubilant when he said he was ready to return to Europe. They spent weeks deciding the best way to travel.

Finally, they settled on a seventeen-day tour of seven countries. After flying to England, where they stayed for two days, they went on to Amsterdam. There the Shadrins boarded a tour bus that took them through Holland, Germany, Austria, and France. The tour did not go to Vienna. Nick was so uncomfortable on the bus —there was no place for his long legs to fit—that they agreed it was the last time they would undertake a tour of this nature.

During their brief stop in Rotterdam Ewa saw a side of her

husband she had never witnessed before. The date was September 1, and Ewa wanted to take advantage of being in Europe to telephone her mother in Poland. Around 9:00 P.M. Ewa began trying to call her mother from pay stations as she and Nick walked about Rotterdam. There was no answer at her mother's number. As she and Nick strolled about and the hour grew later and their wandering took them to increasingly remote spots, Ewa noticed that Nick was growing tense, ill at ease. They stopped intermittently for Ewa to try to place her call, and she was finally able to get through. But while they were walking about, Nick said that they should be careful, that something could happen to them out there at night and no one would ever know it. This, says Ewa, is perhaps the only time she knew Nick to express any fear whatsoever.

The double operation had been running since the summer of 1966. Shadrin's meetings with the FBI's James Wooten and the CIA's John Funkhouser were frequent and regular. Subsequent statements by Wooten support the assumption that Shadrin also was meeting with his Soviet handler in the Washington area. In addition, he made deliveries of purportedly classified information, carefully prepared by the CIA, to dead drops near his home.

A shrewd and observant woman, Ewa Shadrin might have been expected to catch on to what her husband was up to. But she insists rather convincingly that she actually believed Wooten and Funkhouser to be Nick's personal friends, that she thought nothing was peculiar about the frequent telephone calls, that she easily accepted Nick's carrying a nine-millimeter Walther with him when he walked his dog. She even found nothing peculiar about his insisting that she carry the little .38 pistol with her when she walked Julik. Of course, there were the frequent weekends when Nick was hunting and fishing that Ewa cannot possibly account for.

Ewa Shadrin is also convincing when she insists that during their limited foreign travel prior to 1970 Nick never had an opportunity to meet with Soviet agents. She argues that he was never away from her long enough for a meeting. Indeed, this is supported by former highly placed CIA officers, who have stated that they never would have approved the operation if it involved sending a man with Shadrin's background to meetings with Soviet agents outside the United States. There is no evidence that this was done during the early years of the operation.

Reports from other double agents of that period—professionals who were working with the FBI in duping Soviet spies masquerading as diplomats—as well as opinions from former counterintelligence specialists confirm that it is not uncommon for the Soviets, after a period of prolonged contact, to suggest that the subject meet with them outside the United States. Such a meeting confirms in the Soviets' minds the validity of their agent. It is reassuring to know that he is not afraid to meet with them on turf that would be dangerous for a double agent. To convince the double, the Soviets may take the position that higher-ranking KGB officials could not risk entering the United States for the purpose of a clandestine meeting with a Soviet agent engaged in plundering secrets from the United States.

It is unclear whether Shadrin's first meeting with the KGB outside the United States was proposed by the Soviets or set in motion by American initiative. And it is not known to what degree Shadrin resisted taking such an extraordinary risk or how much warning the FBI gave him about the grave risks he faced in leaving the country for such a meeting.*

In any event, Shadrin traveled to Montreal in September 1971 for a meeting with the KGB. The contact took place only a few weeks after the CIA had quietly provided alleged evidence to the Royal Canadian Mounted Police (RCMP) that its longtime chief of counterintelligence Leslie James Bennett was possibly a Soviet penetration agent. Without Bennett's knowledge, but with the assistance of the CIA, a secret investigation was launched by security officers of the RCMP. In building the case against Bennett, the RCMP and the CIA contrived a scheme aimed at entrapping him in a web of his own making. At least twice during the fall of 1971 the Mounties set a snare that aimed at providing strong circumstantial evidence that Bennett was tipping off the Soviets about CIA/RCMP operations.

It appears that in one of these cases Shadrin was volunteered by the CIA as bait for the trap. His meeting was scheduled in Montreal with his KGB contact. Surveillance was planned by the

---

*John Huminik, a Washington businessman who worked as a double agent against the Soviets a few years prior to Shadrin's operation, has told the author that his FBI handlers were exuberant when he reported to them that his Soviet handlers wanted him to leave the country for a meeting. Huminik states there was never any concern by the FBI agents over possible danger to him. However, Huminik was not a Soviet defector, although his family was from Russia and some members remained there.

RCMP security officers who were secretly investigating Bennett. At this point Bennett had not been informed of anything concerning the Shadrin/KGB contact. Then, at literally the last minute, a private telephone call was made to Bennett by someone at the CIA. He was informed that the agency was sending a double agent for a meeting at a certain place in Montreal but that the CIA neither planned nor required any surveillance. The CIA caller was simply paying Bennett the courtesy of letting him know the meeting was going to take place on his turf.

The trap now set, the officers investigating Bennett sat back to observe the Shadrin meeting. Ordinarily the KGB would place such a meeting under heavy surveillance, and extensive precautions would be taken by the Soviet agent to make sure he was not followed or observed meeting with Shadrin. But nothing of the sort happened. The KGB man waltzed to the meeting without taking any evasive measures or ordinary precautions. Right or wrong, this was considered circumstantial evidence that Bennett had tipped off the Soviets that there would be no surveillance of the meeting while, in fact, there was.

Less than a year later Bennett took early medical retirement, and there was a parliamentary investigation of his activities. However, no formal charges were ever made, and at one point Canada's Solicitor General stated: ". . . there is no evidence whatsoever that Mr. Bennett was anything other than a loyal Canadian citizen."*

The crucial point in terms of Shadrin is the astounding risk the CIA took in providing information to a suspect Soviet agent that would undeniably peg Shadrin as a man actually working for American interests. If Bennett had been working in concert with the Soviets, Shadrin's duplicity would have been exposed to the KGB from that moment forward.

Bennett agrees, telling the author: "If I was under suspicion as a possible KGB agent, it would be the height of irresponsibility to have brought me into the picture at all." He added that even

*Ten years after these events Bennett commented to the author on their plausibility as well as the possibility of his involvement: "I am not denying knowledge of this particular operation, but for the life of me I just cannot recall any worthwhile details. But I can assert without fear of contradiction that even if I knew about the Shadrin-KGB meeting in Montreal, irrespective of how sheltered Shadrin's identity had been, I never revealed it to the KGB for the simple reason that I had never worked for them or for any other intelligence service whose aspirations were inimical to our Western democratic interests."

though Shadrin's name probably would not have been provided for security reasons, identification by the KGB would have been simple if it knew the date, time, and place of the meeting.

But of course, Ewa Shadrin was aware of none of this. What she knew was that during the late summer of 1971 Nick was working very hard when she proposed to him that she and a girl friend take a trip to Bermuda together. To Ewa's surprise, Nick was strongly opposed to this, arguing that she and her friend should not travel together to Bermuda. He countered with the suggestion that they, Nick and Ewa, take a vacation in Canada, a country they had not visited. Ewa, of course, was delighted, although surprised at the abruptness of his plans. Nick explained that not only would it be a refreshing interlude, but he had a business associate in Canada it would be useful for him to see.

Before flying to Montreal, Shadrin got in touch with Pete Sivess to see if Pete could find out whether Anatoli Golitsin was in Canada. Golitsin had last telephoned Shadrin from Canada, and Nick wanted to try to see his old friend. Sivess reported that he did not know what had become of Golitsin and had no way of finding out. Golitsin was as deeply hidden as any Soviet defector in U.S. history.

It was late August or early September when the Shadrins arrived in Montreal and checked into the Hotel Bonaventure. Nick wanted to take care of his business appointment right away so they would have the rest of the time for their vacation. After checking in, he told Ewa he was going to meet with his business associate, a Russian who had been working for the United States for many years. It suited Ewa, who had little knowledge of Montreal, to wait for Nick in the hotel room. Before leaving, he gave her a telephone number to call if he did not return from his meeting at the promised hour.

Nick left, and Ewa settled down to watch *For Whom the Bell Tolls* on television. Three hours later Nick returned, clearly in high spirits. He said that his meeting had been a success and that now he and Ewa could enjoy their vacation together. From Montreal the Shadrins traveled north and spent several days at Mont Tremblant; from there they went on to Quebec. Ewa remembers the trip as being thoroughly exhilarating.

Upon their return to the United States she and Nick began planning a vacation for the following September—this time to

Europe, for an unstructured visit to Spain, Germany, Austria, and Greece. No more tour buses for Nick and Ewa. Nick also mentioned that he would have to meet with the man he had seen in Montreal, but that would be only a small part of their trip.

In August 1972, a day or so before the Shadrins were scheduled to leave for Madrid, a man whose face Ewa had nearly forgotten appeared at their front door. It was none other than John T. Funkhouser, whose pleasant voice Ewa had heard on the telephone so many times. She had met Funkhouser only once, at the steak house, and was pleased to see him again.

Ewa greeted him warmly and asked him to come in and sit down. Funkhouser, who was just as gracious in person as on the telephone, explained that he really could not stay long. He told her that he knew she and Nick were going on a European vacation and wanted to see her personally and wish them both a happy vacation. Funkhouser then spoke privately with Nick for a few minutes and quickly departed. Ewa accepted the visit as just what Funkhouser said it was—a friendly farewell to them. After all, Nick spoke highly of Funkhouser, saw him frequently at lunch, and considered him a close friend and associate.

The Shadrins' first stop was Madrid, where they spent two days. From there they flew to Munich, where the Olympics were in progress. While there they rented a car and drove to a resort in Bavaria, which Nick did not like. Soon they returned to Munich. As it happened, Pete and Ellie Sivess were in Munich to visit their son. There was only time to get together at the airport in Munich before the Shadrins flew to Vienna, so they met there for a quick lunch. Ewa recalls that they all were in an exuberant humor.

The Shadrins arrived in Vienna in midafternoon and checked into the Hotel Bristol. Nick told Ewa that he would have to leave the next morning to meet his friend, the Russian who had been working for the United States government for twenty-five years. Just as he had done for the Montreal meeting, Nick gave Ewa a piece of paper with telephone numbers on it to call if he did not return on time. She paid little attention to the paper, simply stashing it in a place where she could find it if she needed it. What was different for the Vienna meeting was that Nick was going to be away overnight, that she was not to expect him back at the hotel until the next evening, around eight o'clock.

Ewa insists that she was so accustomed to accepting anything

Nick told her that she found nothing strange about this. Nor was she puzzled when he did not take even a shaving kit with him. He took absolutely nothing. He left behind his reading glasses, his hypertension medication, and his passport.

Ewa Shadrin had no trouble filling the time that Nick was gone. She went shopping, took tours of the city, and visited museums. In fact, she was about to leave the next afternoon for another tour when Nick appeared—four hours earlier than she had expected. He looked completely relaxed, refreshed, and clean-shaven. He seemed to be in excellent spirits and told her his meeting had gone very well. He said nothing more than that.

The next day the Shadrins flew to Athens, where they spent five luxurious days swimming, water skiing, and admiring the glorious sights of Greece. They stayed at a marina near Athens, and Nick especially enjoyed looking at the great variety of boats he had not seen before. But most of the time they spent lounging on the beaches.

On September 6, 1972, Nick and Ewa were sunning themselves on a beach near Athens. Everyone was talking about the seizure in Munich of the Israeli Olympic quarters. As Nick and Ewa lay there, they heard the latest dreadful news coming over a nearby radio. Nick rushed to the man lying beside the radio and asked if he could listen. The radio reports described the airport shoot-out in which nine members of the Israeli team were killed.

The man with the radio turned out to be Walter T. Haas, a Czechoslovakian who had become a businessman in Montreal. Haas and Shadrin developed an instant rapport as they discussed the horror of the events in Munich. A day or so later Shadrin approached Haas in the hotel lobby and resumed their conversation. Haas and his wife found Shadrin to be a highly engaging, pleasant man to talk to. And they both liked Ewa. Haas says that Nick proposed that they all spend an evening together at a Greek club on the outskirts of Athens, and they did.

Ewa Shadrin was quite taken with Mrs. Haas and so admired the perfume the elegant Canadian woman was using that to this day she uses the same scent. During their conversation at the club that evening it developed that they all enjoyed skiing. The Shadrins told Mr. and Mrs. Haas that they were planning to take a regular skiing holiday each winter.

The Haases told Nick and Ewa about their favorite hotel at St.

Moritz, the Schweizerhof, and highly recommended that they stay there if they decided to ski at St. Moritz. The Shadrins expressed enthusiasm over the idea. The two couples parted on a high note, stating that they hoped to see each other again, perhaps at St. Moritz.

The following year the Shadrins bought their cottage at Solomons Island, an expense that crimped their travel style. They did not leave the country that year. Nick spent an enormous amount of time working on the cottage and getting his boat fixed up to his satisfaction. Even Ewa was lured to the Chesapeake that year and spent some time there swimming with her friends. But it was clear she was not going to make a habit of going there to spend the night, so their obvious course was to rent out the cottage for income—a course that has been followed to this day.

All during 1973 the telephone calls from Wooten and Funkhouser continued as a routine part of the Shadrins' lives. "Is Nick around?" each man would ask politely, after a few amiable words to Ewa, who almost always answered the telephone. She would hand the telephone to Nick and then heard him discussing a meeting or a lunch date. The calls came at least once each week, often more frequently. This went on for years.

As always, Ewa accepted these events as normal. If they suited Nick, they were unquestioned by Ewa. The only oddity she noted was Funkhouser's insistence on eating lunch in the car. This was the antithesis of the long, comfortable lunches that Nick enjoyed with his other friends. But Ewa knew that Nick looked forward to every meeting—even if the circumstances were not quite to his liking.

In February 1974, almost on a whim as far as Ewa was concerned, they decided to travel to St. Moritz for a skiing vacation. Nick had a little vacation time from the office, and this seemed a good way to use it. It also would be a chance to try the Hotel Schweizerhof. Without much more planning than making hotel reservations, they flew to Switzerland.

From the beginning the trip was a disaster. Among other things, Shadrin did not feel good physically. But the chief object of his anger was the Hotel Schweizerhof which struck him as too rigid and stuffy for his enjoyment. In addition, Nick announced there were "too many Germans" there for his tastes.

Despite this, they stayed and signed up for skiing lessons—in different classes, because Nick was far more advanced than Ewa. They met each day for lunch, after their morning classes. But the tone of the stay had been set. Even on the first day, Ewa recalls, Nick was so annoyed by the atmosphere of the hotel that he went to the receptionist in the lobby and inquired about car rental rates. He also picked up maps of the area. Ewa did not know why he did this, and he was in no mood to be questioned.

On the first evening in the dining room the maître d' seated the Shadrins in a location that did not suit Nick. The maître d', a German, promised Nick the seating would be better the next evening. The next evening they were seated at the same table, and Nick flew into a rage the likes of which Ewa had never seen. He made such a scene that the waiter ostentatiously gave them the best table in the house, leaving Ewa utterly embarrassed over Nick's behavior.

Later, in their room, Ewa tried to talk to Nick about the terrible scene he had caused in the dining room. She knew better than anyone that he was capable of becoming imperious with people he either disliked or for whom he had no respect, but she had never seen anything like that evening's performance. Nick flew into another rage about the behavior of the hotel personnel, blaming much of it on the fact that so many of them were Germans.

For a couple of hours Nick ranted on, telling Ewa that only Julik was his friend. He decided that he was leaving, to go home to Julik. He said that at least Julik would be glad to see him. He began packing his suitcase, telling Ewa she could remain at St. Moritz. Ewa has no doubt that he was truly serious in his threat to return home the next morning.

The only reason Ewa could give for Nick's strange behavior was that he had not been feeling good. He had been to several doctors who were not able to diagnose why his stomach was giving him trouble. Just a week earlier he had been in the hospital for tests. She knew this was worrying him. In any case, she was able to get him calmed down that night and convince him not to go home the next day. Still, she had never seen him so furious.

The next day Nick disappeared. He was gone all day.

Ewa was skiing from 9:00 A.M. until 3:00 P.M., and Nick was not on the slopes. He failed to meet her for lunch. Ewa believes he rented a car and took off—perhaps to Austria. Because of the rage he had been in the night before, she decided not to ask him where he had been or what he had done. And Nick never told her. However, that night he seemed much more relaxed, and they enjoyed the rest of their trip.

A day or so after Nick disappeared, they encountered Walter Haas of Montreal, who was at the Schweizerhof with his family for a skiing vacation. Ewa recalls their pleasure at seeing the Haases and their regret that there was so little time to visit.

However, Walter Haas's impression of that trip is a bit different. He recalls that he was at the Schweizerhof with his family and some friends; it was an annual family skiing vacation. The Haases returned from the slopes one day, and there were the Shadrins. "I must say we were surprised to run into them. We came back from skiing one day, and there they were at the hotel. We had our family with us and some friends, and I didn't see how I could fit them into being with us."

But Haas had no trouble recognizing the Shadrins, and he did find time to spend an hour or so with them over a drink. He doesn't remember the conversation, describing it as essentially "meaningless." He expected to see them around the hotel the next day and hoped to have another chance to chat with them.

"But the next day, when we came in from skiing, I asked the hotel manager about them. He said they had checked out rather suddenly, had said good-bye to no one. He seemed puzzled about it. So was I."[*]

The telephone rang frequently in the Shadrin home. There were, of course, the regular phone calls from Wooten and Funkhouser as well as calls in which Nick set up his hunting and fishing dates with friends. Also, there were calls from dental patients. And Ewa's friends, who tried not to telephone her during her office hours, called in the evening. In addition, Nick had become helpful to émigrés and former Soviet citizens who were trying to adjust to life in the United States. This, at least, is Ewa's impression from the heavily accented voices—always Russian accents—of people who called in the evenings to speak to Nick.

Late one summer evening in 1974 Ewa routinely answered the telephone and said, "Hello." She could sense someone on the line for a few seconds, and then she heard a click. The first time it

---

[*]Ewa does not recall checking out early.

happened she paid little attention to it. Then it happened again. And again, four or five times within thirty minutes.

"Finally, I told Nick to pick up the phone," says Ewa. "The person would not even speak to me long enough to ask for Nick." It obviously was not a familiar caller, for those people did not hesitate to ask Ewa for Nick.

When the telephone rang a few minutes later, Nick picked it up. "We were both in the kitchen when he answered," recalls Ewa. "His face suddenly was very strange as he listened to what the caller was saying. Nick didn't really say anything. He just responded in monosyllables. It wasn't possible for me to have any idea what he was talking about."

When Nick finally hung up, Ewa says, he had an odd look on his face, an expression she had never seen before. "I couldn't imagine what the trouble was," says Ewa. He told her that the caller was a Russian émigré who wanted to meet him right away on Lorcom Lane in Arlington, not too far from the Shadrin home.

By then it had turned dark, and Ewa implored him not to go. She is not sure why she felt so strongly about it, but it was clear to her that the call and the request were most unusual. Nick said nothing. He stood there, his hand resting on the phone, with a strange look on his face—one chiefly of confusion, but perhaps some fear. Then Nick said the call was extremely important, that he must go. He said the person had been in the country only a short time and needed his help. Even so, Ewa begged him not to go.

Visibly upset, Nick began trying to call Jim Wooten and John Funkhouser. Neither man was home. Funkhouser had a summer place in the mountains, down in Virginia, and Nick tried to get a telephone number for that, but without success. He tried Wooten's number near the Chesapeake Bay and still had no luck.

Becoming almost frantic, Nick tried to call a third person Ewa was not familiar with—someone around Solomons Island. This time he was successful.* Upset, Ewa left the room and did not hear the conversation. But when Nick finished his phone call and emerged from the kitchen, he had resolved that he would not go to

---

*A search of Shadrin's desk in 1980 revealed a tiny scrap of paper with the name and telephone number written in Nick's hand for "Byrd Turner." That telephone number was for the home of Elbert T. "Bert" Turner, who in those years was the head of the FBI's Soviet Counterintelligence Section. The telephone number is in Solomons, Maryland.

Lorcom Lane. Nevertheless, he seemed quite disturbed. Ewa decided to ask him nothing, to wait and let him tell her whatever he chose to tell her about the incident, whenever he felt like talking.

Two days later Nick still had said nothing. Ewa asked him about the strange occurrence two evenings earlier. He brushed it aside, explaining that it was nothing, just an émigré who was upset. He said it all had been taken care of. "I could tell it was something he didn't want to talk about, so I didn't ask anything else," says Ewa. That, it seems, is how she always handled matters she sensed Nick preferred not to talk about.

For many years Nick had had trouble with his stomach as well as with high blood pressure. His hypertension was controlled by medication, and he never seemed to take it seriously. Concerning his blood pressure, Shadrin once told Tom Dwyer, "If I don't take it, I don't worry about it." But Shadrin was terribly concerned about his stomach, which seemed to plague him constantly.

Finally, after exhaustive examination, doctors determined that appendicitis or the resulting appendectomy—done many years earlier in the Soviet Union—had developed into a condition in which his ureter was being squeezed. Surgery was the only answer, and in September 1974 he entered Commonwealth Doctors Hospital in Fairfax, Virginia, where Dr. Giovanni DiSandro corrected the problem. The operation was a gratifying success.*

During the two weeks Nick remained in the hospital, Ewa had a chance to see some of his best friends—people she normally did not see. Also, it was an occasion for some of Shadrin's more diverse acquaintances to meet each other—people like William Howe and Jim Wooten.

One person Ewa had never met was Jim Wooten, with whom she had spoken hundreds of times over the many years he had been calling for Nick. Around noon one day Ewa went to the hospital to see Nick, and much to her pleasant surprise Wooten was there in Nick's room. She found him to be as gracious in person as he had always seemed on the telephone.

Nick indicated that he and Wooten had business to discuss.

---

*As often was the case, Nick gained another new friend as a result of his association with Dr. DiSandro. The two discovered their mutual interest in hunting and fishing, and today Dr. DiSandro fondly recalls his experiences with Shadrin. Not only did they go hunting together, but Nick took him up to Solomons Island, where they fished the Chesapeake in Nick's boat, *Ewa.*

Ewa cheerfully accepted the hint, left the hospital, and had lunch at a restaurant nearby. When she returned an hour later, Wooten had departed. John Funkhouser also visited Nick in the hospital, and Ewa was disappointed that she did not get to see him again.

The Shadrins remained very close to their first friend, Captain Thomas Dwyer. After thirty-two years, Dwyer retired from the navy, his last assignment being one of the most prestigious in the service: executive assistant to the commander in chief of the Pacific Fleet, Admiral John McCain. Captain Dwyer was also the intelligence officer who oversaw the *Pueblo* incident in 1968. In the fall of 1974 Dwyer informed the Shadrins of his impending second marriage, this time to a charming southern woman in New Orleans. The Shadrins had been fond of Dwyer's fiancée, "T.C." Larue, from the first time they met her two years earlier. Shadrin considered it an enormous honor when Dwyer asked him to be the best man at his wedding. Dwyer insists, though, that the honor was really his—that Nick Shadrin was simply "the best friend I ever had." The wedding took place in New Orleans in November 1974.

Nick and Ewa were enchanted with New Orleans—the food, the wedding festivities, the mix of people. They spent two days seeing the city's sights and enjoying her fine restaurants. For many years Shadrin had been trying to give Tom Dwyer his naval navigator's watch, ever since the first time Dwyer admired it. On this occasion Nick tried again, and Tom accepted it. Dwyer still wears it—the best watch he has ever had.

The month following the Dwyers' wedding, Nick and Ewa went to Holland to visit some of Ewa's relatives. Deprived of his own family, Nick strongly favored Ewa's keeping her ties with her family. Looking for the cheapest possible way to get to Holland, they took Icelandic Airlines. Unfortunately, their flight was delayed, finally took off at 2:00 A.M., and, because of bad weather, was diverted to Brussels. The Shadrins spent the night with some Polish friends of Ewa's who lived there. The next day they took the train to Amsterdam, where her Dutch relatives met them at the station. Nick and Ewa spent five days in Amsterdam before returning to Washington. The weather was dreadful during the entire trip, according to Ewa, and Nick never left her side.

Next, Nick and Ewa turned their attention to a trip to Brazil. Planned while Nick was in the hospital, it obviously ran counter to their proposed regular winter skiing vacations at St. Moritz. But the brochure they read in the hospital offered a tour that "was so cheap we really could not afford not to take it," says Ewa. In February 1975 they flew to Rio de Janeiro, where they spent a week swimming and lolling on the beach. In September 1975 Nick and Ewa again went to Europe—this time to Spain, where they spent a week with Ewa's relatives.

Back in Washington, the several lives of Nicholas Shadrin continued. To people like William and Mary Louise Howe, Nick and Ewa were perfect guests for their elegant parties. Then there was Nick's life with his sporting companions—men like Pete Sivess, Nicholas Kozlov, and many others. Few hunters and fishermen were more determined than Nick to fill his limit on each trip. If he did not use all that he took, he had friends who would, and their freezers grew heavier as the season progressed. Finally, there was Nick Shadrin's secret life—that of a double agent in the Igor operation. That life included James Wooten, John Funkhouser, and a variety of handlers from the KGB with whom he staged secret meetings in the Washington area. It was a life of dead drops and cryptic phone calls. Shadrin carried off this ultimate deception with such skill and finesse that even his wife—a woman so canny and shrewd that many casual acquaintances doubt she could ever be so gullible—would make sense of it all only in retrospect.

There was one major U.S. goal in running Shadrin as a double agent: to enhance Igor in the eyes of the KGB, to promote his rise through the ranks toward the top position in KGB counterintelligence in the United States—or at least to a key position in the KGB's American Department. This would put one of the Soviets' top U.S. spies in league with American Intelligence. So far this had not happened—at least to the knowledge of the CIA Counterintelligence staff.

Meanwhile, the principal movers behind the Igor operation had been busy dealing with other ramifications of his appearance. Indeed, one of the most significant aspects of Igor's appearance in 1966 was his certification of Yuri Nosenko, the deeply suspect Soviet defector who had come over in 1964. Igor had brought information that supported the proposition that Nosenko was just who he claimed to be.

Igor's certification of Nosenko paved the way for the settlement of a wrenching question at the CIA. The top men in the Soviet Division and almost all of James Angleton's counterintelligence staff believed Nosenko to be a phony. For three and a half years Nosenko was confined under Spartan conditions as the CIA tried to break his story. Although his inconsistencies became more hopelessly knotted, he never made a confession.

In the fall of 1966, when Richard Helms brought Rufus Taylor from DIA to take the number two position at CIA, one of Taylor's first assignments was to resolve the Nosenko question. It was after Igor's certification of Nosenko that Helms ordered Taylor to resolve the Nosenko matter, although Helms specifically states that Igor had nothing to do with his decision. To accomplish this, Admiral Taylor assigned Gordon Stewart to study the whole question for several months in 1967. Stewart's finding was that the case against Nosenko was not proved and therefore still open to other interpretation. By then the Nosenko case had been transferred from the Soviet Division and placed under the jurisdiction of the Office of Security. There it was placed in the hands of Bruce Solie, the man who had participated in the original questioning and debriefing sessions with Igor. Indeed, Solie apparently believed in Igor strongly enough to endorse Nosenko's full rehabilitation. With the help of the FBI, which was anxious for its own reasons to accept Nosenko, there was created the Solie Report, which included what really amounted to explanations of past inconsistencies in Nosenko's story.

In any event, in October 1968 an agreement to release Nosenko and resettle him like any other defector was reached. Most of the CIA Counterintelligence staff sharply dissented. Ostensibly for his work on the Nosenko case, Solie was awarded an intelligence medal. Soon after that Nosenko was married, and Solie served as best man at his wedding.

Meanwhile, in terms of Igor's contact with CIA Counterintelligence, there was a lengthening silence. The staff had waited vainly for some word from Igor. Then, in the early seventies, there was a glimmer of hope when CIA Counterintelligence received a message from Igor in the form of a coded cable sent from France. It was a sign of life, an indication that he was alive, traveling outside the Soviet Union, and trying to keep in touch with his American contacts. However, no meeting materialized.

This would appear to be slim payback for the years Shadrin had invested in his role as a double agent, although, perhaps, there were spin-off cases from Igor's information that justified the FBI's apparent continuing enthusiasm. In any case, the structure of the Shadrin operation seemed secure, and there were good reasons for his American handlers to believe the Soviets accepted Shadrin as a true redefector. Indeed, if his American handlers did not feel their deception of the Soviets was secure, it can be presumed they would never have sent him in 1972 on an overnight meeting with the KGB in Vienna—"a snake pit of Soviet spies," in the words of one CIA officer who served there.

Apparently the CIA did not send a control officer to cover Shadrin for his 1972 meeting, although presumably there was some reason for John Funkhouser's unique visit to the Shadrin home on the eve of the meeting. But Ewa Shadrin is not aware of any special person assigned to take care of her in Vienna—as in the case of Ann Martin three years later. Moreover, Jim Wooten has indicated to Ewa Shadrin that there was no surveillance for Shadrin's 1972 meeting.* Following this meeting, there was no time for a debriefing in Vienna. And Shadrin did not return directly to Washington but went instead to Athens, where he struck up his friendship with Walter Haas.

One former station chief in Vienna, who was not there when Shadrin went for his 1972 meeting, but is knowledgeable about such meetings in Vienna, has described what probably happened when Shadrin was gone overnight. He thinks the KGB would have taken Shadrin to a villa near Vienna and polished his ego, pure and simple. He believes it is likely that after so many years of service Shadrin might have been bestowed with a high rank.

"They take the guy to a comfortable setting, feed him well, and sit in front of a fireplace and tell him how great he is," says the former Vienna station chief. "It is a cheap and emotionally effective way to motivate an agent."

But in Shadrin's case the Soviets followed through with substantial hardware. Soon after Shadrin returned to Washington, sophisticated espionage equipment arrived by diplomatic pouch at

---

*One former counterintelligence expert has stated to the author that the absence of surveillance indicates confidence in Igor on the part of the sponsoring agency—in this case the FBI. The presence of surveillance, if detected, might invite Soviet investigations dangerous to Igor. There was, of course, no surveillance of Shadrin's final, fateful meeting in Vienna three years later—perhaps for the same reason.

the Soviet Embassy. He had been instructed in the use of the equipment during his Vienna meeting, according to James Wooten's later explanation to Ewa Shadrin. Oleg Kozlov, the Soviet who was handling Shadrin in Washington, turned over to him a radio transmitter that, according to one high FBI source, was more sophisticated than any the bureau had known the Soviets possessed. The Soviets also provided Shadrin with a code book for secret transmissions.

While at least one former counterintelligence officer has pointed out that frequently the Soviets are willing to sacrifice sophisticated communications equipment in order to enhance an operation—that is, to make Shadrin and his American handlers believe even more firmly that the Soviets were duped—it seems clear from Wooten that the FBI viewed the delivery of the spy equipment as evidence that the Soviets had accepted Shadrin completely. His recruitment by the Soviets seemed secure. The Americans seemed firm in their resolve that the Soviets were duped. They either were duped or were going to extraordinary lengths to make it appear that way.

Chapter 8

LATE IN 1974 Ewa Shadrin noticed an odd letter in
the pile of mail the postman had just brought to her door. There
was nothing particularly distinctive about the envelope that caught
her eye, but it bore a postmark from Oxon Hill, Maryland, a
suburb on the other side of Washington. In a strong hand, it was
addressed to Nicholas Shadrin. Whom did her husband know in
Oxon Hill?

Ewa Shadrin opened the letter. The writing was plain and
bold, very easy to read, and the two pages were sprinkled with
Russian phrases. It did not make any sense to her. The main
references were to Nick's health and to the fact that his operation
that fall had been a success. The questions were short and
simple—almost childlike.

"The tone was friendly, but it was very strange," recalls Ewa.
"It was as though it were written by someone not quite right in the
head. There were all kinds of simple, perfunctory questions about
Nick's health. I could only guess it was one of the oddball émigrés
Nick occasionally tried to help." She recalls that the thrust of the
letter was about Nick's health, the writer expressing satisfaction
that Nick was feeling better and hope that he would not become ill
again. It was signed with an unfamiliar name.

Ewa thought about the letter occasionally through the day, but
she decided against asking Nick about it when he got home. She
thought it might be one of those areas he might not want to discuss.
If he did want to discuss it, she reasoned, he would notice that she

187

had opened the letter and mention it to her. He never mentioned it.

A couple of months later Ewa noticed another letter from Oxon Hill. She recognized the bold handwriting even before noticing the postmark. This time she decided not to open the letter, although she puzzled over it the rest of the day. When Nick came home, Ewa asked him to show her the letter, to tell her whom it was from.

"Nick would show me anything; he had no secrets," says Ewa. "But when I asked him about the letter from Oxon Hill, he looked at me strangely and said he would not show it to me. He looked like a little boy you catch doing something wrong. It was most unusual."

Ewa badgered him gently about the letter, finding it hard to believe he really would not let her see it. But when she saw that he was serious, she said nothing more to him about it. However, at the next opportunity she began looking around Nick's study for the letter so she could read it herself. She never found it.

Shortly after that, however, Nick asked Ewa to type some envelopes for him. He wanted to make sure the address was exactly right, and he was not confident of his own typing abilities. Ewa prepared several envelopes, addressing them to Herr Rudiger Lehman at 116 Berlin, Kottmeierstr. 7, Germany, which is in East Berlin. Without comment, Nick gave her a return address to be typed on the back of the envelope: Philip Duffy, 3509 Deal Drive, Oxon Hill. Ewa immediately recognized Duffy as the name she had seen on Nick's strange letters.*

The letters, a part of Nick Shadrin's lonely secret life, came during a year when his frustrations reached a new intensity.

---

*In 1980, when one of the envelopes Ewa Shadrin typed was discovered in Nick's desk, she instantly recalled that indeed the name of the person on the return address of the Oxon Hill letters was Duffy, a fact that had faded from her memory. Looking into it, the author discovered that there is no 3509 Deal Drive in Oxon Hill, although there indeed is a 5309 Deal Drive. And at 5309 lives one Peter Duffy, a twenty-three-year veteran of the Metropolitan Police Department in Washington, who at one time had the Soviet embassy on his beat. Peter Duffy, when informed that a variation of his name and address had been used in this manner, was incredulous. There was a Philip Duffy who had lived in nearby Hyattsville from around 1970 until 1975, when his name dropped out of the telephone book. In 1980 that person was located at a different address, also in Hyattsville. He expressed incredulity that his name—particularly the spelling of "Philip"—had been used in this manner. Philip Duffy is a handyman and carpenter. The two Duffys stated that they had never heard of each other. Former Soviet counterintelligence personnel have explained that it is not uncommon for the Soviets to pick a name from the telephone book, perhaps create some variation on it, simply to have a return address on an envelope in an operation such as this. The actual form of the variation often represents a coded message.

Despite his satisfactory contacts with high defense and intelligence officials—and the enormous respect he enjoyed at the Naval War College—his professional life was essentially dreary. At the same time Ewa's career became increasingly successful—something her husband seemed genuinely proud of.

Although Shadrin made friends easily, he never seemed to become as attached to anyone as he did to his first and oldest friends—men like Tom Dwyer, Jack Leggat, Bill Howe, and Tom Koines. Few occasions were more important to Shadrin than when he could see old friends and engage in the deep and wide-ranging conversations he loved. Still, there is not even a hint that he ever shared his secret life with the closest of them.

All these friends were troubled by Shadrin's frustrations, that he felt so useless, so unappreciated. They regarded him as potentially one of the most brilliant analysts in the United States, and it was depressing for them to watch such talents being frittered away translating articles at the Defense Intelligence Agency. But every effort made to get Shadrin a security clearance appeared hopeless.

Deep into one of their long, amiable conversations, Tom Dwyer edged toward a subject few people could discuss with Shadrin. It probed the depths of the pervasive inner gloom that ever more frequently flashed across Nick's face during times of special difficulty, especially over his dull professional responsibilities. Shadrin was speaking of the contributions he could have made and comparing his life in the United States to his exalted position as the youngest destroyer commander in the Soviet Navy.

They had been discussing these matters for hours, in a way that only old, familiar friends can. They were talking about all the things that might have been, all the ifs that both men knew no longer really mattered. It was then that Tom Dwyer asked Shadrin a question he had long considered putting to him. "Nick," he said, "if you knew things would be this way when you were considering escaping to the West, would you still have come?"

Shadrin looked intense and gave the question some thought, but not for long. Dwyer knew he must have thought about it before. "No," Shadrin said quietly, shrugging his shoulders in a gesture of hopelessness, looking intently into his friend's eyes. "If I had known this, I would not have come."

It was a moment of terrible poignancy for Tom Dwyer. He, too, felt helpless that his country, with all that it had to offer, could not extend a useful life to a man with Shadrin's brilliant skills.

But Dwyer and most of Nick's friends point out that Shadrin recovered quickly from such low points. Casual acquaintances are surprised when told how somber he could become when he considered his fortunes. But Shadrin was a deeply pensive man, and these moods were an essential part of his richly varied personality.

Nick Shadrin's devotion to Julik, the German shepherd given to him by Anatoli Golitsin, was extraordinary. Julik simply was a part of Nick Shadrin, and it was normal for people who had not seen Nick for a while to inquire about the dog. By many accounts Julik was a ferocious animal, and indeed, he did bite a few people and attack some other dogs. Tom Dwyer can recall once, after not seeing Julik for a couple of years, asking apprehensively if the dog would give him any trouble. "Nick laughed and said that Julik would remember me," says Dwyer. "And he did."

When Julik passed his thirteenth birthday Nick and Ewa knew that his time was limited. Watching Julik become older, slower, more senile made Nick gloomy. On May 8, 1975, Nick had the dog put to sleep. He dug a grave in the backyard garden and buried Julik there. Nick's grief was profound. He had finally stopped smoking, but the day he buried Julik he started again. His only solace was a new German shepherd puppy, Trezor, that Ewa hoped would fill the terrible gap left by Julik. But she knew it would take a long time. Ewa usually had a big party for Nick on his birthday in May. This year he asked her not to because of his grief.

But Nick's spirits brightened later that spring, when he got a new and larger boat, which he christened *Ewa*. It was more comfortable than his previous boat, and he filled the summer weekends with fishing and cruising the Chesapeake Bay. No matter how dismal matters were at his office, Nick could always escape completely by taking off on his boat.

In October Tom Koines met Shadrin for lunch at Danker's and found him to be his normal, cheerful self. Koines did notice that the conversation quickly came around to Nick's always-flickering hope of finding something that would allow him to quit his job at DIA. For nearly two hours Koines and Shadrin talked and drank beer.

After lunch they took a walk through downtown Washington and sauntered into a bookstore—something they did often after lunch. They were looking over the books and discussing them when Nick picked up a copy of *KGB: The Secret Work of Soviet Secret Agents* by John Barron. Published a year earlier, the book was a highly regarded study of the work of KGB activities against foreign countries.

"I know a lot of the people in here," said Shadrin, flipping the pages, stopping at the photographs. "You should read this, Tom. I want to give it to you." Over Koines's protests, Shadrin purchased the book and presented it to him.

"It was just like Nick to do that," says Koines. "And it was the last time I ever saw him."

Indeed, there are many who recall the last time they saw Nick Shadrin. His friends seem to have clung to their last recollections with a special attachment, proof, as it were, that Nick was fine when last seen. But toward the end of the year these last recollections all had a peculiar common thread—an element that stands out when placed against the fact that he was never seen again.

Robert Kupperman had a luncheon date with Shadrin for mid-December. But Shadrin telephoned and said he would not be able to make it, that he had some important business to attend to before going on vacation in Vienna. It was during this telephone conversation that Nick stated that he expected everything to be much better for him after he returned from Vienna. That was the last time Kupperman ever spoke to Shadrin.

Also that December Colonel Bernard Weltman, formerly Shadrin's boss at DIA, received a telephone call from Nick. Although they had not gotten together in several months, they had seen each other socially many times since Weltman left DIA in 1972. He and Nick had common interests in some financial investments.

"Nick was excited, happy when he called," recalls Weltman. "He congratulated me heartily on a recent promotion and then said it had been too long since we had gotten together. He said he and Ewa were going to Vienna on vacation in a couple of weeks, and he wanted my wife and me to go with them."

Weltman told Shadrin that they would like to go, but it seemed impossible just then. Weltman had been deeply involved in a long, complicated assignment, and the end still was not in sight. But he said he would discuss it with his wife.

Then Weltman asked Shadrin if anything had improved in his professional life or if everything was the dreary same for him at

DIA. "I've got a new and good iron in the fire," Weltman recalls Shadrin saying. "My entire professional future is looking up. . . . Things are finally looking really very good for me."

Weltman was almost gleeful in his congratulations. His first question was whether Shadrin finally was getting a security clearance. "No," said Shadrin. "It is even more important than that." Weltman waited anxiously to hear more, but then Shadrin said that he could not discuss it over the telephone, that he looked forward to seeing Weltman in person.

Weltman was delighted over the news from Shadrin, but he considered his invitation to go to Vienna perfunctory. "But Nick called again a few days later," says Weltman. "He wanted to know what my wife had said. He insisted that he really wanted us to go with them, but I explained to him that there were various reasons why it was impossible for me to leave the office just then."

Shadrin's wanting to get together was standard in Weltman's mind, but there was something clearly unusual about his insistence that the Weltmans accompany the Shadrins to Vienna. "He really emphasized that I should go with him to Vienna. The implication was that it would be much more than a social occasion. Looking back on it, I see his request as a pronounced desire to have someone go with him on that trip."

But Weltman did not go, and that telephone conversation was the last time he ever talked to Shadrin.

In early December 1975 Tom Dwyer and his wife visited the Shadrins in Washington. They spent several days together, and on the day the Dwyers were to leave, Nick stayed home from work so he could see them off at the airport. First, they all went to Billy Martin's Tavern for a lunch of clams.

"Nick was not happy," Mrs. Dwyer recalls. "I thought he seemed depressed. He was trying so hard to be gay, but he really wasn't himself." However, Tom had experienced many years of Nick's ups and downs, and he figured this was a low point from which Nick would rebound. But Nick seemed extremely preoccupied and not particularly interested in engaging in the long conversations that usually marked their get-togethers.

After lunch Nick drove the Dwyers to National Airport and let them off at one of the traffic islands in front of the terminal. "I looked back just before we went through the terminal door," says Dwyer. "Nick was standing there by his car looking at us. He looked sad and dejected as he watched us, but then he smiled and waved."

That was the last time Tom Dwyer saw the best friend he ever had.

Then a few weeks later Dwyer received a Christmas card from Shadrin, and it was extremely cheery—the happy side of Nick Shadrin. In it he indicated a good reason for being happy. He had told the Dwyers about the upcoming Vienna vacation, and it had sounded like nothing more than a nice vacation. But in his Christmas card he stated that after the Vienna trip everything would be markedly improved for him from a professional standpoint.

That was the last word Tom Dwyer heard from Shadrin. He never received the torte Nick and Ewa sent him from Vienna a few days later.

The clear implication in all this is that Nick Shadrin finally had been promised a security clearance. And for reasons that eluded his friends, it was somehow tied to his Christmas vacation in Vienna. Whatever happened to stimulate Shadrin to tell so many friends that his professional life would improve after the Vienna trip probably occurred after Dwyer's visit in early December. The glum luncheon Dwyer had with Shadrin on the last day of his visit was in the first week of December. The cards, as well as Shadrin's comments to others, were initiated a week or so later.

Late one bitterly cold afternoon, a couple of weeks before they were to leave for Vienna, a few days after the Dwyers had departed, Nick indicated to Ewa that he wanted her to step into the kitchen. His gestures—avoiding making any noise—were memorable to Ewa because on rare occasions Nick would show signs, such as this, of suspecting that their house was bugged. Over the years this happened only two or three times. This time Ewa could sense that Nick was extremely serious. Once in the kitchen, Nick whispered to Ewa that he wanted to go for a walk, that he had something very important to tell her. He even wanted to leave Trezor, the puppy that had replaced Julik, at home. It was always more relaxing to go for a walk without the strapping, booming Trezor, destined to grow to over 100 pounds.

The cold, crisp air hit their faces as they turned down the sidewalk. The sun was setting. "It was a beautiful afternoon," says

Ewa. Nick was all buttoned up in an overcoat, but not a hat. He rarely wore a hat, except for hunting and fishing. No sooner had the door closed behind them than Ewa could sense a rare optimism, a deep happiness bursting from Nick. She could see it in his eyes, feel it in his voice.

Once down the street a bit, he told Ewa something very important had come up in his work—something that was going to make an enormous difference in his professional life. He told her that he had some business meetings set up in Vienna during their vacation and that these were crucial to the new professional success he envisioned.

It was years since Ewa had seen Nick so happy, and she was thrilled by what he was telling her. She had agonized terribly over his frustration at work, his difficulty in reaching the heights she knew he was capable of. They both were glowing with smiles and happiness as they walked through the cold dusk.

Nick did not offer any specific details about his new horizons, and Ewa did not ask. He volunteered, though, that at last, after sixteen years, he was going to get his security clearance—a clearance that would allow him to rise to his own level in the world of consultation and analysis. Ewa was ecstatic. Nick mentioned that there were going to be other new opportunities, but she paid little attention. What made sense to her was that at long last he would have his security clearance.

It is hard to understand fully Ewa's long and deep frustration over Nick's professional life in the United States. She, of course, had been strikingly successful in her career. But her happiness was profoundly dampened by Nick's terrible and ever-deepening disappointment. At last, she thought as they walked along, this was going to change. Nick was then only forty-seven, and she reasoned there was plenty of time left for him to enjoy the success she knew could be his with the proper clearances.

During the next two weeks Nick was filled with an optimism Ewa had rarely seen during their years in America. For the first time they both felt a satisfaction about their prospects. They had believed that if they were patient, if they worked hard enough, this would come to pass. At last, Ewa could feel secure that after the Vienna vacation everything would begin to fall into place.

About 6:00 P.M. on Monday, December 8, a day or so after Nick had told Ewa about his exciting professional prospects, he made what she thought was a strange request. His jeep had been stolen from the driveway a few weeks earlier—something he believed would never have happened if his beloved Julik had been alive and well. In the gathering dark, Nick asked Ewa to back her car out of the garage and leave it in the driveway. While she did this, he turned off all the outside lights.

When Ewa came back into the house, Nick explained that his old friend Jim Wooten was going to stop by for a few minutes. For some reason Wooten preferred to park in the garage so that his car could not be seen from the street. As always, Ewa asked no questions. She presumed all the outside lights were turned off so that Wooten would not be seen as he stepped from the car into the house.

As they waited, Nick explained that Jim Wooten was bringing with him another person, a woman named Ann Martin. Nick said that Ann Martin would be spending some time with them in Vienna. The purpose of the visit that evening, Nick said, was for Ewa to meet Ann Martin. He indicated that he was already acquainted with Ann Martin. He said that, if asked, Ewa should identify Miss Martin as a dental patient.

By the time Jim Wooten and Ann Martin arrived it was pitch-dark outside. Ewa was pleased to see Wooten again, having met him only at the time Nick was in the hospital, although his telephone calls were as frequent as ever. Ewa invited them to sit down and served tea, coffee, and cookies.

Ewa found Ann Martin extremely reserved, even cold. Instantly Ewa formed an unfavorable impression of her. Soon after Wooten and Miss Martin arrived, Ewa had to leave to attend a Christmas party being given by some of her dental colleagues. She does not know how long Wooten and Miss Martin remained at the house. It was two weeks later, in Vienna, that Ewa next met Miss Martin.

At the time of the strange visit Christmas cards had begun to arrive at the Shadrin home. Ewa never paid any attention to Christmas cards. Thus, she missed the one that Jim Wooten later told her had come a few days earlier, one bearing an important message for Nick. The envelope, Wooten related, was addressed in a bold hand and postmarked Oxon Hill, Maryland.

Chapter 9

THE CIA's wait for Igor had entered its tenth year.

The CIA men on hand for the start of the Igor operation were largely gone from the intelligence services. Richard Helms, James Angleton, Newton Miler, Ray Rocca, and Admiral Rufus Taylor had retired. While the FBI's Hoover and Tolson were dead, James Wooten, William Branigan, Bert Turner, and William Lander continued their interest in the case. But at the CIA the operation had drifted into other hands, its importance surely diminished from that spring day in 1966 when Igor made his peculiar gambit with a telephone call to Richard Helms. "The case had been in the doldrums for years," says one prominent CIA operations officer of that period.

Toward the end of the decade-long operation, wrenching changes had taken place at the agency that would have a fundamental bearing on the handling of the case involving Shadrin and Igor. No longer was it the top-priority operation it had been in the days of its inception as an exclusive brainchild of the highest intelligence officials in the United States. Nevertheless, the case remained tightly held by the FBI's Soviet Counterintelligence Section, the CIA's Office of Security, and the CIA Counterintelligence staff. The ancient Angletonian stricture to keep it from the CIA's Soviet Division—an injunction that had provided security in more ways than one—was apparently intact.

But in a sense the case had gone to the Soviet Division anyway.

This happened when personnel in the Soviet Division moved over to the truncated counterintelligence staff. At least one officer of the very division from which Angleton and his men had concealed the Shadrin/Igor operation was now a key figure in running it. The drastic changes took place following CIA Director William Colby's firing of Angleton and the immediate resignation of his top lieutenants in late 1974 and early 1975.

The CIA's new regime was repelled by earlier suspicions that seemed to involve convoluted thinking and tended to smother genuine operational opportunities. The new thinking called for abandoning or restructuring such operations in order to concentrate efforts on the active collection of hard intelligence. In his autobiography, *Honorable Men*, William Colby, then Director of Central Intelligence, comments on his review of the maze of counterintelligence activities that flourished under Angleton's autocratic rule:

> I spent several long sessions doing my best to follow his [Angleton's] tortuous theories about the long arm of a powerful and wily KGB at work, over decades, placing its agents in the heart of allied and neutral nations and sending its false defectors to influence and undermine American policy. I confess that I couldn't absorb it, possibly because I did not have the requisite grasp of this labyrinthine subject, possibly because Angleton's explanations were impossible to follow, or possibly because the evidence just didn't add up to his conclusions. At the same time I looked in vain for some tangible results in the counterintelligence field, and found little or none. I did not suspect Angleton and his staff of engaging in improper activities. I just could not figure out what they were doing at all.

On December 20, 1974, James Angleton, the enigmatic patriarch of CIA Counterintelligence, retired at the request of William Colby. His closest associates soon followed. Suddenly the long era of Angletonian dominance was over; the agency was rid of the cunning spymaster and his "tortuous theories." Almost immediately work was begun that would, in the words of one of Colby's top operations officers, "bring counterintelligence back into the agency."

This new era must have been greeted with smug satisfaction by those who had been less than content working under the long shadow of the ever-suspicious James Angleton. It promised, among other things, the pursuit and development of sources which had been rendered impotent by the pervasive suspicions that now were gone. And there could be a resurrection and continuation of long-stalled endeavors.

Already there was increasing recognition of the legitimacy of Yuri Nosenko, the Soviet defector who had been under such intense suspicion during his first years in the United States. The harshest manifestations of suspicion lifted after Igor's appearance in 1966, when he had certified Nosenko's bona fides. However, that clearance was only enough to get Nosenko out of custody and settled into American life, as with any other defector. This, according to Director Richard Helms, did not mean that the CIA considered Nosenko bona fide—only that it wanted to be rid of a seemingly intractable problem. But this lukewarm acceptance was not satisfactory to men like Bruce Solie and Leonard McCoy, who had become advocates of Nosenko—no doubt partly because of their belief in Igor's message regarding Nosenko. This message, of course, continued to be concealed from the mainstream of McCoy's Soviet Division.

Going much farther than DCI Helms ever envisioned, Solie and McCoy readdressed themselves to the Nosenko case with an eye toward vindicating him once and for all. Almost incredibly they and others managed to bring Nosenko into the bosom of the agency as a highly paid regular consultant and lecturer on current Soviet intelligence matters and personnel. Even more astounding was Nosenko's employment as a lecturer at the CIA's counterintelligence courses—a post that provided him firsthand association with some of the agency's key clandestine personnel.

Right or wrong, such a drastic reversal in the agency's policy on Nosenko constituted a flagrant repudiation of the nearly universal suspicions voiced by the respected veterans who had handled the Nosenko case just a few years earlier. The crowning touch to Nosenko's resurrection came in 1978, when CIA Director Stansfield Turner issued an internal statement to agency personnel calling the controversial defector "a well-adjusted American citizen utilized as a consultant by CIA and . . . making a valuable contribution to our mission."

With Nosenko's enthusiastic acceptance established, the new regime could turn to the resurrection and genuine acceptance of Igor, the KGB officer who had so boldly certified Nosenko.

Indeed, under the old school, CIA counterintelligence officers had doubted Igor as seriously as they had Nosenko, although the Igor case was much more closely held. But with the old guard gone and Nosenko exuberantly embraced, it was time to bring Igor back into the fold.

Indeed, the fervency with which Nosenko was embraced might well suggest the high esteem in which Igor was suddenly held. One could not be embraced without the other, any more than one could be doubted without doubting the other. Their fortunes were inextricably linked. Now that Nosenko was okay, Igor had to be okay. It was, in a basic sense, a mutual certification society.

At the agency only two officers involved in the Shadrin/Igor case had been in it from the start. Bruce Solie, the faithful defender of Nosenko, had been one of the earliest officers to talk to Igor. He had done so in his position at the Office of Security, which was working to the exclusion of the suspect Soviet Division in the search for a penetration agent. Solie had been aware from the start of the deception and recruitment of Shadrin.

The origins of Leonard McCoy's participation, on the other hand, are not that clear. However, there are indications that McCoy was the only person in the Soviet Division informed about Igor—a move that may have been necessary to acquire McCoy's assistance in recruiting Shadrin into the operation or to acquire substantive guidance for exploitation of Igor's intelligence potential. In any event, McCoy's knowledge of Shadrin stretched back to 1959, when he was the primary CIA officer involved in reviewing Shadrin's debriefing.

Almost immediately after the purge of Angleton and his staff, McCoy moved over from the Soviet Division to the counterintelligence staff. The new chief of counterintelligence was George T. Kalaris, an officer highly regarded by Colby who had served as chief of a Far Eastern station following assignments in Europe. It is not known how much time was expended in briefing Kalaris and McCoy on the intricacies of the Shadrin case and its relation to the remote Igor. It is likely that the whole operation was seen as bearing the earmarks of the sort of Angletonian scheme that was no longer favored by the new CIA leadership. Many years and thousands of hours had been invested in an effort that apparently was generating little hard intelligence, at least for the CIA.

But there was one aspect of the Shadrin operation that would be absolutely tantalizing to the new counterintelligence team—the old promise of Igor's reemergence as a U.S. spy in the top ranks of the KGB. Short of that elusive goal, a resumption of contact with Igor would be completely in keeping with a primary theme of the Colby CIA: the collection of hard intelligence. And without doubt, Igor's stature must have swollen impressively with the stunning resurrection of Nosenko. After all, Igor's original certification of Nosenko had appeared to pave the way for his first clearance.

But contact between Igor and the CIA had been exceedingly rare. The pressing question now was how to reestablish contact with him. There arose a reasonably sure possibility, a link with the past that could provide a serviceable circuit for a reconnection with Igor. There, spinning idly among the ancient Angletonian schemes, was the Shadrin operation—its sturdy structure firmly in place. As outmoded as it was, it would have to do.

An ominous cloud had rolled into place over the Shadrin operation following his 1972 overnight meeting with the KGB in Vienna. On that occasion Shadrin met primarily with Mikhail Kuryshev and Oleg Kozlov, both high-ranking Soviet spies operating under diplomatic cover. Back in Washington after that meeting, Kozlov, who was Shadrin's Washington KGB handler, delivered the so-phisticated espionage equipment—an indication to the Americans that perhaps the Soviets were going to upgrade their use of Shadrin.

But this did not happen. James Wooten has stated that Shadrin never once used the equipment, that it remained stashed in his attic until the FBI collected it more than three years later. Within a couple of months after he delivered the equipment, Oleg Kozlov returned to Moscow. Shadrin's contact with the Soviets mysteri-ously stopped.*

Throughout 1973 and 1974 Shadrin continued his regular dealings with American intelligence officers James Wooten and John Funkhouser. There was always the hope that contact with the Soviets would be reestablished. The wheels of the operation were

---

*One anomaly in Wooten's firm report that contact was lost is Shadrin's 1974 trip to St. Moritz and his disappearance for a day with a rented car (see Chapter Seven). In view of the proximity of St. Moritz to Austria, it appears possible a meeting with the Soviets took place. But Shadrin's American handlers, while acknowledging other meetings, reject this possibility.

kept greased, ready for the Soviets whenever they decided to reconnect with Shadrin. "From a maintenance standpoint, it was simple to keep Shadrin's end of the operation open," says one former CIA officer familiar with some aspects of the case.

In the summer of 1974, nearly two years after the Vienna meeting, the Soviets made their first reconnection with Shadrin. It came in the form of the strange telephone calls Ewa witnessed on the evening Nick told her he needed to leave home to meet someone on Lorcom Lane. Much later Jim Wooten explained to her that it was the KGB making its first contact. Nick had tried desperately to reach Wooten and Funkhouser without success. When he was not able to get the go-ahead from his American handlers, Shadrin made the difficult decision to skip the meeting on Lorcom Lane. There is no account of the Soviet response to being stood up.

Later that year, as the storm clouds intensified over the Colby-Angleton relationship, the Soviets again made contact—this time in the form of the cryptic note mailed from Oxon Hill, Maryland. Then came the firing of Angleton and the resignation of his top men, followed by other messages from Oxon Hill. This new Soviet interest was accepted by the Americans, although there is no indication that at that early stage there was a clear understanding of just how it would be used. This would come later, as the new counterintelligence staff cast about for a way to reestablish contact with Igor.

Sometime in 1975 Shadrin was ordered to request a meeting with his top contacts in Moscow, men he had not seen since 1972. Even though the Soviets had not indicated any desire for such a high-level meeting, the Americans pushed ahead anyway. Some older hands would have counseled that Shadrin's still-unexplained break in contact with the Soviets was an urgent reason for supreme caution, that it would be better to move more slowly, to watch the Soviet hand unfold. But caution was not a guiding light. The success of Shadrin's 1972 Vienna meeting was seen as firm evidence that danger was minimal.

Shadrin did as he was ordered. Much of the communication of that period was in the form of coded messages and secret-writing letters from Oxon Hill. Shadrin's responses were made to the address in Berlin. In light of his comments to many friends, it appears certain that the United States promised him that he was to be given a security clearance— the realization of a dream that had eluded him for fifteen years. This most likely was offered as bait to the Soviets, a sweetening in the Shadrin package to encourage them to renew their association with him. The ultimate goal, of course, was to draw Igor to Vienna, ostensibly for a meeting with Shadrin. This meeting would serve as a cover for Igor to make a reconnection with his handler from the CIA.

Finally, word was relayed circuitously from Moscow—in a letter from Oxon Hill—that Shadrin's top KGB contacts were willing to see him again. There were strong hints that Igor would be present. Shadrin proposed Spain as a meeting site, but the KGB suggested Helsinki. After consultation with his handlers Shadrin demurred. Helsinki, he was told, was too dangerous. For reasons that remain utterly baffling, Shadrin was ordered to counterpropose that the meeting take place in Vienna, a city in which the Soviets dominated the intelligence scene.

The KGB quickly accepted.

Early in December 1975 top counterintelligence officers of the CIA and FBI gathered at a secret meeting to discuss Nick Shadrin's impending rendezvous in Vienna. The highest CIA officer present was George T. Kalaris, Colby's new chief of counterintelligence. Accompanying Kalaris from the counterintelligence staff was Leonard McCoy. Cynthia Hausmann of the counterintelligence section of the Soviet Division was present. Bruce Solie of the Office of Security was also there, along with James Wooten, William Branigan, and others from the FBI.

Various accounts of this meeting sharply dispute whether or not there was discussion of the advisability of providing surveillance for Shadrin's contracts with the Soviets in Vienna. Kalaris reportedly told the gathering that the CIA believed the man known as Igor would make an appearance in Vienna. He added that Bruce Solie would be dispatched to Vienna to deal with Igor because Solie was the original CIA officer who had dealt with the supposed American agent. Cynthia Hausmann would be sent to debrief Shadrin after his meetings.

The CIA's new chief of station in Vienna was informed that the contact would take place and that Shadrin's cover in Vienna would be that he and his wife were on their way to a skiing vacation in Zürs. The Vienna station would serve only as a conduit for the officers from CIA headquarters to transmit the debriefing reports back to Washington. The station would provide support in arranging safe houses and reserving suitable hotel rooms. But it would not be responsible for overseeing Shadrin's contact with the Soviets. It would be up to intelligence officers in Washington to decide questions such as surveillance.

The CIA officer assigned to be in charge of the Shadrin contact in Vienna was Cynthia Hausmann. Tall, thin, angular Miss Hausmann had won good marks for her performance in the Soviet Division, primarily as an assistant to Leonard McCoy in the reports section. She now was assigned to the counterintelligence section of the Soviet Division. Miss Hausmann was known for her competence, if not for her flair. "She was a good, gray intelligent girl who certainly sparked no idea of making her a case officer," says one person who knew her and her work in the Soviet Division.

However, Miss Hausmann had been a case officer even before her tenure in the Soviet Division. After getting her start in the Eastern European Division and becoming a reports officer, Miss Hausmann was assigned during the fifties as an operations officer in Munich, where she utilized her nearly native fluency in German to support her cover as a student in a sensitive covert operation. Following this she served in the Soviet Division until about 1965. By 1966 she was a case officer for the CIA station in Mexico City, a role made public by Philip Agee in *CIA Diary*.

Another observer has described Miss Hausmann as "very clever, quite a fast learner." Underlying all comments on her, however, is the feeling that she could never be regarded as a warm person, never someone who seemed interested in becoming close to others. Indeed, the only sign of warmth Ewa Shadrin witnessed was when the strange woman spoke of her cat, while describing her life alone in Washington. Mrs. Shadrin recalls Miss Hausmann as "polite, nice, cold, and aloof."*

Cynthia Hausmann's arrival in Vienna was delayed by the bad flying conditions that prevailed in Europe that week. However, at 9:30 A.M. on Wednesday, December 17, Miss Hausmann met with the chief of station in his office. After a ten-minute chat the station

---

*In a telephone conversation with the author, Miss Hausmann, who retired from the CIA in early 1981, declined an invitation to give her version of the events.

chief proposed that they move to a secure room at the station where others had assembled to discuss the Shadrin contact.

At some point during the meeting the chief of station asked Miss Hausmann if surveillance would be required for the Shadrin meeting. She replied that it was thought in Washington not to be necessary. According to the station chief, Miss Hausmann explained that the reason the FBI did not want surveillance was that Shadrin was a trusted and experienced operative who had previously met with the Soviets in Vienna and returned safely. Surveillance would only run the risk of exposing the whole operation. After about twenty minutes the chief of station turned the meeting over to his deputy and departed. He was scheduled to go to Washington the next morning for a long-planned Christmas leave. Because he was not going to be in Vienna for the actual Shadrin meeting, he turned the planning session over to his deputy to work out the details. The deputy would be in charge during the absence of the chief of station.*

The station had considered the possibility of surveillance of the steps of the Votivkirche, the site of Shadrin's meeting with the KGB. It was customary for the station's operational personnel to assess the pros and cons of providing surveillance. Difficulties would be weighed against the station's capabilities for providing surveillance and the urgency of the request from the cooperating agency, in this case the FBI. For various reasons, the Votivkirche was a location where the station preferred not to put its personnel on the streets. It was deemed likely that the Soviets would maintain their own surveillance, which would risk exposure of CIA personnel attached to the Vienna station. Two Soviet installations, one a Soviet bank, were in locations that would allow the KGB to monitor any surveillance activity being maintained by the CIA as well as the meeting itself.

Surveillance of the steps of the Votivkirche by the CIA would appear to be a simple procedure from any one of several windows in the nearby U.S. consulate building. The CIA station could have prevailed upon the consul for access to the consulate, but

---

*One former CIA counterintelligence expert has explained to the author that in Angleton's time, chiefs of station would not have been apprised of movements of double agents in their territory. "There would be no reason to let the chief of station know," says the expert. "You can't take a high-level case and bring in people who have nothing to contribute. All it does is spread the secret."

the station personnel preferred not to exercise that option. However, the station was prepared to provide fixed surveillance for the Shadrin meeting if Washington required it.*

The man in charge of arranging hotel rooms and the safe house for the mission was an old friend of Miss Hausmann, with whom she had worked in Washington and Munich. It fell to this officer to facilitate Shadrin's meeting so that Miss Hausmann could debrief him and transmit the information back to Washington.

One person who was not present at the meeting on Wednesday at the CIA station was Bruce Solie. In describing Solie—a very thin man of medium height with a high, balding forehead crowning a rough-hewn face—people invariably say that his appearance is primarily that of a security officer. He had arrived in Vienna a day earlier than Miss Hausmann, but his sole reason for being there was to make contact with the agent Igor if, as hoped and expected, he showed up. Solie had no scheduled duties involving Shadrin's meeting with the KGB.

The veteran CIA officer who was station chief in Vienna felt no hesitancy about departing for his scheduled Christmas leave. The station was to play no role in Shadrin's actual contact—only a supportive role of facilitating communications, providing security for visiting personnel, and arranging hotel rooms with appropriate cover. While the station chief's snow-delayed flight sat stalled at the Vienna airport, Nick and Ewa Shadrin arrived on their flight from London.

However good the reasons, Shadrin's case was being handled by the second team from start to finish. From the moment of his arrival in Vienna he was in the hands of the deputy station chief and Cynthia Hausmann, a middle-level counterintelligence officer. There is no evidence that Bruce Solie ever had any direct contact with Shadrin.

Shadrin's first meeting, on December 18, was with two veteran Soviet diplomats, both of whom he had met on earlier occasions.

---

*Five years after Shadrin's disappearance a controversy continued to simmer over the question of surveillance. Mrs. Shadrin and her attorney, Richard Copaken, insist that the Vienna station was prepared to provide surveillance until Cynthia Hausmann called it off. According to Copaken, Miss Hausmann has stated to him that the FBI told her it did not want surveillance. But other sources indicate that the question of surveillance was not an explicit point on the agenda at the December meeting between the CIA and the FBI to plan the Vienna contact. One FBI source at the meeting has stated that possibly the CIA said something to the effect of "You are not going to require surveillance, are you?"

Mikhail Kuryshev had been attached to the Soviet Embassy in Vienna during Shadrin's 1972 meeting there, and Oleg Alekseye-vich Kozlov, assigned to the Soviet Embassy in Washington from 1968 to 1972, had been one of Shadrin's Soviet handlers.

On the eighteenth, after Shadrin had met Kuryshev and Kozlov on the steps of the Votivkirche, they rode around in an automobile and talked for a time. Kuryshev, who had been reassigned to Moscow and was dispatched to Vienna especially to see Shadrin, explained that he was too well known in Vienna to risk having dinner with Shadrin and Kozlov. It was too likely that he would be spotted by CIA agents who knew him well. But the brash young Kozlov had no such fears. After letting Kuryshev off, he took Shadrin to the fish restaurant that Nick later mentioned to Ewa with such enthusiasm. Also, the two Soviets instructed Shadrin to rent a car the next day and familiarize himself with the streets of Vienna.

Whatever transpired at the first meeting, it made Shadrin very happy. Mrs. Shadrin has testified to his exuberance when he returned to the hotel room that night. When Miss Hausmann debriefed him that night, he told her that he was informed he had been promoted to the rank of colonel in the KGB. She then departed, presumably to cable the results of his meeting to CIA headquarters. Shadrin mentioned to his wife, however, that he had not told Miss Hausmann everything, that he was saving the most significant information for Jim Wooten, his FBI handler. Apparently, Shadrin himself felt little confidence in Miss Hausmann.

On the evening of Saturday December 20, while Nick Shadrin said farewell to his wife for perhaps the last time of their lives, Miss Hausmann attended a dinner party at the home of her old CIA friend and his wife. From an operational standpoint, Miss Haus-mann would not have spent unnecessary time at Shadrin's hotel because of the likelihood that some of the maids and bellhops were employed by the Soviets. Indeed, there is no evidence of any contact by Miss Hausmann prior to Shadrin's meeting on Saturday night.

According to Cynthia Hausmann, the dinner party at her friend's home lasted until 12:30 A.M., at which time he drove her back to the safe house. But her host has a different story. He states that he left to drive her home at midnight. In either case, she should have been back at the safe house no later than

1:00 A.M.—and as early as 12:30, if the host's account is correct.*

But Miss Hausmann did not answer the phone when Ewa Shadrin made her first frantic telephone call to the emergency number at 1:35 A.M. At 1:55 A.M., when Mrs. Shadrin made her second call, Miss Hausmann's initial question—even before being told Shadrin had not returned—was whether Mrs. Shadrin had tried to call earlier. When Mrs. Shadrin stated that she had indeed tried earlier, Miss Hausmann stated only that she had been attending a dinner party. In subsequent interviews with Mrs. Shadrin's attorney, Miss Hausmann has declined to explain her whereabouts for the disputed thirty minutes, stating only that she went directly from the dinner party to the apartment.

It is possible that the discrepancy is academic because Miss Hausmann apparently did nothing once she learned that Shadrin had not returned. At around 5:00 A.M., Miss Hausmann notified the acting chief of station, who urged her to contact CIA headquarters immediately. Miss Hausmann demurred. Basically her decision was to wait for some development. These were the crucial hours when there might have been a chance to reverse whatever course Shadrin had been set upon following his supposed contact with the Soviets—if, of course, there was genuine interest on the part of the Americans in reversing that course.

The Vienna chief of station, who was at home in Washington by the time of these events, has theorized on how Miss Hausmann might have viewed the situation. She first might figure that Shadrin and the Soviets, engaging in lively discussions, had all gotten drunk and that Nick would return the next day with a dreadful hangover. He also pointed out that Miss Hausmann, in deciding not to cable Washington immediately, would know that there was nothing anyone in Washington could do.

For whatever reasons, nothing was done that night. Miss Hausmann told Mrs. Shadrin not to worry, that Nick had been late returning from his meeting two nights earlier. This, of course, was an absurdity; Nick had returned at precisely the time his wife was expecting him. There was nothing else Ewa Shadrin could do but remain in her room, weeping the night through.

Finally, the deputy chief of station raised the alarm at CIA

---

*The host, still active as a CIA officer, was contacted by the author and declined to comment on these events.

headquarters at 10:00 A.M. on December 21, more than eight hours after Ewa Shadrin made her first futile effort to notify Cynthia Hausmann that Nick had not returned. Immediately cables began to move back and forth with details, questions, suggested answers. Soon the State Department was notified that an American citizen was missing, and a second channel of inquiry was opened, a second line of communication flowing back and forth across the Atlantic.

It was fifteen hours since Shadrin was supposed to meet the KGB agents on the steps of the Votivkirche. In one of the earliest cables from the United States to the Soviet Union, the Americans stated that Shadrin had given his wife the names of the Soviet diplomats he was meeting—Kozlov and Kuryshev. To avoid a conflict in stories, Mrs. Shadrin, who had not been given the names by Nick, was then supplied with these names so that she would know them if asked. It is possible that this is the only reason the names ever became known.

From the time Ewa Shadrin informed Cynthia Hausmann that Shadrin was missing, she found it peculiar that she was never questioned directly by Austrian authorities. She had expected the police to want a detailed description of Nick's appearance and clothing when she last saw him. However, this never happened. She wondered how the authorities could be looking for Nick without pertinent descriptions.

Later, Miss Hausmann explained to her that the Austrian authorities could not be notified as long as Ewa remained in the country because they would insist upon questioning her. For reasons that were not made clear to Mrs. Shadrin, U.S. intelligence officials did not want the Austrian authorities questioning the last known person to have seen Shadrin.

Later Ewa was told that the Austrian authorities were notified as soon as she left the country with Bruce Solie, who, she had been told, was dispatched from Washington to escort her home. Former CIA officers with connections to the case confirm this. However, in 1980 Austrian authorities insisted that they were not notified of Shadrin's disappearance until three weeks after it happened—far too late for them to conduct a fruitful investigation.*

---

*There was one report of a maid at the Hotel Bristol who claimed she had seen Shadrin at the hotel after December 20. Hers is the only reported sighting of Shadrin in Vienna after his disappearance. However, the maid was located in 1980 and conveyed to the author a statement that she had never said she had seen Shadrin.

Theories abound as to what happened to Nick Shadrin, but they all fall into one of four categories. Two sets of theories are predicated on Shadrin's being kidnapped, either by the Soviets or by the CIA. Some theories are rooted in a presumption that Shadrin was a KGB agent all along, that his defection in 1959 was one of the Soviets' best-handled provocations. The fourth set of theories presumes that Shadrin became desperately disillusioned with his professional life, his marital situation, and his future and that he took off on his own for parts unknown, to establish himself in yet another life.

The most widely accepted theory at the time of Shadrin's disappearance—one held with apparent sincerity by the FBI, the CIA, the State Department, and high government officials— was that the KGB had kidnapped him and spirited him back to the Soviet Union. There also was a feeling that some resolution was imminent, whether it be parading a broken Shadrin before the world to denounce the West or simply leaking word he had been executed as a traitor. In no case was a resounding silence expected.

The first order of business was establishment of high-level contact between the United States and the Soviet Union. Apparently there was agreement that a plea for Shadrin's return—one cloaked in absolute diplomatic sterility—was the most appropriate channel. Nothing that would pollute the atmosphere should be done. Top U.S. diplomats had to be able to assure the Soviets that if they returned Shadrin safely, there was no risk of embarrassment to them or any public exposure.

There was a feeling of urgency about the contact—that every lost hour contributed to a hardening of the Soviet position and the possibility of Shadrin's execution. There had been no promising response through standard diplomatic channels by the time Ewa Shadrin reached Washington on Christmas Eve, the day Jim Wooten gave her the names of the Soviet diplomats with whom her husband was planning to meet.

At the time Wooten gave her the names, he told her that Secretary of State Henry Kissinger was at that moment preparing to speak privately with Soviet Ambassador Anatoly Dobrynin in Washington to plead for Shadrin's return. Wooten explained that every moment of delay placed Nick in greater potential danger. Ewa's utmost cooperation in containing the story was essential to Kissinger's success.

209

But Kissinger did not get around to talking to Ambassador Dobrynin on Christmas Day. This was deeply disturbing to Jim Wooten and to other officials who were trying to assist Ewa Shadrin. On December 30, the U.S. Embassy in Moscow contacted the Soviet Ministry of Foreign Affairs, which stated that no Soviet official was in contact with Shadrin on December 20. However, the Soviets expressed a desire to "cooperate" and deal with the matter "constructively," according to an FBI report of those events.

Kissinger did not talk to Dobrynin until January 5, a delay that angered Jim Wooten. Dobrynin denied any knowledge of Shadrin. By then Mrs. Shadrin had confided in William and Mary Louise Howe, and the following evening there was the meeting with the Howes and James Wooten at the home of Robert Kupperman. Even at this early stage Ewa Shadrin began to realize that her hopes for success were better placed in individuals like Jim Wooten and the Howes and Kuppermans than in high-level diplomats and officials. Still, she knew it would take the diplomatic might of the American government to move the Soviets.

Quietly but steadily the Howes and the Kuppermans began contacting everyone they knew in government in a position to help. They pressed them to lean on higher officials. Mary Louise Howe briefed William G. Whyte, vice-president of U.S. Steel and a close friend of President Ford's, beseeching him to take the Shadrin matter to the President. A few days later Whyte indicated that he had done so. Other avenues were pursued with success in getting the story to the White House.

The Howes briefed their friend and neighbor Alabama Senator John Sparkman, who contacted Kissinger personally. He reported that the Secretary of State believed that he had done all he possibly could and that the situation seemed hopeless. It was also reported that Kissinger had discussed the matter with Soviet Foreign Minister Andrei Gromyko, who noncommittally referred him back to Dobrynin.

Others briefed by the Howes included House Speaker Carl Albert; Mississippi Senator James Eastland; Albert Hall, who was serving as Assistant Secretary of Defense for Intelligence; and Admiral George W. Anderson, Jr., chairman of the President's Intelligence Advisory Board. All expressed extreme concern and a willingness to try their best to prod those higher officials who might be in a position to help.

On February 5, Brent Scowcroft, President Ford's assistant for national security affairs, telephoned Mrs. Shadrin to say that he had just reviewed the Shadrin file and would be in touch soon to advise her of the administration's plan of action. Later that day General Vernon Walters, Deputy Director of the CIA, telephoned Mary Louise Howe to report that Scowcroft had arrived at CIA headquarters late in the afternoon and was meeting at that hour with CIA Director George Bush to reach an agreement on how to pursue the Shadrin matter.

The next day Ewa Shadrin went to the State Department, where she met with Arthur Hartman, Assistant Secretary of State for European Affairs, Robert L. Barry, and Lawrence S. Eagleburger. During this meeting Eagleburger, according to Mrs. Shadrin, shook his head and stated: "They [the CIA and FBI] got themselves into this with their harebrained schemes. Now they expect us to pull their chestnuts out of the fire." He did not explain precisely what he meant.

But Arthur Hartman followed up immediately by contacting Yuli Vorontsov, a high official at the Soviet Embassy. Later Hartman told Mrs. Shadrin he had minced no words with the Soviet, opening the conversation by saying, "We have a spy case here."

"We don't have Shadrin," was Vorontsov's instant reply.

According to Mrs. Shadrin, Brent Scowcroft told her, "As you know, we do not have much leverage with the Russians," which suggested to her that no plan was forthcoming from the White House. It also was clear that the CIA was not in any hurry to formulate a strategy. Other officials, while sympathetic, obviously were getting nowhere. A puzzled Mrs. Shadrin began to realize that despite the seemingly sincere efforts of a few government officials, nothing had been done.

On February 10, after careful consultation with the Howes and the Kuppermans—bolstered by friendly advice from Jim Wooten —Ewa Shadrin concluded that her husband had been abandoned by the United States government. She had not seen a single sign that it was taking any productive steps to bring him home or even to find out what had happened to him. Reluctantly she was becoming convinced that the government was maintaining a holding action in dealing with her. She knew that she alone could not move an obstinate government.

Ewa Shadrin retained the services of Richard Copaken, a

partner in the old-line Washington law firm of Covington &
Burling. Copaken was recommended by Robert Kupperman, who
once described the feisty young lawyer as "bright and aggressive
—a man who has a willingness to slay dragons." Indeed, in
Copaken Mrs. Shadrin found a man who would lead her not only
against the dragons but down every road that held the faintest hope
of clues to Nick Shadrin.

Chapter 10

FROM the beginning of her quest Ewa Shadrin showed a remarkable faith in the United States government, considering that she had spent her formative years under Soviet domination. She was imbued with a cynicism and suspicion common to many people who have matured under a Communist bureaucracy. She believed that the state, no matter what its pretenses of benevolence, is an adversary—to be feared, hated, always suspected. Her sixteen years in the United States had alleviated this feeling to a degree, but still, the inclination was strong.

The anchor of Ewa Shadrin's life had been shorn away, leaving her adrift in a turbulent sea of confusion and contradiction, while *always* there remained the latent suspicion born of her origins in Communist Poland. What is remarkable is that she could suspend her natural feelings toward government to the extent that she did. Indeed, her initial faith in official Washington's goodwill was strong, though just beneath the surface smoldered her impatience, a bridling against the prospect of waiting for the bureaucracy to move. However, as a lone woman in a huge world she realized that she needed her government. Nick Shadrin probably was in custody 5,000 miles away, in the hands of a hostile bureaucracy that operated in the darkest secrecy behind a sinister veil known to the world as the Iron Curtain. Such an obstacle was so ominous, especially to Ewa Shadrin, that it seemed to her only another

213

strong government could confront it. It was with these feelings that she placed her faith in the highest officials in Washington.

Through the early weeks of Ewa Shadrin's agony there was no more faithful counselor and friend than Jim Wooten. While the Howes and Kuppermans provided critical moral support, Jim Wooten was the bedrock of Ewa Shadrin's faith that Nick would be returned safely. Wooten was the man who understood the intricacies of the operation in which Nick had been involved, as well as the bureaucracy they faced in seeking a resolution.

Wooten's resolute course may have been gratifying for Ewa Shadrin, but it was viewed differently by his superiors. The first storm clouds were spotted around the first of February. Wooten informed Ewa that Secretary of State Henry Kissinger, who by then had made several unsuccessful queries of the Soviets, had written a letter to the FBI indicating that one of its agents had undercut Mrs. Shadrin's faith in Kissinger's efforts. That agent, clearly, was Wooten.

This did not seem to shake Wooten's commitment to Ewa, his promise to fulfill his personal pledge to Nick Shadrin. However, it suggested that his assistance should be conducted with more discretion. He told Ewa that he remained absolutely committed to helping her, but he added that he hoped he would not have to retire early—a strange possibility that Ewa had not heard before.

On February 17, one week after Ewa Shadrin retained Richard Copaken, she asked Wooten to meet with them to brief Copaken on the case. Wooten readily agreed. Ewa suggested that they meet at Copaken's customary lunch spot, the elegant Sheraton-Carlton Hotel. Wooten demurred, saying that the place was crawling with FBI and KGB agents keeping each other under surveillance.

Wooten suggested they have lunch at Goldberg's Delly, also in downtown Washington, but catering to a different lunch clientele. It was a warm day, around twelve-thirty, when Copaken and Mrs. Shadrin arrived. They went through the line and then took their food trays to a corner table. When Wooten entered, he saw them and waved cheerfully, got his own food, and joined them.

For one hour Copaken questioned Wooten about various aspects of the case. The FBI man was helpful, frequently mentioning his own admiration for Nick Shadrin, as a man and as a patriot. Ewa was satisfied that she could continue to count on his support. Toward the end of the meeting Copaken asked Wooten how long it took the FBI to convince Shadrin to go to work as a double agent. "Oh, I suppose it took a couple of days," Wooten replied.

Until that moment Ewa Shadrin had said almost nothing. But when she heard this, she became incredulous. "But, Jim," she said, "you told us at our meeting at the Kuppermans' that it took close to a year to persuade Nick and that Rufus Taylor got him to do it." Ewa's voice reflected perplexity more than anything else.

"Ewa," said Jim Wooten evenly, "I did not tell you these things." He looked directly at her, his large, dark eyes impassive. Ewa glanced at Copaken and started to say something more, but she sensed that her attorney did not think she should. He moved on to other subjects, later explaining to Ewa his feeling that there was no reason to antagonize Wooten at that point by having a confrontation. The meeting ended on a friendly note.

Twelve days later, on February 29, 1976, James Wooten retired from the FBI. He was fifty-four years old and had served the bureau for more than twenty-eight years.* He cited the health of his wife as his reason for quitting. But Wooten continued to be friendly to Ewa Shadrin, even assisting in the preparation of a letter from her to the attorney general asking for financial assistance in her legal fees.

At the end of May Wooten telephoned Mrs. Shadrin to say that he was moving to a western state because doctors believed the climate would be better for his wife's health. In July Ewa went to the office of a real estate agent near Solomons Island to discuss the possible sale of her property there and happened to meet Jim Wooten and his wife, who were negotiating the sale of their home in that area. Wooten was friendly, promising to send Ewa his address and telephone number once they were settled in their new home, which he did. But that was the last time they saw each other.

At about the time of the meeting at Goldberg's Delly efforts by Henry Kissinger took him yet again to Soviet Ambassador Dobrynin. On this occasion the veteran Soviet diplomat stated to Kissinger, in reference to Shadrin: "He is not in the Soviet Union."

*William J. Lander, a top FBI Soviet counterintelligence official at that period, has told the author adamantly that Wooten's retirement had nothing to do with his assistance to Ewa Shadrin—that the reasons were purely personal and aimed at taking certain advantages in the federal retirement system.

Replied Kissinger: "This answer is not sufficient for the United States."

The Soviets clearly were becoming exasperated by discussion of the Shadrin matter. A cable from Moscow advised the State Department to tell those interested in the Shadrin case to direct any further inquiries to the American Red Cross. However, nothing fruitful developed from that suggestion.

Ewa Shadrin was beginning to grasp the magnitude of the troubles she faced. It was increasingly clear that she had to broaden her own efforts. So far not a single answer of hopeful substance had come from the government. And her friend Robert Kupperman was being told by his friends at the State Department that he would be wise to disassociate himself from the Shadrin matter.

Mrs. Shadrin was gratified that she had retained the services of Richard Copaken. At thirty-four, he already was known around Washington for his perseverance, even brashness, in espousing a client's position. A short, robust man with a balding dome, he is intense and outwardly friendly. As an avid fan of spy movies he was particularly well disposed toward their case. There would be much disagreement among Ewa's friends over some of Copaken's tactics, but few ever questioned his absolute commitment to the case. His feisty style—bluntly jumping in with both feet—rankled bureaucrats of every stripe. Discretion did not stand in the way of advocacy, and it soon was clear that he would stop at nothing in this matter.

One of the first orders of business was to get in touch with Admiral Rufus Taylor, to learn more about the role he had played in recruiting his friend Shadrin into the double operation. William Howe had known Taylor for at least twenty-five years, and he had known him best during the years when Taylor was Director of Naval Intelligence. Howe was well aware of the close association between Taylor and Shadrin. He even recalled when Taylor had once gone to bat for Shadrin in trying to get him a security clearance.

Howe called Admiral Taylor, by then retired, to ask him about his old friend Nick Shadrin. "Nick *who?*" Admiral Taylor said to Howe. "Shadrin? I never heard of him."

Incredulous, Howe insisted that it was impossible that Taylor could not remember Shadrin. Finally, the admiral conceded that he had known Shadrin but vehemently denied he had had anything to do with recruiting him into the double operation. He did, however, suggest other people Bill Howe might contact.*

Meanwhile, telephone calls were going out from government officials to people who had known Shadrin, professional associates as well as friends. Colonel Weltman, Shadrin's boss at the Defense Intelligence Agency, was told: "Stay away from Ewa Shadrin." Reginald Kicklighter, Shadrin's old adversary at DIA, telephoned a number of people, including Tom Koines, and told them not to discuss the case with anyone.

The initial White House strategy was to appoint a special person as the contact point for Copaken and Mrs. Shadrin. On February 20, 1976, they met with William G. Hyland, a veteran intelligence man then serving as assistant to the President for national security affairs. Hyland had been designated by National Security Adviser Brent Scowcroft as the White House official to keep tabs on the Shadrin case. Practically from the start, Hyland and Copaken were at odds. While Copaken's distrust of Hyland grew with each encounter, Hyland was increasingly astonished at, in his words, Copaken's "naïveté which led to successive disasters."

Mrs. Shadrin and Copaken had been extremely cautious in deciding with whom they would discuss the case. It was soon clear that the position of the government—the CIA, the FBI, the State Department, the White House—was that the tightest possible security should be maintained. But it also became increasingly clear that if anything was to be accomplished, Mrs. Shadrin and her attorney and friends were going to have to make it happen. This feeling was cemented in late February, when Brent Scowcroft, after having met with various diplomatic and intelligence officials, gave Ewa the impression that the government did not have a working plan to secure Shadrin's return.

In an interview with the author, William Hyland stated that a crucial factor from the beginning was that once the government pressed the Soviets through diplomatic channels and elicited a negative reply on Shadrin, there was nothing more that could be done officially for an appropriate length of time. The U.S.

---

*Amazed that Admiral Taylor would have initially claimed he did not know Shadrin, Mary Louise Howe called him again a few days later. Taylor sounded fine and offered admiring comments about Nick. He told Mrs. Howe that while he had nothing to do with recruiting Shadrin, he believed that Tom Karamessines, head of CIA's clandestine operations under Helms, would know all about it. Unfortunately Mrs. Howe was unable to talk to Karamessines, who has since died.

government could not persist in asking about Shadrin after the Soviets stated flatly that they could not help. Such persistence would only harden the Soviet position.

Hyland asserts that this was why he and others sought to prevent an early meeting between Mrs. Shadrin and President Ford. After the Soviets' denial of knowledge in the early part of 1976 no useful purpose would be served in getting President Ford involved. Hyland and others felt it was far better to hold the Ford card to be played after an appropriate interval.

"But we also felt we had to let Mrs. Shadrin try anything she and her attorney wanted to," says Hyland. "It would have been callous to stand in her way, but there was a limit to what we could do officially to help them." Hyland claims this was the official attitude behind subtly and unofficially paving the way for the efforts to make an exchange.

Copaken scoffs at the suggestion of goodwill on the part of the White House at this early juncture. Satisfied that the government either could not or would not act officially, Copaken moved in early March to contact Wolfgang Vogel, the East German attorney who gained fame in 1962 for arranging the swap of U-2 pilot Francis Gary Powers for Rudolf Abel. Vogel also played a role in arranging less-celebrated swaps of spies in the East-West espionage wars. The suggestion that Copaken contact Vogel came from the State Department, indicating that at least some elements within the government wanted to help.

At an early March meeting with Vogel in Berlin, Copaken suggested an exchange of Shadrin for Günter Guillaume, the East German spy whose capture had brought down the Willy Brandt government. Vogel told Copaken he believed Shadrin was alive and in Soviet custody. The East German warned emphatically that if any information discussed in the private Copaken-Vogel channel were ever echoed in diplomatic channels, the Soviets would interpret it as a signal that the United States did not desire Shadrin's release.

On March 23 Copaken had another meeting with Vogel in Berlin and again came away with heartening news. Vogel informed Copaken that following their first meeting, he had been told by the East German intelligence service that he could have no further meetings with Copaken. However, Vogel claimed he had appealed this to Erich Honecker, head of the East German government.

Copaken says that Vogel told him that Honecker had conferred by telephone with Leonid Brezhnev on the Shadrin question and won permission for Vogel to have a subsequent meeting with Copaken.

Vogel's interpretation of these events, according to Copaken, was that Shadrin was alive, in Soviet custody, and available for an exchange. Vogel told Copaken that it would be tremendously helpful if Copaken could secure a letter from President Ford to Chairman Brezhnev, to be handed to Vogel for his use. Vogel believed that if Honecker could personally deliver such a letter to Brezhnev, he likely would be successful in setting the stage for Shadrin's release.

Again, according to Copaken, Vogel stressed the urgency of allowing no hint of the Copaken-Vogel channel to reach diplomatic ears. That, Vogel warned, would destroy whatever hope there was of winning Shadrin's release. Observers such as William Hyland insist that this was all part of the "soft-soaping" Vogel pulled on Copaken—that Vogel was simply an opportunist on a "fishing expedition" who hoped to win fame by becoming personally involved in an exchange for Shadrin.

Copaken returned to Ewa Shadrin with new high hopes—if he could only get the letter suggested by Vogel. On April 16 the White House did provide a version of the letter requested, an odd offering written on White House stationery from National Security Adviser Brent Scowcroft to Ewa Shadrin. According to Copaken, it was supposed to be a coded message from President Ford to Soviet Premier Brezhnev—*if* Copaken could succeed in selling it as such to Vogel. Copaken scurried about Washington in search of a handsome leather binder for the letter and a variety of imposing ribbons, all designed to dress up the letter to impress Vogel.

That evening, as Copaken was preparing to travel to Berlin for another meeting with Vogel, William Hyland telephoned him at home and explained that he had spoken with Yuli Vorontsov, a Soviet diplomat, who had asked him about Vogel. Hyland informed Copaken that he had told Vorontsov about the letter in Copaken's possession. Copaken was enraged, charging that Hyland had violated the ground rules of the negotiations. Hyland claims he could not lie to the Soviet diplomat by expressing ignorance of the Vogel developments. Such a lie, he says, would undercut the credibility of the whole operation. However, Copaken claims Hyland intentionally disrupted the whole scheme by informing the

Soviet diplomat of the Vogel-Copaken channel. Whatever the truth, Copaken flew off to Germany a few days later for his meeting with Vogel.

It was clear the moment Copaken saw Vogel, on April 22, that something had gone wrong. Vogel showed the lawyer a message he had received from the Soviets, which stated: "The Soviet side wishes no further discussion and warns of possible attempts at political blackmail. What Minister Kissinger was told still remains valid, including the statement that the Soviet side reserves the right to return to the question of Artamonov's return to the Soviet Union."

Copaken was furious. He could only connect the Soviet message with Hyland's informing the Soviet diplomat of the impending meeting. What made it worse was Vogel's assurance that the leather-bound White House letter would have served quite well as an instrument to help him in dealing with the Soviet leaders who might be able to assist in recovering Shadrin.

Also present at this meeting was Francis J. Meehan, a highly respected foreign service officer, later ambassador to Poland. The reason for Meehan's presence is in dispute. Copaken says he was sent because he was long acquainted with Vogel and would be able to make a fair assessment of the merits of the situation. Hyland states flatly: "We sent Meehan to look after Copaken. The last thing we wanted was this kid running around Berlin playing master spy. We were afraid something might happen to him."

In any event, the Vogel initiative seemed to collapse. Copaken returned to the United States, where he informed Ewa Shadrin that the Soviets seemed to have ordered Vogel to cease negotiations. It was, of course, enormously disheartening to Ewa.

On May 3 Vogel telephoned Francis Meehan, who was stationed in Vienna, and told him that his authorization to deal for Shadrin had been withdrawn by the Soviets. Five weeks later Vogel wrote to Copaken stating that his authorization had been withdrawn.

Following the collapse of the Vogel overture, on May 13, Henry Kissinger again asked Ambassador Dobrynin about Shadrin. Dobrynin said the Soviets did not have him, adding that he hoped Kissinger would not raise the Shadrin question again. Kissinger responded that he knew from Vogel that the Soviets had Shadrin. Dobrynin is said to have answered, "Vogel is not authorized to speak for us." While Copaken claims this was yet another violation of Vogel's ground rules by Kissinger, it would seem apparent that the Vogel prospects were, at this late point, hopeless.

What remains today of the efforts to secure Shadrin through Vogel is a seething caldron of accusations between Copaken and Ford administration figures over who did what to whom as the effort evaporated. In the end Copaken bitterly denounced Hyland and Kissinger for wrecking the Vogel channel on purpose. Hyland calls these charges nonsense and states: "If I made any mistake it was in allowing Copaken, an overly enthusiastic amateur, to enter into this with delusions of being a master manipulator."

A year later, when the Shadrin case burst its wraps in a welter of confusing published accounts, Henry Kissinger stoutly denied Copaken's allegations that he had undermined negotiations for Shadrin's release. Telling reporters that the charges represented "an irresponsible distortion," Kissinger added, "There are few cases in which the United States has so exerted itself."

Whatever the truth, Copaken tried frantically to get word to President Ford directly concerning the Shadrin matter. Every effort was frustrated by Hyland and others who believed the President should not yet be involved. On May 14 the irrepressible Copaken found his opening. As a former White House Fellow he was invited to a reception hosted by President Ford. "I believed Shadrin's life was at stake," says Copaken. "It was urgent that President Ford be told what was going on." Copaken sidled up to the President and began bearding him directly about the Shadrin case. Copaken told Ford that he hoped the President would meet with Mrs. Shadrin.

Apparently stunned, President Ford muttered that he was familiar with the case and hoped to become more directly involved after the primaries were over. He suggested that Copaken get directly in touch with John O. Marsh, counselor to the President. At that point, only a minute or two into the exchange, a presidential aide realized what was going on. Indignant and speaking in a way that attracted the attention of much of the gathering, the aide told Copaken that he should not attempt to involve President Ford, that it was important for the President to be removed from direct association with the case. His point made, Copaken politely retreated.

Once back at his office, however, Copaken immediately telephoned Marsh to say that President Ford had personally told him to get Marsh to brief him on the Shadrin matter. Five days later Copaken and Ewa Shadrin met Marsh, who received them graciously in his office, listened to a full briefing, and promised he would try to help. Obviously, none of this suited William Hyland, the man supposedly handling the Shadrin case for the White House, or others who had opposed Copaken's access to Ford.

There is little doubt that by this time Copaken had gotten under plenty of official skins, especially at the White House. "These were sensitive issues," recalls one White House official of that period. "We believed that Copaken was walking on dangerous ground, that he possibly could do something or say something that would reveal sensitive issues, and that he might even endanger Shadrin."

It is not surprising that Copaken recalls the primary issue at that time in a slightly different light. His most important objective, suggested by a Vogel representative, was to secure a letter from the White House that would impress upon Vogel the fact that the United States government would respect his ground rules in the future, particularly the point that called for no diplomatic contacts concerning the Copaken-Vogel negotiations on Shadrin.

In early June there was a meeting at the White House that included Philip W. Buchen, Bobbie Kilberg and William Hyland.* Copaken brought with him Daniel Gribbon, a senior partner of Covington & Burling. The primary purpose of this meeting remains in dispute. Copaken insists that the main issue was to secure the letter promising no future interference in the Vogel channel. Hyland, Buchen, and others recall that there was great concern over Copaken's entire approach to the case and a feeling that it would be better handled under the supervision of someone else. That was the reason for the presence of Gribbon.

Whatever else may have been on the agenda, the White House officials took the opportunity to tell Gribbon that someone with greater experience and discretion should be handling the Shadrin case, someone with more experience in dealing with sensitive matters. A second point raised by the White House officials concerned the fact that the Justice Department had been paying Mrs. Shadrin's bills from Covington & Burling. At least two of the White House officials have stated that Copaken's fees seemed unwarranted in view of the flimsy results he was getting. Still

---

*John O. Marsh recalls meeting at the White House with a senior partner of Covington & Burling who assured Marsh and other White House officials that the firm had confidence in Copaken. Marsh believes there was an indication that there would be some guidance for Copaken from more senior partners of the firm.

shaking his head over the Covington & Burling bills, Hyland says, "It was hard to believe they would charge such fees to someone in Mrs. Shadrin's situation."

The message from the White House seemed clear: Get the abrasive Copaken off the case or the government would stop paying the legal bills. "Of course, we wanted him off the case," says Hyland. "It was nearly impossible to deal with him." But Gribbon instantly dismissed the idea of removing Copaken. He indicated to the White House officials that if the government would not pay Mrs. Shadrin's legal bills, the law firm would absorb them.

When the dust had settled, Copaken was not removed from the case and the government did not at that point stop paying Ewa Shadrin's bills from Covington & Burling.* Copaken succeeded in getting a satisfactory letter for his future dealings with Vogel. But if anything, the contentiousness that existed between Copaken and the White House was greater than ever.

In May 1976 the Japanese arrested a TASS correspondent who had tried to bribe a U.S. seaman for naval secrets. Copaken immediately began dickering with the State Department to see if this might be an avenue for an exchange, but the Japanese quickly released the Soviet spy when the Russians threatened retaliation against Japanese journalists in Moscow.

At last, seven months after Shadrin's disappearance, the press learned about the case. It is astounding that in a journalism town like Washington, Mrs. Shadrin and others managed to keep the story under wraps for seven months following Shadrin's disappearance.† She and Copaken sincerely respected the fundamental point that any chance for negotiations with the Soviets would be destroyed by publicity. That, after all, was the government's basic reason for telling Mrs. Shadrin not to let the case reach the public. In this regard, she lived up to her end of the bargain magnificently.

---

*In all, the government paid about $78,000 in legal bills over three years. This left Mrs. Shadrin owing Covington & Burling about $250,000 in legal fees. Her out-of-pocket payments for Copaken's trips and expenses have amounted to $20,000. It is Mrs. Shadrin's understanding that Covington & Burling has no intention of trying to collect from her, that the firm recognizes it is a bill she is unable to pay. Covington & Burling refuses to comment on whether it plans to collect. Mrs. Shadrin's former congressman, Joseph Fisher of Virginia, introduced special legislation that would have provided for paying the balance of her legal bills; but Fisher was defeated for reelection in 1980, and the bill died in committee.

†During the original spy swap efforts in March, New York Times reporter David Binder made queries at the State Department that suggested to officials that he was close to learning details. In an FBI report of the incident, one official tells another: "His [Binder's] attempted bluff was seen through and no comment was made."

In July Washington columnist Jack Anderson confronted Mrs. Shadrin and Copaken with the facts of the story. They were essentially correct. Copaken turned at once to William Hyland, the highest contact point he had in the government. According to Copaken, Hyland told him to tell Anderson that his facts were all wrong. Hyland warned him that a Jack Anderson story would wreck any chance of securing Shadrin's return.

Copaken, in righteous indignation, responded that he would not consider lying to Jack Anderson or anyone else. Along with Mrs. Shadrin, Copaken went to Anderson's office and told him that his facts were essentially correct. "He was cold and gruff and testy," recalls Mrs. Shadrin. "He told us he would have to recheck all of his facts to see if a story would really hurt Nick's chances of being returned." Meanwhile, Hyland himself called Anderson on behalf of the White House and urged his cooperation.

A few days later Anderson told Mrs. Shadrin that he would hold off publication if he had Copaken's promise that he would be given the jump on the story when it finally broke. Copaken agreed, and Anderson kept his word. A year later, as the story began to tumble out, Copaken urgently phoned Anderson. It was too late to get the story in his column, but he still scooped everyone else with the news on his radio report.

But no sooner had Copaken pacified Jack Anderson than he found himself approaching Stanley Karnow, a columnist who had covered foreign affairs for years. Karnow had been recommended to Copaken by a mutual friend. After the collapse of negotiations with Wolfgang Vogel, Copaken wanted to get in touch with Victor Louis, a Soviet "journalist" who might be able to help. The approach took place in September, with Karnow's assistance.

Much later, on July 25, 1977, after Karnow had been scooped by Jack Anderson, the Washington *Post*, and the *Wall Street Journal*, the following account of the incident appeared under his by-line in *Newsweek*'s international edition:

> Like many reporters, I knew Victor Louis, a KGB operative who ostensibly makes his living as a Soviet journalist. Would I set up a meeting with Louis? I agreed on two conditions: that I be given the full Shadrin story and that I get first rights to publish it when we deemed it could be made public without risking the chances for Shadrin's release.*

---

*Copaken claims he never promised exclusivity to Karnow.

> . . . I contacted Louis and arranged for a rendezvous with him in Helsinki. . . . Copaken and I flew there together and sat down with Louis on a park bench, where Copaken related his tale of Shadrin, an innocent tourist, being kidnapped by KGB agents. . . . Copaken suggested a series of possible trades for Louis to consider.

Karnow stresses that Louis thought it was fairly senseless even to try to get Shadrin released, pointing out that the Soviet military would oppose the release. But Louis told Copaken that he would try to see what he could do. In Karnow's view, Louis did this for reasons of his own—including trying to secure Copaken's representation in a libel action he was pursuing in the United States. Subsequently Louis told Copaken that he had raised the Shadrin question in Moscow and that it provoked "an embarrassed silence."

Also in September, a Soviet MiG pilot named Viktor Belenko flew his plane to Japan and requested U.S. asylum. Copaken tried desperately to get William Hyland and the State Department to tie the Soviet request for an interview with Belenko to providing Copaken some access to Shadrin. The request was considered and rejected.

In October 1976 Copaken spotted another possible opening after a Soviet named Valentin Zasimov flew a small plane into Iran and sought political asylum in the United States. Copaken asked the White House to request that the Iranian government, *if* it decided to return Zasimov to the Soviets anyway, tie the return to Shadrin's release. William Hyland told Copaken there was not the slightest possibility that the Iranians would return Zasimov to the Soviets. However, upon Copaken's insistence, Hyland said consideration would be given to the request.

Many times over the previous nine months Copaken had spoken with CIA Counterintelligence Chief George Kalaris. CIA Director George Bush had appointed Kalaris as the contact for Copaken and Mrs. Shadrin, instructing him to assist them wherever possible. On October 8 Copaken and Mrs. Shadrin drove out to CIA headquarters for a meeting with Director George Bush and Kalaris to discuss, among other things, getting the Iranians to tie any possible return of Zasimov to the release of Shadrin. Also present at the meeting was Chester Cooper, formerly of the CIA, and an old friend of the Howes who had been helpful since the beginning. Bush reiterated what Hyland had said earlier: that there was not the remotest possibility that the Iranians would return Zasimov to the Soviets.

Then Copaken raised a point that had increasingly troubled him. Considering the apparent intractability of the government in doing anything about the Shadrin matter, he was prompted to ask Bush if all the events could be a cover for some sort of assignment Shadrin was on. Copaken said that if they could only learn the truth, they were willing to do whatever the government suggested to maintain the cover. He pointed out that they had been successful in keeping the story under wraps so far.

Bush and Kalaris assured them there was no possibility of that. It was not worth further discussion.

Copaken's most urgent request of Bush, however, was that he intervene at the White House and arrange an appointment for Mrs. Shadrin with President Ford. Copaken explained that he had been thwarted in every effort to have the President personally hear Mrs. Shadrin's plea. He appealed to Bush to use his own personal friendship with President Ford to arrange a meeting for Mrs. Shadrin. Bush promised that he would do his best.

Two weeks later it was announced that the Iranians had decided to return Zasimov to the Soviets. Copaken telephoned William Hyland, who expressed surprise over the development. Because the return had not yet been consummated, Hyland agreed to Copaken's request that he try to tie the actual return to Shadrin's release.

According to Copaken, Hyland telephoned him the next day to say that at President Ford's personal request, Ambassador Richard Helms had raised the Shadrin matter with the Iranians, who said that only the shah could make such a decision—and he was unavailable.* There is no evidence the request was ever acted on one way or the other. The next day the Iranians returned Zasimov to the Soviets.

After months of futile effort Copaken's attempts to get Mrs. Shadrin an audience with President Ford paid off with his end run through George Bush. An unhappy William Hyland met Copaken and Mrs. Shadrin at the White House on the afternoon of

---

*Hyland does not remember what message he relayed to Copaken. Helms's recollection is that he did not raise the Shadrin matter with the shah or other Iranians because the shah had already told him that they were going to send Zasimov back, in accordance with a treaty between Iran and the Soviet Union.

November 5. Hyland was adamant—despite Ewa's pleas—that Copaken could not be present for her meeting with Ford. He told Copaken he would have to remain in the waiting room of the Oval Office, that President Ford wanted to talk to Mrs. Shadrin alone—not with her attorney. "I didn't want Copaken making a scene with the President," says Hyland.

For many months during the presidential campaign Mrs. Shadrin had seen President Ford's smiling face on television and in newspapers. It was not the face that greeted her that afternoon at the White House. Perhaps it was because the preceding day he had lost the presidency to Jimmy Carter. President Ford stood as Mrs. Shadrin entered the room with William Hyland and motioned for her to sit in an armchair across from him. Hyland sat on a sofa.

"He was cold and austere," recalls Mrs. Shadrin. "He never even faintly smiled when he greeted me. And I don't know if he heard anything I said. His eyes seemed glazed over like a bull-frog's while I talked." If anything, President Ford's coldness reminded her of the indifference of another government official—the strange Miss Hausmann who had been in charge of Nick in Vienna.

Mrs. Shadrin was in the Oval Office for less than fifteen minutes. President Ford said almost nothing, only glancing at Hyland occasionally as Mrs. Shadrin told him of her plight. She requested that he write to Soviet leader Leonid Brezhnev and ask directly for Nick's return.

President Ford told her that he would think about it, that he did not want to make a "snap judgment." Mrs. Shadrin's initial reaction to Ford's lukewarm assurances was that he was no more decisive than any of the other bureaucrats she and Copaken had been dealing with.

The exception seemed to be George Bush, who had warmly received Mrs. Shadrin and seemed genuinely interested in helping alleviate her plight. He even went a step farther. In late November, when Bush went to Plains, Georgia, to brief the incoming President about intelligence matters, he informed Carter about the background and status of the Shadrin case.

Finally, on December 3, 1976—nearly one year after Shadrin's disappearance—President Ford sent a letter to Soviet Chairman Brezhnev. The exact wording is not known, but William Hyland informed Copaken and Mrs. Shadrin that the President said that he would like to know what had happened to Shadrin. He asked for Brezhnev's assistance in having Shadrin returned to his wife.

On Christmas Eve, one year from that miserable day when Ewa had flown home accompanied by the enigmatic Bruce, the White House received Brezhnev's response. It was conveyed orally by Yuli Vorontsov, then the second highest official at the Soviet Embassy, to Hyland, who informed President Ford. On December 27 Hyland called Ewa and Copaken to the White House to read them his notes on Brezhnev's response. Copaken expected Brezhnev to say that he could not help, that the Soviets simply knew nothing of Shadrin's last visit to Vienna.

But Brezhnev's message was something quite different, according to the version given Copaken and Mrs. Shadrin by William Hyland. Brezhnev stated that records had been consulted in Moscow and that he could report to President Ford that *Shadrin had never arrived for his second meeting with the Soviets.*

Copaken was stunned. It was one thing for this to have been conveyed through lower channels and quite another to have direct word from Brezhnev. Considering the obvious answers Brezhnev could have given that would have done nothing to risk his integrity with Ford, he gave an answer that was startling in its apparent candor. How could Brezhnev speak with such confidence? How could he know that there was no surveillance by the CIA of the meeting—given the exceptional ease with which surveillance could have been maintained? How could he be sure that during the past year the United States had not acquired photographs, perhaps from some passing tourist, showing that the second meeting did take place?

Why would Brezhnev risk polluting his channel of trust with the American President unless the KGB had advised him with absolute certainty that Shadrin had never shown up for the second meeting? What minion in the KGB would dare risk responsibility for advice to Brezhnev that might later be the basis for exposing the Soviet leader as a blatant liar to the United States President in a direct message—especially when there were so many other things that could have been said.

These questions—all basically unanswerable—contributed to the grim suspicions that were beginning to pester Mrs. Shadrin and her attorney. Was it possible, they wondered, that the United

States—even at the highest levels—knew much more about Shadrin's disappearance than was being admitted? The suspicion fed the growing feeling that maybe the enemy was in Washington instead of Moscow, that for reasons convoluted to the extreme, it somehow served U.S. intelligence purposes to abort Shadrin's second meeting with the Soviets.

Or of course, the KGB could have picked up Shadrin on his way to the meeting—perhaps the moment he stepped from the Hotel Bristol to hail a taxi. That might explain why the KGB could advise Brezhnev to state flatly to President Ford that Shadrin had never shown up at the Votivkirche. Whatever was behind the message, it was compelling evidence that indeed, Shadrin had never reached the meeting site.

By this time Copaken and his sturdy client had little reason to believe the United States authorities were acting in good faith toward them. Despite all the high-level posturing, nothing whatsoever had been accomplished in the quest for Nick's return. Not a single exchange effort had been backed with any consistency by the government. More than ever Copaken and Mrs. Shadrin realized they had to move ahead forcefully, even abrasively, if they hoped to make any progress.

There was some new hope, however, with the advent of the Carter administration. The incoming President had promised that his deep concern for human rights would be a hallmark of his administration, and certainly this bode well for the Shadrin effort. Even before Carter took office, Copaken telephoned Charles H. Kirbo, the man who would come to be known as Carter's "one-man kitchen cabinet." Copaken explained the Shadrin situation to Kirbo, saying he wanted him to know the background of the case. According to Copaken, Kirbo listened and then explained that in his opinion, a man with Nick's background was probably untrustworthy, that if he would betray his native country, he likely would betray his adopted one. It was clear that Charles Kirbo was not going to be in the forefront of any enthusiasm for helping Ewa Shadrin.*

Still, the Carter administration gave Mrs. Shadrin and Copaken an entirely new set of officials upon whom they could try their

---

*Kirbo stated in 1980 that he had no recollection of Copaken's call and that he had never expressed such sentiments about any defector.

skills. As early as February Copaken succeeded in getting Secretary of State Cyrus Vance to raise the Shadrin issue with Ambassador Dobrynin, who stated, as he had so many times before, that the Soviets knew nothing of Shadrin's whereabouts.

Two weeks before President Carter took office, Copaken had received word that it was possible for him to meet again with Wolfgang Vogel in West Germany, that there were new possibilities for prisoner exchanges that might involve Shadrin. After consultations with administration officials, Copaken met Vogel in Berlin on February 22 with a shopping list of about seventy-five names of persons detained in foreign countries in whom the Soviets were known to have an interest. The names had been provided to Copaken by the CIA, at the prompting of the Carter officials,

Vogel reviewed the entire list and told Copaken that he believed there were three possibilities that might particularly interest the Soviets. They were Günter Guillaume and his wife, prisoners in West Germany, and Jorges Montes, a prisoner in Chile. Zbigniew Brzezinski was informed of this Soviet interest and urged to move expeditiously to exploit the interest.

Mrs. Shadrin believed then that prompt action, initiated by President Carter himself, would quickly yield the Guillaumes or Montes for a trade. For the first time in more than a year there was reason for hope—reason to believe that the new administration had Nick and Ewa Shadrin's interests at heart. This quasi euphoria was heightened in February with the nearly thrilling news that the new director of the Central Intelligence Agency would be Admiral Stansfield Turner—a man who had known and admired Nick Shadrin for years. The avenues of possibility were spreading in several directions.

In April Copaken again met Vogel in Berlin. Ewa had prepared a handwritten note to Nick, to be delivered to him through Vogel. Vogel promised to deliver it, stating that if he was told by the Soviets it was impossible, he would return the letter to Copaken. (The letter has never been returned.) Vogel told Copaken there was still considerable Soviet interest in an exchange involving the Guillaumes and Montes. All indications were that high United States officials were working with the West German government and the Chilean government to make available these prisoners for the Shadrin swap.

While these efforts presumably were still going on, news suddenly came that Montes had been used in a trade for eleven East

Germans. So far, in Ewa's view, the Carter administration—while proclaiming its concern for human rights—had shown not the slightest inclination to become involved in getting back Shadrin. Toward the end of June Mrs. Shadrin managed to get Zbigniew Brzezinski on the telephone in her efforts toward a more personalized approach.

She never expected any warmth from Brzezinski, but she was shocked at his coldness when, according to Ewa, he stated: "A lot of U.S. citizens get in trouble while abroad. Your husband is not the only U.S. citizen in a foreign prison. We have many cases like this."* Stunned, Mrs. Shadrin tried to explain that this really was not just another case of an American in trouble, that her husband had been on a very special assignment in service to the United States—an assignment that now had been acknowledged by the government.

Brzezinski told her that if she believed President Carter should be involved personally, she should write a letter requesting an appointment with him. Immediately Mrs. Shadrin wrote a formal request to Brzezinski, asking to see Carter. Again she felt the old faint hope rising.

But there was little reason to hope. A prompt reply came from Brzezinski stating that a meeting with President Carter was unlikely, although everyone in the administration who was aware of her problem could "fully sympathize with your sense of frustration and anxiety." Ewa Shadrin wondered if, indeed, there was anyone at the White House who could sympathize with her terrible and growing predicament. Unbeknownst to Ewa, but according to Brzezinski, the White House continued to press top Soviet specialists in the State Department for a resolution, and Brzezinski raised the matter with Dobrynin "more than once."

As a last desperate effort to make some personal contact at the White House, Mrs. Shadrin sent a plea in the form of a letter to Rosalynn Carter, appealing to her on a woman-to-woman basis for help in getting her husband returned. Two weeks later Mrs. Shadrin was informed that Mrs. Carter would not respond to the request—even to answer the letter—but that she sent her sympathy.

---

*Brzezinski recalls the exchange somewhat differently, explaining that he was comparing Mrs. Shadrin's difficult situation to that of families of POWs and MIAs. Still, Ewa felt Nick's assignment was not comparable to military duty.

Meanwhile, Copaken was still rattling every door in town as he tried to initiate an exchange. His highest hope was with the Guillaumes, who were being held in West Germany. Chancellor Helmut Schmidt was due to arrive in Washington on July 13, and Copaken did everything possible to ensure that President Carter would raise the matter with him.

But just before Schmidt's arrival, Copaken was given a message from the State Department—a message that a White House deeply concerned about human rights did not have the gall to deliver. Copaken and Mrs. Shadrin were officially informed that in light of the current difficulties in relations between the United States and the Soviet Union, no extraordinary efforts could be made to win Shadrin's release. Two high government sources informed Copaken that in the official view of the United States government, Shadrin was simply too expendable to be handled in such a high-level manner.

"They were telling me there was no longer any reason for me to count on my government doing anything to get Nick back, beyond just waiting for something to happen," says Ewa Shadrin.

Thus, it became clear that the United States government had abandoned Ewa Shadrin in her quest to find her husband. Moreover, and perhaps worse, it was clear that the government had abandoned Nick Shadrin as well. For more than eighteen months Mrs. Shadrin and Copaken had largely played everything the government's way, scrupulously avoiding publicity that might have borne unfavorably on the government's purported efforts to win Shadrin's release.

Finally, it was clear that they had been led down a garden path, that no one high in government was actively interested in getting back Nick Shadrin. Every indication of good faith, in the final analysis, had been only an effort to pacify Mrs. Shadrin and her supporters. It was as if the government wanted only to contain the story, to cover itself, to conceal from the world that it had abandoned a good citizen who was working in its service. Ewa Shadrin realized the time had come to accept that the government had lied to her, that it had shown only bad faith. It was a performance she would have expected from the sort of government from which she had escaped. There was but one avenue left—one that hardly another country in the world could offer.

It was time to go public.

It probably will never be known at what point the CIA sensed that Copaken and Mrs. Shadrin had been played to their limit. But by early July 1977 bits of the story had begun to find their way to the Washington *Post*—bits of the story infused with bitter drops of poison that not a single source in the government had ever intimated to Mrs. Shadrin or to Copaken. The implication was that really, after all, Nicholas Shadrin was probably a traitor to the United States, that it was likely he had gone back to the Soviet Union on his own.

When Copaken learned that the story was about to break in the Washington *Post*, he had no illusions about how it had got there. In Copaken's opinion, it had been handed to the newspaper by people within the government whose purposes were served by getting its version out ahead of Copaken's. He also learned that the *Post* story was going to contain the allegation that Shadrin was a phony defector to begin with, that he had been suspected all along as being such. Copaken realized that this account was precisely what would best serve the purposes of the CIA.

Copaken did not wait to react to the story that would appear in the *Post*. He had already prepared his strategy in case something like this happened. He had been in frequent touch with an old friend who was a reporter for the *Wall Street Journal*. He and Mrs. Shadrin had briefed the reporter thoroughly and in confidence about the Shadrin case. When the time came, Copaken wanted someone to be able to tell the story as his client saw it.

The time had come. Copaken alerted the *Wall Street Journal* reporter. More than that, he made certain the Washington *Post* knew he had alerted the *Journal*—a move Copaken hoped would make the *Post* look more carefully at the sources of its own information. Not only did Copaken intend to get out what he considered to be the true story, but he intended to force the *Post* to be exceedingly careful in printing what he considered reckless allegations leaked to it by the government. Copaken clearly had learned enough about the bureaucratic mentality to realize that there was no greater guiding influence than the threat of being exposed as foolish. That, he hoped, was what the *Post* would consider.*

Of course, the *Wall Street Journal* did not take Copaken's word

---

*Robert Kaiser, the reporter who wrote the *Post* story, dismisses Copaken's contention. Kaiser has told the author that the information was not handed to him. He was given a lead on the story by a source he considers reliable and then pieced together the rest of it.

for anything. Before printing the story, the *Journal* went to a variety of its sources, including the FBI, which referred it to the State Department. On July 13, 1977, the telephones at Copaken's office began to ring. He had already made sure Mrs. Shadrin was on hand. The earliest calls were from an official who said the White House wanted to know how the information had gotten to the *Wall Street Journal*. Then came equally frantic calls from officials at the State Department. Other government officials called. Copaken informed them all that he and Mrs. Shadrin were going public, that they had disseminated the information.

Then came an almost-desperate telephone call from a high official representing the White House, pleading that if Copaken could just hold off the publicity, something could be done. Helmut Schmidt was in Washington that very day, due to see President Carter. Perhaps it would be possible, after all, to raise the issue of trading the Guillaumes for Shadrin. The official begged Copaken to give America's self-professed champion of human rights one more chance to act honorably toward Shadrin.

After consulting with Mrs. Shadrin, Copaken told them all that it was too late. They had waited for eighteen months and borne the brunt of lies, deceptions, and bad faith. Their only hope was to go it alone, trusting that the bright light of publicity would bring new revelations. But the editors at the two newspapers were cautious, wanting to be certain they publicized nothing that would jeopardize any hope for Nicholas Shadrin. Then Ben Bradlee, editor of the Washington *Post*, consulted directly with Mrs. Shadrin about how she thought the publicity would bear upon her husband's fate. In the end, the editors decided to go ahead.

The next day the stories ran in the Washington *Post* and the *Wall Street Journal*; the wire services wrote their own. Copaken and Ewa appeared on ABC's *Good Morning America* show, and were interviewed by Jack Anderson.

The story was flowing across the land and around the world.

Jack Leggat was having lunch alone in a restaurant in Southern California. He customarily saved his newspaper to read during lunch. There before him was the astounding story about his old friend Nick Shadrin. "I could hardly believe what I was reading," says Leggat. "It was all incredible—that Nick would have been pulled into such an operation, that someone would have been stupid enough to let him go to Vienna."

Leggat finished reading the story and went to the nearest pay telephone. After several attempts, he finally reached Herman Dworkin, a mutual acquaintance of Leggat and Nick's who had been with the Office of Naval Intelligence. Leggat asked Dworkin what on earth was going on. "Remember, Jack, you always said intelligence was a dirty business," Leggat recalls Dworkin saying. Leggat questioned him more closely and realized he was becoming intensely upset. "Dworkin would tell me nothing," says Leggat. "He was clearly scared to death of something."

As Leggat probed further before getting in touch with Ewa, he found that lips everywhere were sealed. Even the closest friends refused to discuss the case. The word had gone out that nothing was to be said to anyone about the Shadrin case.

During this period Mrs. Shadrin was trying to arrange to see General Sam Wilson, then the head of DIA. General Wilson had initially declined to see her, claiming that he really did not know enough to be of any assistance. But Robert Herrick, who was doing what he could to help Ewa, got in touch with the general and convinced him to see her.

Herrick accompanied Mrs. Shadrin to see General Wilson at his office in the Pentagon. Ewa recalls Wilson as being friendly, open, and speaking very highly of Nick. Wilson also told them that the first thing he had done when he heard that Nick had vanished was to get in touch with all the people he could think of who knew anything about the case and tell them not to discuss it. That, perhaps, is why men like Herman Dworkin suddenly were mute.

Of course, there were extraneous ramifications from the publicity. A young man who said he was from North Carolina telephoned Mrs. Shadrin and told her he had information that might help her locate her husband. He proposed a meeting in the Washington area. Ewa, accompanied by Mary Louise Howe and backed up surreptitiously by an armed neighbor in law enforcement, met the young man at noon in a parking lot in Arlington. Standing in front of a large department store, she listened to his tale of being a former FBI agent. He said that he believed he could help her. But, he added, he needed $2,000 for his expenses in doing the work. Ewa told him that she did not have $2,000 and that if the Soviets had Nick, there really was not much he could do. There was no further contact, and Ewa saw no reason to report the young man for trying to get money under false pretenses.

During the first few days of the publicity a wide range of stories appeared across the country and in the foreign press. Copaken's handling of the press seemed to have neutralized to an acceptable degree the message spewing from some government sources that Shadrin was believed to be a phony defector. The account in the Washington *Post* raised the possibility but then tended to discount it.

The story in the *Wall Street Journal* adopted a tone that even Copaken could not have improved upon: "And U.S. officials aren't anxious to disclose the bureaucratic bungling that preceded his disappearance and the diplomatic blunders that may be keeping him in captivity. . . . When news of Mr. Shadrin's presumed kidnapping hit Washington, the bureaucracy scurried for cover."

In an account a few days after the story broke, the Washington *Post* again returned to the matter of Shadrin's bona fides in a rendition perhaps accurately reflecting what was going on during those days:

> Those who have cast doubts on Shadrin to this reporter are generally professional skeptics, including people whose job it is to be suspicious about Soviet defectors.
>
> But suspicion remains: the President's Intelligence Advisory Board, for example, investigated the case and said it could not thoroughly dispel suspicions about Artamonov/Shadrin's true status.
>
> Perhaps the doubters have an unfair advantage. No matter how persuasive the testimonials of friends and colleagues, no matter how strong the circumstantial evidence, a skeptic can always reply: "Yes, but if he was a brilliant triple agent, then of course he could fool anybody." Just so.

Many high officials have reacted strongly to the leaks that Shadrin was a suspect defector all along. The feeling is summed up by the comment of former DIA Director General Daniel Graham: "Such a suggestion is a calumny against the man I will not accept."

The most compelling evidence that Shadrin's bona fides were never in serious doubt lies in the fact that following his disappearance in Vienna—presumably into Soviet hands—there was never an investigation to assess the net damage generated by his loss. Shadrin had worked and socialized with people who held the highest security clearances in the United States. In the course of the author's interviews with dozens of these former friends and colleagues, not a single one recalled any signs of an investigation along these lines. While many agree that Shadrin would be a valuable source of information for the Soviets—whether or not he ever held high security clearances—not one was ever questioned about this in terms of his relationship with Shadrin. (The only wide-ranging investigation came years later when the Intelligence Oversight Board sought to determine any wrongdoing in the whole affair.)

So, if the government at some late date decides to take the stance that it all along suspected Shadrin's bona fides, it will have to answer the question of why it did nothing to determine the value of its loss at the time of his disappearance. That determination, after all, is the first step in neutralizing potential damage.

It seems ironic that if any government bureaucracy was helpful to Ewa Shadrin and Richard Copaken during the first eighteen months of their effort, it was the Central Intelligence Agency. One of the first CIA officers appointed by Director George Bush to help them was George Kalaris. Neither Copaken nor Mrs. Shadrin had any inkling of his role in playing Nick to the Soviets, but they found him apparently interested and helpful.

One of the most extraordinary, perhaps even unprecedented, moves of the CIA under Bush was to produce several of its clandestine officers for questioning by a private attorney, Copaken. Indeed, over her obvious objections, Cynthia Hausmann was taken before Richard Copaken, who, on two separate occasions in March 1976 grilled her for several hours about the night Shadrin was lost.

It was a poignant moment for Ewa Shadrin when she emerged from Copaken's office on the day of Miss Hausmann's first visit for questioning. There in the waiting room, seated a few feet from Ewa, was Miss Hausmann. A CIA attorney was sitting next to her. Ewa looked at her for a long moment, but Cynthia Hausmann studiously avoided her gaze. Ewa quickly left.

Of those CIA officers familiar with the Shadrin matter who have spoken to the author, most have had only criticism of the handling of matters in Vienna. William Colby, Director of Central Intelligence at the time of Shadrin's disappearance, said in an interview that he had been critical of the "deficient handling, the absence of countersurveillance, the fact no one was at the emergency number. Something really went wrong." No matter what else, it is simply beyond anyone's comprehension that Cynthia Hausmann would not be available at the emergency number when Mrs. Shadrin needed to reach her.

Among the puzzlements that night in Vienna is the period of time between the hour Miss Hausmann was dropped off at her apartment and the time when she was actually in the apartment to answer the telephone. Copaken went over this area with her dozens of times. She steadfastly refused to provide an answer. It is perhaps significant that she would not offer even a flimsy excuse, such as saying she was in the shower and not able to hear the phone ring the first time. According to Copaken, she simply states that she went directly to her apartment when she was dropped off, offering no explanation of the discrepancy that exists between her story and that of her host for the evening.

While the Vienna station chief at that time says without hesitation that he would give "poor marks" to Miss Hausmann for failing to be at the emergency number, stronger words come from veteran intelligence observer General Sam V. Wilson: "Primarily, it was just sloppy handling. It was a case being run on sort of the boundary line between the FBI and the CIA, and it just didn't get the attention it deserved. Somebody went to sleep at the switch. Somebody had a higher priority for some reason—or somebody had a slight head cold or what have you—and said the hell with it. It will work out all right. It was just a case of going to sleep and booting one as far as I'm concerned."

What would General Wilson do about such sloppiness? "If I had anything to do with it, the person would get fired. I would never give them another chance to do a thing like that. I feel hard about that sort of thing. Unless there were overriding circumstances of an extenuating nature, it should be just curtains for the individual as far as I'm concerned. From my distant view of this operation, the person responsible for this operation was guilty of gross malfeasance."

In addition to making Miss Hausmann available, the CIA arranged for Copaken to interview the station chief himself, who was in Washington on the date Shadrin vanished. Still, nothing revealing has been forthcoming—only the general account that has appeared here.

The CIA went quite a ways in cooperating with Copaken, but it could not call in all its personnel for polygraph tests just because of questions being raised by Copaken, a private attorney. That, clearly, would violate the basic trust that must exist between those running the CIA and the officers in the field.

But it wasn't necessary. The Vienna station chief, who was on leave at the time Shadrin vanished, recognized that a polygraph examination of those involved would be useful. He also realized that it was difficult for headquarters to order such examinations. So the chief of station—the highest CIA officer serving in Vienna at that time—made the extraordinary suggestion to the director of security that he be polygraphed. He also suggested that others involved do the same. In the end, everyone in Vienna who had had anything at all to do with the Shadrin meeting was put on a polygraph machine, which indicated that all of them were telling the truth.

It was not until March 1978 that Copaken was able to interview John Funkhouser, the CIA officer with whom Shadrin was close. Funkhouser, by then retired, met Copaken and Mrs. Shadrin for lunch at the Sheraton-Carlton. Apparently he was not concerned about the KGB and FBI agents Jim Wooten had feared were swarming over the place. The luncheon was pleasant enough, according to Copaken, but Funkhouser insisted that he knew Nick primarily as a friend. Although he indicated to Copaken that he did have a professional relationship with Shadrin, he said he could not discuss it. When Copaken pressed Funkhouser on what he and Nick spent so much time talking about, the naval expert insisted that they always discussed the Soviet Navy. At one point Mrs. Shadrin referred to the fact that Funkhouser and Shadrin had lunch together every Wednesday.

"It was every *other* Wednesday," Funkhouser corrected her. All this seemed strange to Ewa, especially since Jim Wooten had implored her never to mention Funkhouser's name. Why should there be such secrecy about the relationship if it was hardly more than a friendship? Why should Nick's admitted FBI handler, Wooten, make a point of telling her never to mention Funkhouser's name?

Compared to all the other questions in Ewa's mind, these were minor ones.

Chapter 11

At two minutes before eleven on the morning of August 5, 1977, three weeks after the Shadrin story broke in the press, Richard Copaken answered his telephone at the Washington offices of Covington & Burling. A bright, cocky voice, laced with an apparent British accent, said airily, "I understand you are looking for Nicky Artamonov."

Identifying himself as Benson, the caller described himself as a former British agent interested in assisting in the search for Shadrin. He told of "a mercenary character" named Agnew who had supplied Shadrin with false documents in Zurich six days after he had vanished in Vienna. He told Copaken that he believed that for money Agnew might lead him to Shadrin.

Benson stated that Copaken might be able to attract Agnew by placing the following ad in the *International Herald Tribune*: "Harry wants German Bank Notes of 17th century origin." The ad was to be followed by an unlisted telephone number to be installed in Copaken's Washington office. Benson instructed Copaken on the code phrases to use when the elusive Agnew telephoned. He also mentioned several details that Copaken would later claim were of "riveting significance," a significance that could have been known only to Nicholas and Ewa Shadrin.

Moments after the mysterious Benson hung up, Copaken called Ewa. She was with a patient, but Copaken told her to drop everything and come at once to his office so they could have lunch together and talk. Urgently Copaken related details of the strange telephone call. Ewa was able to point out the areas where Benson's comments struck responsive chords with her and Nick's past.*

After lunch Copaken telephoned Leonard McCoy, the officer CIA Director Stansfield Turner had assigned to replace George Kalaris as the contact for Copaken. McCoy listened to details of the bizarre call and told them to come to the CIA at once. In a rush, Copaken and Ewa Shadrin sped across the Potomac River and out the George Washington Memorial Parkway to the CIA headquarters in Virginia. Copaken was so preoccupied with his discussion of events that he drove past the entrance to the CIA. He wheeled to a stop and made an illegal U-turn. As he sped back toward the CIA, he saw flashing lights in his mirror. It was a traffic policeman. Frantically Copaken explained to the policeman who he was and what he was trying to do. He stated that a man's life might hang in the balance, that the officer had to let him be on his way to the CIA. Finally, the policeman relented and let him go.

Their two-hour meeting with McCoy began at about three-thirty. The meeting took place in a "secure room" about twenty by fifteen feet that seemed to be used primarily for filing. McCoy mentioned that the CIA file on Nick Shadrin filled a room about this size. It was on this occasion that McCoy assured Mrs. Shadrin that he recalled meeting her at their home so many years earlier (see Chapter Six). Mrs. Shadrin recalls McCoy as being very tall, polished, gracious, and polite, a gentlemanly sort of man with whom she was comfortable.

Copaken enthusiastically reported every detail of the telephone call from Benson. McCoy listened patiently, coolly, seemingly unimpressed. Despite Copaken's enthusiasm to get on with placing the ad in the *International Herald Tribune*, he told McCoy that he was planning to leave almost immediately for a four-week vacation. McCoy stated that he thought it would be best to wait until Copaken returned from his vacation before placing the ad. McCoy believed that if the caller were a fraud, he would call back soon.

---

*To this day, Ewa Shadrin remains unimpressed with Copaken's claim that the clues were of any special significance. One involved the name Benson, which was the false name used by Walter Onoshko during the earliest days of the Shadrins' arrival in the United States. Another clue was a reference to the nickname Nicky, which is a name that, according to Tom Dwyer, most of Shadrin's British friends called him. Then there was Benson's reference to a brand of vodka that had a small plant floating in it, which happened to be a vodka Shadrin occasionally gave friends. In Mrs. Shadrin's view, these "clues"—and there are several others—are either coincidental or fairly easily available to anyone who wanted to determine them. But Copaken to this day believes the clues were sufficiently convincing for pursuit.

With agreement reached not to respond to the Benson suggestions for at least four weeks, one might have expected a lull in the developments spawned by the burst of publicity. But there was no lull. Copaken, who was spending his vacation at Cape Cod, had made sure there was no telephone in the house he and his family had rented. But he spent a good part of the month of August in a pay telephone booth near the post office, keeping up with breaking details on the Shadrin case.

On August 17 there appeared in the Soviet Union's *Literary Gazette* an extraordinary account of the saga of Nikolai Artamonov/Shadrin.* Written by Genrikh Borovik, the article was entitled "They Shoot Horses, Don't They?" Knowledgeable observers agree that it was extremely unusual for the Soviets to present such a detailed account of their version of events leading to Shadrin's disappearance—an account that holds up unusually well in areas that can be checked. While there are clearly some allegations that are purely reflective of the Soviet position, it cannot be dismissed as just another piece of propaganda.

According to this Soviet version, Shadrin had approached a diplomat from the Soviet Embassy in Washington in 1966 and outlined his miserable life in the United States, explaining how painfully sorry he was that he had ever left the Soviet Union. He told the Soviets of his dismal professional life, including facts that are indisputable. Shadrin offered to spy for the Soviets while he continued his work for the United States Defense Intelligence Agency. By doing this, he hoped to make amends for his treasonous activities and pave the way for his safe and honorable return to the Soviet Union. The *Literary Gazette* saw Shadrin as a good Soviet who had great success in the Soviet Navy at a young age, a man who became infatuated with himself and with Ewa Gora.

Then, in an almost coquettish gesture, the author pulls from his hat an assumed name for the Soviet diplomat who became Shadrin's handler: Igor Aleksandrovich Orlov. The first and last names are those of the little man at the framing gallery. A very common nickname for Aleksander is Sasha. The article quotes Igor Orlov extensively as he comments on Shadrin:

He slid down the slippery slope. However, his quest for contacts with Soviet people might have indicated that deep down there

---

*The full article appears in the Appendix.

242

was still a germ of humanity which at some stage began to sprout again and made the moral torment unbearable. . . .

Often people who are voluntarily cast into the capitalist world and deprived of links with the motherland begin, albeit belatedly, to realize what a terrible mistake they have made and try their best to retrieve their right to serve the motherland. Some are grateful even for a chance to confess. This word sounds strange on the lips of a traitor, yet Artamonov repeatedly used it in later conversations with me when he talked about his misadventures abroad.

While there has never been any other account, among many differing ones, that has Shadrin making the initial approach to the Soviets, the rest of his "confession" is plausible. Indeed, he had to offer something as a reason for wanting to return to work for the Soviet Union, and this probably makes as much sense as anything else he could say.

But then, in the very next lines of Igor Orlov's account in the *Gazette* article, there appears an ominous suggestion:

There was another possibility: Artamonov-Shadrin could be lying to us. He was in fact not repentant at all and, on instructions from his masters, could be trying to become a so-called "double agent" in order to play a "game" with us.

At first glance it may seem strange, but when we agreed to contact Artamonov both alternatives were real. At his first meeting with me, Artamonov said he was seeking contacts with Soviet people on instructions from his American masters in order to play a "game" with us, but this assignment coincided with his sincere desire to at least go some way toward making amends to the motherland.

Igor Orlov then explains that he and his colleagues discussed this strange situation, weighing the pros and cons of going along with it. It was finally decided to continue the contacts, that Artamonov would get nothing of value from the Soviets, and on the chance that Artamonov was "half-sincere," there could be much to be gained. Thus, Igor Orlov says, began his regular meetings with Shadrin/Artamonov.

In the account that follows, Igor Orlov states that once the Americans had gleaned all of Shadrin's information, they "surrounded him with a gang of traitors, who henceforth were to be company for him." One of these traitors is identified as Nicholas (Nikolay in the *Gazette*) Kozlov, who indeed was an old colleague of the real Igor Orlov as well as one of Shadrin's hunting companions. In fact, Shadrin and Kozlov had a hunting date set up for two days after Nick's planned return from Vienna in January 1976—a date he could not keep.

Calling Kozlov a "profoundly immoral and unprincipled person," the *Gazette* article goes on to describe him in extremely vicious terms. Kozlov, who is highly admired within the American intelligence community for his contributions as a former Russian, states that he had nothing whatsoever to do with Shadrin's activities as a double agent and that, in fact, he is complimented that the Soviets have seen fit to describe him in such venomous terms.

The article describes Shadrin's frustrations over having to deal with former Soviets such as Kozlov and one Sergey Gordeyev as a prime reason for his wanting to return to the motherland. Shadrin supposedly could see that he was becoming more and more like these people with whom he was associating—and he wanted out.

Quoting Igor Orlov, the *Gazette* sees all this as a marvelous coincidence: "And, however, strange as it may seem, the Americans themselves facilitated [Shadrin's] decision to come to us by setting him the task of seeking contacts with us."

The article calmly and rationally explains why the Americans would want to send Shadrin on such a mission, using the very reasons that Mrs. Shadrin had been able to learn in her quest for information. It also raises the grim possibility of what might happen to Shadrin if American intelligence officials ever learned that in reality he was providing the Soviets with much more information than he was supposed to.* The article also explains that as the years wore on, Shadrin seemed to be growing more tired and frustrated.

Igor Orlov's account includes the first Vienna meeting on December 18 near the Votivkirche. Placing himself at the meeting, Orlov states that Shadrin told him that he was ready to return to the Soviet Union. Orlov states that he told Shadrin that he was doing what he could, that he would make further inquiries and try to give Shadrin a decision and meet again on December 20.

---

*Careful analysis of the *Gazette* account fails to provide even one item of exclusive information that Shadrin might have passed to the Soviets without authorization. If the account were true, it would seem, the Soviets could effectively "prove" it by including here information that only Shadrin could have given them. It is significant that they did not.

244

Then Igor Orlov reports: "Artamonov did not show up at the appointed time for the meeting in the agreed place on 20 December."

Igor Orlov's assessment of events concludes on this note:

A few careless phrases attesting to a change in the mental state of Shadrin/Artamonov, and the specialists surrounding him might have suspected that the "double-agent" . . . had come under our influence. We had foreseen this danger and warned him of it. . . . Perhaps Artamonov made some tragic mistake after 18 December and the CIA, learning of his upcoming return home, realized that the game was lost and that it was a scandalous failure, hastened to remove Artamonov and accused the other side to cover the traces. I would not like to think the worst but, knowing the CIA's methods, I find it hard to assume he is being kept prisoner; it is too dangerous for them. . . .

Then the author, Genrikh Borovik, takes the podium to agree with Igor Orlov's opinion that the most likely possibility is that Shadrin was kidnapped by the CIA or FBI while on his way to the meeting of December 20. Borovik theorizes that the Americans could not bear to have Shadrin—a man in whom they had shown such faith—appear in the Soviet Union to denounce the United States.

". . . the American special services have for a long time been resorting to killing people who are a threat to them . . ." writes Borovik. "The Artamonov case fits into this train of thought."

Moving then to a tone of moral indignation, Borovik makes a plea for Shadrin's former wife and purported son in the Soviet Union: "We have a right to join them in demanding a reply from the American authorities: Where is Nikolay Fedorovich Artamonov, and what has become of him?"

Regardless of what else it might be, the article is an exceedingly clever presentation of the Soviet side of the Shadrin matter. It completely turns the tables. Ewa Shadrin, while repelled by some of the allegations about her in the account, found it hard to argue with much of the basic logic. It would become increasingly disturbing to her as events unfolded.

The appearance of the article, however, had grim implications for seasoned observers of the Soviets. General Sam V. Wilson, who himself served in Moscow, made this observation after reading the *Gazette* account: "This means Shadrin already had to be dead.

As long as there was any possible chance of Shadrin reappearing to prove them false, they would not dare imply his demise was at the hands of the CIA. They would not dare come forward with such an allegation if there were any possibility that he could surface and prove that allegation spurious. They try very carefully to make sure things don't boomerang in terms of accusations or allegations that they make."

This interpretation of the article, coupled with Brezhnev's absolute statement to President Ford that Shadrin never reached the meeting site in Vienna on December 20, was grim fodder for Ewa's thoughts. It certainly suggested strongly that Nick had been intercepted before he reached the Votivkirche—simply because there would have been an assumption of surveillance that would inhibit fiddling with the facts on that particular point. The dreadful, gnawing question was: *Who intercepted him?*

Even though there were compelling reasons for Ewa Shadrin to lose faith in her government, she tried to believe that most of the ineptitude she had seen was not spawned by ill will. But she was convinced of the government's bureaucratic inability to act forcefully, and she doubted that finding Nick was high on any agenda. In its feeble fashion the government was moving as effectively as it could.

In a curious way the meetings at the CIA seemed to hold more promise than anything else Ewa was doing. And it was particularly gratifying that Admiral Stansfield Turner—one of Nick's great admirers—was the Director of Central Intelligence, the highest intelligence post in Washington. It did not seem unreasonable to expect from the CIA the sort of strong unilateral action that might get results. It also was encouraging to be dealing directly with men like George Kalaris and Leonard McCoy, men who so clearly seemed to have Ewa's interests at heart. She knew nothing about the role they had played—indeed, were even then playing—in the Shadrin operation.

Two weeks after the presentation in the *Literary Gazette* of the Soviet version of matters, Admiral Stansfield Turner appeared on the *CBS Morning News*. He was interviewed by CBS correspondent Fred Graham, who asked him about the claim by the KGB in the *Literary Gazette* that the CIA had murdered Shadrin.

"That's utter nonsense," replied Turner. "Utter nonsense."

"Are you denying that now?" asked Graham.

246

"Absolutely," stated Turner emphatically.

Then Graham asked Admiral Turner what he thought might have happened to Shadrin. Answered Turner: "A double agent went to Vienna for a proposed rendezvous that the KGB suggested with two KGB officers. He never returned from that rendezvous. One can hypothesize that he defected on his own voluntarily. One can hypothesize that he was abducted. *I think the fact he was last known to be in the company of two KGB officers is very incriminating.* [Emphasis added.]"

Ewa Shadrin was aghast. Stansfield Turner, Nick's old friend and associate, had implied that Nick probably had redefected to the Soviets, that the version of events in the *Literary Gazette* was correct—minus the part about the CIA's murdering him. This was the impression made upon Mrs. Shadrin, Copaken, and their supporters. Turner's comments amounted to an enunciation of the CIA leaks six weeks earlier which suggested that Shadrin had been a phony defector to begin with. Ewa Shadrin was almost speechless over what she perceived to be abandonment by a man in Turner's position who had claimed to be Nick's friend.*

On September 8 Copaken and Mrs. Shadrin met with Leonard McCoy to resume their discussion of whether to place the ad in the *International Herald Tribune* in an effort to lure Agnew, as the mysterious caller named Benson had instructed. At this meeting Copaken and Mrs. Shadrin also wanted to know why Admiral Turner had made what they interpreted as a statement of betrayal.

McCoy stated that he had checked and learned that the statement was a carefully prepared utterance by Turner, that he said precisely what he intended to say. McCoy told them that some people within the agency had pleaded with Turner not to say what he did, while others encouraged him to do so. McCoy said that unfortunately Turner more often listened to the colleagues he had brought into the agency from the navy than he did to seasoned intelligence veterans.

During this meeting, according to Copaken and Ewa, McCoy

*One former counterintelligence officer points out that if the CIA had reason to believe that Shadrin was alive and in Soviet hands, the Soviets would be more apt to give him better treatment if they believed the CIA thought he had voluntarily redefected to the Soviet Union. Therefore, Turner's statement could have been calculated to help Shadrin. Still, this was not a thought that occurred to Ewa Shadrin. Others have interpreted Turner's statement as meaning the scenario was incriminating to the Soviets. Turner has refused to comment.

expressed his own opinion about what probably had happened to Shadrin. He believed the Soviets had tried to kidnap him and that if Shadrin had resisted, he had been killed in the ensuing altercation and then buried on the grounds of the villa where they had gone for their meeting. McCoy elaborately described the manner in which the Soviets might have later disposed of the remains so that they would never be discovered.

Raising another possibility, McCoy asked Mrs. Shadrin where she believed Nick might go if he had not been taken captive or killed. Ewa replied that she was aware that he liked what he knew about Australia, with its bountiful open country and water. She remembered that Tom Dwyer once told Nick it was "like California without the crowds." She said she supposed he might go there.

Also at this meeting it was decided that Copaken would go ahead and place the advertisement in the *Herald Tribune* as a means of attracting Agnew. Although McCoy showed little enthusiasm for pursuing Benson and Agnew, he indicated that the CIA would support whatever Copaken decided to do.

As they were walking out of the CIA headquarters building, just beside the statue of Nathan Hale, McCoy was talking about how much Admiral Turner admired Nick Shadrin. Nearly at her wits' end, Ewa asked, "If Admiral Turner thinks so highly of Nick, why has nothing been done? Why hasn't the director seen the President?"

"Turner has talked to the President," replied McCoy.

"When?" said Copaken, unable to contain his excitement. "When did he talk to the President? What did the President say?" McCoy declined to say anything more. But he did suggest that Copaken use his upcoming meeting with Turner to allow the CIA director to tell him about his meeting with President Carter.

Not for the first time, confusion was foremost in Ewa Shadrin's mind. But this appeared to be good news. It seemed certain that McCoy would not have told them Turner had seen the President if he had not. There was not a single, even obscure purpose that would be served by that. Ewa hoped that this signaled new feeling in the Carter administration, which spoke so passionately about human rights.

The day after this meeting McCoy flew to Australia, later setting off myriad suspicions in Richard Copaken's fertile mind. He wondered if the visit to Australia was directly connected to the fact that Ewa had stated, in response to McCoy's question, that Australia was the most likely spot Nick would go if he were on his own. McCoy's flight to Australia also had interesting connections with the developing matter of Benson and Agnew.

As Benson had instructed, Copaken had a private, unlisted telephone installed in his office. On September 15 the ad appeared in the *International Herald Tribune*. At midmorning the special telephone rang in Copaken's office. He picked it up. "Hello, Harry," said a voice. Copaken began chattering away with the details Benson had told him to provide. By the time he finished the caller had hung up. The line went dead.

Befuddled, Copaken did not know what he had done wrong. The next morning around ten, there was one brief call on the private phone, followed by a second call twenty minutes later. The caller said that he was Agnew. He reported that Shadrin was alive, safe, and well and living in a Western country. Agnew said he would speak with Shadrin and then get back in touch with Copaken.

A few days later Agnew called again to say that he had discussed with Shadrin the possibility of returning, that Shadrin was anxious to be reunited with his wife, but that he feared the CIA would try to silence him. Quite businesslike, Agnew gave specific instructions for an elaborate meeting in Buffalo, New York. He did not seem concerned about money. He said that Shadrin would pay his fee, that he would look to Copaken only for his travel expenses. He stated that he wanted $3,000 sent to the National Bank of Paris in Monaco. It was to be put in an account under the name of W. Flynn. Copaken wired the money immediately.

Not long after that, Agnew called Copaken in a rage, claiming that he had been warned by a friend to stay away from Buffalo. He blamed Copaken for compromising him. He said he would get back to Copaken later. Thus began a six-week wait. During that period Admiral Turner prepared a letter to Shadrin assuring him that the CIA would welcome his return—a letter Copaken would have in his possession to give Shadrin if necessary.

By then, of course, it could be presumed that Agnew had collected the $3,000. That, certainly, is what Ewa Shadrin had thought was going on from the start. She had felt serious doubts all along that any of this was worth pursuing—on the basis of her absolute belief that if her husband could have acted freely, he would have been in touch with her. Still, highly respected and intelligent people like Marshall Shulman at the State Department and Robert Keuch of the Justice Department believed it would be foolish not to follow the matter to its conclusion. Ewa Shadrin knew she could never live with herself if she did not try everything.

On November 6 Copaken, tired of waiting for the next telephone call, concluded the episode was a fraud, but he still "wanted to find out who was running the sham and why." He and Mrs. Shadrin went to Monaco. Checking at the bank there, they found that the $3,000 had been collected by a W. Flynn who had used a passport as identification. The passport had been issued in Brisbane, Australia, in August 1975.

Copaken, who now insists he was skeptical from the beginning, clung to the notion that no matter who Benson really was, he had provided information that Copaken found highly convincing. By the time the passport chase ended Copaken had determined that it had been falsely issued in the name of William Joseph Flynn, a railroad conductor in Australia, who, when confronted, was as confused as everyone else.

The culprit in the scam turned out to be one Walter James Flynn, also of Australia, who had fled the country the preceding March, when a million-dollar real estate deal fell down around his ears. When Copaken finally got his hands on Flynn in France in December, Flynn airily admitted using the name Agnew and making the calls—but insisted that there *was* an Agnew who knew Shadrin's whereabouts. Flynn said he was willing to take a polygraph test about all the events—if the test were given in London and if Copaken would pay his fare to get there. It was nothing more than the old burlesque come-on—pay a little more to see a little more. Copaken finally got Flynn to London, where he promptly flunked the polygraph test.

Two weeks later Copaken's special telephone rang. It was the ever-hopeful Flynn, offering to show a little more leg. This time he offered the "real name" of Agnew and gave the name of a respectable international businessman. Flynn stated that everything else about the story was true. If Copaken would just meet him in Vienna, it could be to his and Mrs. Shadrin's advantage. Copaken agreed to pay Flynn $2,500 if he could answer three questions—all related to establishing his bona fides. In London soon after that, Copaken paid Flynn one-half of the $2,500, the rest

250

to be paid after Copaken confirmed the answers. All the answers were wrong, of course, two of them implicating reputable people. It was then that Copaken turned the flimflam over to the London police.

Undeterred by his flimsy record of success, Flynn made Copaken one last offer. For a mere $250, he would produce Shadrin's Brazilian driving license which contained a photograph taken after Shadrin's disappearance. Copaken wouldn't even listen, but he used the opportunity to set up Flynn for arrest.

For another full year the Flynn case dragged on. Finally, in March 1979, Flynn was convicted in Knightsbridge Crown Court of London for swindling Mrs. Shadrin out of $1,250. He was sentenced to eighteen months in prison. An FBI report on the matter notes that Flynn "has an extensive background in peddling false information for profit to media and unfortunate victims."

Flynn's conviction closed the single most expensive, maddening episode in the whole quest to find Nick Shadrin. To this day, bitterness creeps into Ewa Shadrin's voice as she speaks of the Flynn escapade and the thousands of dollars and hundreds of lost hours spent chasing a fairy tale.

The CIA had joined in the chase to some extent, revealing a few unusual aspects of its own finesse. One of the most curious episodes involved a CIA man called Captain Whitey Gooding. A naval aide Admiral Turner had brought to the agency, Captain Gooding was dispatched with Copaken and Mrs. Shadrin to Europe for one of the Flynn tricks. They all were at the United States Embassy in Paris when Captain Gooding mentioned that he had some photographs taken of Shadrin when he was meeting Soviet agents. Mrs. Shadrin was stunned when she heard his casual comment. She had never seen photographic evidence of Nick's meetings as a double agent. Captain Gooding apparently had brought the photographs along to help identify Shadrin. They immediately presented Mrs. Shadrin's considerable cunning with a challenge.

"Oh, let me see them!" she said cheerfully. "I have so few pictures of Nick." Captain Gooding removed the photographs from an envelope—there were at least a half dozen—flipped through them, and handed them to Ewa. She quickly studied them, her heart pounding.

"This one is so clear," she said, plucking out one of Nick greeting a KGB agent.

"Yes, so you like that one?" said the helpful Captain Gooding.

"Yes," said Ewa, brimming with enthusiasm. "It is a wonderful picture of Nick. I have so few. Do you think I could keep this one?"

"Why not?" said the good-natured Captain Gooding, assuring her that he had plenty of others for identification purposes. Ewa could hardly conceal her pleasure as she pocketed the first absolute evidence she had of Nick's activities as a double agent. In retrospect, she only wishes she had asked Captain Gooding for more. "I think he would have given me several if I had just asked," says Mrs. Shadrin, smiling and shaking her head.*

The CIA was so helpful on the Flynn caper—even sending Inspector General John Waller to Europe to assist—that Copaken became suspicious. What could be more convenient than to have him and Mrs. Shadrin absolutely absorbed for more than a year following an utterly worthless trail? Copaken even suspected an ingenious fabrication by the CIA—if not actually by staging the entire affair, at least by having helped it along once it got started.

To the point was McCoy's sudden visit to Australia the day after Copaken informed him that he was going to place the ad in the *International Herald Tribune*. It was much later, and only by coincidence, that Copaken even learned of McCoy's trip. Tom Dwyer reported that McCoy had stopped in Honolulu to see him on his way back from Australia, where, he told Dwyer, he had attended a conference on counterintelligence.

Copaken's theories included the possibility that somehow McCoy, acting for the CIA, stimulated the appearance in an Australian newspaper of details about the real Flynn—details that, in fact, did lead Copaken to find him. "There's just too much coincidence to overlook," says Copaken. He even told the court in London that he suspected that the entire episode might be part of a CIA "disinformation campaign."

Early in the Flynn debacle—the second week of October 1977—Mrs. Shadrin and Copaken had their first meeting with Admiral Turner. It had been arranged by Leonard McCoy, just before he flew off to Australia. The CIA Director had indicated his eagerness to assist Mrs. Shadrin.

---

*An FBI source intimately familiar with the Flynn affair later offered the author a curious, yet friendly warning: "If I were you, I would be very careful handling that story about the photographs." His suggestion was that there was more to it than met the eye. All efforts to reach Captain Gooding have failed.

Admiral Turner was expansive in greeting Mrs. Shadrin and Copaken, assuring her of his warm feelings for Nick and his tremendous admiration for him as a man and as an analyst. He left nothing unsaid in showing his respect and in saying how much he hoped the CIA would be able to help in retrieving Nick. Then Admiral Turner pointed out that the entire matter was actually the business of the FBI, but that the CIA was willing to assist because of the international connections and, of course, his own personal warm feelings for Nick Shadrin.

Mrs. Shadrin felt like Alice in Wonderland as she listened to Turner's comments. Could he be the same man who only a few weeks earlier had, in her opinion, clearly implied that Nick was a traitor who had gone home to the Soviet Union? Copaken pricked the illusion.

"We were shocked at your statement about Shadrin on CBS," said Copaken.

Turner was visibly startled, even irritated. He explained that he had not meant the remark the way it had sounded, that he had even been caught off guard by the television interviewer. He was about to brush the subject aside when Copaken, who is direct in all things, stated: "But, Admiral Turner, we know that you were given several subjects that were to be covered in the interview. Shadrin was one of them."

"That's not true," retorted Admiral Turner, anger rising in his voice. Again he explained that he had been caught off guard, that he had not meant to imply that Shadrin was likely a traitor. Copaken did not argue.

After ironing out details of ways in which the CIA could assist in the Flynn matter, Copaken raised the subject of Turner's meeting with President Carter on the Shadrin case. Turner exploded with fury and shouted: *"Who told you that?"*

"Leonard McCoy," answered Copaken.

"Then Leonard McCoy is a bold-faced liar!" Turner screamed as he leaped up from his seat and stormed about the room. He denied vehemently that he had ever raised the question with the President.

"It was perfectly clear to us that Turner had indeed seen the President," says Ewa Shadrin. "He couldn't conceal it. His rage was too great toward McCoy."

The meeting ended soon after that. A few weeks later McCoy

253

received a formal letter from the CIA general counsel's office ordering him never again to speak to Richard Copaken or Ewa Shadrin or anyone else involved in the case.

Seven months later, in May 1978, McCoy met Tom Dwyer for lunch in Washington. The relationship between McCoy and Dwyer is strong, and Dwyer dismisses much of the criticism of McCoy. "Leonard is an extremely honest man," says Dwyer. "He is very careful with the truth. He admired Nick, and he did everything he possibly could to help in his personal and professional capacities. I think he feels he got kicked in the teeth. It got him into deep professional trouble."

It was only a matter of months before McCoy was transferred from headquarters to a post in Germany. It was his first overseas assignment. There is no evidence that the transfer was viewed as a promotion.*

From the beginning of her quest Ewa Shadrin had longed to get in touch with Nick's good friend Anatoli Golitsin. She recalled the profound respect the men had for each other, and she also remembered how shrewd and canny Tolka was in matters such as this. He might offer excellent insights into the operation Nick had been involved with, and he could provide intelligent theories about what might have happened to Nick if he were in Soviet hands. Mrs. Shadrin spent hours poring over telephone books at the Library of Congress, looking for names in various towns where she had heard he might be. Each new rumor about Golitsin's identity —or a tip on where he might live—sent Ewa scurrying back to the telephone books. For some reason, there were always bountiful rumors about Golitsin's name and whereabouts.

But she could get nowhere. Few defectors have ever been as well hidden as Golitsin. Finally, Admiral Turner agreed to get in touch with Golitsin to convey Ewa's ardent desire to talk to him. At the end of August 1978 a letter to Copaken came from Stansfield

---

*In December 1980 Jack Anderson reported that the CIA's deputy chief of counterintelligence was transferred from his headquarters position and posted overseas as a result of preparing an "operational analysis" of a Soviet cable concerning former Secretary of State Henry Kissinger. The cable, which was turned over to the CIA by its top Moscow agent known as Trigon—since arrested by the KGB—concerned an allegedly improper meeting Kissinger had with Ambassador Dobrynin in which Kissinger made various comments on the Soviet policies of the Carter administration. The CIA operational analysis, according to Anderson, concluded that "what Kissinger had done 'bordered on treason.'" Though Anderson did not name McCoy, the transfer and position in Counterintelligence coincide with McCoy's own employment history.

Turner. In his best Turner style, the admiral began by saying he had acted as "expeditiously as possible consonant with pertinent security considerations." He continued to say:

> Your request was conveyed to Mr. Golitsin on August 11. He has categorically refused to consider contacting, or meeting with, Mrs. Shadrin. Mr. Golitsin's position is that he has never really been a close friend of Nick Shadrin and as he has not had any contact with Mr. Shadrin since 1964 he cannot conceive how he could be of any help to Mrs. Shadrin in determining what happened to her husband, or to make any intelligent contribution on questions concerning his present condition or whereabouts.
>
> I am sorry to have to convey this negative response from Mr. Golitsin. However, he is adamantly opposed to any proposed contact. . . .

If this was really Golitsin's answer, it was a terrible disappointment. But Mrs. Shadrin had scant reason for believing anything Admiral Turner or the CIA told her on a matter such as this. She remained unconvinced that Golitsin would so callously assert that he had not been a close friend of Nick Shadrin.

In the fall of 1980 the author put Mrs. Shadrin in touch with Golitsin by delivering to him an appeal Mrs. Shadrin had recorded.* Speaking in Russian, Mrs. Shadrin told Golitsin of Turner's letter claiming Golitsin said he had never been a close friend of Nick. "Please get in touch with me," she pleaded. "I know you want to help your friend Nick."

Using a personal friend as an intermediary, Golitsin sent a message to Ewa Shadrin through the author asserting that Stansfield Turner's letter had been truthful, that Golitsin could see no possible way he could be of help to her. He added, however, that during his association with Shadrin he had warned him that it was dangerous for Ewa to be in telephone contact with her parents in Poland.

What did this mean? "I don't know," says Ewa Shadrin. "But it sounds just like Golitsin."

During the spring of 1978 Copaken and Mrs. Shadrin continued their struggle to understand the larger picture of which Nick's

---

*It was done in this fashion out of respect for Golitsin's expensively contrived new identity. Indeed, the author, who discovered Golitsin's whereabouts, never shared the information with anyone, even his editors. In an earlier telephone exchange with the author, Golitsin had courteously declined to discuss the Shadrin case.

case was a part. This effort coincided with the publication of *Legend: The Secret World of Lee Harvey Oswald* by Edward Jay Epstein. "I probably bought the first copy in Washington," says Copaken. "I know of no single thing published that had a greater impact on what we were doing than *Legend*. It moved us many miles ahead of where we were."

The book revealed for the first time the intricacies of the investigation going on within the CIA in the mid-sixties over the possible presence of a Soviet penetration agent. It also discussed the Nosenko case and its ramifications. As Mrs. Shadrin read the book, she could feel a perplexing sense of familiarity. There was quite a bit in the book about a CIA officer named Bruce Solie. Something told her that he just might be the miserable character named Bruce who had accompanied her home from Vienna.

"His name jumped off the page at me," says Ewa. "I don't know why, but I knew he was the one." In her quest to find out what happened to her husband, she had tried unsuccessfully to learn the identity of the strange man named Bruce. Quickly she began calling the Washington area information operator, asking for a Bruce Solie. She found a listing. It was midmorning when she dialed the number.

"A woman answered and said that Bruce was at work," Ewa recalls. "She gave me a number where I could reach him." Ewa called the number and reached Bruce Solie in the Office of Security at the Central Intelligence Agency.

"Yes?" Solie said.

"My name is Ewa Shadrin, the wife of Nick Shadrin. Are you the man who came with me home from Vienna on Christmas Eve in 1975?"

There was a pause, and then the man said that no, he was not—or, at least, he could not recall doing that. Ewa pressed him, pointing out more details about their trip together. Finally, Bruce Solie was able to recall that yes, indeed, he had accompanied Ewa Shadrin home from Vienna at that time.

"Will you see me?" Ewa asked urgently. "Can we talk?"

Solie stated that he would have to think about that, perhaps seek some advice. He told her he would get in touch with her.

A few days later Ewa again called his number. His secretary answered and said that he was not there. Ewa told the secretary to tell Solie that she wanted to meet him at the National Air and

Space Museum, under the Wright brothers' airplane. One of the cryptonyms for the Shadrin/Igor operation was Kitty Hawk, and this was Ewa Shadrin's way of letting Solie know she had learned a good bit about what was going on. Ewa asked Solie's secretary to give him the message, that he would understand it. She said she would await his call confirming the meeting.

Solie never called back.

Two years later, in an extremely rare interview, Solie was asked by the author why he had failed to meet Ewa Shadrin at the Wright brothers' exhibit at the museum. "I couldn't find it," replied Solie. Then he laughed.

Chapter 12

PART of Copaken's frustration and Ewa's agony was the continuing confusion over just what Nick's role had been as a double agent. During the first days, of course, when Ewa was in the hands of Cynthia Hausmann, she believed Nick had been an innocent American citizen snatched off the streets by his former Soviet masters. Two months later, when Copaken entered the case, there was a general acknowledgment of what Jim Wooten had first told Ewa: that Nick was performing a great patriotic duty to the United States by serving the FBI and the CIA as a double agent working against the Soviets. Many of the government officials Ewa met readily told her that Nick had been engaged in an extraordinarily noble service for his country.

Just what he was supposed to have been doing as a double agent was far from clear. However, it seemed certain that he was passing CIA-doctored information on the U.S. Navy to the Soviets. He was also able to report on KGB personnel working in the Washington area and to provide details on the espionage techniques of the Soviets. Shadrin's first trip to Vienna for an all-night session with KGB agents presumably had provided substantial information, followed, of course, by the delivery in Washington of the sophisticated spy equipment. Indeed, there would seem to be value in these activities.

It was impossible for Ewa to make a knowledgeable assessment of the truth. Everything was so remote and murky that she had little choice but to accept that Nick had been doing just what Jim Wooten and others claimed he had been doing. From the beginning

—the meeting with Jim Wooten at the Kuppermans' house—there was the hint that Nick had been sent into the double agent role against his will. But there was not the slightest indication that he had done so without knowing all the facts. Ewa Shadrin remained perplexed that he could have done something so dangerous, but it had not occurred to her that he might have been tricked into doing it.

By the spring of 1978 Mrs. Shadrin and Copaken felt they had an understanding of the operation Nick had been involved in. They believed that he had been approached by the KGB, reported that approach to the FBI, was advised to play along, and did so. As risky as it all sounded, the theory made as much sense as anything else.

But during that year a writer was conducting research for a book on the subject of possible Soviet penetration of the CIA. His research took him, by his own account, to numerous former intelligence and counterintelligence officers. One of the sources mentioned, almost as an aside, that right under the noses of everyone in Washington was an excellent example of either witting or unwitting cooperation between the CIA and the KGB. He mentioned the Shadrin case and said that the secret key to it all was the presence in 1966 of a Soviet agent named Igor.

None of this had too much to do with the writer's line of research, but he had heard about the Shadrin case and knew that Richard Copaken was the attorney retained by Mrs. Shadrin. He went to Copaken and told him about the existence of Igor and the role he played in the recruitment of Shadrin. Copaken was electrified. It was the overlay that made all the patterns fit, the shadows come into focus. He begged the writer to tell him his source. The writer refused. Finally, however, the writer agreed to go back to the source and try to convince him to talk to Copaken.

A few days later Copaken received word that the source would talk to him on a promise of absolute confidentiality. The source even insisted that Mrs. Shadrin not know his identity. Copaken agreed and, as promised, never told Mrs. Shadrin the source's identity. Copaken and the source met in a private home in the Washington area for several hours. The source revealed apparently everything he knew about Igor.*

---

*Copaken has refused to confirm or deny this account of his discovery of Igor. However, the author has confirmed it with other sources.

On April 1, 1978, Copaken called Ewa Shadrin. He told her that it appeared they were the victims of a staggering deception by the United States government, that there was new evidence that Nick Shadrin had been compromised with the Soviets from the first moment he agreed to go to work as a double. Stunned, Ewa listened to this new tale—more overwhelming than all those that had come before. For two and one-half years officials of the CIA, the FBI, the State Department, and the White House had affirmatively deceived her. Nick Shadrin had not been approached out of the blue by the Soviets; he had been set up by the Americans, slowly ripened, and then sent to Vienna for the final plucking by the Soviets.

Every latent suspicion and hostility Ewa Shadrin had for bureaucrats and government officials came to the surface. She felt she had been a fool to believe anything told to her by George Bush, Stansfield Turner, Zbigniew Brzezinski, Leonard McCoy, James Wooten, George Kalaris. They all had deceived her in their names and in the names of the highest government officials in the United States. For the first time she was possessed by a pervasive feeling of profound bitterness. Indeed, she could see no reason to accept the American officials' word over that of the Soviets, as reflected in the article in the *Literary Gazette*. In view of everything else, was there any reason for her *not* to believe that the CIA had either actively or passively brought about the disappearance of her husband? By Ewa's lights, there was no reason whatsoever.

One of the first people Ewa called after learning about Igor was Jim Wooten at his new home in the West. She could hear a radio playing in the background when he answered the telephone. "We have learned about the Soviet agent who asked for Nick in the spring of 1966," Ewa said at once.

"What?" yelled Wooten. "Wait a minute!" Ewa heard him turn off the radio and return to the line. Cautious at first, Wooten gently tried to elicit from Ewa additional information while confirming nothing she said. When Ewa asked if Wooten knew about Igor, he replied, "If I were aware, I could not comment." Each of his statements was carefully covered with caveats that he was in no way confirming anything she said.

Within a few minutes, however, Wooten had clearly confirmed the story, insisting that the telephone call ("*if* there was a telephone call") to Helms was in the summer of 1966—not the spring, as Ewa initially suggested. Wooten repeated and emphasized dozens of times during the next several telephone calls that the call could have come no earlier than late June.

Mrs. Shadrin declined to tell Wooten how she had got her information about Igor, although she begged him to tell her whatever he knew. From the start Wooten seemed intensely interested in learning how Ewa had found out about Igor, and he told her he was almost certain he knew. He explained that the person who had revealed such information had committed a gravely serious deed. He said that even now he should discuss nothing with Ewa, that he could lose his pension or be prosecuted.

Wooten made an impassioned plea to Mrs. Shadrin to understand that Soviet knowledge of her information about Igor could bring about the death of a valuable agent working for American intelligence interests. He clearly indicated that Igor was an extremely important agent for the United States, strongly implying that he was still active and that disclosure of his activities would probably mean his immediate arrest by the Soviets, probably his execution.

Wooten told Ewa that if she allowed the news about Igor to reach the Soviets, "He is finished, because if he [Igor] did this [approached the Americans], we have to figure the Soviets did not know he did it . . . he may still be alive . . . if you want to play God . . . if the man was sincere, and he did this for the United States without the Soviets knowing it, that guy is finished." He explained that just the revelation of the story would be enough to tip the Soviets since their records would quickly show who had been the first to contact Shadrin.

Several telephone calls later, according to Mrs. Shadrin, Wooten named his suspect as the source for the revelations about Igor, the one man who presumably concluded early on that Igor was a Soviet provocateur. "Jim Angleton must have told you," Wooten said. "He's the only one who could have told you or *would* have told you."

Mrs. Shadrin said that to her knowledge, James Angleton had nothing to do with the revelation of Igor's role in the Shadrin case. She told Wooten that she did not know how Copaken had got his information, but that it was being confirmed bit by bit by those in a position to know, including, ironically, James Wooten.

Ewa Shadrin told Wooten that she would like his help in

ascertaining Igor's last name. She wanted to identify him and try to get in touch with him. Wooten said flatly that he would not help, that he would get into serious trouble by discussing any aspect of Igor. He told Mrs. Shadrin that even he was not supposed to know Igor's last name, that he had learned it by pure coincidence. Ewa Shadrin did not press the point, but she knew she would be calling Wooten again.

On May 14, 1978, Igor made his public debut in Time magazine, when its edition of May 22 was released.* Several days later the story appeared in The New York Times; it included this statement: "Several present and former intelligence officers told The Times that the publication of Igor's name and the details of his case endangered 'his life and others,' as one source put it, and was detrimental to United States security."

Ewa Shadrin, of course, saw it in a completely different light. How could officials be worried about Igor—a Soviet spy of questionable loyalty—when her own husband, a tried and true American citizen, apparently had been sacrificed to promote him? Where was the concern of these same officials when they were sending Nick to Vienna, into the jaws of the KGB? It was not Ewa Shadrin's place to weep over the exposure of Igor.

With the new leads on Igor, Ewa Shadrin and her band of supporters went to work to try to determine his real identity. William and Mary Louise Howe began spending hours at the Library of Congress and the State Department, going over lists of Soviet diplomats. They pursued every diplomat with the first name Igor. From the start, however, their task was probably hopeless.

Meanwhile, Ewa was calling Jim Wooten nearly every day, often several times a day, badgering him for tips that might lead to the identification of Igor. As a man who seemed to have a genuine concern for Ewa, Wooten could not resist at least giving the impression that he was helping. Mary Louise Howe has described Ewa's approach: "She was calling him three and four times a day, pleading and begging and crying over the phone. She would try to get him to say a name that would rhyme with Igor's real name or to tell her which part of the alphabet held the correct first letter of his real name."

---

*Richard Copaken refuses to confirm or deny that he had anything to do with Igor's name appearing in Time magazine. Ewa Shadrin asserts that she did not reveal the story of Igor.

More than two years later, when the author confronted Wooten at his desert home, he categorically refused to discuss any aspect of his connection to the Shadrin case. "I have no choice," were the words he kept using.

Finally, on the basis of what was perceived as a clue from Wooten, Ewa became convinced that Igor's last name started with *K*. However, she never could get Wooten to confirm the name of her top suspect, one Kupkov. In any event, Wooten kept trying to explain to Ewa that it would do no good to learn the last name of Igor. Once, in a discussion of the letter *K*—and what might follow it—Wooten said, "You might as well say Kozlov."

A few days after he learned the details of Igor's role, Richard Copaken advised the Justice Department and the State Department of the new revelations, which, if true, showed without question that he and Mrs. Shadrin had been actively deceived by the highest officials in the United States, officials who knew Shadrin was an unwitting part of a much larger operation involving Igor. Copaken was assured that his new information would be evaluated at the highest levels.

On April 19, 1978, Copaken was called to the Justice Department and informed of a decision on how to handle the matter of new information pertaining to Igor and its obvious implications for Mrs. Shadrin's quest to find her husband. The decision was to make no further attempt to assist Mrs. Shadrin, to decline any inquiries on the subject of Igor, and to cease providing access to Mrs. Shadrin and her attorney. Henceforth the FBI and CIA directors—both of whom had met with Mrs. Shadrin in the past and offered full cooperation—would no longer see her or her attorney.

In essence, the government was saying it regarded the Shadrin case as closed. The apparent reason was that it could not tolerate Mrs. Shadrin's pressing her quest beyond the walls of ineptitude and silence she had been shown by the government. Such a reaction on the part of the government confirmed to Ewa Shadrin her suspicions that something even more sinister was being concealed. It seemed obvious that the government felt any real probing on its part for Shadrin might tip the scales against Igor—an agent it apparently *still* viewed as viable, despite his exposure in *Time* magazine.

On May 24, 1978, Copaken, as a last resort, turned to the

Senate Intelligence Committee, seeking relief for Mrs. Shadrin's terrible quandary. In a letter requesting a formal investigation, Copaken told the committee: "The callous disregard for her feelings that has been exhibited by the United States government is not in keeping with its responsibility to the family of a man who served it so valiantly for so many years."

Nearly three months later the committee's chairman, Birch Bayh, responded innocuously by thanking Copaken for his interest and advising him that the committee "has been working on the Shadrin case for over a year and will continue to do so as a part of its oversight duties. . . ." To Ewa this response was the final evidence of an uncaring, self-protective and untruthful bureaucracy.

After the revelation of Igor, Copaken requested a meeting with James Angleton, former counterintelligence chief of the CIA. They met in July, after Copaken agreed to Angleton's stern stipulation that no one ever know any details of the meeting. Later this pledge was breached when one of Ewa Shadrin's ardent supporters circulated an account of it in a newsletter of developments.

Seated at a window table at the elegant Sheraton-Carlton Hotel, Angleton and Copaken talked for five hours.* Angleton acknowledged to Copaken the existence of Igor—a point which by then had been confirmed by various sources—as well as the general outlines of the Shadrin operation. Although he said he had personally never met Igor, Angleton stated that he understood he was young and seemed brilliant, demonstrating extensive knowledge of several KGB directorates.

While Angleton clearly acknowledged Shadrin's role in the Igor matter, he stated that he absolutely would not have allowed Shadrin to leave the United States for a meeting with the KGB. When asked about the Canadian meeting in 1971, the former CIA man stated that it was not dangerous because of the proximity to the United States. He asserted that he had not known about the 1972 meeting in Vienna and that he would not have allowed Shadrin to go if he had known.

Most important, Angleton told Copaken that he concluded fairly early that Igor was a phony defector, a provocateur sent to deceive the Americans. Although others accepted Igor, he was not

---

*Neither Copaken nor Angleton would confirm or deny any aspect of this meeting.

among them. Angleton explained the intricacies of why all knowledge of Igor was kept from the CIA's Soviet Division, a stricture that remained intact until Angleton's departure nine years later. He told Copaken it was important to have the Soviets believe that United States Intelligence accepted Igor, that this was the heart of turning the tables on the provocation.

While Angleton and his men pretended to believe in Igor, he explained to Copaken, the FBI had fully and genuinely accepted Igor as an agent working for American interests. It was because of the FBI's genuine acceptance of Igor that it perceived no difficulty in sending Shadrin to Vienna and no special risk in doing so without surveillance. Angleton reiterated his belief that Shadrin was safe carrying out the operation in the United States and that he would have never allowed Shadrin to go to Vienna. When Copaken pressed the point of Shadrin's 1972 Vienna meeting—well before Angleton's departure—Angleton insisted he never knew about it.

Angleton also intimated to Copaken in deepest confidence that at the requests of advisers to Presidents Ford and Carter, he had provided his analysis and advice on how to respond to Shadrin's loss. He said he told Ford administration officials that the only hope of getting Shadrin back was to give up some tremendously important asset—something on the order of the exchange of Rudolf Abel for Francis Gary Powers. His advice to the Carter officials was that the best course was to make a large cash settlement with Ewa Shadrin, that this was the only way the United States could redeem itself. He recommended that Carter make a public apology to Mrs. Shadrin. If this were not done, Angleton reasoned, it would leave an impression with potential defectors that the United States did not care what happened to Shadrin, thus seriously affecting the climate for defection.

In addition to these points, Angleton stated that he had had nothing to do with originating the Shadrin operation. The best news from Angleton was that he believed the Soviets would not execute Shadrin, that they would keep him in fairly comfortable custody for long-term debriefing.

Copaken had hoped to have additional meetings with Angleton, but after the first meeting the retired Chief of Counterintelligence became hostile and refused further contacts. Apparently he was angered by indications that somehow word of his confidential meeting with Copaken had reached the public.

In the spring of 1978, a couple of months prior to his meeting with Angleton, Copaken again wrote to President Carter, pleading for the self-professed champion of human rights to meet with Ewa Shadrin. Carter refused, but he did instruct the Intelligence Oversight Board (IOB) to review the case and to prepare a report. That got under way in the summer of 1978. The IOB then included former Pennsylvania Governor William Scranton, former Tennessee Senator Albert Gore, and Washington attorney Thomas L. Farmer. The staff was headed by Burton Wides, who had been a counsel to the Senate Intelligence Committee.

On April 16, 1979, Copaken received a letter from Robert L. Keuch, deputy assistant attorney general of the United States. Keuch explained that not only was he responding to Copaken's letter to President Carter of nearly a year earlier, but he was speaking on behalf of the entire United States government: ". . . this response reflects all the investigations and inquiries that have been undertaken by the Government to determine Mr. Shadrin's fate."

Keuch reviewed the scope of various government investigations into what happened to Shadrin and then noted that the IOB investigation alone took "more than five months and involved both the detailed review of large numbers of documents and files and the interviews of more than eighty witnesses. . . . In the course of the investigation, [the IOB] had access to all documents and persons in the intelligence community deemed relevant and necessary to its investigation. This investigation . . . attempted the exploration of every credible lead. . . ."

Then Keuch—though promising to keep the matter open for new developments—went on to effectively close the case forever:

> Unfortunately, despite these intensive efforts, the Government has been unable to determine what happened to Mr. Shadrin when he disappeared in Vienna, Austria, in 1975. None of the investigations, analyses, and inquiries that have been conducted disclosed evidence of any hostile action against Mr. Shadrin by the United States Government, any of its agencies or agents. Beyond that, however, it can only be concluded that Mr. Shadrin is a missing person.

Another stone wall. Ewa Shadrin had not expected anything much different. She did go through the motions of asking if she could see the report prepared by the IOB. Her request was rejected on the ground that the report contained sensitive information. Ewa Shadrin has no more reason to believe in the integrity of this investigation than in that of the countless officials who lied to her, misled her, allowed her to believe things the government knew were not true.

As for Keuch's letter itself, there was little to say. It failed to address the crucial points, such as the government's use of an unwitting Shadrin in the Igor operation, which certainly appeared to be gross malfeasance toward an American citizen. And the fact that Shadrin was allowed to walk unprotected into Vienna again suggests malfeasance of the highest order.

Copaken believes it is impossible for the IOB to fail to find wrongdoing. If, in fact, the Soviets did abduct Shadrin, then the wrongdoing is obvious—the lack of any surveillance, the disappearance of Cynthia Hausmann for an hour, the fact that she was not at the emergency number, the fact that she did not immediately notify Washington, and other things that happened in Vienna. In Copaken's view, the IOB cannot have it both ways. Somehow something very wrong was done, or otherwise Shadrin would not have been lost. The people who sent Shadrin into the scheme were wrong—if for no other reason than the generally conceded fact that he was deceived and sent into the espionage wars without understanding the terrible risks he faced.

Copaken suggests that the transparent wrongness of the IOB's conclusion renders its entire investigation a whitewash. The wrongdoing seems perfectly obvious to anyone. The question is whether there is anything sinister behind it.

In June 1978 William Colby appeared as a guest on the Fred Fiske radio talk show in Washington. Colby had been Director of Central Intelligence at the time Shadrin was sent to Vienna for his last meeting. Mrs. Shadrin telephoned the radio show and spoke over the air with Colby. She asked him directly if the CIA had killed her husband or continued to hold him in custody. Colby's response was:

"I am absolutely sure that the CIA did not kill your husband, Mrs. Shadrin. I am absolutely sure the CIA never had custody of your husband. This case has been looked into very carefully, as you well know. I know there are some questions about it. The FBI, I think, is the major agency responsible for that activity, and I

267

know that the CIA was of some assistance to them, but that the responsible agency was the FBI at the time."

Then Mrs. Shadrin asked why the agency and others had lied to her about Igor, and Colby deflected the question by speaking of his own involvement during that time with the congressional hearings into CIA activities.

A few days later Mrs. Shadrin telephoned Colby at his office, and he agreed to meet her the next day at Copaken's office. Colby spent an hour with them and explained that the Shadrin disappearance occurred during the transition period as one director was going out and another one was coming in. According to Copaken and Ewa, Colby stated that he really could not remember much about the incident.

Ewa Shadrin did not believe anything he said.

Ewa Shadrin and her attorney believe there is far more to this story than they have been told or have found out. They are convinced that the government continues to deceive them at the highest levels, that real efforts were never made to locate and free Nicholas Shadrin. It is now clear to Mrs. Shadrin that no single real effort was ever made to arrange an exchange of spies for Shadrin —despite much breast-beating that seemed to create the appearance of efforts. And the constant chirping of the Carter administration on the subject of human rights rings in Ewa Shadrin's ears as brutal mendacity. At every turn, it seems, the greater concern was that the government might do something to jeopardize Igor.

In the spring of 1978, with all hope of government help gone, Copaken began efforts to acquire information under the provisions of the Freedom of Information Act. The government, as might be expected, initially responded that it would take many months to pull together the Shadrin files just to review them for possible release under the law. The stonewalling that Copaken had come to know so well continued, even as he sought relief under an act of Congress.

A year later *Reader's Digest* became interested in the case and launched a suit against the government seeking access to the Shadrin files, citing provisions of the Freedom of Information Act. At first the government, initiating its response with a stalling maneuver, indicated it would take many months to locate the disparate material on Shadrin. Attorneys for the *Digest* reminded the government that the IOB had just conducted a detailed review of "large numbers of documents and files" on the Shadrin case and that the government obviously already had all the material at hand.

The *Digest* suit was filed in the Southern District of New York. In the early stages of the proceeding, Judge Robert J. Ward made it clear to the government that he would not tolerate any evidence of bad faith. Said Judge Ward: "I will not stand still while national security is used as a cloak rather than as a protective shield."

But the CIA seemed as lackadaisical in dealing with Judge Ward as it had been in dealing with Ewa Shadrin. Months passed with the CIA seemingly unable to process any of its voluminous files on the Shadrin matter. At one point Judge Ward said in a tone of amazement: "How does our intelligence agency work? No wonder we have problems overseas. . . . You have so many files by the time you find them, the situation has come to fruition. . . . Has the bureaucracy gotten so monumental that before the elephant can move, the crisis is upon us?"

Joseph P. Kimble of the CIA's Office of General Counsel persisted in describing in great detail just how the agency was going about moving the papers around in this case. He explained how four senior counterintelligence officers had been brought back to review the documents, which he stated pertained to "an extremely sensitive counterintelligence operation by the CIA." At one point Kimble asserted that the documents in question bore heavily "on the equities of other agency components," a bit of phrasing that would make Admiral Turner proud.

Admonished Judge Ward: "Never talk to me in bureaucratise. Talk to me in English." Finally, after listening to a great many more words from Kimble and Assistant United States Attorney Janis Farrell, Judge Ward commented wearily: "The convoy will travel at the speed of the slowest vessel. I understand your point."

Finally, Judge Ward warned the government that "if someone down in Washington wants to play games on this, so long as I have a say in it, anybody that wants to play games will lose."

In the end, the government produced nothing but hundreds of newspaper clippings from the files of the CIA and the FBI. In addition, there were hundreds of pages of documents in which every single letter of type—even dates—had been blacked out in deleting purportedly sensitive material. No one ever explained the difference between the totally blacked-out pages and the ones that were never released at all.

Finally, when it was obvious that the government had not

shown an iota of good faith during the entire course of the proceeding, attorneys for the *Digest* requested that Judge Ward review a government-prepared summary of the documents that the CIA had refused to produce. The agency maintained that even this index could not be considered in open court. With great reluctance the judge agreed to review the index *in camera*.

On August 20, 1980, a solemn Judge Ward called in attorneys for the *Digest* and the government. He stated that in reviewing the summaries of classified documents, he had made one assumption: that the government's summaries were "accurate and fair."

He then rendered his judgment that release of the documents described in the summaries would "seriously compromise our foreign intelligence-gathering operations and certain aspects of our foreign relations." He added: "If it were ancient history from a closed book, I would have no problem with the matter; but it is not, and that is where my problem lies, and that is even though many of the events occurred a number of years ago. But I would regard the book as still being open, and that is what troubles me."

It is not known what the government gave Judge Ward in its summaries to stimulate such a response. However, the *Digest* decided to contest the ruling, primarily because the court had not reviewed a single document in question. Moreover, there is no compelling reason to believe that anything prepared by the government in this case would be fair and accurate. For four years it consistently demonstrated its bad faith and duplicity toward Mrs. Shadrin and all others who tried to find out what had happened to her husband. There is no reason to believe that the government, when allowed by Judge Ward to operate in a cloak of secrecy, would perform any more honestly than it had in the crucible of public attention.

The fate of Nick Shadrin may never be known. The most likely source for an eventual answer is some future defector from the KGB—unless, of course, Ewa Shadrin is correct in her staunch belief that there are U.S. officials who have known all along exactly what happened to her husband.

Although the CIA refuses to discuss the Shadrin case, its position on agency responsibility for defectors is clear. Robert W. Gambino, the director of the CIA's Office of Security, made the following statement to a congressional committee in 1979: "The

Agency assumes an awesome responsibility when it takes under its wing any defector. . . . If bodily harm were to come to a defector inadequately protected by our Security Officers, there would be a devastating impact on all potential defectors."

Two former directors of central intelligence, in commenting to the author, agreed that Shadrin's loss affects the climate for defection. Said Richard Helms: "The worst feature of the case was permitting Shadrin to travel to a city in Europe where the KGB could control the environment. Potential Russian defectors would understand a double-agent operation, so I would have to say that the loss of Shadrin is discouraging mostly in the sense of faulty tradecraft on the Americans' part."

William Colby, who was Director of Central Intelligence at the time of Shadrin's disappearance, declared: "The handling in Vienna was certainly deficient—especially the absence of any counter-surveillance measures." And he expressed concern that Shadrin's loss would create "psychological disincentives to Soviets considering defection."

Colby added: "In the closed world of Soviet society and especially the KGB, it is very much in their interest to indicate that defection leads to frustration, punishment or degradation, and we know that they actively promote such impressions. Whether the Soviets internally portray Shadrin's disappearance as a result of their own action, which I doubt, or as the inevitable fate of one who leaves their service does not make a great difference. The effect of either on potential Soviet defectors is certainly depressing."

Perhaps the most disturbing aspect of the story was highlighted in the cryptic comments of Judge Robert Ward five years after Shadrin vanished. The judge stated that the case remained an open book, that it appeared to have "ongoing relevance." Authoritative observers interpret this as an indication that Igor continues to be regarded as a bona fide agent working in the KGB for the United States.

Those who doubt Igor's credentials are appalled by this prospect. They regard Igor as one of a number of false defectors, including Fedora and Nosenko, who have seduced and confused sensitive elements of our intelligence services for more than fifteen years. Even if Igor had been a true defector, some point out, the news stories that began to appear in 1978, telling of his approach to the CIA, would have sealed his fate in Moscow. If he were still dealing with the CIA or the FBI, his every move would be controlled by the KGB. Yet others believe that Igor is a true defector, who has escaped KGB detection, provided this country with valuable information on a continuing basis, and serves to this day as a spy for the United States. It may be decades before the public knows the truth.

Of all the mysteries spinning in the wake of the elusive Igor, none is more tantalizing than his timely certification of Yuri Nosenko. It occurred at the nadir of Nosenko's crumpled fortunes, at a time when there was nearly unanimous agreement among the professionals assessing Nosenko that he was a dispatched agent. His story, oozing deception, was in shambles. But no matter how tightly knotted his lies and contradictions became, Nosenko refused to admit that he was a dispatched agent. The coming of Igor may have been a terrible tragedy for Nick Shadrin, but it was a welcome blessing for Yuri Nosenko.

In the annals of Soviet defections to the West, there is no case as bizarre and of such continuing perplexity as that of Yuri Ivanovich Nosenko. His first contact with the United States was in Geneva on June 3, 1962, and following his return to Moscow he was considered a defector in place. His next contact was in January 1964, and the following month he was brought into the United States. After four and one-half years of tumultuous internal debate the CIA granted Nosenko his bona fides. Finally, on May 11, 1977, fifteen years after Nosenko's original contact, the FBI and the CIA officially concurred that he was a bona fide defector to the United States. This concurrence was based on an examination of "the totality of information furnished by him."

There is no precedent for such strenuous examination of a defector's bona fides. In the wake of the torrid debate over Nosenko, there remains a quagmire of dissension. The professionals who originally suspected Nosenko are on one side. On the other are those who, in subsequent years, have managed to win enthusiastic support for him from the highest intelligence officials in the land. Today his doubters are mostly gone, and the few original doubters still in the intelligence services are mute. Even some of Nosenko's hottest CIA detractors, long retired, seem almost resigned to the proposition that Nosenko has won lasting acceptance. Only a few believe the case should be opened yet again to examine the whole question of what Nosenko's acceptance means to the U.S. intelligence services.

One of the most bizarre aspects of the affair is the urgent and fierce intensity one encounters from Nosenko supporters when merely questioning reasons for his total acceptance. According to an official statement from the CIA, Nosenko "continues to be used as a regular lecturer at counterintelligence courses of the Agency, the FBI, Air Force OSI, and others." In this capacity Nosenko is in direct contact with this country's most carefully concealed covert personnel—by any standards a peculiar place to put a man who required fifteen years to win complete acceptance by the CIA and the FBI. But these supporters are hampered as they try to explain why Nosenko should be considered a true defector. In the end they say there is no way to show a reporter the significant reasons why they can be so sure Nosenko is okay because doing so would reveal sensitive information.

Nosenko's supporters today claim that he has provided tremendously important information to the United States on various cases which, understandably, if this is all true, cannot be revealed. The story is that Nosenko, who apparently offered little worthwhile information during his years of confinement and hostile interrogation, blossomed when the FBI finally got its hands on him. Estimates from his current supporters suggest that he can be credited with providing vital information on more than 200 cases of great significance, information that has sharply damaged Soviet intelligence efforts. When told of this, his detractors suggest that perhaps, once he was released from CIA custody, he was provided with new information by the Soviets—much of it very good intelligence—to heighten his chances for full acceptance.

A common suggestion from Nosenko's widely and highly placed supporters is that he underwent treatment by the CIA so cruel and unusual that the Western world would be scandalized if details ever reached the public. Nosenko himself has privately described horrible things he claims the CIA did to him while he was in its custody, things that supposedly are so awful they cannot be described in public. Several Nosenko supporters have told the author that one clear sign of his intense patriotism and loyalty to America is that he never revealed what was done to him during the years of his hostile interrogation. (The word "torture" is not used, but that clearly is the implication in all these comments.)

Whatever the truth, Nosenko has generated an enormous degree of support since 1968, when the CIA, under Richard Helms, set him free. Helms has made it clear that he never envisioned that Nosenko would be resurrected, awarded his bona fides, and put to work in a sensitive position in the intelligence community. All Helms had in mind was getting rid of a terrible, unsolvable problem—a man in custody under Spartan conditions with no prospect for release. Nosenko had demonstrated that he could not be broken, and the best course, short of shipping him back to the Soviets, was to try to insert him into American society in the most benign manner possible.

But in the hands of men like Bruce Solie, Leonard McCoy, and others, Nosenko soon rose to respectability. By the time the FBI got its hands on him he was able to provide information that the bureau deemed valuable. (When Nosenko was finally cleared by the CIA in 1968, Rufus Taylor sent a memorandum to DCI Richard Helms noting that at least nine new cases had been developed from Nosenko's information. Almost always, in intelligence considerations, there is debate over the value of any bit of information. In a particular case, some may think an item is crucially important while others may argue that the information is being "thrown away" by the Soviets in order to promote their dispatched agent.) In any case, it is clear that Nosenko's postdetention information was enthusiastically received by the FBI and that later the CIA gave him the same warm embrace.

By early 1981 Nosenko had established himself as a legitimate, even honored participant in the U.S. intelligence community. A negative suggestion about Nosenko in the company of his supporters provokes angry scorn, almost irrational diatribes about questioning any aspect of his peculiar background.

Short of a full-blown presidential or congressional inquiry, it is all but impossible to prove who is right in this ferocious debate. If might makes right, then Nosenko has won hands down. He is accepted by the men who run the U.S. intelligence community. No major newspaper reporters continue to raise questions about Nosenko's acceptance. The issue is so old and confusing that even the best reporters on good newspapers covering national intelligence matters yawn at the questions of his legitimacy. An inquiring reporter faces the stone wall of national security when probing the matter, and Nosenko's supporters simply say that the information that is most convincing about him cannot be revealed.

No doubt the next step in the saga of Yuri Nosenko will be the final trumpeting of his honor and value by leaking to selected reporters the "real truth" about specific cases he has helped the West break. Nothing really can be proved by this because the public would be asked to take only the pieces handed to the selected reporters—reporters who would not be selected if they were inclined to challenge the assertions aimed at the irrevocable resurrection of Nosenko.

But along Nosenko's rocky rise to respectability, there was one serious stumble—one that should have left his supporters in a state of humiliation, if not full-blown suspicion. It happened in 1978, when the House Select Committee on Assassinations, looking into the history of Lee Harvey Oswald, undertook an examination of Yuri Nosenko. Worse yet for Nosenko, he was called to testify in executive session. Even his strongest supporters, hoping for a public vindication of Nosenko following negative suggestions about him that year in Edward Jay Epstein's *Legend: The Secret World of Lee Harvey Oswald*, were left in a mild state of shock by the revelations and findings of the committee.

The only nonpartisan, nonintelligence group ever to have access to the full file on Nosenko, the committee reached the official conclusion that he had lied on the subject of Oswald. The committee, explaining that its purpose was not to determine the validity of Nosenko other than in his statements about Oswald, stopped short of drawing wider conclusions. But it was firm in its assertion that Nosenko, the man who brought the message from Moscow that the KGB never had the slightest interest in Oswald, is a liar.

In addition to the committee's thorough review of the files, a variety of intelligence agents and officials were called to testify about Nosenko. These men had rarely uttered a public word about Nosenko or anything else. At nearly every juncture, their testimony—even when trying to support Nosenko—was devastating to the proposition that he was the sort of man to be drawn into the halls of the clandestine services to give lectures on counterintelligence and be handsomely paid.

Take, for example, the testimony of Bruce Solie of the CIA Office of Security, the man who orchestrated Nosenko's original clearance in 1968. Solie and Nosenko became friends; when the Russian married, Solie served as his best man at the wedding. In a sworn deposition Solie quickly conceded that he was uninformed about Nosenko's positions on Oswald. But Solie agreed that the Oswald aspect of Nosenko's testimony was "an important part to be considered" in any evaluation of Nosenko's bona fides.

Reading Solie's testimony can best be likened to chasing quicksilver. Staff counsel Kenneth Klein struggled valiantly to understand why Solie was willing to accept Nosenko's statements on Oswald, even though he claimed he had never asked Nosenko a single question about Oswald during his extensive investigation. The best answer Klein could elicit was that Solie was willing to accept whatever Nosenko said as true unless he was shown information to the contrary—certainly a peculiar philosophy for a security officer.

Finally, Klein asked Solie that if it were proved that Nosenko was lying about Oswald, "Do you think that would change your opinion as to whether he was bona fide?"

"It sure would," Solie replied.

John Hart, a former high CIA official, who, in 1976, orchestrated yet another shoring up of Nosenko, was brought out of retirement in 1978 by CIA Director Stansfield Turner to explain to the committee the agency's position on Nosenko. Curiously, Hart announced he knew almost nothing about Nosenko's Oswald connections, even though the committee had asked the agency to send someone to speak to that point. Instead, Hart excoriated his CIA colleagues who had placed Nosenko under hostile interrogation years earlier. It is difficult to imagine Hart's conjuring up more venomous terms to describe the men who had handled Nosenko.

But Hart had an even more curious message about Nosenko, whose information on Oswald he believed was given in good faith. Straying from his theme and pressed by an incredulous congressman, Hart ineluctably arrived at this statement: "Let me express an opinion on Mr. Nosenko's testimony about Lee Harvey Oswald. I, like many others, find Mr. Nosenko's testimony incredible. . . . Therefore, if I were in the position of deciding whether to use the testimony of Mr. Nosenko in this case or not, I would not use it." This was in striking contrast with his own statements and an agency response to an interrogatory submitted to the committee two weeks earlier, stating that the CIA believed Nosenko's statements about Oswald were "made in good faith."

But none of this was as damaging to Nosenko as his own

appearance before an executive session of the committee. His two appearances followed two days with the committee staff. Kenneth Klein opened his questioning with the following summary of what Nosenko had told the staff up until that point: "You have testified that the KGB did not even speak to Lee Harvey Oswald because he was uninteresting; and that you decided he was not interesting without speaking to him."

From that point on, Klein elicited astonishing conflicts and inconsistencies from Nosenko. Repeatedly Nosenko retreated to the explanation that Klein was using material that he had provided while under hostile interrogation. But when Klein asked if the hostile interrogations had ever led Nosenko to lie, Nosenko stated, "No, I was telling the truth." Actually, most of Nosenko's information on Oswald—including details that the committee concluded were lies—is contained in an FBI debriefing report of early March 1964, a full month before Nosenko was placed under hostile interrogation.

Nosenko complained bitterly to the committee about the Spartan, solitary conditions of his long and surely dreadful confinement. No one has disputed that he was kept under miserable conditions as part of the effort to break him, but his custodial situation had been approved by the attorney general and was being monitored at a high level of the CIA. Nosenko had presented the intelligence community with an extraordinary problem, and extraordinary precautions were taken to be certain that technical legalities were observed.

But Nosenko repeatedly insinuated that his treatment went far beyond simple harsh conditions, telling the committee: ". . . a number of interrogations I was under drugs, and on me was used a number of drugs, and I know that, and hallucinations and talking during night and sodium and everything, even many others, and a number of things were absolutely incoherent." Nosenko later added: ". . . on me were used different types of drugs and sleeping drugs, hallucination drugs, and whatever I do not know, and don't want to know." At another point he made a reference suggesting he had been slapped but quickly amended it by saying "not physically but I mean psychologically."

Finally, as Nosenko sank ever deeper into a morass of contradictions, he begged Committee Chairman Louis Stokes to stop the questioning. He submitted that he should not be questioned about anything he had said during the period he was under hostile interrogation, although he swore that he always told the absolute truth about Oswald, even under hostile questioning. He described the "inhuman conditions" of his imprisonment, which indeed were far worse than those of any modern U.S. prison. He was deprived of daily showers, reading material, exercise, television, writing, any form of entertainment. He was kept first in a small atticlike room in a safe house and later in a vaultlike room. Nosenko also stated in his plea to Chairman Stokes that "I never went [to the] press because I am loyal to the country which accepted me, and I didn't want to hurt the country. . . . Who would like to defect, reading in what conditions and what treatment defectors is receiving."

The committee granted Nosenko's request, and the questioning stopped.

But the general investigation went on, with particular emphasis on the drugs Nosenko claimed had been used against him. The CIA, which was doing everything it could to support the wavering Nosenko, presented the committee with a list of every drug administered to him during the period in question. During August 1965 four different drugs, including a simple antibiotic, were administered; he was also given Zactirin and Donnatal, medicines usually prescribed for minor pain and stomach acidity. On one occasion in August Thorazine, a major tranquilizer, was administered. With the exception of Thorazine, the only drugs given were routine, such as antihistamine and cough syrup.

David Murphy, chief of the Soviet Division, which had custody of Nosenko during the period in question, swore to the committee that no drugs had ever been used other than the ones on the CIA list. Other officers from the CIA and FBI swore they had never seen any evidence of Nosenko being drugged or having been physically abused. Moreover, the CIA officer assigned to debrief Nosenko on his career in the KGB swore to the committee that he never heard Nosenko make a complaint about his conditions during the many hours he spent with him during the period. If Nosenko is telling the truth about being drugged, or if his insinuations about physical abuse are true, then a number of intelligence officers with distinguished careers have perjured themselves before the United States Congress.

One of the most intriguing findings of the committee's review of the Nosenko file was that the agency spent relatively little time questioning Nosenko about Oswald. Indeed, the vast majority of the interrogations focused on other aspects of Nosenko's knowledge. It is ironic that given Nosenko's miserable public performance on the Oswald question, this was not the chief area where Nosenko ran aground with the CIA. Indeed, this committee finding tends to support a major thesis of his detractors—that this odd defector's knowledge was particularly vacant and contradictory in areas of routine KGB operations.

In its final report the committee made the following statement concerning Nosenko:

> [The committee] questioned Nosenko in detail about Oswald, finding significant inconsistencies in statements he had given the FBI, the CIA and the committee. For example, Nosenko told the committee that the KGB had Oswald under extensive surveillance, including mail interception, wire tap and physical observation. Yet, in 1964, he told the CIA and FBI there had been no such surveillance of Oswald. Similarly, in 1964, Nosenko indicated there had been no psychiatric examination of Oswald subsequent to his suicide attempt, while in 1978 he detailed for the committee the reports he had read about psychiatric examinations of Oswald.
>
> In the end, the committee . . . was unable to resolve the Nosenko matter. The fashion in which Nosenko was treated by the Agency—his interrogation and confinement—virtually ruined him as a valid source for information on the assassination. Nevertheless, the committee was certain Nosenko lied about Oswald—whether it was to the FBI and CIA in 1964, or to the committee in 1978, or perhaps to both. The reasons he would lie about Oswald range from the possibility that he merely wanted to exaggerate his own importance to the disinformation hypothesis with its sinister implications.

Although the committee believed that its mandate fell short of requiring a conclusion on Nosenko's bona fides, its chief counsel, G. Robert Blakey, later wrote that "the credibility of [Nosenko's] story about Oswald . . . becomes not just one factor but the linchpin in the assessment of his bona fides." That linchpin, the committee clearly felt, offered feeble support for the bona fides of Yuri Nosenko.

One might expect such a conclusion by a committee of the

United States Congress to have a negative bearing on Nosenko's position in the intelligence community. Not at all. It was as though all this had happened in secret behind closed doors—not in the bright light of a public forum. Not a single major publication is known to have even mentioned that the congressional committee concluded that Nosenko is a liar. Any attention the fact might have received was smothered by the sensational aspects of the committee findings—that indeed there probably was a conspiracy to assassinate President Kennedy.

Whatever the reasons, Yuri Nosenko continues to be regarded with a certain reverence by his supporters. He is in regular contact with U.S. covert counterintelligence personnel and is paid around $40,000 per year. Most troubling of all is that Nosenko's very acceptance is linked to other defectors—Fedora, Igor, and others—who have come under intense suspicion.

The thorniest of these linkages involves Fedora, a Soviet KGB officer who operated under diplomatic cover at the United Nations from the early sixties and became a prized FBI source. Not only did Fedora verify specific points in Nosenko's story that later were shown to be lies, but he went much farther. He told the FBI that the KGB was so distraught over Nosenko's defection that all its operations in New York were shut down. This odd and unsubstantiated claim looked even more peculiar when the CIA confirmed that KGB operations were continuing in Switzerland, where Nosenko had served and about which, presumably, he could reveal information. Just as in the case of Igor's certification of Nosenko, Fedora's certification of the defector created a bond of mutually supportive credibility that cannot be dismissed casually.

The basic questions about Fedora's bona fides were first made public in 1978 by Edward Jay Epstein in *Legend*. Still highly protective of its source Fedora, the FBI began a secret investigation to determine the source of Epstein's information on Fedora. In fact, there was such alarm within the intelligence community over the exposure of Fedora that serious stories circulated that he probably had been tortured and executed by the Soviets as a result of Epstein's revelations. The result of this search for Epstein's source is unknown.

Far more crucial, however, was a subsequent investigation by the FBI aimed at assessing Fedora's bona fides. In 1980 the investigation—one of the most tightly held secrets in the intelligence community—ended with the FBI's astounding conclusion that Fedora was a dispatched agent, that he was under Moscow's control during all the years of his association with the bureau, including the period when he was giving urgent support to Yuri Nosenko.

One might expect such a conclusion about Fedora to lead to a reexamination of all related cases and sources, including Nosenko and Igor. (Igor, of course, had also certified Nosenko.) As of the spring of 1981, this had not happened. The finding on Fedora was viewed as a piece of history unrelated to anything going on today in U.S. Intelligence. It was decided, at least for the time being, to do nothing.

It is far from clear why officials have refused to pursue the seemingly pointed implications of the new Fedora findings or why they do not want to reopen the bewildering Nosenko case. And it is astounding that every sign indicates that the United States continues to consider Igor a valid source—even in light of his certification of Nosenko, even after his preposterous and tragic manipulation of Nick Shadrin.

But a public revelation that any one of these curious defectors is phony could have awesome bureaucratic repercussions. If one falls, others must fall, creating havoc inside intelligence services where crucial analyses and long-term plans may have been built upon the supposed reliability of these sources. The most ominous question is whether it has become simpler to live with Nosenko and other sources with whom he is linked than to cast any one of them out and risk tumbling the whole internal structure of cases and strategies.

Ewa Shadrin has waged a magnificent battle on behalf of her husband. With a fierceness and tenacity born of love, she has challenged the most powerful and indifferent bureaucracies in the world. She has fought through lies and deceptions, never taking her eyes from the goal. But the generous faith she had in the beginning has been eroded, washed away by the crashing waves of deceit. Not only is her faith gone, but so is her hope.

She believes that she will never see her husband again. Does she think he is dead or alive? "He is either dead or in a Soviet prison," she says. "There is no difference." Silently the tears well up in her eyes, years after Vienna.

There is no doubt now that Nick Shadrin originally was provided to Igor to promote his credentials within the KGB. The question is whether Shadrin later was sacrificed to protect the very man he promoted. Did a situation develop on December 18, 1975, that presented intelligence officials with a dreadful dilemma, one that demanded a decision either to sacrifice Shadrin or to lose Igor? Did it come down to one or the other? Historically, good men have faced just such decisions. They have had to stand by and see innocent lives lost to protect the greater common welfare, to protect an intelligence source or operation that was of inestimable value. Could that have happened in the case of Nick Shadrin?

"That is not something that matters to me," says Ewa Shadrin, the grim fierceness returning to her eyes. "If they killed Nick, or let Nick be killed or kidnapped to save Igor, there is no reason good enough to justify it. They deceived Nick and tricked him into doing this. If Nick had been a spy, if he had even been paid for what he was doing, if they had told him the truth about the danger he was in, perhaps it would be different."

In the end there is only one certainty: Ewa Shadrin has been the victim of one of the greatest deceptions the American government ever perpetrated on one of its citizens. The lies, calculated wittingly or otherwise to protect Igor, reach all the way to the top of the government. Despite the numerous overtures by American officials, Ewa today feels that no real effort was ever made to find out about her husband. She believes that is why President Ford stared at her sullenly, silently. It is why President Carter, the fervent supporter of human rights who promised never to lie, refused to see her at all. That is why Rosalynn Carter refused even to answer Mrs. Shadrin's letter. They would leave the actual lying to their underlings.

Of all her tribulations, Ewa Shadrin faced nothing quite so cruel as the realization that some of Nick's best friends had been in the vanguard of the deception. It was, of course, the emergence of news about Igor that brought about the ultimate collapse of the deception. In the spring of 1978 the dreadful reality of it all began to seep into Ewa Shadrin's brain. It came during a time when she was spending many hours each day trying to unravel the complexities surrounding Igor. Over the telephone, she found herself crying, screaming at Jim Wooten: *"But if you knew about Igor, how could you not tell Nick?"*

"If Nick had known the truth," replied Wooten evenly, "he could never have played his role."

Appendix

LITERATURNAYA GAZETA REPORTS ARTAMONOV-SHADRIN STORY
LD190947Y Moscow LITERATURNAYA GAZETA in Russian 17 Aug 77 p 14 LD
[Article by Genrikh Borovik: "They Shoot Horses, Don't They?"]
As translated by U.S. Department of State.

In July 1977 leading papers and magazines in America carried sensational headlines using the words "agents," "double agents" and even "triple agent." They all referred to the same person—Nicholas George Shadrin—who, the papers assured us, had been a U.S. special services "double agent" and had "mysteriously disappeared following a meeting with KGB employees" in Vienna in December 2 years previously. Here are some press reports:

"One evening in December 1975 a Russian-born American citizen, Nicholas Shadrin, left his wife in a Vienna hotel and set out for the Votivkirche, where he was to meet two KGB agents. To this day his fate and his true role in the shadowy world of espionage remain unknown . . ." (NEWSWEEK).

". . . He was a double agent representing American intelligence and, at the same time, pretending to spy for the Kremlin . . . His case . . . is as intriguing as a spy novel. . . ."

"The case of Shadrin, who disappeared in Austria 18 months ago, was the subject of numerous official and unofficial American-Soviet contacts . . ." (the Washington POST).

At KGB headquarters the author of these lines was shown materials pertaining to the case the Western press is currently writing about. These materials shed light on the true fate of the man whom the American papers call a U.S. citizen, Nicholas George Shadrin.

Washington, May 1966

It was a Saturday. A Soviet Embassy employee made a routine trip to the shopping center to buy some provisions for the family. In a remote corner of the store he was addressed sotto voce, in excellent Russian, by a tall man standing next to him.

283

"Excuse me, but are you an employee of the Soviet Embassy?"

"Yes."

"I have often seen you here in this store, and from your conversation I realized what you were."

The man was about 40, thin and well dressed.

"My name is Shadrin. Nicholas George Shadrin."

"I am listening, Mr. Shadrin."

"I absolutely must meet one of your comrades and have a talk . . . I beg you. . . . I am a Soviet citizen. . . ." The man was clearly upset.

"Ring the Soviet Consulate. Write down the number. . . ."

"No, no, I can't go to the consulate . . . The thing is that my real name is Nikolay Fedorovich Artamonov. No doubt you have heard of me. . . ."

"Nikolay Fedorovich Artamonov? No . . . doesn't ring a bell. . . ."

The stranger appeared surprised at this reply. . . .

"I was an officer on one of our—that is," he corrected himself, "a Soviet destroyer. I fled to Sweden . . . in 1959. Do you see? I sought political asylum there. And I have been here since then. . . . I must talk with your comrades . . . and tell them how it all happened. . . . In Leningrad I have a wife and a son. . . . I beg you. . . ."

"OK, I'll tell the consulate about your request. How can I find you?"

"I live not far from here, in Arlington . . . but you mustn't phone."

"Don't you want to go to the consulate? If you can't be 'phoned, how will you be contacted?"

"Every Saturday between 1700 and 1705, over a period of a month, I will wait for your man near the Hecht store on Wilson Boulevard, at the parking lot. Have you got that?"

"Right, supposing I remember that," the embassy employee shrugged his shoulders, not ruling out the possibility of provocation. "But I'm not promising anything."

"I understand. But you must convey the request," the man looked anxious, beseeching.

"Please tell them of my request . . . For a long time I didn't dare . . ."

The next day, the Soviet Consulate in Washington asked Moscow for some facts about Nikolay Fedorovich Artamonov, allegedly a former Soviet Navy Officer who had fled to Sweden in 1959 and sought political asylum there. The consulate also asked for a photograph of Artamonov.

Gdynia, June 1959

(From the testimony of Ilya Aleksandrovich Popov, born 1934, native of Vorone-zhskaya Oblast, Russian, education, seventh grade)

. . . I have known Subcommander Nikolay Fedorovich Artamonov since March 1956. In September 1958 our ship began an assignment in the Polish port of Gdynia . . . on Sunday 7 June 1959, around 1700, Artamonov ordered me to make a cutter ready for fishing in the estuary of the Wisla. In the evening he arrived at the cutter with a girl he knew called (Yeva) and ordered us to set off toward the Wisla. We passed the Polish border guard post and sailed into the open sea. A thunderstorm blew up in the night. Two or three times Artamonov checked to see that I was holding the right course and took a turn at the wheel. . . . [paragraph continues]

At dawn he told me: "We're lost—we took the wrong course, the storm upset our compasses." As we were approaching shore, Artamonov changed into a dark blue civilian suit in his cabin, lowered the cutter's naval flag and disembarked with Yeva. He told me he now knew where we were; he said he would go off to get some fuel and we would return to Gdynia in the morning. . . . After Artamonov left two civilians came up in a car. One said "police" and signaled to me to get into the car. Several times I uttered the word "watch" to make him see that I was on watch and didn't want to go anywhere. Then the two of them twisted my arm up my back and put me into the car. They took me to a building—police headquarters, as it turned out. I demanded the right to phone the Soviet Consulate. The chief said I couldn't phone the consulate at that moment because everybody was asleep. . . .

In the morning they took me to another police building in the center of the city. I saw Artamonov in the corridor. . . . He told me: "Looks like you'll be going back to Gdynia alone; I'm stuck here." I took it that, being an officer, Artamonov would be held for a while, but I told him I would wait if he wasn't going to be long.

. . . On the evening of the same day I was summoned for questioning by the chief of police through an interpreter—a tall, elderly man, a Russian emigree [sic], about 60.

I was asked whether I still maintained that Artamonov had become lost and ended up in Sweden accidentally. I said that we had gone fishing and became lost, the storm having affected our compasses. The interpreter laughed maliciously and said that the storm couldn't have affected the compasses. . . . He picked up a newspaper from the table and translated for me something that went roughly as follows: "A Soviet officer has quit his country and fled to Sweden." There was a picture of our cutter. I said to the interpreter: "Why do your papers print lies?" He said: "Perhaps it is the truth."

. . . At the end of the interrogation the interpreter asked me whether I wanted to stay in Sweden. I told him I was a Soviet person, born on Soviet soil, and would continue to live there; there was nothing for me in Sweden. . . .

It was hinted several times at the interrogation that Artamonov would be staying in Sweden, so I asked permission to see him. After the interrogation I was taken below—to Artamonov's cell. They did not let me talk to him alone.

Artamonov asked me: "Well Popov, why have you come?" I told him I had spoken on the telephone with a representative of the Soviet Consulate and that they would be coming to Kalmar at 2000. I expected Artamonov to be delighted at this news, but he just lowered his head and told me: "What do I need the consulate for now, Popov? It's waiting for me here. . . ." And he pointed at the cell wall. I thought he meant the "wall" was waiting for him, that is, he was going to be shot. I told Artamonov that the Swedish newspaper had said that he would be staying in Sweden, and I asked him whether this was true. He bowed his head and said nothing . . .

I realized that he had nothing to say to me. I asked Artamonov what I should tell headquarters when I got back. He pondered and then said: "Tell them that as soon as they let me go. I will return. . . ."

285

. . . On Sunday 14 June 1959 I flew into Moscow. . . .

Stockholm, June 1959
(From the papers DAGENS NYHETER and STOCKHOLM TIDNINGEN)
". . . It is reported that a love affair between a 33-year-old Red Navy officer and a beautiful 22-year-old dark-haired girl led to their fleeing from Gdynia on Sunday evening. A day later, on Monday, around 2100 they arrived at Oland and landed in the eastern part of the island. The officer and the girl asked for political asylum. . . . According to a statement by the public prosecutor the Soviet officer, despite 3 days of interrogation, has not yet given a satisfactory explanation of his flight to the West. . . .

". . . The commission on aliens decided on Thursday to grant the refugees political asylum. . . ."

Kaliningrad, September 1959
(From an indictment)
". . . On the basis of the facts Nikolay Fedorovich Artamonov is accused of betraying the motherland while carrying out a special assignment on a ship in the Polish port of Gdynia and of fleeing to Sweden, where he sought political asylum which was granted; that is, of committing a crime as stipulated by Article 1 of the law on criminal responsibility for state crimes. . . ."

Washington, May 1966
Our consulate in Washington received materials pertaining to Artamonov and a photograph a few days following its request. He was not an imposter. He was a citizen of the Soviet Union who had committed a most grave crime against the motherland and who was abroad and seeking a meeting with a Soviet consular representative. For some reason he could not come to the consulate and he did not want any Soviet consular official to ring him at home. However, this did not change the essential nature of the case—a Soviet citizen had appealed to the Soviet Consulate. Therefore, Artamonov's request could not be ignored. And on the Saturday a representative of the Soviet Consulate arrived at the prearranged place in Washington.

"Our meeting lasted about 30 minutes. Artamonov told me that he had been half-drunk when he fled to Sweden. His passion for the woman had gone to his head and this had led to the very grave error which he now deeply regretted. He had no other serious reasons for fleeing. Artamonov said this crime had led to another crime—in order to live abroad he agreed to cooperate with American intelligence and told a representative much of what he knew about the state of Soviet Navy. He realized that these crimes merited severe punishment. He said that all these years he had been unable to rest, thinking about the way he had betrayed his people, his family and his friends. Recently he had been unable to live with the thought. He believed that he was able to do something for the motherland and, in that way, at least to some extent, expiate his grave sin.

"I asked him how he intended to do this. Artamonov said that he was working as a consultant for the U.S. Defense Intelligence Agency [DIA] and that he could give us what he thought was valuable information essential to the Soviet Union's security.

"In conclusion I told him I would report the contents of our conversation to the consulate. He thanked me and said: 'What do you think—is there a hope?' 'Of what?' I said. 'That I might be of some use.' I replied that I couldn't say anything about that. Artamonov said where he would be every Saturday between 1700 and 1715 over a two-month period, waiting to meet a consular representative. . . ."
[Signed] An employee of the USSR Consulate in Washington.

Two weeks later Soviet representative Igor Aleksandrovich Orlov—this is the name we will use in this documentary sketch—turned up at the prearranged place to meet Artamonov.

I. A. Orlov:
What was the basis for our agreeing to make contact with Artamonov-Shadrin in 1966?

A careful study of documents—comments by Artamonov's colleagues and friends and the testimony of engineer Popov—convinced us that Artamonov's treachery and his flight to Sweden with his lover were not caused by any serious, say, ideological motives. He had many friends, a wife and a son whom he loved. Following his flight undispatched gifts wrapped for his family were found in the ship's cabin.

What happened to him? By all appearances, his rapid career had gone to his head: He had been promoted to the rank of subcommander third class at an earlier age than usual. He had begun to be affected by conceit, arrogance, egoism, a sense of "anything goes." The emergence of these qualities alienated his friends against their will; they knew him in another way. He began to seek new "friends." They were officers of foreign navies who were in Gdynia at the time (some of them, it turned out later, had links with Western intelligence). They paid him compliments and unambiguously hinted that a man with his qualities could go a long way. He came to think of himself as exceptional. This coincided with his intoxication with (Yeva Gura), who told him she was pregnant by him. He had scarcely prepared for the flight. To him it was an unexpected and seemingly easy way out of a nasty personal situation, one promising interesting adventures. Even Swedish counterintelligence was unable to understand what made a man like Artamonov leave his motherland, home and the service and flee to a foreign country without money, unable to speak the language. The Swedes even suspected that Artamonov had been sent to their country as a Soviet agent.

None of this mitigated the crime committed by the traitor Artamonov, but it gave grounds for believing that it had been committed not by a malicious, long-disguised enemy of Soviet power but by an overly self-confident, vainglorious man infatuated with a woman and above all with himself.

Yet once the man had begun to betray, he could not stop. Artamonov agreed to cooperate with American intelligence. His crime became worse. He slid down the slippery slope. However, his quest for contacts with Soviet people might have indicated that deep down there was still a germ of humanity which at some stage began to sprout again and made the moral torment unbearable. And he might have decided to make amends for at least part of his guilt.

Often people who are voluntarily cast into the capitalist world and deprived of links with the motherland begin, albeit belatedly, to realize what a terrible mistake they have made and try their best to retrieve their right to serve the motherland. Some are grateful even for a chance to confess. This word sounds strange on the lips of a traitor, yet Artamonov himself repeatedly used it in later conversations with me when he talked about his misadventures abroad.

This was one train of thought we pursued. There was another possibility: Artamonov-Shadrin could be lying to us. He was in fact not repentant at all and, on instructions from his masters, could be trying to become a so-called "double agent" in order to play a "game" with us.

At first glance it may seem strange, but when we agreed to contact Artamonov both alternatives were real. At his first meeting with me, Artamonov said he was seeking contacts with Soviet people on instructions from his American masters in order to play a "game" with us, but this assignment coincided with his sincere desire to at least go some way toward making amends to the motherland.

You will agree that the situation was somewhat unusual. But, having looked at it and discussed it from all angles, we decided to continue contacts with Artamonov. In practical terms we were not risking anything even if his assurances of sincerity were sheer provocation. Naturally, he was unable to get from us any information which would be useful to an enemy. There could, however, be a lot to gain from the contacts if Artamonov was even half-sincere. All this had to be looked into. . . .

Thus began my regular meetings with Artamonov.

From conversations with him we soon learned the details of his life abroad.

In July 1959, that is, just 1 month after fleeing, Artamonov was approached by Americans who suggested cooperating with U.S. intelligence. For this he was guaranteed transport to the United States, financial assistance and, subsequently, permanent work. He agreed. In September he was taken to the FRG and kept for 1 month in a small detached house belonging to U.S. intelligence near Frankfurt-am-Main. His physical and mental condition was checked, and ideological indoctrination was carried out. Conversations were held with him by the traitor Prodskiy, who had worked in Leningrad before the war and gone over to the Hitlerites.

Artamonov was then taken to the United States (now under the name of Nicholas George Shadrin) and given accommodation [sic] in Alexandria near Washington, where people began systematically and painstakingly extracting information about our armed forces from him. I did not ask him what he told the Americans; there was no point in asking. We simply believed that he had revealed to them everything he knew, and of course, a senior [as published] naval officer's knowledge could do us palpable harm when handed to the enemy.

Having pumped Artamonov dry, they surrounded him with a gang of traitors, who henceforth were to be company for him. One Nikolay Kozlov was appointed his guardian.

From information on N. V. Kozlov:

". . . Born in 1918. In 1943 he went over voluntarily to the side of the Hitlerites. In May of the same year he graduated from a school for propagandists near Berlin. Served as chief of staff of the 2d Regiment of the 1st Russian

288

Liberation Army Division. After the war he was in (Shlyasgaym) prisoner-of-war camp, where he participated in preparing false documents for Russian Liberation Army employees. In 1948 he became a secret employee of U.S. intelligence. Employed in selecting and training cadres for the CIA with a view to getting them into the Soviet Union's territory. A profoundly immoral and unprincipled person. Fears and despises Americans. Conceals from the bosses the fact that he has a mother in the Soviet Union, fearing that this fact could damage his position in the special services. Detests the Soviet Union. . . ."

I. A. Orlov:

Nikolay Kozlov reported regularly to his bosses on his "ward's" frame of mind. But Kozlov was just one of the people surrounding Artamonov. There was, for example, one Sergey Gordeyev, who was morally thoroughly corrupt and who fled to the Americans from West Germany in 1952. Both the Russians and the Americans knew that this individual was, on top of everything else, paranoid.

Artamonov observed these people and was gradually seized with horror, as he put it: He was becoming—if he had not already become—the same as they were. But he was not free to choose a different society for himself. And he had to keep company with such as Kozlov and Gordeyev. The danger of irretrievably losing everything human was, in his words, growing.

In the mid-sixties Artamonov was appointed DIA consultant on the Soviet Armed Forces. His function was to read Soviet newspapers and make use of the information supplied to him by the Americans to analyze the situation in the USSR Navy, to prepare reports for his bosses and to give lectures on these subjects for U.S. naval officers.

He was quite well off, above all thanks to (Yeva) (They were unlawfully married, despite the fact that he was not divorced from his wife, who was living in the USSR), who had a dental practice. The Shadrins had no children.

He knew nothing of his wife and son. Only once—in September 1965—did he manage to convey to a female relative in Leningrad through an American lady tourist (Artamonov was afraid to send her to his wife) the fact that he was "alive, well and missing the family."

It was against the background of all this that Artamonov, as he put it, was increasingly coming round to the idea that he had to seek a way out of the conditions under which he placed himself. And, however, strange it may seem, the Americans themselves facilitated the decision to come to us by setting him the task of seeking contacts with us.

From Artamonov's statement to the USSR Supreme Soviet:

". . . The years after I committed the very grave crime served as a hard lesson for me . . . I was never a deliberate, inveterate enemy of my motherland. At the same time it is necessary fully to recognize the whole gravity of the crime and its results, which are in no way different from the actions of the USSR's foreign enemies. While in no way freeing myself of responsibility for what I have done, I beg to be given the opportunity to expiate my guilt, to help my motherland in some way if I can, and then to return home. . . ."

I. A. Orlov:

Artamonov handed me this statement at one of our meetings. It was Artamonov's dream, to use his words, to return home. He realized he would die if the Americans found out about this.

It is hard to believe someone who has committed a grave crime against his own people, and it is perfectly natural that we certainly could not trust him completely. He sensed our mistrust, felt it deeply and tried to do everything possible to prove his sincerity.

Of course, the Americans did not give him important secrets. But we were able to judge from his information where the Americans were directing their efforts in order to fill in gaps in their knowledge of our armed forces. Thanks to Artamonov, we received important information on many people working in U.S. intelligence, particularly in those sections dealing with deserters from the Soviet Union, on their work methods, on the organizational structure and so forth. Of course, he also brought us the information which has been compiled for him beforehand by his U.S. bosses so that he could play his "game" with us. And several times we indirectly "allowed" the Americans to come to the conclusion that we were "taking seriously" the information which Artamonov was bringing us on their instructions.

What were the Americans' intentions in sending Artamonov to meet us? For they were perfectly well aware that Artamonov would obtain no information on the Soviet Union during these meetings. So why did they play this game? First, with a view to the misinformation which, as they thought, they could send us through Artamonov. Second, so that Artamonov, by gaining our confidence, could seek out an opportunity—albeit after a long period of time—to draw some conclusions on "the work of Soviet counterintelligence." And, third, Artamonov was maintaining in his bosses the illusion that with time we might assign him to meetings with a Soviet "secret agent" [*nelegal*] on U.S. territory.

In this complex situation Artamonov acted at considerable risk to himself, perfectly well aware that the U.S. special services would deal with him on his very first mistake. The strain and the constant danger in which he found himself told on him. In the last years it was increasingly felt that Artamonov was tired. He frequently spoke of missing his motherland and family and remembered his naval service.

When we learned in the fall of 1975 that Artamonov would be able to come to Austria, we agreed on a meeting with him in Vienna to discuss questions of his return home. The meeting was fixed for a place near the Votivkirche. This place is directly opposite the U.S. Consulate. Artamonov, as he had warned us, had informed the Americans about this meeting. Perhaps we were photographed. Of course, this troubled neither him nor me.

Vienna, 18 December 1975

Orlov and Artamonov met near the huge cathedral building, as agreed, at precisely 2000.

Despite the rather cold weather, Artamonov was hatless—Orlov had never seen him in headgear—and scarfless, although his topcoat was neatly buttoned right up.

He smiled with joyful relief, went up to Orlov and could not restrain himself from embracing him:

"I've escaped at last! . . . How afraid I was that we wouldn't meet!"

Crossing the square, they turned into one of the streets, went several blocks, turning now right and now left, and finally stopped by a car which was waiting for them. No one "led" [*vel*] them. The snow-covered streets were deserted. They got into the car, executed several control maneuvers to lose any possible "tail" and headed for the part of the city where the conversation was to take place.

". . . Artamonov complained of fatigue. This difficult operation was also telling. He said his work for U.S. intelligence was a burden to him. He once again mentioned his statement addressed to the USSR Supreme Soviet. He very keenly raised the question of returning home. I said that the solution of this question was drawing to an end and that I would obviously be able to inform him of official permission at one of our subsequent meetings. Artamonov continued to press me. I replied that I would do everything possible. We agreed to meet on 20 December."

[Signed] I. Orlov

Vienna, 20 December 1975

". . . Artamonov did not show up at the appointed time for the meeting in the agreed place on 20 December."

[Signed] I. Orlov

I. A. Orlov:

And there were no signals from him on subsequent days. We had already decided to organize a search, using our possibilities, but on 30 December the Foreign Ministry received notification from the U.S. Embassy in Moscow. . . .

Moscow, 30 December 1975

At 1530 the USSR Foreign Ministry consular administration was visited by Counsellor Clifford Gross, chief of the consular section at the U.S. Embassy in Moscow, who handed over the following note: "As has become known, Nicholas George Shadrin, who is now a U.S. citizen, met with two Soviet officials in Vienna on 18 December. . . . He again met with them in Vienna on 20 December but did not return after this meeting and has been missing since that day. . . ."

I. A. Orlov:

I do not know to what extent the Americans suspected Artamonov or when mistrust of him began to predominate in their assessment of the "double agent."

Latterly he was filled with a sense of gratitude toward us for having definite faith in him and because he now had the prospect of returning home and justified hope that his severe sentence would be reconsidered. A few careless phrases attesting to a change in the mental state of Shadrin-Artamonov, and the specialists surrounding him might have suspected that the "double agent" of the U.S. special services had come under our influence. We had foreseen this danger and warned him of it. But I am not sure that he could have coped and followed our advice to the end. Perhaps Artamonov made some tragic mistake after 18 December and the

291

CIA, learning of his upcoming return home, realized that the game was lost and that it was a scandalous failure, hastened to remove Artamonov and accused the other side to cover the traces. I would not like to think the worst but, knowing the CIA's methods, I find it hard to assume that he is being kept prisoner; it is too dangerous for them. . . .

From the author:

I did not know Artamonov, and so I have tried to set down this story in such a way as to exclude the author's subjectivity as far as possible and to reduce to a minimum the retelling of this man's tragic fate "in my own words." I was familiarized at the KGB with the documents relating to this case. I spent many hours in conversation with Igor Aleksandrovich Orlov, who is now in Moscow, listening to his story, a small—but, in my view, very significant—part of which has been cited in this feature.

In conclusion, however, I would like to share with the readers some of my own thoughts, which do not require special knowledge, just logic.

I, like Orlov, have no doubt that the "disappearance" of Shadrin-Artamonov was the handiwork of the CIA. It was hardly revenge against him—the CIA is a powerful enough organization to allow itself to disregard emotions. No, it was an essential—from the CIA's viewpoint—measure and the only one which could save the already dishonorable organization from another scandal. For almost 10 years—starting in the spring of 1966—the CIA, the FBI and the DIA reported to the top leaders of the U.S. administration (first Democratic, then Republican) on Shadrin's "vigilant" operation against Soviet counterintelligence. And it suddenly turns out that their "most valuable agent" is nurturing the idea of returning home. And, God forbid, he will do so at a time of emotion uplift [*dushevnyy poryv*]!

Imagine for a moment the faces of CIA, FBI and DIA leaders at the thought, for example, that on returning to the USSR Artamonov would address a press conference at which he would describe how everything happened in actual fact. After all the scandals and exposures which had recently rained down on the heads of the CIA and the FBI this would be a new, shameful failure for them, and on the eve of the 1976 presidential election, moreover!

. . . On 20 December 1975, as the U.S. press reports, Artamonov set out at the agreed time from the Hotel Bristol, where he was staying in Vienna, for his meeting with Orlov (immediately after the previous meeting on 18 December Artamonov—once again as the U.S. press reports—had informed his CIA guardian of the upcoming meeting). But he did not turn up for the meeting: He was kidnaped on the way by a special group of the CIA or the FBI (I do not know which of these establishments had come out in front in fulfilling the last mission regarding the "double agent"), and the U.S. administration was informed that Shadrin, who had set out for a preplanned meeting with a KGB employee in Vienna, "did not come back" and had thus been "kidnapped by Soviet intelligence."

This, or something like this, might be a representation of the operation against Shadrin-Artamonov which, according to its authors' plan, was supposed not only to allow U.S. special services to protect their innocence but also to make capital out of it. Of course, this is only supposition, and scarcely anybody, apart from a very limited number of people in the American special services, can confirm its authenticity. But the logic of the events inexorably leads one to believe that this was how it happened, more or less.

There is indirect evidence of this:

—For 18 months the American authorities did not publicize the events connected with Shadrin-Artamonov. Yet the United States always makes the best of an opportunity to fan an anti-Soviet campaign, particularly for the purpose of spy mania. The U.S. State Department even expressed regret at the fact that it had been unable to avoid the publication of the materials on the Shadrin case despite all the measures it had adopted;

—(Yeva Gura), whom the American special services had brought out of Vienna immediately after 20 December 1975, was "recommended" not to talk to anyone about Shadrin's disappearance. The American press got hold of this information only recently, thanks to the activity of (Yeva Gura's) lawyer;

—And, finally, the American special services have for a long time been resorting to killing people who are a threat to them, and not only political enemies but also their own servants who for some reason have become a nuisance. The Artamonov case fits into this train of thought. Are the world and the Americans themselves really not aware that the CIA and other U.S. special services have repeatedly deceived their own administration, not to mention Congress? The recent investigation of the CIA's activity by the Church Senate committee was a fine illustration of this.

Lastly, Artamonov committed the gravest sin against the motherland —treason although later, by all appearances, he tried to find a way out of his predicament. Nobody deprived him of his Soviet citizenship. Artamonov did not cease to be a USSR citizen because U.S. Congress declared "Nicholas George Shadrin" an American citizen. His wife and son are in the Soviet land. We have a right to join them in demanding a reply from the American authorities: Where is Nikolay Fedorovich Artamonov, and what has become of him?

Index